the *Lacemaker*

Books by Laura Frantz

The Frontiersman's Daughter
Courting Morrow Little
The Colonel's Lady
The Mistress of Tall Acre
A Moonbow Night
The Lacemaker

THE BALLANTYNE LEGACY

Love's Reckoning
Love's Awakening
Love's Fortune

the *Lacemaker*

LAURA FRANTZ

Revell

a division of Baker Publishing Group
Grand Rapids, Michigan

© 2018 by Laura Frantz

Published by Revell
a division of Baker Publishing Group
PO Box 6287, Grand Rapids, MI 49516-6287
www.revellbooks.com

Printed in the United States of America

Library of Congress Cataloging-in-Publication Data
Names: Frantz, Laura, author.
Title: The lacemaker / Laura Frantz.
Description: Grand Rapids, MI : Revell, [2018]
Identifiers: LCCN 2017031367 | ISBN 9780800726638 (pbk.)
Subjects: | GSAFD: Love stories. | Christian fiction.
Classification: LCC PS3606.R4226 L33 2018 | DDC 813/.6—dc23
LC record available at https://lccn.loc.gov/2017031367

Scripture quotations, whether quoted or paraphrased, are from the King James Version of the Bible.

This book is a work of fiction. Names, characters, places, and incidents are the product of the author's imagination or are used fictitiously. Any resemblance to actual events, locales, or persons, living or dead, is coincidental.

Published in association with Books & Such Literary Management.

18 19 20 21 22 23 24   7 6 5 4 3 2 1

To Susanna Thorne Hightower,
my fifth great-grandmother
and a recognized Virginia Patriot,
who supplied the Continental Army
during the American Revolution.
I promise you your own story.

1

MAY 1775

Elisabeth took a breath, breaking an intense hour of concentration. Mindful of the pinch of her stays, she straightened, the ache in her back and shoulders easing. In her apron-clad lap was the round pillow with the new lace she'd worked. Delicate as snowflakes, the intricate design was crafted of imported linen thread, now a good two yards of snowy white. She preferred white to black. All skilled lacemakers knew that working with white was kinder to the eye.

Raising her gaze, she looked out fine English glass onto a world of vivid greens broken by colorful splashes of blossoms. Elisabeth's favorites, butter-yellow roses and pale pink peonies, danced in the wind as it sighed around the townhouse's corners. Nearly summer at last. But not only almost June. 'Twas nearly her wedding day.

"*Oh là là!* What have we here?" Around the bedchamber's corner came a high, musical voice. "Surely a bride does not sew her own laces!"

"Nay, Isabeau. I've not patience enough for that."

"Not for an entire wedding gown, *merci*." The maid rounded the four-poster bed as fast as her girth would allow, holding a pair of clocked stockings. "You have been busy all the forenoon and likely forgot 'tis nearly teatime with the countess. Lady Charlotte surely wants to discuss your betrothal ball. 'Tis rumored Lord and Lady Amberly will be there."

Elisabeth nearly smiled at her maid's flaunting of titles. A humble Huguenot, Isabeau was still as bedazzled by the gentry as the day she'd first landed on Virginia's shores. Elisabeth set aside her lace pillow and watched her maid pull two tea gowns from a large armoire.

"Are you in a blue mood or a yellow one?"

"Yellow," she said. Yellow was Lady Charlotte's favorite color, and Elisabeth sought to cheer her all she could. In turn, the Governor's Palace served up a lavish tea table that surely rivaled the British king's.

Glancing at the tiny watch pinned to her bodice, Elisabeth left her chair so that Isabeau could undress and redress her.

"'Tis such a lovely day, likely the countess wants a turn in the garden. Do you think her girls will be about?"

"I should hope so. Fresh air and exercise are good for them, though their father oft keeps them inside of late."

Isabeau darted her a fretful look. "On account of the trouble, you mean."

Elisabeth tried not to think of that. "The sun might spoil their complexion, Lady Charlotte says. And she's right, you know. Look at me!" Though faint, the freckles across the bridge of her nose and the top of her cheekbones gave her skin a slightly tarnished look that even ample powder couldn't cover. Her fault for slipping outside with her handwork in the private corner of the garden she was so fond of, forever hatless.

"You are *tres belle*, even speckled," Isabeau said, lacing her stays a bit tighter. "And you've won the most dashing suitor in all Virginia Colony, no?"

"One of them." Elisabeth swallowed hard to keep from saying more on that score too. Her fiancé, Miles Cullen Roth, was many things, but he was not cut of the same cloth as fellow Virginians William Drew and George Rogers Clark and Edmund Randolph.

Isabeau's voice dropped to a whisper. "Though I do wonder about love."

Elisabeth shot a glance at the cracked bedchamber door. Papa always said she gave the servants too much room to talk, but the truth was she preferred plain speaking to the prissy airs of the drawing room. "'Tis a business matter, marriage."

"So says your father." Isabeau frowned her displeasure. "I am a romantic. One must marry for love, no?"

"Is that the way of it in France?"

"*Oui, oui!*" her maid answered.

Though she was an indentured servant, Isabeau did not have a father who orchestrated her every move. Given that, Elisabeth could only guess the gist of Isabeau's thoughts. *I am free. Free to come and go outside of work. Free to marry whom I please.*

And she? Who was Elisabeth Anne Lawson? The reflection in the looking glass told her little. When the history books were printed and gathered dust, what would be said of her?

That she had the fortune—or misfortune—to be the only child of the lieutenant governor of Virginia Colony, the earl of Stirling? Daughter of a firebrand mother who used ink and quill like a weapon? Possessor of a pedigree and dowry the envy of any colonial belle? Friend and confidante of Lady Dunmore? Wife of Miles Cullen Roth? Mistress of Roth Hall? End of story.

The scarlet seal on the letter was as unmistakable as the writing hand. Noble Rynallt took it from his housekeeper and retreated to the quiet of Ty Mawr's paneled study. Sitting down in a leather chair, he propped his dusty boots up on the wide windowsill overlooking the James River before breaking the letter's seal.

> *Time is of the essence. We must take account of our true allies as well as our enemies. You must finagle a way to attend Lord Dunmore's ball 2 June, 1775, at the Palace. 'Tis on behalf of your cousin, after all. Gather any intelligence you can that will aid our cause.*
>
> *Patrick Henry*

'Twas the last of May. Noble had little time to finagle. His cousin was soon to wed Williamsburg's belle, Lady Elisabeth Lawson. He'd given it little thought, had no desire to attend any function at the Governor's Palace, especially one in honor of his nemesis's daughter. Lord Stirling was onto him, onto all the Independence Men, and none of them had received an invitation. But 'twas as Henry said, Noble's cousin was the groom. Surely an invitation was forthcoming or had been overlooked.

Noble frowned, thinking of the stir he'd raise appearing. Lord Stirling was likely to have an apoplectic fit. But if that happened, at least one of the major players barring Virginia Colony's fight for independence would be removed. And his own attendance at the ball would announce he'd finally come out of second mourning.

∞

The unwrinkled copy of the *Virginia Gazette*, smelling of fresh ink and Dutch bond paper, seemed to shout the matrimonial news.

> *Miles Cullen Roth's future bride, Lady Elisabeth Lawson, an agreeable young Lady of Fortune, will preside at the Governor's ball the 2nd of June, 1775 . . .*

The flowery column included details of the much anticipated event right down to her dowry, naming minutiae even Elisabeth was unaware of. As she turned the paper facedown atop the dressing table, her smile faded. A ticklish business, indeed.

Isabeau, quick to catch her mistress's every mood, murmured, "The beggars! I'd rather it be said you have a sunny disposition and Christian character. Or that you are a smidgen over five feet tall, flaxen haired, and have all your teeth save one. And that one, *Dieu merci*, is a jaw tooth!"

"I *am* Williamsburg's bride," Elisabeth said as her maid pinned her gown together with practiced hands. "The locals feel they can print what they want about me. After all, I was born and bred in this very spot and have been catered to ever since."

"You don't begrudge them their bragging?" Isabeau studied her. "Having the particulars of one's dowry devoured by the masses seems shabby somehow."

"It does seem silly. Everyone knows what everyone else is worth in Williamsburg. There's no need to spell it out."

"Tell that to your dear papa," Isabeau answered with furrowed brow. "He had a footman pass out multiple copies of the *Gazette* this morning like bonbons on Market Square."

Unsurprised, Elisabeth fell silent. Turning, silk skirts swishing, she extended an arm for Isabeau to arrange the beribboned sleeve. Below came the muted sound of horse hooves atop cobblestones.

"Your intended? On time? And in such stormy weather?" Isabeau looked up at her mistress with surprised jade eyes.

Turning toward an open window, Elisabeth listened but now only heard the slur of rain. "Mister Roth promised he'd come. 'Tis all that matters. He didn't say when."

"How long has it been since you've seen him?"

"April," Elisabeth admitted reluctantly, wondering why Isabeau even asked. Her maid well knew, being by her side night and day. Isabeau's pinched expression was a reminder that Miles was not a favorite, no matter his standing in Williamsburg. Elisabeth dug for another excuse. "He's been busy getting Roth Hall ready for us, his letters said."

She felt a twinge at her own words, for his letters had been but two over six months. He sent unnecessary, extravagant gifts instead. Gold earrings in the shape of horseshoes. A bottle-green riding dress. Pineapples, lemons, and limes from his estate's orangery. A London-built carriage. So many presents she soon lost track of them. And not a one had swayed Isabeau's low opinion of him.

Despite his generosity, Elisabeth felt a sense of foreboding for the future. She did not want his gifts. She wanted his presence. If he was like her oft absent father . . . 'Twas difficult to see clear to what she really hoped for. A happy home. A whole family.

"Your coiffure is *magnifique*, no?" The words were uttered with satisfaction as Isabeau produced a hand mirror for her to better see the lovely twisting of curls falling to her shoulders, the wig dusted a costly powdered pink. Twin ostrich feathers, dyed a deeper rose, plumed near her right ear.

"I don't know." Reaching up, Elisabeth slid free the pins holding the wig in place, displacing the artfully arranged feathers. "Powder is going out of fashion like patch boxes. Tonight I will move forward with fashion."

Her maid's brows arched, but she took the wig and put it on a near stand, where it looked forlorn and deflated. Catching a glimpse of herself in the mirror, Isabeau smoothed a silvered strand of her own charcoal hair into place beneath her cap. At middle age, she was still an attractive woman, as dark as Elisabeth was fair.

"We must make haste, no? But first . . ." Isabeau retrieved the ostrich feathers and refastened them in Elisabeth's hair while her mistress glanced again at the watch lying faceup on her dressing table.

Late.

Miles was nothing if not perpetually late, while she happened to be an on-time sort of person. Fighting frustration, she set down the hand mirror. "I wonder what Mama is doing tonight."

Isabeau looked up, a telling sympathy in her eyes. "Your *mere* will rejoin you when all this talk of tea and taxes blows over, no?"

Elisabeth had no answer. Mama had sailed to England—Bath—months ago. All this talk of tea and taxes had no end.

A soft knock sounded on the door, followed by another maid's muffled voice. "A gentleman to see you, m'lady, in the drawing room."

A gentleman? Not her intended? She smiled wryly. Likely the servants didn't remember Miles.

She went hot, then cold. Miles's visits were so few and far between, he seemed a stranger each time she saw him. Because of it they spent the better part of an hour becoming reacquainted at each meeting. Tonight would be no different. Perhaps they'd recover the time lost to them in the coach.

Isabeau steered her to the stool of her dressing table. With deft hands, she clasped a strand of pearls about Elisabeth's neck. The routine was reassuring. Familiar. Selecting a glass bottle, Elisabeth uncapped it, overwhelmed by the scent of the latest cologne from London. Rose geranium. Again Elisabeth peered at her reflection in the looking glass with a sense of growing unease.

Everything seemed new tonight. Her scent. Her shoes. Her stays. Her gown. She'd never worn such a gown, nor felt so exposed. Despite the creamy lace spilling in profusion about her bare shoulders, the décolletage was decidedly daring. Made of oyster-pink silk, the gown shimmered and called out her every curve. The mantua maker had outdone herself this time. Fit for Queen Charlotte, it was.

Moving to the door, she grasped about for a glimmer of anticipation. "I'd best not keep company waiting."

At this, Isabeau rolled her eyes. "I should like to hear Mister Roth say such!"

Isabeau followed her out, and they passed down a dimly lit hall to a landing graced with an oriole window and upholstered seat. The velvety blackness beyond the shining glass was splashed with rain, not pierced with stars, and the warm air was soaked. This was her prayer place. Isabeau paused for a moment as Elisabeth bent her head briefly before going further.

Then down, down, down the circular steps they went, Isabeau pulling at a stray thread or straightening a fold in the polonaise skirt before reaching the open door of the sitting room, its gaudy gold and scarlet overpowering and oppressive even by candlelight. The colors reminded Elisabeth of red-coated British soldiers. She stepped inside as Isabeau retreated. Her eyes shot to the marble hearth where she expected Miles Roth to be.

"Lady Elisabeth."

She swung round, her skirts sashaying, her head spinning as well. Mercy, her stays were tight. She'd eaten little at tea.

Behind her stood a man, the shadows hiding his features. She put out a hand to steady herself, missing the needed chair back by a good two inches and finding a coat sleeve instead. The gentleman looked down at her and she looked up, finding his dark head just shy of the wispy clouds skittering in blue oils across the ceiling. Whoever he was, he wasn't Miles. Miles was but two inches taller than she.

"Mister . . ."

"Rynallt. Noble Rynallt of Ty Mawr."

What? A recollection returned to her in a rush. Noble Rynallt was a distant cousin of Miles. So distant she had no further inkling of their tie. Quickly she calculated what little she knew of him. Welsh to the bone. Master of a large James River estate. Recently bereft of a sister. A lawyer turned burgess. The Rynallts were known for their horses, were they not? Horse racing? The finest horseflesh in Virginia, if not all the colonies.

She was certain of only one thing.

Noble Rynallt was here because Miles was not.

Surprise mellowed to resignation. She gave a small curtsy. "Mister Rynallt, what an unexpected pleasure."

"Mayhap more surprise."

She hesitated. He was honest, at least. "Is Mister Roth . . ."

"Delayed." He managed to look bemused. And apologetic.

She tried not to stare as rich impressions crowded her senses. A great deal of muscle and broadcloth and sandalwood. The cut of his suit was exceptionally fine, dark but for the deep blue waistcoat embroidered with the bare minimum of silver thread, a creamy stock about his neck. The color of his eyes eluded her, the remainder of his features failing to take root as she dwelt on the word *delayed*.

Dismayed, she anchored herself to the chair at last.

"He asked me to act as your escort till he arrives." He struck a conciliatory tone. "If you'll have me."

He had the grace to sound a bit embarrassed, as well he should. This was, after all, her betrothal ball given by Lord Dunmore at the Governor's Palace, with the cream of all Williamsburg in attendance. And she was coming not with her intended but with a . . . stranger.

Nay, worse. Far worse.

Yet good breeding wouldn't allow a breach of manners. She forced a small smile. "I thank you for the kindness. Will my intended's delay be long?"

"As brief as possible, I should hope," he replied, extending an arm.

No matter who Noble Rynallt was, his polite manner communicated that he had all in hand. Yet it failed to give her the slightest ease.

"As I rode in I noticed your coach waiting," he remarked as he led her down the front steps, past the butler to the mounting block. "I'll ride alongside on my horse."

Behind them the foyer's grandfather clock tolled one too many times. The ball had begun. Lord Dunmore hated latecomers.

They'd be fashionably tardy, at best.

2

They rode down the long, puddled avenue of Palace Street, past catalpa trees and townhouses winking with candlelight. Noble's eyes were drawn to the Palace lanthorn aglow atop the flat, balustrade roof at the end of the grassy avenue. All sorts of conveyances were drawing up before the governor's residence, though none as fine as the coach he rode beside. Painted a rich cream with scenes of the four seasons on its panels, the vehicle was drawing notice. Noble hadn't seen its equal anywhere in the colonies.

Whatever his faults, Miles Roth had good taste. Expensive taste. This contraption, with its German steel springs, hardly gave a lurch as it glided north. No matter how disappointed she was at her ill-timed escort, the coach wouldn't add to Elisabeth Lawson's dismay. Though the curtains were drawn and he couldn't hear past the staccato clip of horse hooves, he could well imagine the scene playing out inside. Lady Elisabeth's maid had been as displeased to see him as her ladyship had been surprised.

Standing in his stirrups, he cast a look back over his shoulder in the direction of the Raleigh Tavern. He'd head there as soon as he could excuse himself. For now, the black edges of the humid night weighted him on every side. He much preferred a new day kindling at the rim of the horizon, suffusing storefronts and gabled roofs and fragrant Williamsburg gardens with soft light. Night reminded him of what he'd lost. Even this night seemed a tad melancholy, pressured and rushed and filled to the brim with unwanted obligations. To push the shadows back he rehearsed what he knew of the young woman in the coach in case he had to converse.

Pretty in a pale sort of way, Elisabeth Lawson had handled the news of her fiancé's tardiness with grace. Likely she'd had a great deal of practice. Although this was the first time Noble had acted as her escort, the joke round town was that Miles Roth had pressed all sorts of cohorts into similar service, as if by sending other men in his stead, he hoped she'd become smitten with one of them. Well, just this once he'd play the fool and attend the ball at Henry's request. He couldn't deny that when spirits flowed freely, tongues were loosed and the Patriots had plenty to gain. But 'twas the last time he'd undertake such hazardous duty.

Since leaving his lodgings at the Raleigh, he'd petitioned Providence all the way that Lady Elisabeth not press about the real reason for Miles Roth's delay. Noble wouldn't lie. *Delayed* seemed the safest term, though *easily swayed to his own pleasure* was more like it. Dice in hand, Miles seemed to live and breathe the motto gilded over the tavern's Apollo Room mantel: *Hilaritas sapientiae et bonae vitae proles.* Jollity, the offspring of wisdom and good living.

He doubted Patrick Henry had trouble muddling Miles's senses with draughts and spirits. But tonight of all nights his wayward cousin was not only gambling but keeping a willing woman waiting, sure to rile both Governor Dunmore and

Lady Elisabeth's powerful father. Noble felt at sea himself, having shed his mourning garb after long months of shunning society, about to attend a ball that was as appetizing as last week's she-crab soup. He craved the tranquility of Ty Mawr farther down Quarterpath Road. The abundance of sated laughter and raucous talk emerging from the Governor's Palace tainted the lovely night. Betimes Williamsburg was a boil that needed lancing.

Elisabeth shifted on the velvet cushion of the coach seat, glad the utter blackness hid her tense features. Yet she knew Isabeau sensed her turmoil, just as plainly as she sensed her maid's. It seemed to ooze and roil in the close air between them.

"Your pink feathers are ruffled, no?" Isabeau murmured, her rapid French laced with alarm. "Your intended should be ashamed! Tardy for his betrothal ball!"

"'Tis not Miles Roth I'm thinking about," Elisabeth confessed, "but *him*."

"Monsieur Rynallt? *Oui, oui*, he has finally come out of mourning."

"'Twould appear so," Elisabeth replied dryly.

In the coach's heated confines, Isabeau swished her fan. "A great many belles at the ball will be smiling even if you are not. I simply wish that he did not look so much like a scoundrel."

"Scoundrel?" Elisabeth peered at her maid through the darkness. "That is not how I would describe him."

"No?" Isabeau's voice pitched. She was all but wringing her hands. "He is—how do you say it? A rascal? A rogue? Swarthy as a buccaneer with his dark looks. Some say he has more gypsy blood than Welsh."

"How is it that you know so much about him?" The question seemed silly. Isabeau knew nearly everyone in and about Williamsburg. Her pride was in taking the pulse of the place.

"There is plenty of tittle-tattle about town."

"Can you not find something good, then, to say in his behalf?"

"*Oui, oui!*" Isabeau pursed her lips in thought. "The hospitality of Ty Mawr is well known. No one who comes a-begging is turned away. Not only that, the maids at the Raleigh say Monsieur Rynallt is the very best patron they have, tipping so generously."

Elisabeth snapped her fan open, stirring the too-warm air. "I'm not interested in his benevolence but his politics."

"His politics?" Isabeau's voice fell to a disgruntled whisper. "He is one of the Independence Men, you mean."

The words *Independence Men*, oft uttered like an oath by her father, now returned to Elisabeth like a thunderclap, as did something equally ominous that fought its way to the forefront of her memory. "He's also a dissenter and no longer comes to church."

"Not your church, no? He is a Pi—Pe—"

"Presbyterian?" She knew as little about that as Isabeau. There was but one church, according to her father. The Church of England. Her fan fluttered harder. "Perhaps I should have refused his offer of escort. But I was caught so unawares."

"*Oh la vache!*" Isabeau's voice climbed. "I have no words! Think on it, mistress. You coming in on the arm of not Monsieur Roth, your intended, but a—a—"

"An independence-loving, church-shunning radical," Elisabeth said, then amended, "There are plenty of that sort in Williamsburg these days."

"Your papa—he will be enraged, no?"

"Indeed." Elisabeth paused, a tiny tendril of amusement taking root. "But I think Mama would be pleased."

"*Oui*. But your dear *mere* is not here."

Elisabeth took a steadying breath. "I'd plead illness, but this ball has been planned for months. Lady Charlotte is acting in my mother's stead. Her girls are to be my bridesmaids . . ."

The coach rolled to a gentle stop, and the remaining words went unsaid. The Palace entrance was bustling despite the rain, the humid air thick with aromas from the kitchen. She could hear the sweet trill of violins. An undeniable spark of excitement pulsed on the heavy June air, even if it wasn't her own. Before her shoe struck the first coach step, Elisabeth determined to play her part to secure her future, regardless of her feelings.

⟡

Noble's prayer for a discreet entrance to the Palace's festivities was answered. At the precise moment he and Lady Elisabeth stepped into the flower-strewn entry, a woman swooned at the far end of the ballroom, and several liveried footmen rushed to her rescue. Every eye was fixed on the ailing Lady Grey, and Noble simply guided Elisabeth Lawson by the elbow into the midst of the glittering assembly. A first minuet was struck, and they moved onto the polished parquet floor with the other dancers as if they'd been there from the first.

She looked up at him, her intelligent eyes assessing, a relieved pleasure pinking her powdered features as if he was—dare he think it?—some sort of hero. When she looked away from him, his eyes traced the delicate oval of her face, noting every detail.

A dimple in her left cheek, visible even without a smile. Darkly arched brows. Aquiline nose. Remarkably blue eyes. Smooth white shoulders sloped down to an elaborately embroidered gown that seemed to catch the light of every candle.

She hardly looked besmirched, yet she was. Not only by her rake of a fiancé but by he himself and his less than honorable intentions squiring her. Beside her he felt less than gallant, using her ladyship for political purposes, though his cause was noble enough.

Though he hadn't danced in what seemed a decade, she made the reacquaintance almost effortless. A discarded memory pulled at him and fell into place. Lady Elisabeth was the same woman he'd seen with Lord Dunmore's daughters in the royal gardens not long ago, trying to master the steps of some complicated country dance. He remembered her laugh, not high and flutelike as he thought it would be, but throaty and rich as a violoncello. The dancing master had not been amused, he remembered, when he and his fellow burgesses had slowed to watch as they left a meeting at the Palace.

Her eyes were no longer on him but swept the room restlessly. She was looking for Miles Roth, obviously, and he felt curiously let down. His cousin deserved a sound thrashing for his wayward ways. If only Miles was made of sterner stuff, immune to Henry's wiles. Yet Patriots like him and Henry relied on Miles's weaknesses to strengthen their own cause. Still, Noble's own part in the scheme sat uneasily.

He was suddenly aware of a great many eyes upon them now, for a great many reasons. Without prior arrangement, without forethought, the two of them were the only wigless, unpowdered people in the room. And her lovely gown with its avalanche of lace was a perfect foil for the dark ribbed silk of his suit. For the moment they seemed to be creating as much a stir as Miles's absence and Noble's own unannounced end to mourning.

By the time Miles finally entered, the shimmering ice sculptures had begun swimming in crystal punch bowls in the adjoining supper room, and the spun sugar frosting on the enormous tiered cake had succumbed to a slow melt. One look at him and Noble knew someone had had to pry the dice from Miles's hand to get him here. In his yellow satin suit, he looked like a giant honeybee, a port stain splotched across his waistcoat, his stock askew. Noble felt a blistering embarrassment for Elisabeth Lawson.

Duty bound, he squired her about the crowded edges of the ballroom to Miles's side, struck by the horrendously incompatible picture they made. She so pure and genteel, his cousin debauched and half drunk.

It seemed a grim prediction of their future.

Before Elisabeth could recover her manners and thank him, Noble Rynallt had turned his back on them and made his way to the knot of gentlemen near an open window. He slid through the perspiring summer crowd—no easy task, given the crush of three hundred people in attendance. She watched him go with a mixture of relief and regret.

At his exit, her father was soon at her elbow, looking down at her. To the casual observer he seemed unruffled, but she knew better. "I'd thought to see you here long before now."

The stern words were directed at her, not her intended, as if she was somehow to blame for both Miles's tardiness *and* her own.

"My apologies, sir." Miles reached up a hand to straighten his stock, eyes roving the overwarm room. "I was detained."

At least Miles had the gumption to speak for her. Whatever his faults, he was one of the few men not cowed by her father. He was, for better or worse, unapologetically . . . Miles.

Elisabeth looked in dismay at the deep purple stain blooming on his chest, the hue of Noble Rynallt's impeccable attire. Moving in front of Miles, she reached out a gloved hand and drew his suit coat closed with a steel-cut button, hiding the offending mark.

His voice held a trace of tenderness. "Ah, m'lady, always looking out for me."

She softened at the unexpected words. Aware of her father's scrutiny, she resisted the urge to tuck in a strand of fair hair falling free of Miles's wig. Truly, yellow was not a good color on him. He looked washed out, a wastrel. Had he no valet? Once they'd wed she'd help manage his wardrobe with suitable shades.

"I suppose we should dance," he finally murmured, eyeing the crowd.

Her father looked on as a Scotch reel was struck, as lively as the minuet had been sedate.

Once in Miles's arms she was overcome by the distillation of sweat, snuff, and spirits. He moved a bit wildly, limbs loosened by too much port.

Through the melee of whirling, swirling dancers, Noble Rynallt's face stayed steadfast. Now standing near the supper room doors, he resembled one of the paintings on the ornate walls. Guarded, watchful, unsmiling.

Not far from him was Lady Charlotte, her crimson silk a fiery counterpoint to her oldest daughter's ice-blue taffeta. Any displeasure she felt about the presence of one of the Independence Men was well hidden. Indeed, Lady Charlotte was smiling at Elisabeth benignly, making anything else of little consequence.

And her fiancé? He looked bored. Irritated. At the very ball in his honor.

Oh, Miles, you are enjoying none of this.

All the heart went out of her. Her father's disapproval, Miles's sated disinterest, her own inability to partake of any merriment, all worked to snuff any flicker of joy. "Sunny," folks about Williamsburg sometimes called her, on account of her felicitous disposition.

Tonight she felt sunny no longer.

3

The following day, Elisabeth moved down the shadowed hall and paused at her mother's bedchamber. The answering silence spoke volumes. She pushed open the door, and fresh sentiment sliced through her. Usually sitting in a wingback chair by an open window, Priscilla Lawson was always busy with handwork or her writing, her slender figure clad in painted silks and satins from France and Britain, all adorned with lace she'd worked. Her French ancestry was apparent in the lacemaking tradition of five generations beginning with her great-grandmother, Gabrielle, and then her grandmother, Isabelle, who'd moved to England and taken her lacemaking there. Elisabeth's mother had in turn brought her lacemaking to Virginia colony, even founding a small group of local Williamsburg lacemakers, of which she was patron.

Years before, Priscilla Carter had been the belle of Bath. Traces of that loveliness still lingered in her rich auburn hair and diminutive hands and feet. Would she be much changed when she returned from England?

"Don't you worry none, m'lady." 'Twas Mamie, her moth-

26

er's maid. Despite her bulk, she moved quietly and entered through the dressing room doorway. "She be back soon."

Taking the handkerchief Mamie offered, Elisabeth dried her eyes, bypassed the vacant chair, and sank down on an embroidered footstool, pondering all she'd hoped to do with her mother in the days leading up to the wedding. "This afternoon is the final fitting for my bridal gown. Margaret Hunter sent round a note saying the wedding fans Mama selected have just come in."

"Miss Cressida goin' with you?" Mamie asked from where she now sat spinning on a small wheel in a corner.

Nodding, Elisabeth struck a lighter tone. "When we return from the mantua maker's, perhaps we shall have tea in the arbor. I'll stop by the bake shop for those chestnut tarts Mama is so fond of."

Mamie smiled, her plump body moving in time with the wheel. "Doctor Hessel's due any minute."

"Doctor Hessel? Why?"

"Now you know better'n I do 'bout that." Mamie's fondness for the young physician overrode the subtle annoyance in her tone. "Your papa called him in to see you one last time before the weddin'. I told the butler to send him on upstairs."

On the heels of Mamie's words came a footfall. Resigned, Elisabeth left the bedchamber as quietly as she came, nearly bumping into the doctor in the hall.

"Ah, there you are," he began, his voice booming in the quiet. His lack of pretense, even a proper greeting, was one of his most endearing traits. He seemed almost a member of the family. In the feeble light of the hall, his eyes sought hers and seemed to assess the situation with a glance as he followed her into the sitting room. "You look unwell."

"Do I?" Clutching Mamie's damp handkerchief, she did

feel in need of some remedy. "Perhaps being up half the night dancing and feasting has left me lifeless as a rag doll. But I shan't complain." Truly, missing her mother was the malady, yet she wouldn't bemoan that.

"I've brought some medicines should you need them," he said, opening his medical kit as Mamie hovered.

"Best save them for another of your patients," Elisabeth told him. "I feel fit as a fiddle."

"You're to honeymoon in the West Indies, your father tells me. I thought it wise to prescribe quinine for the trip."

"Kind of you."

"Kind? 'Tis what I do." His wry smile called out one of hers. "You're fully recovered from the spring fever, Mamie said. I must confess I wouldn't have prescribed a wedding this soon."

"Soon? 'Tis been months in the making." She raised her shoulders in a ladylike shrug. "Papa has his plans."

"Is your father here?"

"Nay, he's often away these days, closeted with Lord Dunmore." Could he sense her relief at that? "Since the gunpowder incident . . ."

"Of course. Say no more." Sympathy softened his fair features. Even in the shadows, his Dutch descent was apparent—and his youth. Though he was not yet five and thirty, his training in Holland had made him one of the most sought-after doctors in the colonies. "You have your mother's frail constitution, your father feels, and every precaution is due."

He was one word away from calling her an invalid. All the times she'd nearly died while in his care rose up, clouding the day. First a virulent fever, then a near fatal chest infection, followed by other, smaller maladies.

She reached out and laid a pale hand on his coat sleeve,

gratitude eclipsing her dismay for a few fleeting seconds. "All will be well. Soon I shall wed at Bruton Parish and be happily situated at Roth Hall, close enough to send word should I have need of you."

"Indeed." He patted her hand, more her friend than physician. "If only all my patients were half so obliging."

What had Mama last said to her before she had boarded the *Sparling*?

"What an ever-changing world is this beyond the shifting shadows of our brick townhouse."

Adjusting the brim of her hat to deflect the afternoon sun, Elisabeth tried to push aside thoughts of weddings and trips abroad as the open chaise glided down Botetourt Street. Colonial Williamsburg seemed to pulse with the beat of dissent. This very morn the local militia was mustering at the new courthouse, and men were flocking to Charlton's coffeehouse to discuss the latest news from England. Women weren't allowed inside Charlton's, but she took a long look at its wooden façade, her mouth watering at the fragrant Caribbean chocolate carrying on a teasing breeze.

Her beloved Williamsburg was no longer entirely a Tory town, all citizens loyal subjects of King George III. 'Twas fast becoming a den of rabid radicals, Papa said. Could it be that the tension beneath their roof was linked more to the revolutionary activity all around them than the more personal conflict between her parents?

"Front or back, m'lady?" The coachman turned his head as they neared the Shaw residence.

"Back, please."

Cressida lived on the street just beyond. Like usual, she was waiting inside the delicate tracery of wrought-iron fencing in the rear garden, her face alive with impatience. Set back from the street, the Shaw residence was sprawling and genteel as befitting a leading merchant. Elisabeth particularly liked the bricked walk to the house shaded by linden trees. But today she hardly noticed, readying herself for the volley of questions Cressida was sure to ask.

They'd scarcely spoken at the ball. Cressida, like Elisabeth, was endowed with a bountiful dowry and had been set upon by widowers and bachelors alike. Unlike Elisabeth, Cressida showed no ill effects from too much dancing and too little sleep.

The coal-colored hair and sloe eyes Cressida had inherited from her West Indies mother, coupled with the fiery Scottish pedigree of her father, made Elisabeth seem colorless in comparison. If Elisabeth Lawson was Williamsburg's bride, Cressida Shaw was Williamsburg's belle.

"London, drive the long way," her friend said, pressing a sixpence into the coachman's gloved hand. "Slow as molasses, if you please."

He nodded, helping her into the chaise before shutting the door.

As she sat beside Elisabeth on the upholstered seat, their gowns clashed in a profusion of sea green and raspberry taffeta.

"Where is Isabeau?" Cressida asked.

"Sick with a headache," Elisabeth answered.

"How fortunate. I've given Molly leave for the afternoon," Cressida said of her own maid. "We've much to discuss, you and I." At Elisabeth's silence, Cressida turned and looked her full in the face. "Why, Lizzy, you're dark as a thundercloud! You're not having second thoughts, are you?"

"About?"

"Your wedding!"

Second thoughts? Not once in her life had she been allowed them. Her father had dictated her every move from the cradle. And she'd never questioned it till Cressida came into her world. Dear Cress, whose father let her do whatever she willed.

"I'd hoped Mama would accompany us today," Elisabeth said, careful to keep her emotions in check. "But she has yet to arrive."

"It must be hard having an invalid in the house, needing relief from Virginia's heat. But I do wonder if chilly Bath is of any more benefit, not to mention the long sea voyage." Raising her fan, Cressida gave a languid wave to a passing carriage as they turned onto the rutted lane leading to the outskirts of town. "But we've no time to waste talking of mothers and maids. Not with Noble Rynallt just come out of mourning."

The unexpected words returned Elisabeth to the matter at hand. So Cressida had noticed him? Thinking of his rapid departure from the ballroom, she said, "He was hardly there. He didn't even stay for the midnight supper."

"He prefers the Raleigh Tavern, probably because of his politics," Cressida murmured. "'Tis no secret he and Lord Dunmore don't see eye to eye. 'Twas gallant of him to escort you. Quite brave, actually, given the Palace's stance concerning Patriots. And I'm quite sure it offended your father's sensibilities also."

Elisabeth didn't like the reminder. She'd not seen her father since the ball, as he'd kept to the Palace. But soon he'd take her to task.

"Hmm." Cressida continued her speculating. "Perhaps something nefarious is at play."

Nefarious? Cressida had always been a tad dramatic.

"Mister Rynallt was simply doing Miles a favor. They're cousins, remember. Neighbors."

"Ah, neighbors, indeed, as much as thousands of acres will allow. Roth Hall pales in light of Ty Mawr being on the river. Have you not seen it?" At the shake of Elisabeth's head, Cressida made a sorry face. "A shame. Every marriageable female from here to Boston should. Ty Mawr is in sore need of a mistress."

"Since Mister Rynallt's sister passed, you mean." She'd hardly known Enid Rynallt. Enid was older. A spinster. A woman who preferred Ty Mawr to Williamsburg. "I've not seen the Rynallt estate, but you do tempt me."

"Dearest Lizzy." Leaning back on the seat, Cressida looked vastly satisfied. "How glad I am that you have bypassed the most eligible bachelor in all Virginia."

Elisabeth studied her, understanding dawning. "Are you smitten with the master—or Ty Mawr?"

"Perhaps both." Cressida's eyes narrowed. "You can well imagine my dismay when you entered on his arm. And then I remembered that he is Miles's kin and will soon be your cousin-in-law."

"But what of Mister Bennett?"

"Poor Mister Bennett." She gave a sigh worthy of the recent comic opera they'd seen at the theater erected on Palace Green. "A lowly tradesman, is all. Father thinks I need to reconsider our . . . arrangement."

Seeing her friend so dismissive left Elisabeth feeling slightly sick. Had she no memory that her own father was a tradesman? He'd been middling at best before rising to the heights of Virginia's gentry as far as an ambitious Tory merchant could.

"The Bennetts are a fine family," Elisabeth said. "And devout believers."

Cressida had the grace to turn a slightly sheepish pink. "Fine for someone else. Think of it, Lizzy. With you at Roth Hall and myself mistress of Ty Mawr, we'll be neighbors."

"There is the small matter of your groom, mind you—and his politics."

Cressida gave her a sly smile. "I'm sure I can manage on both counts. What of you? Can you manage the roguish Mr. Roth?"

The probing question was so bruising Elisabeth nearly winced. "In time, perhaps." Did that sound as flat as she felt? "But Papa has made the match and I must honor it."

"I say let your father marry him," Cressida replied irreverently.

Ignoring this, Elisabeth continued on. "It helps, of course, to think of Miles's good qualities."

"Has he any?" A look of outright humor shone on Cressida's face. "Besides his inheritance?"

Embarrassment flooded Elisabeth. For Miles. For herself. Her mind emptied then righted itself. The words of Philippians wove through her head like a song.

Whatsoever things are true, whatsoever things are honest, whatsoever things are just, whatsoever things are pure, whatsoever things are lovely, whatsoever things are of good report; if there be any virtue, and if there be any praise, think on these things.

"He's generous," Elisabeth said at last.

"Extravagant, you mean," Cressida returned.

"I'm sure, after we're wed, more of his good qualities will make themselves known to me."

Cressida looked doubtful. "Noble Rynallt of Ty Mawr has so many exceptional traits it would take me from here to Charles Town to enumerate them all."

"Thankfully, we're only going to the mantua maker's, so you won't have to," Elisabeth said with a bit of bite as the sign for Margaret Hunter's came into view. She glanced at her watch, feeling the need to hurry home.

What if today was the day Mama finally docked?

Straight pins sticking at odd angles between her thin lips, Margaret Hunter examined the wedding gown from every angle, a dent of concern in her brow. Elisabeth sensed the mantua maker's disapproval. Cressida roamed the once richly appointed shop, perusing the silk masks and remaining fans with an assistant, far enough away to miss the mantua maker's strained whisper.

"Lady Elisabeth, 'tis the third time I've taken in this gown. Are you not eating?"

Elisabeth hesitated, remembering how none of the delicacies at the Governor's Palace had tempted her and she'd managed but half a scone and some nonimportation tea this morning. Silence was the best answer, she guessed.

Turning before a full-length mirror, Elisabeth was easily lost in the luxury of the gown, ill-fitting or no. Since the boycott of British goods, Williamsburg's seamstresses had been hard-pressed to stock their shelves. Elisabeth's wedding dress had been made from a quantity of silk Margaret Hunter had tucked away and forgotten. Likely Providence had prompted the notoriously meticulous Margaret to remember an item she should never have overlooked in the first place.

Who could forget Spitalfields silk?

Cressida came up from behind, peering over Elisabeth's shoulder into the looking glass. "I do hope you have more

34

quality fabric stashed away. I've decided on painted silk for my wedding dress."

Plucking the pins from her mouth and returning them to the heart-shaped pincushion dangling from her waist, Margaret said, "I've read nothing in the *Gazette* of your nuptials, Miss Shaw."

"You soon shall," Cressida replied. "Best begin stitching straightaway. I have my eye on a gentleman along the James River. And I don't believe in long engagements."

Margaret's voluminous skirts swished out of sight before Elisabeth hissed, "You would marry an *Independence Man*?"

"Indeed. Those unpredictable rebels are far more dashing than the staid Tories." Once again, Cressida smiled like a cat with cream. "I shall see Mister Rynallt before the week is out and must say I am counting the hours."

Tongue-tied with dismay, Elisabeth fell silent. Cressida always seemed one step ahead of her. A planned rendezvous, perhaps? Her friend was bubbling over with glee. Poor Mister Bennett.

Or perhaps . . . Elisabeth allowed herself an ungracious thought.

Perhaps poor Mister Bennett was blessed indeed.

⊸⊷

Sitting in the shaded arbor, Elisabeth opened the box of chestnut tarts, the flaky crusts and nutty centers oddly unappetizing. Once again the chair across from her yawned empty. Cressida had declined tea, citing another engagement. Mama had yet to materialize. Perhaps it would do Elisabeth good to *pretend* her mother sat there, not just air. Feeling a burst of whimsy, she shot a glance at the house's back windows before talking to herself in low tones.

"My gown is finished, Mama. Well ahead of the wedding." She reached into her pocket and produced a bridesmaid's fan, unfolding it and placing it atop the small table. "I think the design you chose for these is beautiful. Margaret Hunter agrees."

Pausing in her monologue, Elisabeth lingered on the fan's artful lines. Her name was gilded directly on the leaf paper, complete with her wedding date of June 16, 1775. "We had a lovely betrothal ball at the Governor's Palace. Several ladies asked about you and said they've kept you close in prayer."

Seeing the maid approach with a tea tray, she bent her head and said silent grace. She could almost sense her mother's presence. Hear her beautifully modulated English voice. But it was her father who often overrode her mother's heartfelt petitions, the prayer he said at each meal easily remembered.

"Submit yourselves for the Lord's sake to every human institution, whether to king as one in authority, or to governors sent by him, for such is the will of God. Honor all people, love the brotherhood, fear God, honor the king."

The maid poured tea beneath the fragrant, rose-covered arbor, smiling her thanks as Elisabeth snuck a pastry into her pocket.

At that, the girl began clearing her throat—the telling signal that Father was approaching. All of Elisabeth's delight vanished. Down the bricked path he came, stern of face and stiff of figure. Usually he clutched a pipe and freshly inked copy of Rivington's *Royal Gazette*. Always he was dark as a storm cloud. Had he ever been any different?

Today his hands were empty, his dismissal frightfully curt. "Leave us. I would speak with my daughter alone."

The maid gave a quick curtsy and withdrew.

For a moment his gaze drifted over the hollyhocks and

phlox Mama had cultivated with the help of Governor Dunmore's gardener. Such beauty in the face of such sternness. The beloved statuary of a small child releasing a dove from a cage in the heart of the garden drew Elisabeth's eye. Even as a child she'd wished to fly away like that dove whenever he was near.

In the glare of sunlight his once-handsome face was compromised, cheeks deeply pitted from the pox. The heavy powder concealing the scars gave him a wan appearance when he was, in fact, quite robust. "Elisabeth Anne."

"Yes, Father."

Their eyes met, and for the briefest second his seemed to thaw. Their silvery depths, so shrewd and assessing, took in the only child he'd ever had, and Elisabeth was again reminded that all his hopes were pinned on her marriage to Lord Dunmore's protégé—a king's man and, more importantly, heir to what seemed like half of Virginia.

"You've recovered from the ball?"

She hesitated. Had she?

The shadow of Noble Rynallt seemed to fall across the tea table between them, and it was no surprise when her father said, "How is it that you arrived on the arm of one of the Independence Men?"

She expelled her breath in a soft rush. "'Tis somewhat a mystery." She wouldn't speak ill of him, or Miles, though Miles's liquored breath had told her volumes. "Mister Rynallt simply said he was doing his cousin a favor. I believe he is acting as best man."

His eyes narrowed. "You should know there's a plan afoot to take Lord Dunmore's life. And 'tis originating with the Liberty Boys, the Independence Men."

She felt her jaw go slack. Noble Rynallt seemed a gentleman

to the core, as did all the other Patriots she knew of. "The Independence Men aren't lunatics and murderers, are they?"

"Ever since the gunpowder incident, they're murmuring about taking up arms against the king. Noble Rynallt is one of the chief dissenters. Desperate times drive men to desperate measures."

Elisabeth took a sip of lukewarm tea. Desperate times, indeed, though Lord Dunmore had never been popular, even among the top tier of Virginia society. Yet she was able to say in truth, "Lord Dunmore and Lady Charlotte have always been exceedingly kind to me. I'd hate to see any harm come to them. Or their children."

He looked at the uneaten tarts, and his expression shifted from tense to sullen. "Your mother's arrival is imminent. I fear her health has taken another bad turn. I'm considering sending her to Berkeley Springs to recuperate."

Imminent? How did he know? As for the springs—they were so far.

"If she returns in the same mental state, I may have Doctor Hessel admit her to Publick Hospital."

For a moment she sat speechless, the teacup in hand suspended in midair. "Papa—nay!" The outburst was uttered before she could school her emotions. He would punish her mother for her politics? "But the wedding—"

His reproving look assured her she'd overstepped her bounds. "Would you have her at the wedding on a cot—or in a strait dress?"

"Papa, please."

"When are you going to accept the fact that she's of fragile constitution and unsound mind?"

The flagrant lie nearly made her flinch. She caught sight of Mamie at an upstairs window looking down at them. Mamie knew the truth. Dear, guileless Mamie, who'd tended her mother since she was first wed. In an especially cruel twist, her father had denied her accompanying Mama to Bath, sending a maid of his own choosing instead.

Elisabeth recalled Mamie's words.

"Yer mama may be frail, but she's of sounder mind than yer papa. 'Tis just her politics he hates. What sort o' man names his wife a lunatic and threatens her with a strait dress lessen she change her views?"

"She's no more distressed than anyone else with all this talk of tea and taxes," Elisabeth began, mounting a pitiful defense of a woman who wasn't present to defend herself. "I'm sure Bath was a blessed respite from colonial politics."

"For a score of years or better she's been unsound. Before she sailed she had the gall to speak in defense of the Independence Men. Such talk smacks of treason. There are times when I suspect you are following in her footsteps. Your arrival at the ball with Rynallt gives me pause."

So he would blame her for that too? "'Twas Miles Roth's doing, not mine," she replied with rare fire. "He simply sent his cousin to escort me, as he was belated. I had nothing to do with it—"

"Indeed. That's how it begins, you know, all this rebellion. A sharp departure from the truth."

Oh? Just who was dealing in unreality? Setting her jaw, she looked down at her tea, the Lowestoft cup and saucer a watercolor of blue and gold.

Reaching out, he snapped a rose from its stem to tuck in his lapel. "Tell Mamie to ready your mother's bedchamber for her return."

4

Noble Rynallt stood by the hitch rails beneath the gnarled oaks outside Bruton Parish Church in a haze of dust and filtered sunlight. Guests were gathering for a morning wedding that should have been under way a quarter of an hour ago. The bride was missing, someone said. 'Twas his distant cousin, Lucy Croghan, but as she was so besotted with her bridegroom, no one seemed to think anything of it, he least of all.

The stray thought returned his attention to another cousin, another wedding in the offing, mere days away. Miles had asked him to act as best man. He would, though the thought aggravated him like a burr.

Moving out of sight of the late arrivals, he went into the fenced graveyard. Enid was buried at the back beneath the shade of a stately oak. He bypassed other graves with their urns and willows, cherubs and drapery, to his sister's box tomb with its simple engraved hourglass noting the flight of time.

Here lieth the body of Enid Rynallt, beloved daughter of Kennard and Catrin Rynallt, who departed this life in the twenty-ninth year of age . . .

Eyes smarting, he looked west, where the churchyard gave way to pastoral fields that reminded him of Wales. Times like these he contemplated returning to his homeland. But as a second son who'd made his stake in the colonies, he'd left his elder brother to go it alone years before. Enid had soon followed. On this side of the Atlantic, once at home, he now felt adrift save for a few distant relatives. Enid had been an anchor, the heartbeat of Ty Mawr. She had never married, not for lack of offers but because she loved Ty Mawr too much.

The momentary stillness of the graveyard was cut off by a trilling laugh near the entrance. He turned to see the Shaw family arrive. Cressida descended from the carriage onto the mounting block near the church steps in a flurry of lavender silk and lace. Their eyes met briefly across the ground, and it seemed her face assumed a rosy hue even at a distance.

Later, at the wedding reception, if there was no way out of it he'd claim her for a minuet or reel before excusing himself. If he could master his dislike of society. Make polite small talk. The weight of his responsibilities pressed in on him, and he rued being at a wedding when he had better things to do. Today he needed to be in a great many places all at once. The tobacco warehouse in Port Royal. Assessing the militia companies encamped in Williamsburg about the capital and magazine. Or better yet, taking stock of his new stallion gotten from Maryland to sire a brood mare.

Running a finger around the ivory folds of his stock, he loosened the clip at the nape of his neck. Strangle-tight it was in the summer heat.

The subtle tug he always felt to be home was checked by the emptiness he encountered without his sister there. He turned toward the church, his melancholy tempered at the sight of the bride arriving in a chaise. Expression joyous, she waved a gloved hand at him, her attention diverted as her groom rushed out of the church to meet her. Noble felt as if he were on the outside, a handsbreadth beyond all that joy. He turned away, his resolve to attend the ceremony for Lucy's sake ebbing like sand through a sieve.

Had it been two years since Enid died? As he stood at her grave, it felt fresh as yesterday. He'd come here today to deal with the sorrowful memory more than attend a wedding. Since her passing he'd shunned family occasions. Time to move on, mayhap, away from the loss, putting aside his mourning clothes along with any lasting melancholy. Best honor the ceremony then head for Christiana Campbell's, where the reception was to be held. He'd congratulate the happy couple, shuffle through an obligatory dance or two, and hope for brighter days.

𝕯

There were but two places on earth entrenched in Elisabeth Lawson's head and heart. One was her chintz bedchamber, and the other was the Palace gardens where James, the aging gardener, held sway. There everything was fresh and delightful and so artfully arranged it stole one's breath. Everywhere she looked was color and light and beauty. There was the little bagnio, or bathhouse, with its charming hexagonal lines, bed upon bed of riotous flowers, and the boxwood parterres that gave way to gently sloping terraces ending at the enormous fish pond below. It seemed the embodiment of green pastures and still waters.

A breeze gusted, turning her dress a swirl of buttery linen around her. For a few moments she was able to forget the ache of her mother's absence and her father's latest outburst.

The familiar sight of Lady Charlotte's maid, hurrying down the garden walk toward her made her pause. And then, like colorful butterflies released from a cage, Lord Dunmore's daughters swarmed Elisabeth, fluttering past the maid on a warm wind in matching silken dresses.

"Lizzy, Mama has need of you," Lady Augusta called, her fair features turning a deep pink as if she realized she misspoke.

"'Tis *Lady Elisabeth* to you," the exacting maid reminded, ever attempting to curb their exuberance.

"You'll find Mama in the wisteria arbor," Lady Catherine said as she slowed, lifting a skirt hem to view a wayward slipper. "Drat! I've turned my ankle and lost half my shoe!"

"You shouldn't be galloping about like wild horses," the maid scolded, snatching up the offending heel before shooing the girls away. "Miss Galli is ready to resume your lessons."

Giggling, the girls turned and saw the governess's shadow near the Palace. The gardener had slipped away, and Elisabeth was left to trail the lady's maid to where Lady Charlotte waited beneath the arbor freshly painted for summer, a weathervane bearing the English coat of arms atop it. This was the place of many happy hours, of talks and tea and shared laughter, and Elisabeth was only too glad to obey the summons to come.

Ever since Lord Dunmore's family had arrived from England three years prior, Elisabeth had been a frequent guest at the Palace, acquainting them with the moods and rhythms of Williamsburg. Though her husband's popularity was in question, Lady Charlotte's graciousness and beauty had won the heart of nearly everyone she met. But Williamsburg wasn't England, and the years had done little to ease her homesickness. Always Elisabeth sensed a sadness about her, and today was no different.

"Ah, Lady Elisabeth, the sight of you does me good." Reaching across the wrought-iron table, Lady Charlotte squeezed her hand. "'Tis uncommonly warm for June, is it not? I can scarcely bear another summer like the last one."

"Mama said the same before she left for Bath," Elisabeth remembered, settling in the chair opposite. The sight of Lady Charlotte's mottled complexion reminded Elisabeth what a trial it was for her and every European she knew. Despite the heaviness of the mosquito-laden air, she felt at home in its heat, as she'd never known any different.

"Your father tells me she'll go at once to Berkeley Springs."

Elisabeth shifted her gaze from the flawlessly powdered, bewigged woman before her to the gardener as he tamed a yew hedge across the way. "Mama has been overly tired since her last attack of the ague. Papa is zealous for her return to health."

"If I can do anything . . . if you should need any help with the wedding . . ."

Elisabeth smiled. "The lovely ball you gave was gift enough."

Lady Charlotte nodded. "We shall miss you sorely once you leave Williamsburg. The girls are moping about already. Roth Hall seems so far, yet you must be anxious to be its mistress."

Elisabeth paused, the estate's hazy lines and angles unfolding in her mind. She'd visited but twice since she and Miles had first met, and it failed to make a lasting impression. "Miles says the new wing overlooking the deer park is nearly complete." *But he has yet to let me see it*, she didn't add. On the other hand, might he be saving it as a delightful surprise? "You and the girls are always welcome."

"I well remember what 'tis like to be a bride," Lady Charlotte said, studying Elisabeth with thoughtful azure eyes. "I was so besotted with John I would have wed him had he been a chimney sweep."

Truly? The very thought of "Dandy Dunmore," as he was called, covered in soot and clutching brushes almost made Elisabeth laugh. But her amusement faded when Lady Charlotte added, "I'd hoped your liaison with Miles Roth would be a love match."

Was it so obvious, then, that it was all business? Elisabeth's spirits sagged. "I'm fond of him." The admission grieved her, and the sympathetic light in Lady Charlotte's eyes made her feel somewhat cheated. "Love. What is it, truly? I don't love Miles Roth and he doesn't love me. But my father has use of him, and he of us."

There. She had confessed it—as bluntly as her father might have done. But it didn't expunge her longing or change her circumstances.

Lady Charlotte shifted in her chair, and tiny flakes of powder sifted from her wig onto the shoulders of her periwinkle gown. "Marital affection, one hopes, grows in time. And then, when the children come, one's heart is full."

Elisabeth sat completely still, letting the gracious words seep into her and temper her strange yearning. Since she'd been in leading strings, besotted with her dolls, that desire had flowered into a longing for a happy home. A family of her own unlike the one she'd known.

"I say such things because you've become a daughter to me. When I consider your many kindnesses and the infinite help you've shown since we first came here, friendless and ignorant of colonial customs and society, how you've continued to stand by us when so many have fallen away . . ."

Lady Charlotte's eyes shimmered and Elisabeth sensed her deep struggle, her longing for England. "I simply want the very best for you—your future happiness."

This impassioned speech, so unusual for the genteel, polished woman Elisabeth had come to know, began to chip away at the edges of her own composure till she felt adrift and near tears herself.

Lady Charlotte reached into her pocket and brought out a letter bearing her personal seal, made more beautiful by her elegant penmanship. "Keep this close till you're home and have a private moment. I'd thought to tell you these things in person, but such details are better penned. Please burn this once you've read it." She passed the letter to Elisabeth and rose with a rustle of silk, chin trembling. "I'm needed at the Palace. Baby Virginia has sprouted a new tooth and is peevish. Your father is inside. Shall you wait for him?"

Elisabeth could see his carriage near the stables. "Nay. I'm in need of a walk. Please tell him I've gone home." As she turned away, she felt a check to stay, if only for a moment. Turning back around, she reached out to embrace Lady Charlotte. But she was already hurrying back to the Palace, weeping.

Down Palace Green Elisabeth walked, grieved by Lady Charlotte's tears and clutching the mysterious letter. Something more had been penned than wedding salutations, surely. Letters and gifts had been arriving from all over Virginia. Smoked hams. Saddles and riding gear. Peacocks for Roth Hall's expansive lawn. The servants were busy cataloguing and displaying each item in a little-used formal parlor before boxing them up to move to Roth Hall after the wedding. The noisy peacocks were placed in the garden, their wings clipped so they wouldn't fly away. With the wedding day almost upon them, all the little details were falling into place but one.

Would Mama arrive in time?

Lady Charlotte's outburst suggested something even more pressing was afoot. But what?

The glorious June sunlight, coupled with all of the familiar, reassuring sights and smells and noises about town, seemed to mock her suspicions. She took Nicholson Street, careful to avert her eyes from the public gaol. As it was crammed with pirates, debtors, runaway slaves, and thieves, the gaol keeper was hard-pressed to keep order. Even now she heard banging and shouting. 'Twas a relief to turn onto Duke of Gloucester Street and pass the King's Arms Barbershop, Pasteur and Galt's Apothecary, the printer and bookbindery, and numerous taverns.

At the far end of the street sat Bruton Parish Church on a sunny stretch of ground, its sedate pink brickwork solacing her a bit. She'd been christened there and sat in the Lawsons' box pew nearly every Sabbath since. Was it just yesterday it had held the nuptials she'd been forbidden to attend? Papa had thrown the invitation into the parlor fire, blacklisting Lucy Croghan's family as Patriot sympathizers like so many others in Williamsburg.

But Cressida had been an eager guest, sending a note round afterward to say a great many Independence Men had been in attendance and she'd even managed a dance or two with Noble Rynallt. Somehow, inexplicably, that tiny detail stung. Her Tory friend seemed to be changing allegiance before her very eyes. Or was it only Cressida's attraction to Rynallt that swayed her loyalties?

Frowning, she began to realize she was garnering attention.

Men doffed their hats and ladies waved at her from carriages, their looks lingering. Because of no escort? Rarely did she walk the streets like this, and never without her lady's maid. Yet the breach seemed of little consequence and gave her the freedom she craved. Though she was fond of Isabeau, her maid was a chatterbox, every outing fraught with peril.

Your hem is getting hopelessly soiled. Beware of those horse leavings. Mind your hat, as your fair complexion shan't recover from so much sun.

On her right was the Raleigh Tavern, the place that never failed to intrigue her with its stalwart white lines and gabled roof and seditious reputation. Tantalizing aromas from its kitchen and bake shop were advertisement enough, and a number of fine horses were hitched to black iron posts out front. This was the favored haunt of a great many compelling men like George Washington and Thomas Jefferson and that flaming radical, Patrick Henry.

Her steps slowed, and she tried to imagine what lay beyond that handsome front porch and entry door with the lead bust of Sir Walter Raleigh above. Cressida had tried to describe it to her, as she'd attended assemblies in its Apollo Room, something Elisabeth's own father had forbidden. Even now at midday, though the courts weren't in session, it hummed with hospitality. Laughter and conversation spilled from its open, green-shuttered windows, a calling card to come inside.

She sighed. Betimes she wished she was a bit saucy and could cajole and do as she pleased. If so, the first place she'd head was the Raleigh.

She started to cross the street, but a number of convey-ances slowed her. She spied some Independence Men across the way, Patrick Henry foremost. A silversmith by trade, he was silver-tongued and fiery by turns. Mourning his late wife had not put a dent in his politics. Though Elisabeth had never met him, she'd formed a lasting dislike.

Give me liberty or give me death.

He was part and parcel of the trouble with her mother. When Papa saw Mama's last incendiary poem written under her pen name alongside Henry's rousing, equally inflammatory speech, he had sent her to England. But Elisabeth doubted her mother had forsaken pen and ink on the other side of the Atlantic.

She walked on, toward Market Square. The intersection of streets was a blur of busyness, carts and wagons and carriages abounding, the usual ankle-deep springtime mud slowly becoming summer's powdery dust. It settled on her skirts and straw hat as she fanned Lady Charlotte's letter about her face to keep the grit away, suddenly aware of a black roan making straight for her.

Merciful days!

Caught between a racing cart and the spirited horses, she felt a flicker of panic. The pounding of hooves, a woman's scream, and then the sickening shatter of splintering wood. She was trapped in the center of the busy thoroughfare, hemmed in on every side—

A hand shot out, grasping her none too gently by the forearm and half dragging her up atop a strange horse, its pommel bruising her thigh as she collided with the saddle. Stunned, she sat sideways, crushed by the rider's hard arms but out of harm's way. He maneuvered his mount away from the worst of the congestion and then, when the traffic cleared, shot across the road toward Queen Street—and home.

Before she even twisted her head around to look at his face she identified the unmistakable scent of him—a distillation of new broadcloth and sandalwood worn like a brand.

"We should make a new law that genteel, nearly married ladies be barred from city streets on market days," he said in stern tones near her ear.

She took a breath, feeling anything but genteel atop the unfamiliar horse. "Make such a law then. You're a burgess, are you not?"

"Nay, now a delegate. And mayhap I will." His voice, though firm, was warm, even amused. "Lady Elisabeth Lawson, soon to be mistress of Roth Hall."

"You left out my middle name."

"You have one? Most do not."

"'Tis Anne, after our beloved queen."

"I've heard tell your mother calls you something else entirely."

How did he know? Miles? But Miles had rarely been around her mother. "Yes," she confirmed. "Mama calls me Liberty."

"Not Bess or Betsy or even Lizzy?" He sounded approving. "I much prefer Liberty. In all its forms."

"I suppose you do. My mother named me that in keeping with her ideals, despite my father's displeasure. He refused to honor such, so he calls me Elisabeth Anne." Talk of her father always turned her glum. With effort she struck a more cheerful chord. "I suppose I should thank you. Twice now you've come to my rescue."

He said nothing to this, and she realized he might find her coquettish. Not a pleasing trait for his cousin's bride-to-be. She quieted, missing their banter, more uncomfortable with his closeness than needs be.

Beneath the shade of oaks and elms they cantered down Williamsburg's back streets, away from probing eyes and wagging tongues. When he dismounted in back of their townhouse garden on North England Street and helped her down, she met his eyes and found them odd, a shimmering gilt-brown beneath the sooty strands of his hairline, reminding her of the millpond at the edge of town. He turned away from her to adjust the saddle's girth, and she was startled by the length of his queue. Long as a horse's tail it was, and unfashionably so, falling to midback and bound with a dark ribbon tie. At the ball it had been looped under.

Had he not cut his hair all the time he'd spent mourning?

She caught herself blinking in a haze of brilliant sunlight and realized with a bumbling embarrassment that she'd lost some belongings. "Oh my."

He swung back around to look at her.

Putting a hand to her bare head, fingertips touching the remaining pearl-tipped pins, she stared back at him entreatingly. "I've lost my straw hat—and a paper."

His eyes pinned her. "And you want me to retrieve them."

His tone was obliging despite his fierce expression that told her he had no time for unnecessary errands. Swinging back into the saddle, he looked like he wanted to curse.

Her spirits plummeted. She didn't know why she felt so undone. She was home, unhurt, yet desperately missing her mother. About to be wed. And this man, soon to be a relation by marriage, was everything her groom was not. A remarkable contrast to Miles's sour port and snuff. Would she resign herself to smelling sour port and snuff the rest of her life when what she really preferred was broadcloth and sandalwood?

He reined his horse around with a terse, "Mayhap I'll be back."

But he didn't come back. And she was bereft of both her favorite hat and Lady Charlotte's letter.

5

Low oak beams were slung across the Raleigh Tavern's ceiling and painted a crude cream, melding with walls decorated with hunting scenes, guns, swords, and assorted relics from the French and Indian War. Little had changed in the twelve years Noble had been coming here. He was glad for an anchor in the face of so much change, a place that was as welcoming as an old, worn coat. Tipping his hat in greeting to a few men across the room, he made for Patrick Henry's corner table.

"About time, Rynallt. I've been on tenterhooks waiting."

"You're always on tenterhooks," Noble returned. "Ever since April."

"True enough. For now we've more than stolen gunpowder to fret about. But settle yourself and have a pint first, aye?"

Henry held on to his own ale with his right hand, the callused fingers of his left drumming mindlessly upon a piece of paper. Noble eyed it curiously. The Raleigh's dim interior worked against closer inspection, though the personal seal of Lady Charlotte was plain enough. At once his thoughts emptied of the needed drink and fastened on Lady Elisabeth.

"How did you come by the letter?" Noble asked as Henry held it aloft like a gold guinea.

"I was on Market Square yesterday afternoon when Lord Stirling's daughter lost it. Right about the time she nearly got run over and you rode to her rescue."

"Do you happen to have her hat?"

Henry's chuckle worked itself into a robust laugh. "What need have I of a mere hat when the mighty Dunmores' plans are in hand?"

"You jest."

"Nay, I do not." Henry paused long enough to take a sip of ale.

"Now that you've confiscated the letter, do you intend to return it to Lord Stirling's daughter?"

"Nay, I do not." Henry looked offended that Noble would ask. He set the paper squarely between them. "It seems Lady Charlotte is quite fond of Lady Elisabeth, enough to spill a few choice details." His shrewd gaze weighed Noble's reaction. "I promise I won't see it printed, if that appeases you."

A commotion at the door gave them pause. Noble glanced up at the tavern's entrance, heartened by the arrival of a few more Patriots. All looking grave. Unsmiling. Men of quiet deliberation to temper Henry's fire. Noble needed no letter to tell him something was afoot.

Soon Peyton Randolph and George Mason were at their table, Henry still tapping his fingers atop his prize. More ale was ordered and small talk was made till the requested tankards were in hand.

Henry passed the letter to his left. Randolph unfolded it, his stoicism shifting to disbelief. "Surely it cannot be this easy. The Dunmores are to flee? In the night?"

"Aye, tomorrow after the stroke of midnight." Henry had never looked so pleased.

Noble waited his turn, tamping down his impatience with another sip of ale.

"Let them flee Williamsburg then. Leave all Virginia," Mason said, his Scots color deepening. "But let them go without a fight. And make certain they take no powder or munitions with them."

Noble finally held the fine paper, Lady Charlotte's lovely penmanship lost to him as he hurried past her sentimental address of Lady Elisabeth to the particulars.

> *I fear for your safety should you remain. Meet us in the dark of 8 June when the church tower strikes midnight. We shall be at the very end of North England Street. Bring nothing but a bundle of necessities, as we are traveling light.*

Noble shot a glance out a near window in the direction of Lady Elisabeth's townhouse, the glass framing a spectacular sunset. The planned rendezvous was tomorrow night. So her ladyship would leave with the Dunmores? He passed the letter and took another sip from his tankard, more at odds with how he felt about it than the facts. Something akin to Enid's loss chipped away inside him. A smaller loss with Lady Elisabeth, aye, as he barely knew her. Yet still a telling emptiness. But why? 'Twas about more than her leaving, surely. 'Twas the letting go of larger things. A way of life. Beauty. Comfort. Routine. Youth.

He listened to his companions discuss the matter at hand. Talk moved from the letter to the political situation, which was now naught but a powder keg, like those Dunmore had stolen from the town's magazine in spring. In retaliation, George Washington was named head of the thirteen colonies' unified fighting force in case there was further trouble, be it here or Boston or New York or elsewhere.

Yet all he could think about was Elisabeth Lawson.

The letter lay open at the table's center, candlelight flickering over the purple seal. So the plan to flee Williamsburg was in place, the Dunmores exchanging the largely Patriot capital for the Loyalist-laden Yorktown a short distance away.

Only Lady Elisabeth had never read the letter. She'd lost it. But might she have told that to Lady Charlotte? Or learned of the plan another way?

What did it matter? She was Miles Roth's responsibility. For all he knew, Miles was running too.

Noble would wash his hands of the lovely Elisabeth.

'Twas nearly midnight. Looking at the small clock by her bed, Elisabeth wanted to groan. Would sleep never come? Her wedding was several days hence, the reception to follow. And she was, at best, a very skittish bride. Across the room, hanging from a peg, the voluminous silken gown stood in stark contrast to the shadows, provoking her to think of all that awaited her once she said "I do."

Till now the weeks leading up to the wedding had eclipsed any serious pondering, preoccupied as she was with largely frivolous pursuits, feeding the strutting peacocks, counting julep cups for the reception, deciding which dresses and underpinnings went into honeymoon trunks, overseeing the wedding menu in her mother's absence. She usually fell into bed exhausted. But tonight sleep would not come.

When sleepless, she usually took refuge in the music room,

playing her harp. She had Mama to thank for that. Mama, who had a pedal harp shipped secretly from France for her daughter's sixth birthday. Georges Joubert, a French harpist living in the Colonies, had given her lessons. By the time she was ten, she was playing for guests at the Governor's Palace and musical soirees about Williamsburg. Whatever she left behind as a bride, it must not be her harp.

Did Miles like music? Shouldn't she already know the answer to that?

Though tempted to return to the music room tonight, she shut her eyes and tried not to think of anything beyond her bedchamber walls. To no avail. Lady Charlotte's lost letter haunted far more than her missing hat. Noble Rynallt had likely gone back to hunt for both and had found neither. If he returned with them, it would save her returning to the Palace and confessing what had happened. She wasn't usually so careless.

The clock struck midnight. She finally slept. Hazy hours later, she turned over, the sheer lawn of her nightgown clinging to her. Through the open windows, the sultry stillness of the night seemed to echo with every sound. A barking dog. A crying baby. The clip-clop of a cart. Muted voices. Ribald laughter.

Breaking glass.

Her senses sharpened and she came awake. In seconds her whole world shifted. Her first fear—the fear of all Williamsburg—was fire. But she didn't smell smoke. She sensed danger. For the first time in her sheltered, cosseted life, she felt it hovering like a dark presence.

Clawing at the mosquito netting around her bed, she broke free and pressed bare feet to the floorboards before rushing to an open window. Below, in the garden, a host of uninvited guests were capering, the light of pine-knot torches illuminating their mischief. A rush of images assailed her—feathers, war paint, fringed buckskins. Indians? Was it the tea debacle in Boston all over again? White men dressed as savages, singing songs of liberty?

Patriots.

She heard their laughter, saw them raiding her father's wine cellar, watched as they trod upon the prized peony beds and tore down trellis upon trellis of climbing roses.

Where was the gardener? The boy of all work? Where were the other servants? Father? He seemed to reside at the Palace of late. She began to shake. Her unsteady hand yanked on the nearest bell cord, but no one came. The raucous party in the garden heightened. More laughter and drunken voices. More breaking glass.

"Father!" She choked on the word in her panic as she ran down the dark hallway to his bedchamber. Empty. Next she backtracked to the top of the stairs. Shadows darted about in the foyer below. Mamie was there, shouting, holding an iron fireplace poker as if it was a musket. The shadows continued to dart from room to room, all unfamiliar, as if playing some macabre game.

Stark fear give way to a churning nausea. Elisabeth took the stairs, shoulder pressed to the curving wall, unmindful of her state of undress.

Mamie looked up at her, poker waving, voice cracking with alarm. "Nay, chil', it ain't safe. Go on back upstairs and lock yo'self in."

Heart hammering with such force it seemed to shake her very rib cage, Elisabeth hurried down, her feet nearly winged as she flew past a cowering, sobbing Isabeau and into her father's study. The room was empty of ne'er-do-wells but had been ransacked. Papers lay like leaf litter across the elegant carpet, every cupboard and desk drawer torn open. Moonlight spilled through shards of broken window glass.

Her stomach rose to her throat. Would her father's body be beneath all the mess? The possibility thrust her backward, out of the room and into the hall where Mamie was arguing with a tall shadow.

"Give me the keys to the governor's locked study cupboard." The man's Scottish brogue set her on edge, as did the dark eyes that swiveled toward her. They lingered on her for one dismissive moment before shifting to a shouting cohort. "Kill yer torch, mon. D'ye want us all tae be known and in gaol by morning?"

The torch was extinguished, but other men began filling the stairwell, surrounding them, the stench of unwashed bodies and spirits overpowering.

"I done told you I don' know where my master's key is." Mamie stood her ground, poker pointing ludicrously toward the Scots giant before her. "He's away, and the servants have fled—every last one of 'em. And if you lay a hand on Lady Elisabeth, there'll be more than gaol for you, you hear?"

Widening his stance, he swung his claymore carelessly, missing Mamie by mere inches. "Dinna threaten me, woman. I've nae quarrel with ye or yer lady. 'Tis Dandy Dunmore and Lawson's leaving we're celebrating, and we'll no' settle for less."

"Law, but you gonna get more than that," Mamie flung at him. "When Miles Roth sees you've torn apart his betrothed's house—"

"Oh, the mighty Miles is it, ye say?" A rumble of laughter filled the inky foyer. "Another dandy I'd as soon thrust my sword through. I suppose he's run with the rest o' them Tories."

Restive, they began to move away just as she sensed Mamie's resolve crumble. In moments the rabble had returned to the garden. Elisabeth could hear the peacocks protesting as she stepped to the back door left ajar by the mob's exit. Many of the men who were making merry at their expense were in their cups. She'd seen gentlemen intoxicated in a slurringly genteel sort of way, but never the outright debauchery of this horde. She felt besmirched by their very presence. Not once had Papa permitted such a one over his threshold. To think these were among those promoting the cause for liberty made her shudder.

They huddled in a tight knot, she, Isabeau, and Mamie. Isabeau had somehow managed to light a single candlestick, which pushed back the darkness—and magnified the mess all about them.

"I keep thinkin' we'll wake up and it'll be your weddin' day and all will be well." Mamie let go of the poker with a clatter. "And all this be naught but a bad dream."

Unable to watch the havoc in the garden or stand on her shaking legs any longer, Elisabeth turned away. As she did, she caught sight of herself in the gilded mirror opposite, her face as white as her nightgown.

❧

All night they kept vigil in Elisabeth's locked bedchamber, long after the melee had faded away. Nary a neighbor came to check on them. Such indifference hurt worse than the damage. Was all of Williamsburg against them, then? The cocoon of ignorance she'd lived in for so long began to unravel.

Toward dawn the three of them ventured forth.

"La!" Isabeau's voice held a shrillness unheard before. "Every window on the first floor broken, no?"

"'Tis a blessing 'tis summer," Elisabeth replied, amazed that she could sound so calm. "'Twould be cold indeed in winter."

They went from room to room, stepping over once beautiful things now broken. Elisabeth's soul seemed to shrink at the damage. Benumbed, she couldn't even cry. A look of desperation filled Isabeau's face, and she grabbed Elisabeth by the shoulders and gave her a gentle shake.

"Mistress! Why are you so calm? Your home, your future, is in shambles! And no one comes!"

Moving past her, Elisabeth walked woodenly through the gaping back door, Isabeau trailing. Instantly she was sorry she'd come outside. Even in the muted morning light the havoc was appalling. Entire beds of peonies and lilies had been trampled, sundial and statuary overturned, every trellis torn to pieces. The picturesque arbor where she had taken tea and tarts on countless occasions was naught but rubble. Looking over it, she felt a flash of fury.

Isabeau's gasp spun her around. A few feet away the once lovely fountain at the very heart of the garden no longer bore sparkling water but a mass of hardened tar and feathers. Her own heart—so at home here in this garden, the place among her happiest memories—twisted till she thought it would break. And then cold reason rushed in.

At least Mama was away—safe.

❧

It was there Miles found her. Isabeau had gone inside while Mamie went about the garden, trying to right what she could. Suddenly Elisabeth's intended was behind her. A look of patent disbelief marred his features as he took everything in. Had he come all the way from Roth Hall? Or had he stayed the night at one of the taverns in town?

"When did this happen?" he asked.

Her thoughts tripped backward to the sound of breaking glass. "After midnight."

"Who did this?" Eyes that had always looked at her with languid interest now seemed to interrogate. To blame.

"I-I don't know. 'Twas dark. They were all besmeared with paint and powder—"

"Did they harm you, your maid?" His terse question seemed absurd.

"Nay." But she felt she lied. They—whoever they were—had destroyed her home, her hopes.

"The sheriff is on his way." He began to pace, leather boots crushing the few flowers that remained bent and broken along the garden walk. Spinning around, the tails of his frock coat flapping in a sudden wind, he said, "The gaol keeper—Peter Pelham—he did not come?"

"Nay." The strangeness of it swept over her. No one had come. Not the rector of Bruton Parish Church who was to wed them. Not Doctor Hessel. Not a single neighbor. No one. Perhaps because no one thought she remained. That she had fled with her father. Or because their house sat at the end of a private street on the outskirts of Williamsburg. Yes, that was it.

"Do you know where your father is?" He stood near her now, hands on her shoulders. At her hesitation his fingers dug into her skin. "Are you hiding anything from me?"

"Hiding? I—nay." Her bewilderment seemed only to aggravate him. "I have no inkling where my father is. I feared finding him amid all the rubble."

"I'll have the broken windows boarded up and a guard posted. You and your maid should stay upstairs till I speak with the sheriff and think matters through."

She felt more benumbed. She stared at him in disbelief. He strode away from her, fury stiffening his stride. He didn't look back. And she felt her future turn to crumbled stone like the garden bench beside her.

From Port Royal the heavily traveled Tobacco Road took Noble to Williamsburg. Just outside of town he drew up short at the wrenching sight of nearly naked slaves, necks yoked with rusty chains, being brought in for auction on market day. The brands on their sweating, emaciated thighs were plain in the harsh summer sunlight. He looked away till the clink of metal and the dust settled before reining his horse right onto Botetourt Street.

A bit lamed, Seren was. Noble dismounted and led his stallion on a slow walk down Francis Street, thoughts full of the previous day spent hashing out tobacco prices in Port Royal ahead of the coming harvest. 'Twas Friday, and the town, usually a maelstrom of activity, appeared somewhat subdued. Even the Raleigh Tavern seemed to be humming a quieter tune. Yet the sunlit familiarity of it all was pleasing, a reminder he was almost home.

Taking his horse round back to the alley, he was met by a small boy, barefoot and in dusty breeches, shirttails flapping.

"Mornin', Master Rynallt."

"Morning, Billy." He reached into his frock coat, flipped the boy a guinea, and noted his look of delight. "Seren looks to be a bit lamed."

The napped head bobbed up and down. "Sure enough, sir. Don't give it another thought. Just go on inside and have yourself a fine stay."

"I'll do that." Noble unfastened his saddlebags, swung

them over his shoulder, and moved toward the ordinary's back entrance. Before he'd set foot on the door stone, the proprietor stepped into view to greet him.

"You're likely naught but sweat and dust in this heat," James Southall said, clapping him on the back.

With a smile, Noble ducked beneath the eave and felt the cool shade embrace him. "You'll soon set that to rights, I'll wager."

"Aye, and what's yer pleasure today."

"Ale. And one of Purdie's papers."

"Yer hungry for news then. Well, we've got plenty o' that."

Noble heard the words but almost missed the innkeeper's cryptic look as he went ahead of him into the taproom.

A few patrons nodded as they smoked clay pipes and read competing copies of the *Virginia Gazette* and *Norfolk Intelligencer* or talked in hushed tones at the latticed bar. Moving to his usual corner table, the sturdy surface marred by time and dice boxes, he removed his cocked hat before taking his chair, aware of the serving girls peeking out at him from behind the nearest door.

Before he could acknowledge them, James Southall plunked down two pewter tankards, blocking his view and muttering, "I've news, all right, but 'tis not yet made print. Best take a sip or two to brace yerself. Or celebrate."

Without a blink, Noble clasped the tankard handle and swallowed the chill brew, surprised when Southall slid into the chair opposite and said, "Dunmore's fled. Last night, in the wee sm' hours. Took Lady Charlotte and the children, every last servant, and naught but the clothes on their backs."

Noble schooled his reaction, surprised the plan had come off. He hardly had to feign ignorance as Southall hurried on, spilling the details.

"They've gone aboard the man-o'-war, HMS *Fowey*, on the York River." Southall paused, sipping his own ale. "And what's more, Lieutenant Governor Lawson's gone with them—but not his lovely daughter, sorry to say."

Mid-swallow, Noble nearly choked. He set his tankard down so forcefully, droplets of ale sloshed onto the scarred tabletop.

"'Tis rumored Lord Stirling's wife, the countess, is expected in port any day from England. As for the daughter, she's still at the townhouse, or what's left of it."

"What do you mean, what's left of it?" Noble fastened on the tired eyes of the tavern keeper, alarm scoring his chest. "Was there a mob?"

"Aye, first at the Palace, then the townhouse. A great many windows broken." He expelled a breath. "Now why d'ye think they have to turn mobbish and disgrace a good cause? I'm ashamed to call them Patriots. Freedom isn't won by shattering glass and guzzling stolen Rivesaltes and Perpignan. We'll all pay the price for a few fools, I tell ye."

Leaning back, Noble let the unwelcome news sift through him. "All of Williamsburg is aware, aye?"

"Aye, word spread like wildfire and all the papers have gone to print. An express has been sent to Mount Vernon and Monticello and other parts. Wash and Jeff are likely on their way. A meeting's been called for right here as soon as everyone can assemble."

Noble took in the front door as it opened to admit another Patriot. "What of Miles Roth?"

Southall seemed to have to work to minimize a smirk. "Flying high here at the Raleigh on the eve of all the trouble. So sotted he could barely hold his dice cup. Word is he met with the sheriff, who posted a guard and hired some men to board up the sacked townhouse. Then Roth left town a few hours ago without paying his bill here."

Ire spiking, Noble took another sip of ale. "He likely fears his Tory leanings will get him tarred and feathered."

"Aye, so it seems. He's about as popular as the dandies Dunmore and Lawson. I do feel for Lady Elisabeth left behind. And all on the eve of the Roth-Lawson wedding, no less. A sweeter, spritelier lass you'll ne'er find." Southall shook his head. "I'm well aware he's your kin and all, and I mean no disrespect, but why would a man turn tail and run? They were betrothed, were they not? Why not go ahead and wed and take his bride to Roth Hall? 'Twould be the honorable thing to do, would it not? Tory or no? Why, I ask ye?"

Because Miles Roth hadn't an honorable bone in his body.

Noble swallowed down the criticism and stood, not bothering to finish his ale. "Tell the kitchen to save a veal chop for me. I've some business to attend to and then I'll be back."

Elisabeth stood looking at her harp, the only thing in the music room that seemed to have withstood the previous night's onslaught. Around it lay sheets of music, a broken metronome, and her mother's harpsichord turned on its side. The once lovely chenille carpet bore tar and feather boot marks. Both windows overlooking the garden were shattered, as was the Parisian mirror above the marble hearth.

She kept her eyes on her instrument, lovingly counting the strings like a mother counted the fingers and toes of her newborn. All there, as was the graceful neck with its brass action plates, the tuning peg and pedal, every decorative fern and flourish in gold leaf. The instrument remained miraculously intact. As she looked at it in wonder, she pushed past her pain and disappointment to give silent thanks. The harp was still standing for one reason and one reason only. The Lord, or His angels, had kept it from harm, knowing how much it meant to her, knowing how its destruction might well have meant her own.

She longed to sit on her stool and play, touching its familiar keys and pouring out her broken feelings in song. But she couldn't. Not here amid all the mess. Not yet. Not amid workmen hammering boards over the outside windows, the sound rivaling her thudding pulse.

She barely heard Isabeau behind her, treading over the litter to half shout, "Mistress . . . to see you."

Elisabeth looked at her in question. "Someone has come, you say? Please send them in."

Someone sorry for their plight, likely. At last. Perhaps someone with news of her father or the servants. Or Mama.

The doorway darkened. Again she felt sharp surprise. Noble Rynallt's searching stare seemed to strip away her forced composure to expose every bruised feeling beneath. Or perhaps his shock at finding her in the midst of the ransacked room was as profound as her own.

Heat inched up her neck and left a damp line above her upper lip. Though she wore an embroidered silk dress and pearls, she felt as exposed as if she was in her underpinnings. Her humiliation was complete.

She started to gesture to a chair for him to sit down, then realized it was overturned. He righted it without a word and seated her. Sinking down atop its slashed brocade cushion, she realized how weary she was. Across from her he sat on a stained loveseat, dwarfing it with his long, lean form. The formality between them seemed to melt away. There was a sympathetic light in his face, so unlike Miles's, that drew her dangerously near the edge of her emotions.

"This isn't about you, you know," he said quietly.

Did he mean the mess? The violent clash between Patriots and the Crown? Blinking back tears, she looked at her lap, meting out words like she'd seen her stern father mete out affection. "I know."

"I'm not the first to come."

He was inviting her to talk. But doing so required the staunchest effort. "Miles Roth was here, then Cressida Shaw." She felt oddly embarrassed, knowing his ties to each.

"And?"

He was proceeding carefully. Did he sense she was as fragile as the broken glass all around them?

"I don't know where Miles is now. Cressida asked if I was all right."

"No one offered you safe harbor?"

"Nay." Fresh disbelief skittered through her. "I think they are as stunned as I am. Unsure of what to do." She swallowed, fixing her eyes on her harp. "Even if they had, I can't leave here without knowing what's happened to my father or the servants."

"If I tell you, will you go with me?"

Her gaze swung back to him. "Go with you? Where?"

"To rejoin your father."

Did he know the details she didn't? The realization pierced her numbness and exhaustion and gave rise to new questions. "Tell me, please, what has happened. Why." Her voice shook. She hated that she sounded pleading, about to break apart.

"Lord Dunmore and his family fled Williamsburg in the night, as did your father. They're said to be aboard a British warship on the York River. From what I've heard, many of their servants went with them. Once word spread, a mob stormed the Palace and then came here." His gaze lifted to the ceiling, where swords had hacked at the fine plasterwork. "I could take you to the ship—"

"Nay." Her voice firmed. "I shan't leave my mother. She's due any day."

"I could make arrangements to send her back to England in your wake."

To England? Why was he being so obliging when everyone else had turned away?

"Nay." She stood, angling her face toward the window to hide her agitation. "She's been unwell and may be unable to make another lengthy voyage." She turned back to him, uttering yet another uncertainty. "Besides, I'm about to wed."

"Your betrothal still stands."

It was a statement, not a question, so why did it jar her so? "Yes, when Miles returns . . ." Her voice died out along with her hopes. She was certain of nothing. Miles's angry face rose up to taunt her. He'd not said when or if he'd return. She'd just waited, thinking the best of him. But the hours passed, leaving her with more unanswered questions.

Noble rubbed his bewhiskered jaw. "I can't leave you here. Your safety is in question."

"I'm safe enough. There are three of us remaining—my maid and my mother's maid. But we have nowhere to go."

"You'll go with me. To Ty Mawr."

To the home of her father's enemy? Could he see the reluctance in her eyes?

"'Tis near Roth Hall, if you've forgotten. I'll hire a coach. Once we're at Ty Mawr, you can send word to your father that you're well. I'll notify Miles and the rector and you can wed there."

He would do all that? As kin to Miles? Miles must have thought it best to leave town lest the trouble touch him. Or perhaps he was behind her going to Ty Mawr and a hasty ceremony. But if so, why wasn't he here himself? Exhaustion forced her to take a seat again, her thoughts in a fog.

"I'll have a coach sent round for you and your maid in half an hour. Collect whatever you wish to bring. I've business at the Raleigh till then." He looked at her a tad longer. "In the meantime, the guard my cousin posted will ensure your safety."

She started to protest, to offer the use of her new carriage, and then she remembered there were no servants and likely no horses. The light coming through the windows was fading, and she looked longingly at her harp, wanting to take it with her. Suppose another mob returned to destroy what was left standing from before?

With an air of practiced calm, she got to her feet once again and said, "A half hour is fine. We'll be ready."

6

"Take a look at them fine mounts, Patriots all," Mamie murmured as their hired coach slowed behind the Raleigh Tavern. Head bound tightly in a bright blue kerchief, she peered through a small window, eyes narrowing. "Misters Henry and Jefferson just rode in. I'll wager all the Patriot gents are in fine fettle now that Governor Dunmore's gone."

Elisabeth felt a beat of sadness override her shock. Would Lady Charlotte return to England now that her husband had been relieved of his duties? Uppermost were their many kindnesses to her. How they had loved their home and garden. How they oft laughed and romped with their children. She recalled their penchant for music and the arts. Their frequent fetes. Once, Lord Dunmore had told his guests she played the harp like an angel.

This was better dwelt on than the emotional earthquake of the last few hours. How could her father have left without a word to her? And the servants, who had been with them since her childhood? How could they have cut ties without so much as a whisper? She rubbed her temples beneath the brim of her second-best hat, which only reminded her that her favorite hat had gone missing—and the letter with it. What if Lady Charlotte had written to warn her? Telling her of their plans to flee Williamsburg?

Whatever had happened, she could not ignore a simmering resentment toward whoever had brought this about. Till now the Patriots had been mere shadows in the perimeter of her life, unable to harm or change the ordered routine of her existence. She knew about them, had heard tell of Patrick Henry's ferocious temper and Thomas Jefferson's brilliant eccentricities, had smiled behind her fan at George Rogers Clark's derring-do, and had even stood awestruck at the immense physical vitality of Colonel Washington.

Like her mother, she knew the ins and outs of colonial politics, had been schooled in them like the art of lacemaking, and could converse sensibly about them with whoever wanted to. She had done so when her mother couldn't—or wouldn't. Beside her father at every social function, she had accrued far more at two and twenty than most young women ever cared to. But now, in just a few hours, someone had jerked the sumptuous gros point rug out from under her costly calamanco slippers and sent her reeling. And she didn't know who to blame.

"Here he comes," Mamie said, reaching for the door handle of the coach. She got out as quickly as her bulk would allow, claiming all Elisabeth's attention.

At the back of the Raleigh, a tall, tricorned shadow appeared, clothed in shades of black and gray again, as if he'd returned to mourning. Leaving the coach door wide, Mamie bustled up the walk to face Noble Rynallt, her hands moving like punctuation marks to her words.

"You see, sir, I can't leave my mistress. The countess'll be back any day now, and the sight of her torn-down house and all her torn-down things will all but finish her. She needs me to be right here, waitin'."

Noble listened, hat in hand in a touching display of respect to an elderly, displaced servant. His reply was lost to Elisabeth, but it seemed to pacify Mamie. She took a small black pouch from his outstretched hand and waved at Elisabeth before turning back toward the tavern. Elisabeth had no heart to argue. Mamie would indeed help cushion Mama's shock.

A stable boy led out a sleek chestnut thoroughbred with a speckled rump and one white hind foot. Elisabeth tried not to stare as their soon-to-be-host swung himself into the saddle with the grace of a man born riding. Without further ado, Noble Rynallt followed their hired coach out of Williamsburg as it left a trail of dun-colored dust in their wake. They soon took the Quarterpath Road that led from Williamsburg to Burwell's Landing on the James River.

"'Tis so hot," Isabeau murmured, raising a window shade. "This hired coach is so very black, no? I fear it is Monsieur Rynallt's favorite color."

Elisabeth took in a slant of sunbeam as it spilled across the shabby interior reeking of tobacco and . . . worse. A far cry from the fairy-tale one Miles had sent her. Had the mob damaged her wedding coach as well? She had not checked the coach house. But did material things matter when they themselves had not been manhandled?

As they bounced atop the sagging seat, Elisabeth withdrew one of the wedding fans Mama had chosen, reminded of that last day they'd spent together before her mother sailed. The very feel of it seemed to weight her hand.

Tucking the fan away, she focused on the scene unfolding beyond their window. "Do you smell the honeysuckle, Isabeau?" Her eye was drawn to fields overflowing with wheat and tobacco, others left fallow, an occasional cottage tucked in.

"A long time it has been since we rode out like this." Isabeau dabbed at her damp brow with a handkerchief. "I remember how well your mother liked a Sabbath jaunt."

"Ah yes." Elisabeth felt a bittersweet stirring. "Soon we'll see the James." Before the words had left her lips the coach crested a small hill and the wide river lay before them, vaster than she remembered, a number of boats on its shimmering surface. Somewhere along its banks sat Ty Mawr, halfway betwixt Williamsburg and the road to Norfolk. The Rynallt estate was beyond Roth Hall. She remembered its eye-catching wrought-iron gates.

"What will it be like, do you think?" Isabeau said with more dread than enthusiasm.

"Who's to say? I've never been there." But if it was anything like its master, it would be refined. Enduring. Memorable. She unearthed what little she knew. "'Tis situated on Mulberry Island."

"And sports a racetrack, said to be the finest in Virginia." Isabeau's pensive expression was almost comical. "And the horses! So many of them! 'Tis rumored he has as many horses as servants, all Welsh."

"Welsh horses?" Elisabeth tried to elicit a smile, wondering if her maid's musings were fact or fiction.

Isabeau fell into a sour silence. Then, as if the coach windows had slammed shut, the day turned a mourning gray. Overhead, thunder growled like an unruly mastiff, and lightning slashed the sky. Used to Virginia's fickle moods, Elisabeth searched the horizon and could feel the horse's confident stride turn skittish. In minutes the sky let loose. She could smell the dust dampened down as the world got a good washing. The lumbering coach slowed and then rolled to a bumpy stop altogether.

Voices. A horse's shrill whinny. The sudden gaping of the coach door. Isabeau sprung from her seat as if ejected, joining Elisabeth on her side as their host entered in. The door shut with a thud and their ride resumed without a word, each of them pretending to ignore the other.

But there was, Elisabeth decided, no ignoring the master of Ty Mawr.

⁂

Rain dripped from Noble's cocked hat as he removed it and set it atop the seat, surprised when Elisabeth leaned forward and offered him a handkerchief. The fine linen was soft in his callused hand, and when he brought it to his face to wipe the rain away he was stung with a scent he knew all too well.

Rose-carnation cologne. Yardley of London.

'Twas as if she'd handed him a penknife instead. Enid's favorite scent. The remembrance cut at him unmercifully, but he stayed stoic. Though his sister's door had been shut since the day she died, the hall beyond still hinted of the fragrance.

His eyes traced the delicate rose embroidery and the initials *EAL*. The strangeness of Lady Elisabeth's predicament settled over him. He was still questioning the wisdom of his involvement. If he'd taken Lady Charlotte's letter away from Henry and returned it to Elisabeth in time, she'd not need rescuing. But here she sat across from him, her world on end. Yet not a hair was out of place, nor did a single line of worry mar her flushed features. He'd seen more emotion from marble statues in Rome. Still, he sensed her inner turmoil, given away by the taut line of her jaw.

Her maid wasn't weathering the change as well, at least

outwardly. Or mayhap she suffered from travel sickness. Or the less than genteel contraption offended her humble sensibilities. The aged coach lurched along, draining her florid French complexion by degrees. Lightning and thunder continued a merry dance, and he was concerned that Seren was tethered like a lightning rod behind the coach.

Thunder boomed again, and the conveyance gave a tremendous lurch as it hit a rut, nearly sending them colliding into each other.

"La!" the maid shrieked, gripping the seat with frantic hands.

Noble's gaze shot to her mistress, who had not so much as winced. What was going on inside that fair head of hers?

Another couple of leagues and the gates would greet them. He wanted to tell them the journey was near an end if only to ease the tension that sat between them as solidly as a fourth party. Despite the tap of rain atop the roof, the silence within was funereal.

At least he'd sent word ahead to warn of their coming. He hadn't said *who* and *now*, but traveling down Ty Mawr's shaded avenue, he tried to imagine his housekeeper's reaction. They'd not had company in almost two years of mourning. Of all his staff, Mistress Tremayne seemed to miss Enid the most and was the most anxious for him to bring home a bride. The confusion that was bound to ensue made him wish he'd explained himself better in the note. She'd think him courting, at least.

His longtime housekeeper was in the open doorway crowned with its pineapple motif, waiting expectantly for that very thing, or so it seemed. She wore both a smile and that giant mobcap he found ridiculous, a creaseless cambric apron about her doughy waist.

A groom stood by, waiting to help his guests down from the coach. Noble was hardly mindful of the torrential rain, eyes on a stable hand who unhitched Seren from behind and led him away as thunder cracked a final time and sent them all scurrying inside.

A dozen different images struck Elisabeth as hard as the storm when she alighted from the coach. A servant in simple homespun, not the usual British-styled livery. Wet flagstones underfoot. Moss-covered bricks. Immense Palladian windows. A front door open wide in welcome, leading to a high-ceilinged foyer. Oil paintings gracing the walls in ornate frames, most of castles and horses and weather-beaten coastlines. If their host had told her they were in Wales, she would have believed him.

And then Noble Rynallt's voice sounded like a rumble of thunder in the rising storm as he made introductions. First in Welsh, then English.

When her rounded eyes finally rested on the rotund woman she guessed was his housekeeper, Elisabeth realized she'd already been assessed inch by inch. Amid the flurry and confusion of gloves and hats being removed and introductions made, she became aware of something amiss.

"Isabeau, are you all right?" she asked.

Isabeau swayed and put a hand on a paneled wall. "The coach driver, he is violent."

"Well, he is now gone and we're on firmer ground. Perhaps ginger tea would help. I shall ask Mistress Tremayne for some."

Out of the corner of her eye she saw Noble and his housekeeper step to the side, then came her surprised whisper, "Lady Elisabeth, is it? Lord Stirling's daughter?"

"Aye, Miles Roth's soon-to-be bride."

Not mine, his intensity seemed to say. With that, he turned into a room on the right.

The housekeeper's keen gray eyes met Elisabeth's right then. A cloud of questions gathered there, and Elisabeth felt a sudden twinge. Was the housekeeper hopeful of a new mistress?

Stepping forward, she clasped the older woman's hands warmly in her own. "Thank you for welcoming us. We shan't impose on your hospitality for long."

Pleasure seemed to eclipse Mistress Tremayne's disappointment, and she squeezed Elisabeth's hands in return, recovering her smile. "Well, just long enough to savor some of Ty Mawr's pleasures, surely. There's a fine pot of English tea at hand."

"Oh?" Amusement took hold. Tea in the house of an Independence Man seemed odd indeed.

"'Tis rebellious, aye?" Mistress Tremayne smiled wryly. "But you look in need of a generous cup. If you lean real close and take a whiff, you'll smell that 'tis the finest hyson too. But we'd best not tell Master Rynallt. He thinks there's naught but nonimportation tea in the cupboards."

"I won't breathe a word," Elisabeth said. "Might you have some ginger tea? For my Isabeau? She's feeling indisposed."

"But of course. I'll see to it straightaway, m'lady." Pulling on a bell cord near a painting, Mistress Tremayne rang for a maid and requested refreshments.

Elisabeth lifted her eyes to take in a freestanding circular staircase just behind the housekeeper's bulk. It climbed two floors as if on wings with nary a support she could see. Elegant. Airy. Even mysterious. Where did it lead?

Had their host gone into his study? She could see him through a near doorway, his rugged profile a silhouette of solemnity as he looked down at a desk. Sober as a barrister he was. The black armband he once wore and the dark cockade atop his hat lay on a chair, telling reminders of his loss. On the darkly paneled walls hung Indian artifacts of every shape and description. Bows and arrows. A headdress. Antler rattles. Myriad things she couldn't name. From the frontier?

The foyer was empty, absent of all servants save Mistress Tremayne. The coachman simply deposited their baggage in an alcove while the housekeeper took her and Isabeau up the winding stairway. The hall seemed endless, most doors closed, and they were led to a room on the third floor, a gabled haven that smelled faintly of dust and milk paint. As a smiling servant shouldered Elisabeth's trunk across a colorful carpet, she felt overwhelmed with their ready hospitality.

"Just tug on the bell cord should you have need of me," Mistress Tremayne told her. "Supper is served at eight. I shall bring a tray to your room if you like. Mister Rynallt is expecting company, though they've been delayed."

More company? "Thank you," Elisabeth answered.

Isabeau came to stand beside her, both of them gaping at the speech-stealing view from the riverfront windows. Together they took in mint-green paint and delicate white plasterwork on the ceiling and walls before Elisabeth returned to her maid's wan face. In minutes, both ginger tea and hyson turned their surroundings into the equivalent of an aromatic tea shop.

Elisabeth gestured to the silver service. "Let's freshen up and have some civility, shall we?" She moved to a washstand and poured tepid water into a porcelain bowl. After cleaning her face and hands, she sat in a delicately turned chair by an open window and waited for Isabeau to collect herself.

So lost was she in the lovely river view, she nearly failed to notice Isabeau's continued disquiet. "Mistress, what will become of us? We are . . ." She struggled as she often did for the proper English word. "Beggars!"

"Beggars? Nay." Elisabeth reached for a teapot, the fragrance telling her it held ginger. "Beggars seldom grace so lovely a room with so fine a host." She poured the tea with a steady hand. "I don't know what will happen to us beyond this present moment, truly, as we cannot impose on Ty Mawr's hospitality for long. But we shan't be beggars, ever."

"But Tories, *oui*? Mister Rynallt is a Patriot, and you—your father is most decidedly Tory!" Isabeau looked like she might wail. "Should we not go to Norfolk, which is full of Loyalists?"

"We are all British subjects still." Elisabeth held her cup beneath her nose, finding the rare tea's fragrance almost like perfume. "My prayer is that Lord Dunmore will compromise and make peace with the Patriots. And that the king and Parliament will see reason and stop taxing us to death."

"Then you are a praying woman indeed," Isabeau murmured, taking in hand her own cup.

Elisabeth took a steadying sip. For Isabeau's sake, she would be optimistic, but privately she feared colonial politics were long past compromise. In Boston, soldiers and citizens had taken up arms against each other, and increasing numbers of colonists were obsessed with the notion of liberty. Her mother had long watched its workings, and Elisabeth was not ignorant of the Patriot-infused passion behind her pen.

"There is still your dowry." At this, Isabeau looked triumphant, a bit of color filling her wan face. "And 'tis the most agreeable dowry that ever graced Virginia Colony, Tory or no."

"Now who is being silly?" Elisabeth returned. "Just where would this dowry be? My trunk?"

Isabeau's gaze slid to the one piece of baggage they'd managed to come away with. "You are still betrothed, are you not?"

Elisabeth said nothing. And that in itself spoke volumes.

7

For the first time in her entire life aside from being indisposed, Elisabeth did not dress for supper. She tried to relish the freedom of it, the loosening of her stays, the delicious privacy. Clad in a dressing gown, she waited for any sound that foretold Mistress Tremayne. As the ceramic clock on the mantel struck eight, a light knock sounded on the closed door.

Isabeau was in the next room, putting away her own few belongings, so it was Elisabeth who answered. The burgeoning tray separating her and Ty Mawr's housekeeper nearly made her gasp. Welsh fare? Did they mean to make a hogshead of her?

"A small supper," the housekeeper said, hastening to the table situated between two windows. She set down the tray with a heaving bosom and a slight clatter. "Climbing fifty-six steps is not for the faint of heart."

"You needn't wear yourself out on my account," Elisabeth said gently. Surely there was a younger, more agile servant? Or was the ploy to keep them hidden away on high? Known to as few of the other servants and guests as possible?

With a flourish of her hand, the housekeeper removed a cover from a chafing dish. "*Cawl*, a stew of lamb and leeks, served with *caws pobi*—baked cheese—and *bara brith*, what you might call speckled bread."

The Welsh words rolled over her, winsome sounding if strange. Elisabeth staunched a sigh. There was enough fare for her and Isabeau and several attic guests. Her stomach growled in a most unladylike manner. "I could feast on bara brith and little else."

It was the right thing to say. Mistress Tremayne's satisfied smile resurfaced. "If you should need anything more . . ."

Probably not for a fortnight. Elisabeth snuck a pinch of bread. "Thank you. 'Tis a feast."

As if deciding not to bore her or she had run out of breath, Mistress Tremayne simply uncovered the other half-dozen dishes without naming them and poured cider from an iron-stone pitcher. "I leave you to your supper, m'lady."

Isabeau reappeared once the door was shut. "What I wouldn't give for some French fare—*beignets* and *bouilla-baisse*."

Their eyes met, communicating a wordless question about the whereabouts of Pape, the French chef who had dominated the Lawsons' townhouse kitchen. Elisabeth had a soft spot for Pape, who'd snuck her rhubarb tarts, even ice cream, before dinner on countless occasions since she was small.

"God bless Pape." Elisabeth sat without ceremony, for there was no servant to pull out her chair and drape a servi-ette across her lap. "Shall we?"

"Are we to dine together at supper too?" Isabeau took the chair opposite. "A strange position, this!"

"You are fine company. But first a prayer," Elisabeth said, bowing her head. "Lord, we beseech Thee for all our needs and thank Thee for this, our daily bread." Raising her spoon, she sampled the Welsh stew, aware of Isabeau's scrutiny. "Delicious."

Her maid tasted. Made a face. "If there is *petit lamb* in my dish, I cannot eat it."

"Try the cheese then. Caws pobi, I think Mistress Tremayne said."

This was met with more approval. Isabeau finished her portion and had seconds. "How long are we to be here?"

"We shall soon find out," Elisabeth told her, turning back to the window. "For now, I like our secret bower on high."

The sunset was an astonishing pink, the very hue of her favorite roses in the Palace gardens. Savoring it, wanting to seal it on her memory, she fought a strange wistfulness. The blooms brought to mind a world lost, a girlhood gone. Just as the sun was now setting on the James, she knew the sun had also set on a way of life. And she herself had come into something new and multihued when once her existence had been more black and white.

Oh Lord, thank You for such beauty. New possibilities. Blessed memories of old. Protect us. Lead us. Please.

∞

Winded, Noble slowed Seren into a lazy canter down Ty Mawr's lengthy drive. In the saddle since dawn, he'd covered all his acreage in the forenoon, even checking the new gristmill at Roundtree Farm before remembering the hour. While there he'd been detained, as the workings weren't operating properly. Shucking off his frock coat, he'd set his shoulder to the giant stone in front of half a dozen tenants, soon restoring it to working order. And now, looking like a field hand, he returned to find Miles Roth waiting for him, no doubt impeccably if foppishly attired, having brandy for breakfast in his study. Or so Mistress Tremayne told him.

"And Lady Elisabeth?" Noble asked her, glancing upstairs to rooms he couldn't see. "All is well?"

"Snug as a songbird beneath the eave," his housekeeper replied in contented tones. "I'm about to bring up luncheon."

She eyed his muddy boots, which he'd momentarily forgotten. He backtracked to the boot scrape beyond the riverfront door and wiped the soles as clean as he could while she went on her way.

Weary, in no mood for company, he exchanged the freshly mopped foyer for the room that was the most broken in. Everything was as he'd left it the night before. The journal he kept lay open on his desk. His violin rested atop a low, glassed-in bookcase. He couldn't play as well as Thomas Jefferson or John Randolph, but he did try. The air was redolent of spirits and tobacco, lemon oil and beeswax candles. Miles Roth was the only discordant feature in it.

"You're late," Noble said. He'd sent Miles a note as soon as Lady Elisabeth was beneath his roof.

"I beg your pardon. I came as soon as I could," Miles returned, looking at his cousin's begrimed clothes over the rim of his glass. "As I've said before, you take this plantation business far too seriously."

"Mayhap you don't take it seriously enough," Noble mused, shutting the dark walnut door. "Seems like we could find a middle ground."

They stood facing each other as if sizing the other up and preparing for a wrestling match like in days of old. Even as a boy Miles Roth had a wayward bent. And Noble, older by two years, had felt an inexplicable concern for him, and an unbending affection. Miles was the younger brother he'd never had, who had run and ridden with him over every inch of Ty Mawr's acreage.

They'd been kings of their own little principalities back then, till they'd been packed up and sent to William and Mary with their manservants. Noble had been ten, Miles eight. With Miles's parents recently lost at sea, Noble's father had held his estate in trust till he turned twenty-one. Seven years had passed since then, much of it spent in London. Though Miles had long since returned from England, the effects of its dissipations still lingered. Roth Hall was in dire need of a mistress, and so an alliance was formed with Elisabeth's powerful father for her hand.

At first Noble had been surprised, even impressed by the match. Perhaps Miles had some good sense after all. It was rumored around Williamsburg that Elisabeth was as intelligent and engaging as her father was ironfisted and arrogant. A good wife might help reform Miles, even if one had to deal with so intimidating a father-in-law, not to mention a mother-in-law with a literary bent. And then the whole scheme unraveled.

God be praised. The thought came unbidden but was heartfelt. Elisabeth Lawson had escaped disaster. But Noble wasn't going to let Miles off the hook without a chance to shame him for reprehensible conduct before severing their tie completely.

Miles's bloodshot eyes regarded Noble warily as he rounded his desk, its congested bulk between them. Stacks of daybooks and ledgers crowded the surface alongside inkwells and quills of every feather. Though it looked cluttered and disorganized, Noble knew where everything was instantly, even if it took patience to unearth.

"I don't have much time," Miles told him. "There's a game set to begin at Chownings."

"A game?" Noble echoed, shutting his journal. "As our mutual friend Landon Carter once said, no African is so great a slave as a man obsessed with gambling."

"Don't be so quick to judge, Cousin. I've other business in Williamsburg besides."

"Have you considered living in town?" Noble asked, sitting down behind his desk. "There's a house on England Street available, or so I've heard."

"The Lawsons', you mean." Miles looked toward the door as if contemplating his exit. "Unfortunate, that."

"Aye." He inked a quill. "What are you going to do about it?"

Miles shrugged narrow shoulders. "Distance myself from the Tory cause as quickly and completely as I can."

"What are you going to do about your betrothed?" Noble looked up from the document he'd just signed. "Lady Elisabeth?"

The terse question fell flat in the suddenly still room. All conviviality left Miles's face. "What does it matter to you?"

"It matters because she's here beneath my roof."

"Here? Why?"

"No one would take her in. Not even the rector of Bruton Parish Church."

"Do you blame them? She's Lord Stirling's daughter. A Tory. Tories get tarred and feathered. Best take her to the *Fowey* and her father and be done with it."

"You have an agreement. Rather, an obligation."

Miles raised a hand to his ruffled stock as if he found it too tight. "We *had* an agreement."

"You and Lieutenant Governor Lawson signed a contract in my very presence."

"A contract that is no longer binding—"

"Don't try to tell me what's legally binding and what's not.

I studied law, remember. You signed a contract for transfer of ownership of goods—her maid's indenture and a dowry of several thousand pounds—with the understanding that her father would no longer care for her, and you, the groom, would assume those responsibilities, including the properties to be hers in Virginia Colony and the West Indies."

Miles took a step back at the airing of the facts. "I doubt even her father would enforce it given the circumstances—"

"I would enforce it."

Alarm flared in Miles's eyes, but Noble felt no pleasure in trumping his wayward relative. "You have no feeling for her?"

"I—nay." The stain of guilt finally showed on Miles's features. "She's a lovely girl, but . . ."

Though he suspected as much, Noble felt a sweeping relief at the confession. He knew Miles's tastes ran to tavern wenches. Simply put, the genteel Lady Elisabeth bored him to death.

Miles focused on his buckled shoes. "The lady in question is a bit tepid for my tastes."

"Then the fault is not hers but yours."

The condemning words brought an end to the maddening conversation. Without another word, Miles turned to leave. Taking up his hat on a table by the door, he let himself out, leaving Noble to wonder how he'd spare Lady Elisabeth the sting of a broken betrothal if not a broken heart.

8

Though she'd been at Ty Mawr but a short time, the place was gaining a foothold in her heart. Elisabeth sat on the riverfront portico with the best view while Mistress Tremayne served, a tea table before them. It seemed all they did at Ty Mawr was eat. Or did Mistress Tremayne find her too thin?

'Twas Dimity who usually served at the townhouse. She missed her, missed them all. Betsy. Jade. Paris. Thomasin. Had they fled with her father? Would she ever see them again? Only Isabeau remained. Dear, protective, half-hysterical Isabeau. And Mamie, awaiting Mama in Williamsburg.

A vase of pure white roses anchored the equally white linen cloth. On a small ironstone platter sat bara brith, the rich fruit loaf.

"And this?" Elisabeth gestured toward a tiny pot.

"Welsh salted butter," the housekeeper replied proudly. "From Ty Mawr's creamery. It goes splendidly with speckled bread. The bake ovens are always busy here. 'Tis Master Rynallt's favorite, you see."

Elisabeth smiled her pleasure. "Why is it called Ty Mawr?"

"Why is it?" The housekeeper chuckled. "For a town-bred colonial lass, you have a great many questions. But I'm glad to answer them. *Ty Mawr* simply means 'big house' in Welsh."

"Is there a Ty Mawr in Wales?"

"Indeed. It was there that the Welsh Bible translator was born. Bishop William Morgan, kin to Master Rynallt."

"A Welsh Bible? Wonderful history there." Savoring the speckled bread, Elisabeth detected cinnamon and ginger and a spice she couldn't name. "So there are two Ty Mawrs."

"Master Rynallt's older brother is heir to yon Ty Mawr, an upland stone farmhouse two centuries old." Mistress Tremayne looked east as if gazing across the entire Atlantic. "Virginia's Ty Mawr is not so old nor so honored. Yet 'tis more beautiful."

So Noble had a brother. Elisabeth wanted to learn more but took a second piece of speckled bread instead. Mistress Tremayne poured coffee, not tea, and Elisabeth was reminded anew of the conflict. But she was glad for the bracing black brew, having spent a near sleepless night kept up by Isabeau's snoring.

A breeze blew up from the river, redolent of the changing tide. Wrinkling her nose, Elisabeth put a hand to her lace pinner.

Mistress Tremayne put a hand to her own cap. "Glad I am you're properly pinned. Many a hat has ended up in the James. Though we've not had many visitors to warn of late. The master is often away, due as much to his sister's absence as his politics, I fear." She looked down at her apron. "I'll not pretend 'tis been easy here since Miss Enid left us. All the little pleasures of life seem to have gone with her."

Enid. Even if the name hadn't been unusual, Elisabeth knew she'd never forget it. The circumstance that had caused

Enid's death was a mystery. Being a stranger here she felt un-qualified to speak of it, either in sympathy or out of curiosity.

"You've likely heard the sad details. Out riding she was when she fell and caught her shoe in the stirrup. Nearly killed her outright, but she lingered for days. Master Rynallt and Doctor Hessel did all they could, but she died of her injuries within a fortnight. Her brother blamed himself, you see. Something about a saddle in need of repair."

Did Noble feel he'd caused his sister's death? "I'm terribly sorry. I have no words."

"Forgive me. You've come through a storm yourself." Mistress Tremayne's eyes were damp. "But you'll soon be settled at Roth Hall, I suppose. Mister Roth has finally come. He's in the study with Master Rynallt as we speak."

Here? Now? Was Miles the coming company mentioned? The image of him striding away from her in the townhouse garden made her doubly surprised. It had smacked of a finished affair.

Elisabeth sipped her coffee, focusing on the James while Mistress Tremayne glanced down the long portico as if she'd heard something or someone. Elisabeth followed her gaze and saw Noble approaching. He uttered something in Welsh to his housekeeper, who gave a slight bow of her head and went inside.

His quiet voice with its deep measured tones was so low it sometimes escaped Elisabeth's ear. But not this time. Not now. There was a new note within of careful consideration, even uneasiness. She knew he brought ill news before he stepped into her line of sight.

Pressing her back against the upholstered chair, she clasped her hands in the deep folds of her skirt and kept her eyes on her half-empty cup. He took the chair next to her so that they weren't facing each other but looking outward at the sloping lawn and river. The gesture was gallant, allowing her a bit of privacy and the dignity she'd lost.

For long moments Elisabeth waited for him to speak. When he didn't, she turned her face to him. This close, in stark daylight, she could see a few strands of silver in his charcoal hair. And once again her focus shifted from herself to him. What sorrows beyond Enid had he borne that had aged him so? He could be no more than thirty, surely.

Even now his eyes reflected a dozen different things as they met hers, resignation foremost. The lengthy silence was excruciating. She was at a loss for words herself, so she dug deep and borrowed someone else's. "Silence propagates itself, and the longer talk has been suspended, the more difficult it is to find anything to say."

At this he grimaced. "Or so opines Mister Samuel Johnson." He leaned forward. Elbows on the table, he fisted his hands together, eyes on the shimmering river again. "'When the mind is thinking, it is talking to itself.' Plato. Fourth century." He cleared his throat. "Miles Roth was just here."

"I know. Mistress Tremayne told me."

"Did he speak to you?"

"He seems to make a point of not doing so."

"Then the fault is his, not yours, as I told him."

She looked to her lap. Her heart twisted at the humiliation of it all. "I wasn't privy to your conversation, but I sense our betrothal is broken."

"Aye," he said. "Though I could, as a lawmaker, try to enforce the contract."

"By no means. You cannot dictate honorable conduct." She forged ahead in a way she wasn't entirely comfortable with. "Some contracts are made to be broken. Perhaps this is one of them. Providence spares us a great many pains we'd inflict on ourselves otherwise."

"You don't love him." There was no censure in the words. No rebuke.

"I've never been in love," she confessed. "The marriage was arranged, start to finish, by my father."

"You deserve better."

"Do I?" She liked that he said so. She longed for something unarranged. Something heartfelt. "I appreciate all you've done on my behalf." She smoothed the lace of her fichu with nervous hands. "But I shan't impose on your hospitality any longer—"

"You're not an imposition."

Their eyes met and she saw an unclouded invitation there. Or was it simply concern? 'Twas hard to tell where politeness ended and personal interest began. As she pondered it, her heart did an absurd little dance.

"Ty Mawr is yours for as long as you like," he said matter-of-factly. "Till you decide your best course of action."

"I—thank you." What could she say to this? She had nowhere else to go. She turned her eyes to the colorful garden beyond a wide shell path. "Do you really *not* mind having a Tory beneath your roof?"

He winked at her. "I don't know that you're a true Tory. Your very name is Liberty."

"According to my mother, yes." Her smile turned wistful. "I don't know who I am, truly. Other than the daughter of Virginia's last lieutenant governor and the former fiancé of Miles Roth."

"You are simply the very lovely Lady Elisabeth Lawson, daughter of the earl and the countess of Stirling, and as such you've done nothing wrong."

She smiled self-consciously, then got up as gracefully as she could, the wind making a wide bell of her skirts. He stood along with her, his own hair whipped into a black froth, strands pulled free of his queue. It was then she noticed he'd been riding. His clothes were a bit dusty and his boots muddy, as if he'd been laboring alongside his field hands.

He placed tanned hands on the back of his chair. "If you want to send a letter to your father or bring your mother here once she docks, I can arrange for that."

"No need." She took a step back, nearer the door to the foyer, her voice rising above the strengthening wind. "I must make my own way, you see. I shan't be a burden. Your benevolence, though much appreciated, must have an end."

The little speech burst forth with such uncharacteristic vigor she immediately wished the words back. Surprise shone in his eyes, and she felt a stinging remorse at such plain speaking. Unable to even murmur an apology, she simply turned and fled in a swirl of linen and lace.

Isabeau was nowhere to be found. Elisabeth entered their attic rooms to find the windows open, light spilling across the polished walnut floor. The clothespress was gaping enough to reveal that the few gowns they'd hurriedly stuffed into a trunk were now carefully sorted and arranged as if they were here for an extended stay. The change bespoke permanence and seemed to underscore Noble Rynallt's gracious invitation. But it only heightened Elisabeth's dismay. She didn't belong here—and they couldn't remain.

She sank down on an ottoman, eyes on a little writing desk through the sitting room door. The quill and paper atop it reminded her she needed to send a note to Doctor Hessel, perhaps even Cressida. Cressida wouldn't believe she was at Ty Mawr.

As she pondered it, Isabeau finally appeared, a dozen questions in her eyes. "Oh, mistress. I saw you speaking with Monsieur Rynallt. And I was told that Monsieur Roth just rode off."

"Yes to both." The details seemed to stick in Elisabeth's throat. "Our betrothal is broken. Roth Hall isn't to be our home after all."

The bedchamber door snapped shut as Isabeau came inside, slack jawed. "But, mistress, the wedding—has it not been months in the planning? What—"

"It seems I'm not the right mistress for Roth Hall." Elisabeth felt all the remaining emotion drain out of her. Empty as a sieve, she was in no mood to answer questions. "Perhaps Providence has prevented a marital disaster."

"Providence, la!" Hands waving about, Isabeau seemed to be grasping for words. "Your opinion of the Almighty, it is high indeed. I'd be shaking my fist instead of thanking Him. What a fine tangle we are in!"

"Isabeau, have you ever considered going on the stage?"

The gentle check brought a touch of pink to her maid's pale face. "Pardon, mistress. But this is all so . . . sudden."

Elisabeth put a hand to her aching head. "When I was taking coffee on the portico I saw you speaking with a man in the foyer."

"*Oui, oui*. Monsieur Rynallt's valet. He was showing me about Ty Mawr. 'Tis very different than town."

"And his name?"

"Monsieur Landeg. Ninian Landeg."

"A Welshman, no doubt."

Isabeau wore an odd smile. "Welsh, *oui*, and . . . *oh là là*."

High praise coming from Isabeau. Perhaps the valet could be trusted with a letter. "I shall write Doctor Hessel. He always sees things clearly. He may have word of Mama too."

The thought of Hessel brought stark relief. Elisabeth moved to the cloisonné-backed chair, surprised to find not only quill and ink but pounce and wafers atop the desk. A fleur-de-lis seal was in the drawer. All she needed was a messenger. She got down to the business of writing the tersest letter she'd ever penned, biting her lip at the pained plea.

Dear Doctor,

I am at a secret location. Have you any word of my father? My utmost concern is for Mother. Have you any news of her?

Yours affectionately, EL

Isabeau was at her elbow. "I'll have it sent to town."

"By way of the valet, I presume."

"I can think of no faster way to dispatch it. Can you?"

"Make sure no one tells of our whereabouts."

Her father's words returned to her, full of vehemence and suspicion.

These are times in which loyalties are continually in question. You do not know whom you can trust.

9

The French doors of the White Parlor were open wide to the river. A cool, misting rain was falling, the weather shifting like Noble's mood. As he'd left the stables after inspecting a horse just arrived from Rhode Island, his delayed company had appeared. The Dinwiddies and Prescotts, longtime friends of the family, mostly Enid's. His guests were now scattered about the elegant room awaiting supper, obviously aware he'd come out of mourning.

Before she'd died, his sister had redecorated most of Ty Mawr, and now each female present was exclaiming over every niche and fixture, from the papered walls to the carpets at their feet. Enid would have been pleased with their praise. As the White Parlor was her favorite, he'd let her have her way with it and was glad of the outcome. But tonight the buzz of voices around him was hardly heard. He couldn't keep his mind off Lady Elisabeth—and the unexpected arrival of Doctor Hessel.

Ever since the doctor had ridden in, Noble had been aware of a new undercurrent in the house. Though they'd shaken hands cordially enough in the foyer as was their custom, the doctor had seemed a bit distant. At one time he'd been within Ty Mawr's walls so often he seemed as much a fixture as the immense case clock hugging the foyer wall or the smirr of tobacco permeating the study. And then, after Enid died, his sudden absence was just as jarring. Now when they met, it was by chance on the streets of Williamsburg or at a tavern. Noble wondered if Ty Mawr's memories were too dark even for the doctor.

The darkness. The cold baths and bloodletting. The smell of purgatives. Noble had worked hard to eradicate the most wrenching memories, but the shadows were stubborn and deep. The house seemed lonesome and empty and lacking, his sister's redecorating a continual reminder she was not coming back. Sometimes his soul still seemed lined with lead.

"I apologize for arriving unannounced," Hessel had said to him, handing a housemaid his hat and medical bag. "Your guest sent me a note earlier today, and though she didn't say where she was, I managed to wheedle it out of the delivery boy who told me it came from your valet."

"I didn't know her ladyship had written," Noble told him.

Hessel's deep-set dark eyes darted to the shadows of the foyer and lingered on the stairs. "How is she?"

"Under the circumstances, well enough."

"No signs of melancholy? Hysteria?"

"Aye," Noble said. "Her maid."

"Isabeau?" Hessel paused as if he'd forgotten. "So there's one servant, at least, who didn't jump ship."

Noble wondered just how many of the servants had fled. He swallowed down a wave of sentiment thinking of Elisab— *Liberty's*—disarming smile. The name had echoed in his thoughts. How was it possible to lose everything familiar and dear in one glass-breaking, soul-shattering night and

LAURA FRANTZ

not have a crack in one's composure? Though she'd been near tears, not once had she broken down. Yet Hessel was looking at him like he was lying.

"She's quite fragile, if you didn't know. Subject to every fever and malady, it seems. Nearly as much an invalid as her mother."

"I didn't know."

A burst of laughter from the parlor drew Hessel's chagrin. "I'm interrupting, I fear. You have other guests?"

"Just arrived from Savannah."

Hessel cast another curious glance about. "Where is *she*?"

Easy, Doctor, Noble wanted to say. He'd never seen Hessel so earnest, so eager. "She's upstairs in her rooms."

Mistress Tremayne had ushered the doctor to a seldom-used sitting room on the second floor well beyond prying eyes and ears. Noble's staff was closemouthed, most of them, but in these times one could never be sure. And he wouldn't be able to keep Elisabeth's presence secret forever.

He was left to greet his guests and endure a lengthy if congenial supper, during which Hessel remained upstairs. And the reason for it had finally penetrated the logical constructs of Noble's mind with disturbing clarity.

Hessel was in love with Elisabeth Lawson.

Even now, though his guests called him out for conversation, thoughts of the doctor inserted themselves at every possible opportunity.

"We had hoped, Noble, that your coming out of mourning might mean you had found a mistress of Ty Mawr." Mistress Dinwiddie voiced the burning issue at last.

When he said nothing, her husband leapt to his defense. "Surely the end of mourning does not signal the beginning of courtship, my dear. One must proceed cautiously."

97

Overhead, Noble heard the scraping of a chair. Muted voices. Tense minutes ticked past. Another stab at conversation was made. For the moment everyone was listening with rapt attention to a recital of all the flora in Tidewater Virginia.

Except him.

"I've never seen Turk's cap lily in Williamsburg proper." Professor Dinwiddie looked quite perplexed. "What say ye, Noble?"

He directed his attention back to the company at hand. "'Twas in the governor's garden," he replied, hoping to end further comment.

Spoken in the past tense like it no longer existed. When he'd been at the empty Palace with a few of his fellow delegates, they'd not gone into the gardens. Were they largely intact, or had they been destroyed like Elisabeth's? He lifted his eyes to the second floor, where the good doctor had her cornered—and the voluble Isabeau, or so he hoped.

"Are you certain the Turk's cap resides there?" Mistress Prescott questioned. "Thomas Jefferson himself has lately written about the lack of it."

Reaching for his pipe, Noble swallowed down a biting retort. Flora and fauna seemed of small consequence given the state of affairs in Virginia Colony.

And Ty Mawr.

As if sensing his aggravation, Mistress Dinwiddie changed course. "I fancy our host would rather talk horses. You have a fine new thoroughbred in your stables, so I've heard."

"Aye," Noble said. "A Narragansett pacer, recommended by Paul Revere."

"The silversmith?" Mistress Dinwiddie looked shocked. "The one said to ride about Massachusetts Colony alarming individuals of British activity?"

"The very same."

"Oh my." Mistress Prescott swished her fan in agitation. "I'm hopelessly ignorant of all things equine, I'm afraid. And not much better with politics. I'd rather talk botanicals."

To his relief, Colonel Prescott came to the rescue. "Professor, I've been meaning to ask you about a particular species of andromeda, if you don't mind a brief walk in the garden. There by the door is a parasol should you need it."

The rain was falling harder, making a gentle slurring sound as the June dust was dampened down. Soon all his guests had left the parlor and he was alone, wanting to take the stairs by twos.

A match could not be made between a middling doctor and the top tier of Virginia society. Could it? If so, it would certainly solve the quandary Lady Elisabeth found herself in. The social complexities that usually amused him tonight simply grated. He fixed his eye on the open French doors, the garden and guests beyond now cast in a sudden ray of light. The clouds were clearing, but his thoughts remained muddled.

Soon the Dinwiddies shuffled in again, and a game of whist was struck. Noble was acutely aware of the precise moment Elisabeth and the doctor ended their lengthy conversation. Above, a door clicked shut, and the steady tread of someone coming down the stairs trained Noble's gaze on the open doorway leading to the foyer.

He felt sharp relief when Hessel came into view. Donning his hat, the doctor left without ceremony. At the sound of his horse clipping down the drive, Noble excused himself and took a back stair. Isabeau stood on the third-floor landing, talking in low tones with Mistress Tremayne. His housekeeper looked at him a final time before excusing herself, clearly concerned. Was she thinking he'd gotten in over his head this time? Perhaps he had.

He pondered his next move, at sea in his own house. The one woman he wanted to see was missing. Had she gone with Hessel? Nay, he'd seen him leave alone. Relief peppered him, and his attention fixed on her maid. "Where is Lady Elisabeth?"

"In her rooms, monsieur," Isabeau whispered. "Penning another letter."

He weighed the wisdom of that. Would she write to all of Virginia Colony?

With a quiet knock, he waited for her voice before stepping into the sitting room and leaving the door open behind him, nearly bumping his head on the low eave. Elisabeth looked up, her pen midair, her expression a question. Hessel said she was fragile. Given to illness. Noble detected a slight tremor in her hand as she held the quill aloft, as if all her agitation had settled in her fingers.

He took a settee by the window, his back to the pane. The moment he stilled she sprang into action. Setting down her quill, she stood and began pacing as if she found his sudden presence unsettling. Or mayhap the doctor was to blame.

Her wrinkled silk skirts swirled around her, the pointed toes of her blue damask slippers making a soft impression in the carpet as she walked. Even a few feet away she was emanating some sweet scent he couldn't name that set his every sense on fire. He wanted nothing more than to reach out and take her hands in his and still her slight trembling. Whatever had transpired had upended her, nearly cracked her composure, and it brought out every protective instinct he had.

Then, just as suddenly as she'd begun pacing, she sat down

on the settee beside him. He allowed himself the thought that she did so for no other reason than to draw strength from him. He'd become a refuge for her. Or so he hoped.

"I have a letter." She looked toward the desk holding a paper marred with a heavily inked hand. "From my father."

He swallowed, feeling he'd waded deeper into water he might well drown in. So the good doctor had brought her a letter. Was Hessel acting as emissary between Elisabeth and Lord Stirling?

Without preamble, she reached for it and began reading aloud every wavering word.

My dear daughter,

By now I trust your intended has come to your aid and you are ensconced at Roth Hall as a bride, or soon will be. Given that colonial Virginia is in rebellion, I, along with Lord Dunmore and family, have taken measures to ensure our safety and are now aboard a man-of-war on the York River. Once matters resolve in our favor, we will return to Williamsburg. Your mother's imminent return is on my mind. As your new husband has the means to sustain her, it seems most prudent to leave matters in his hands.

Noble saw Elisabeth firm her jaw, knowing full well she couldn't hide her distress much longer. The weight of the letter settled around them, all the repercussions and consequences. He loathed the man and his actions with a loathing that went far beyond politics. He loathed himself because he should have intervened that fateful day and hadn't.

"I have something to confess." At her surprise, he let the details spill. "Remember the letter you lost from Lady

Charlotte on Duke of Gloucester Street? The one you wanted me to retrieve?" He swallowed hard, detecting sudden suspicion in her eyes. "I didn't find it, but Patrick Henry did. I had the chance to tell you before your father and the Dunmores fled but decided it was beyond my ken so left it alone. Now I wonder if you would be in these straits had I given you warning."

She shook her head. "I wouldn't have gone with my father, letter or no."

His conscience eased. Still . . .

"If I was truly meant to go with the Dunmores, I never would have lost that letter." She looked down at her hands, fingers laced together. "Patrick Henry's finding it might well have saved me in the end."

Saved her? What did she mean? When she fell silent, he said, "I go to Williamsburg tomorrow. Do you want me to do anything for you while I'm there?"

Her head came up, and he saw new questions mirrored in her eyes. "There's the matter of my maid's indenture. My father's house. My dowry."

He simply nodded, not wanting to tell her the truth of what was coming, unwilling to smother the glimmer of hope he saw resurface in her comely face. The Revolution he'd helped bring about had dawned, and their lives would never be the same again. Neither his nor hers. A steep price was yet to be paid.

Elisabeth Lawson was among the first casualties.

10

*J*oy cometh in the morning.

Damask roses. Hollyhocks. Peonies. Cardinal flowers. Elisabeth stood amid the sun-soaked garden path the next day, feeling God had given her a gift. Before dawn she'd escaped her room, unable to sleep, and had found her way to Ty Mawr's formal box hedge. Within its green folds she was hidden. The big house's guests had departed the day before, and the garden at this hour seemed hers alone.

She shut her eyes, wanting to hold on to the quiet, the sounds and colors. She was in the shade of a gazebo surrounded by bluebells and lily of the valley. A fountain splashed somewhere beyond the yew hedge. Birds flittered about and traded songs. And a small, stoop-shouldered man was a blur of homespun as he came toward her, toting a shovel. Her quiet interlude was about to be broken. Yet this was the gardener's domain, after all.

"Pardon, miss. I thought you be someone else."

"Please, no apologies." She flashed him a forgiving smile. "I'm merely a guest." Did he even know who she was? Going around the gazebo to deeper shade, she gestured to a tall-stemmed, deep purple lily. "I've found a flower whose name I don't know."

"Queen's trumpet," he said straightaway. "One of Miss Enid's favorites, God rest her. A gift from her brother. Used to try to interest Master Rynallt in gardening before she passed. Get him away from the stables some."

A difficult endeavor, perhaps. They continued down fragrant paths, the gardener pointing out statuaries and particularly unusual species as they walked. She felt a tug of recognition at the placement of the flowers, the design of the beds.

"Aye, there's a Williamsburg gardener to thank for all this. Before he was employed by Lord Dunmore, he was here. You might have heard of him, from the Palace."

"Indeed I have. Mister James." As though he was an artist working on canvas, she could see his creativity everywhere she looked. It bore his characteristic mark. Where was the head gardener now? With her father and the Dunmores? "You tend it beautifully."

"I simply caretake what the master gardener put into place. 'Tis yours to enjoy, miss. I'll not hinder you."

Unwilling to go in and miss a stirring sunrise, she walked on toward the river on a path of crushed shells. The wind settled, and she breathed in the strong scent of the shifting tide and heard the cry of a gull. The sweeping bird flew overhead as she stopped just short of the dock. A number of vessels were tied up, including a rowboat and skiff, all straining at their moorings in the current.

She removed her slippers and wandered down the sandy shoreline. She spied a large piece of driftwood and sat down, her back to Ty Mawr, hoping no one was awake enough to notice her, or if they did, they would not inquire who she was. The mostly Welsh staff was a clannish bunch who spoke in unintelligible whispers as they moved about on light feet. Mistress Tremayne was clearly in charge, and the servants seemed to have a healthy respect for her oversight. Especially the valet whom Isabeau seemed fond of.

"Lady Elisabeth?" A voice carried from the above bank. "I awoke and could not find you. What are you doing out here at break of day?"

Ignoring the rebuke in Isabeau's tone, Elisabeth gestured to the sunrise. "Isn't it a wonder?"

Shadowing her, Isabeau ignored the beauty. "Is it not odd that the sun rises and sets without fail while we have no set course, no compass?"

"Empty your mind of such," Elisabeth chided, patting the place beside her. "At least for the glorious present."

Isabeau scrambled down the bank, her shoes sinking into the sand. Reaching her mistress, she blew out an exasperated breath. "M'lady, such dishabille! Your hair is loosely bound. You are in your plainest gown. *Aidez moi!*" She gawked at Elisabeth's shoeless feet. "What if *he* should see you?"

"*He* has gone to Williamsburg to try to set some things right for us." Elisabeth focused on the sunrise, trying to tease out its many colors. Oyster pink, the very hue of her gown for her betrothal ball. "When he returns, we shall have answers, and then I will determine what to do."

"You should not be in full view." Isabeau cast a look back at the stirring house. "You must keep to your rooms."

"I shan't be cooped up like a chicken. Not even by you."

"Ah, mistress! I fear some of our host's talk of independence has infected you. What would your papa say?"

Elisabeth lifted her shoulders. "Father has no say any longer. Besides, what harm can come to me in so peaceful a spot? I've only the birds and flowers . . . and a cantankerous maid."

"Come." Isabeau rose and began backtracking to the house. "The sun has nearly risen. It shall soon be so hot you'll need a hat. Besides, I requested breakfast at seven o'clock. Tea and toast."

"Not bara brith?" At Isabeau's scowl, Elisabeth said, "When in a Welsh household, you must do as the Welsh do."

"But I am *Français*!"

"*Oui, oui.* I doubt tea will be served but rather coffee. This is a Patriot household, after all."

"Do not remind me." Isabeau put a hand to her furrowed brow. "I abhor coffee and the speckled bread. I feel a headache coming on."

Lacing her arm through her maid's, Elisabeth helped her navigate the bank. "Then I shall give you some of Doctor Hessel's headache powders and all will be well."

Ty Mawr rose up in front of them, the bricked back and portico burnished a pleasing rose gold in the sunrise. She would miss this house. This place. No matter Noble Rynallt's politics.

'Twas the Sabbath, and the town, a seething maelstrom of activity on any other day, seemed asleep. Much of Williamsburg would be at church this morning, its members required by law to attend at least once a month or be fined. As a new Presbyterian, Noble was no longer bound by the Church of England, though he continued paying taxes to Bruton Parish Church. He himself was usually in the pew of the far humbler stone church near Ty Mawr, which was pastored by a tenant.

But this Sabbath was like no other. At least where Lady Elisabeth was concerned. He rode slowly down Duke of Gloucester Street, past rustling leaves and filtered sunlight, wishing he could right circumstances, at least for his houseguest.

For some reason the Raleigh seemed less like home to Noble today, and he felt disinclined to stay for even a pint. Outwardly everything was the same, but inwardly he felt an inexplicable shift.

He'd not arrived first. Several mounts of fellow Patriots were in evidence. Standing by George Wythe on the tavern's shaded front porch, Patrick Henry raised a hand and motioned him over. Though Lord Dunmore had been aboard the *Fowey* but a few days, talk was already circling about naming Henry as his successor. Despite his fiery reputation, Henry had a keen intellect and was a close ally. Noble couldn't think of a better man for the job except George Washington, but Wash's talents ran more toward soldiering.

"What say ye?" Henry greeted him, lifting his felt hat to swipe at his damp hairline.

Noble staunched the sweat from his upper lip with a dusty sleeve. "Well. And you?"

No one answered. John Laurens was studying him, examining his person without comment, and Noble well knew why. He'd finally cast off all the trappings of mourning, even shorn his hair. His cocked hat and coat, minus their usual black band and cockade, looked a bit less forlorn.

"So you've come back to the land of the living at last," Laurens said not unkindly, a telling glint in his eye. Having lost his wife a few months prior, he'd remarried a distant cousin rather swiftly. Marriage had many pains, he'd said, but celibacy few pleasures.

Noble simply nodded, trying to keep his mind on the

matter at hand, not the one at home. But Elisabeth Lawson had a way of storming his thoughts without warning and stealing his attention.

Henry passed him a sheaf of papers tied with string. "I need you to look over these documents. Jeff and Wash have perused them and only have a quibble with two clauses. Barring that, we need a final copy before printing."

"When do you want them?"

"As soon as possible. They're to be introduced at the next convention. Perhaps you could lodge here tonight and have them ready by morning."

"Nay," Noble replied with uncharacteristic haste. "I'm needed at Ty Mawr."

"Ty Mawr? Why?" Henry's thick brows arched. "You've been more at home here in Williamsburg since your sister's passing."

George Wythe flashed a yellow-toothed smile. "You'd be saying nay too, if you had his houseguest."

Confusion filled Henry's face, and then it cleared. His eyes glinted with wry humor as they fixed on Noble. "So 'tis *you* who rescued Lord Stirling's lovely daughter. I heard the gossip but could scarce believe it. Careful lest ye be accused of Tory leanings."

"I'd gladly do it again," Noble said, eyeing the papers in hand.

"You always did have a hospitable bent," Laurens muttered. "Though her ladyship's presence is more complicated than the usual vagabond or beggar."

"Lord Stirling's daughter is complicated indeed," Wythe mused, running a hand through thinning hair, his aristocratic voice a touch dire. "'Tis a risk, to be sure. We have enemies, remember, who'd like to make much of that."

"Then let them," Noble replied quietly, meeting his gaze.

Henry waved a fly away. "All right, gentlemen. Back to the business at hand. Nature abhors a vacuum, 'tis said, and never more so than a political one. We have to act quickly or time and opportunity will be lost to us. Shall we?"

They began a slow but purposeful walk down the street toward the Governor's Palace, looking much as it did in former days save the telling emptiness. Passing the elaborate iron gates with its heraldic beasts and crowns, they went single file through the forecourt to the double front doors. Taking out a ponderous chain, Henry riffled through the keys to one in particular. The front door was unlocked and left open as the men filled the foyer.

Noble's gaze rose from the marble floor to the walnut-paneled walls. He'd always thought the entrance less than welcoming, but now, stripped of its many weapons, it seemed less forbidding. Over a hundred muskets had once been mounted amid a great many swords and other weapons. The red damask chairs looked untouched, as did the hall and artwork beyond. Clearly it was weapons the mob was after. Noble rued the loss of munitions.

Henry led them through the lower rooms, including the blue ballroom and adjoining supper room, assessing any damage before going up the pine staircase. Through the arches at the top of the stairs was a middle room or royal audience room where Virginia's royal governors had conducted business for more than fifty years.

Henry sat in the throne-like chair, once Dunmore's own, looking quite at home. Noble and the others stood about the immense desk, their gazes never settling as Henry spoke.

"Virginia's government is now in the hands of the people,

who have no intention of returning it to royal authority without a fight."

Noble listened without comment as Henry and Wythe discussed the coming Virginia Convention and its new purpose.

Eventually they retreated to the Raleigh for a pint and a pipe. Noble was anxious to excuse himself, taking the necessary paperwork with him.

"About those documents. How soon shall we see them?" Henry asked.

"If I ride out within the hour I can have them back to you on the morrow," Noble told him.

"Done." Henry's satisfaction turned probing. "Now do I sense a wedding in the offing?"

Noble studied him thoughtfully. "Yours, mayhap?"

The men rumbled with laughter. Newly widowed, Henry had six children at home and little time for courting yet little reason to delay. He looked a bit shamefaced, as if he'd been keeping secrets. "Very well then. Since rumors are flying you might as well know firsthand. After the political dust settles I'm to wed Dorothea Dandridge."

Wythe chortled loudest, pounding Henry on the back in congratulations. "Now *that* confession calls for some oysters and Virginia ham," he crowed loudly to the approving nods of the rest.

Noble delayed his departure for a half hour more as they ate amid the clink of utensils and curl of tobacco smoke in a private room free of passersby. Finally, Laurens and Wythe slipped away for a game of whist in the adjoining taproom, leaving Noble and Henry alone.

Noble pushed his empty plate away, preoccupied with a final matter. "What's to be done with Tory holdings?"

Henry hunched over a glass of Madeira, pipe stem between his teeth. He seemed to take an age to answer. Noble was surprised to find that he himself was sweating, more indicative of his angst than the summer heat. With Elisabeth Lawson's entreating face firmly in mind, the matter assumed unusual importance.

"Lawson's townhouse, ye mean?" At Noble's nod, Henry said, "All Tory property is to be confiscated by the Americans in time—servants and furniture auctioned, and all the rest." He puffed on his pipe, gaze never wavering. "Don't look so glum, man. Could be worse."

Worse. The word sat uncomfortably between them. "Mayhap we should revise the wording of the document."

At this, Henry's affability soured.

"Life, liberty, and the pursuit of happiness," Noble said, "for all but Lord Stirling's daughter and fellow Tories, and every slave in the thirteen colonies."

Henry expelled a ragged breath. "Now, my good man, 'tis not a perfect world."

The answer was patently unsatisfying. Noble fixed his eye on a beam of sunlight slanting through a tall window to his left. Dust motes danced in the warm air, and his mind began to drift, cast back to long nights spent laboring over Virginia's fledgling independence papers. Hand cramped from writing, he'd pressed on till dawn, never dreaming of the consequences.

Henry cleared his throat. "How personally involved are you in all this?"

Noble wanted to sidestep the issue, knowing full well Henry wouldn't let him. "In independence?"

"Nay," he growled. "Lord Stirling's daughter."

Noble met his searching gaze directly. "I've just come out of mourning. Ty Mawr lacks a mistress. Lady Elisabeth is not without personal charm. If I told you she has no effect on me whatsoever I'd be lying."

"Ah, Noble. You've always had a tremendous gift for understatement." Henry partook of his pipe, his voice dropping a notch. "I sense you're enamored of her, and it couldn't happen at a more inopportune time."

"One cannot be in love in a fortnight. Infatuated, mayhap, given the little time I've known her. But not in love."

"Man, are you daft? Affection doesn't consult the clock! 'Tis that barrister brain of yours trying to make sense of what you yourself cannot deny, is it not?"

"Then what is your recommendation?"

"Get her out of your house immediately. 'Feed not thy affections,' as my father used to say. For all we know she might be a Tory spy. When word of this spreads, I shudder at the consequences."

"Her ladyship has nowhere to go."

"There are fifteen ordinaries in and around Williamsburg, by my last count." Henry's tone turned a trifle exasperated. "Has she no one willing to take her in? No friends?"

"Few faithful ones," he said, thinking of Cressida Shaw.

"No relatives elsewhere in the colonies?"

"None that I know of."

"Why doesn't she join her father and fellow Tories aboard the *Fowey*?"

"Her mother is expected any day, and that is where her loyalties lie."

"Ah, the countess. Banished to the mother country on account of her patriotic pen."

"Aye, the one we'll soon be at war with."

Henry sighed. "What a fine kettle of fish this is."

Their attention swung to the taproom's entrance, where

a few more Patriots gathered. George Rogers Clark's booming voice warned Noble he'd be further delayed. Mayhap he could slip out the back.

As Noble rose from the table, Henry fixed him with a fatherly stare. "I admire you for coming to her aid when no one else would, but be careful, man. And don't be so quick to trust the lass in question."

From her position at the window, Elisabeth watched for the return of Ty Mawr's master and was at last rewarded. Never had she been so enamored of approaching horse hooves. Her insides did a riotous dance as she set aside her lacemaking and rested her hands in her lap. The piece she was working was complicated. And as black as Isabeau's mood.

"So he's finally come." Isabeau flew to the window, her mouth slanting disapprovingly. "All day we wait and now he comes late—with half a dozen rogues on his heels?"

Joining her at the window, Elisabeth counted five additional riders, each nearly obscured by dust. Other than Noble, she most easily recognized the unmistakable figure of Washington. "He keeps fine company."

But Isabeau did not hear her, for she'd gone to the door to let Mistress Tremayne enter with a supper tray. Elisabeth turned away from the glass reluctantly. For once Mistress Tremayne looked tired, as if something more was stirring than Ty Mawr's expected company. The sumptuous contents of their supper wafted into the room. Roast lamb. Tintern cheese. Welsh cakes. An abundance of butter and preserves.

Isabeau relieved her of her burden, and Elisabeth took a seat at the small supper table, thanking her. "You look tired, Mistress Tremayne. Won't you sit for a moment?"

"I'm afraid not, your ladyship." The housekeeper glanced at the nearest chair longingly. "I've another supper to oversee before the night's through. These Patriots are very fond of dining."

The arrival of so many men at once sounded like a small storm. Elisabeth felt both keen disappointment and curiosity. 'Twas an empty house she wanted, if for no other reason than to be alone with her host again. Pleasurable pieces of their time together kept returning to her even now. "Ty Mawr is a hospitable place."

"Once upon a time it was. For now it will host a few of the Independence Men, including George Rogers Clark, just returned from the Kentucke territory."

The rebels. Elisabeth saw the fire in Isabeau's eyes.

"I wish some feminine company for you," Mistress Tremayne murmured, sympathy in her gaze. "I daresay 'twill be a bit mundane with all the male talk."

She went out, leaving Isabeau to hiss, "Tar and feathers! Are we not hemmed in on all sides by the treasonous beggars?"

"Tar and feathers, indeed. There's not an ungentlemanly one among them, although I've heard George Rogers Clark is a bit knavish at times." Elisabeth turned her attention to their supper. "Look, Isabeau. Strawberries!"

Isabeau waved her hands, ignoring the crystal dish. "I have no appetite. These men convene like a murder of crows. There is to be war, I feel it to my marrow."

"'Tis a tempest in a teacup."

Isabeau glared at her, gaze dropping to the edibles.

"I'm ravenous," Elisabeth replied, wondering what to partake of first. "Now kindly dismiss any thunderclouds and join me."

"*Non, non.* I am to dine with the other servants below."

"With Ninian Landeg, I presume? Surely *that* is cause for celebration."

Isabeau pinked, staring at her mistress's heaping plate in disbelief. "What is this? You rarely eat more than a thimbleful at a time."

"Must be the country air," Elisabeth mused, biting into a berry.

"That, or you are looking to the day we go hungry, no?"

The strawberry's exquisite sweetness turned sour. She'd never known hunger in her life. But she'd seen it on the streets of Williamsburg and had witnessed their French chef ease it in a small way by dispensing victuals out their kitchen door. "God hasn't forgotten us, Isabeau. There's been no revolution up above, remember."

Still, the faith-filled words were touched with uncertainty, and Elisabeth felt a tendril of fear take root.

Isabeau went out, and the room was blessedly still save for the snap of a curtain in the warm, coastal wind. Elisabeth was left to her private supper and the distinct sound of male voices on Ty Mawr's ground floor.

Ty Mawr assumed a different feel depending on who was in it. Tonight was rife with power and quiet dignity and purpose, no doubt owing to the men beneath its roof. Elisabeth felt a welling inside herself of unbridled curiosity and grudging admiration that these men who had so much would risk their very lives and all they held dear to turn against the Crown and be labeled traitors.

Her fascination kept her rooted to the attic's riverfront window, which gave her an exceptional view of broad backs

115

and striking profiles. These Independence Men had been below in the study, Mistress Tremayne told her. But now, as if tired of being cooped up and wanting to stretch their legs, they'd moved onto the rear lawn.

Of all the men, other than Noble, Washington intrigued her the most. Past forty, he was a physical giant, slim of shoulder and long of leg, a touch of youthful red still lingering in his queued hair. She'd never seen such enormous hands.

Most of these men had been in her father's drawing room before they'd posed a threat. More often she'd seen them within the Governor's Palace or about Williamsburg. Then and now she was struck by the vast differences between her father and Governor Dunmore and these unpowdered Patriots. None of these liberty lovers wore wigs. All were in plain but fine broadcloth, not only because there were no Spitalfields silks or other fine exports coming out of England, but because their tastes ran along simpler lines. Only one wore expensive lace at his cuffs, making her take a second look.

"Careful, mistress, lest you learn something you shouldn't," Isabeau cautioned, having returned from her supper. She went about putting freshly washed underpinnings away. In a strident whisper she said, "What are they doing now?"

"Admiring the view, talking. Supper is about to begin."

"Any dames about?"

"Nary a lady, nay."

Isabeau began mending a dress hem, singing under her breath, "God save great George our king. Long live our noble king. God save the king! Send him victorious, happy and glorious, long to reign o'er us. God save the king!"

Elisabeth winced, but the masculine talk below was so robust she didn't shush her maid. She had a mind to remind

Isabeau that as she was French, King George was not her liege, but left it alone.

Twilight crept in, lit by the glitter of fireflies. The evening promised to be a late one. Tonight there would be no answers for her from Williamsburg. Something far more pressing was afoot with these Patriots.

Before turning away from the window, she lingered on Noble. How quickly she'd taken to heart the whole of him.

In the span of that tender thought as she stared down at him, he looked up. Across the expanse of slate roof and emerald lawn his gaze lingered, and it seemed he'd reached out and touched her. Delighted, she leaned in to the glass, hands flat upon the sill. Her breath held.

Dangerous, that.

She spun away, chiding herself. Now was not the time to flirt. To be coy. In an already unsettled world she needed to stay grounded. She needed to just be . . . Liberty.

Free. Enterprising. Independent. Beholden to none.

She must change her name. Hereby, from this night forward, she would be known to all as Liberty Anne Lawson.

11

When Enid died, Noble had considered leaving Ty Mawr and moving to Ty Bryn. As he'd never been one for flinching at shadows, he'd abandoned the idea, only to take it up again after the doctor's recent visit to Elisabeth. He mulled it again after midnight when his fellow Patriots had left for home and the house was still.

Leaning back in his chair, he passed a hand over eyes still burning from too many late nights and an abundance of tobacco smoke and intense talk. Mayhap he'd ride over to Ty Bryn on the morrow and see if the cottage was in good enough repair to move into. Of all his properties, Ty Bryn was the dearest. Since his parents had passed, the place had sat empty. A waste, given its unparalleled river view.

Yet once all the work was done—all the painting and moving of furniture and possessions, and the few staff who needed transferring—would the darkness still follow? What if he just let the past play out in his head and heart? What if when a memory surfaced, he let it alone and did not try to dislodge it? Would he then find a measure of peace?

He'd been in his study but half an hour, the longest un-interrupted half hour he'd had in a fortnight. Ledgers and daybooks were open, but he looked past them into the library, where Elisabeth had gone when she'd ventured downstairs once his guests had left. Seeing him, looking embarrassed and surprised as if she'd expected him to have gone too, she'd turned and hurried up the staircase, candle flickering. But the image she'd left remained, a surprising blend of loosened hair and bare feet and pale blue dressing gown.

Now *that* was a thought he'd best abandon.

She was growing tired of her attic cage, no doubt. Perhaps looking for a book. Once she'd had free roam of Williamsburg, everything at her whim. But now . . .

He'd put her off long enough. He knew she wanted word from Williamsburg. But he was loath to tell her the news.

Or was it because once he told all, he sensed she would leave?

He climbed the stairs to bed, listening for any attic noise. None. Yet the thought of her sleeping beneath his roof, in the very room above his own, was enough to keep him wide awake all night.

Noble glanced at the mantel clock as the cock crowed and decided to ride. Then he'd meet with his houseguest. Riding had once cleared his head and given him answers he'd never gained clear of the saddle. Aye, a good, hard ride was what he needed, if he could master his memories. If Enid didn't overshadow him. He pushed all thought of her to that corner of his conscience he revisited all too often.

He'd not been to Ty Bryn in a month or better. 'Twas long overdue. He left the stables, determined not to let Enid's memory intrude as she herself had that last day, following him on her mare at a precarious gallop despite the damp and his repeated warnings. If he could only rewind time, be less preoccupied with his own interests and more of Enid's. He'd have made sure that saddle was not faulty, the ride from beginning to end more than a dark memory.

In a low-lying meadow dotted with a tangle of wild honeysuckle vine, Noble cleared one stone fence and then another. The thoroughbred came down hard and nearly stumbled, then rose with tremendous grace and took him along the lane that led to Ty Bryn. Only a fraction of the size of Ty Mawr, what it lacked in grandeur it made up for in charm.

With a tug on the reins, he guided the unfamiliar mount around the west side of the house, admiring the climbing roses clinging to one of four chimneys. As his gaze traveled to the well a few feet beyond the kitchen dependency, a flash of insight took hold. Mayhap Ty Mawr wasn't for him but for *her*. Warmth seeped through him like brandy.

Ty Mawr had a hold on his heart that few material things did. His father and mother had come from Wales and spent their last years within its walls. Happy memories for the most part, till age and infirmity ruled the day. Simply sitting atop his horse in the house's cool shadow solaced him as little else could. Mayhap Elisabeth Lawson could find happiness here. Mayhap he could find his happiness in hers.

As he passed beyond the house's north wall, he heard a horse's shrill whinny at the front. His mount's ears flicked, and he drew up short. Across the yard, his farm manager sat atop his roan, looking relieved.

"You've not been here much of late, sir."

"In Williamsburg mostly."

"Much afoot there, aye?"

"Afraid so. How hard would it be to get Ty Bryn ready for occupancy? Can we spare the labor?"

They discussed the particulars, the need for interior paint and a repair to the well. The garden was overgrown but not beyond a good weeding and pruning. With the stable already in constant use and the kitchen house in good order, Ty Bryn would soon be set right.

"Let's see it done then," Noble said, leaving the details in his farm manager's hands. He himself would deal with Lady Elisabeth.

Up and down Liberty walked, waiting. All afternoon she'd tried to occupy her wayward thoughts with a stint of lace-making, followed by bara brith and lemonade with Mistress Tremayne and now a solitary turn in the portrait gallery, a place the servants seldom ventured. All the while waiting for Noble's return.

"Best keep to the house, m'lady." Mistress Tremayne seemed to tread lightly, softening the caution as best she could. "The master feels it behooves us all to keep your where-abouts secret for now. He said to tell you he'll meet with you later today and apologizes for the delay."

She sensed much had happened when he'd gone to Williamsburg. By now he surely had news of what might transpire with her home and Isabeau's indenture. She waited for him like she waited for Doctor Hessel to bring word about Mama. Only Hessel didn't set her insides aswirl.

She paced the gallery, noting work by Gainsborough and Reynolds and a few of the Old Masters. The scent of aging canvas and oils was overpowering in the airless room. As the clock tolled three she came to a standstill before the accomplished John Singleton Copley. The artist had left the colonies for England shortly after painting Margaret Gage, the wife of the commander-in-chief of British forces in America, Thomas Gage. The duchess, as Gage's officers called her, was rumored to be aligned with the Patriot cause. She was also a close friend of the countess, Liberty's mother.

Next was a painting of a woman in a jade velvet gown. Enid. Looking a tad like her handsome brother. The cut of the gown, the lace sleeves resembling the very lace Liberty worked, turned her thoughts to other matters. Her girlhood. The carefree jaunts to the millinery shop or the Raleigh bakery or bookshop lectures. For the first time in her almost three and twenty years she felt she stood on the cusp of old age, looking back on past pleasures she'd never truly appreciated before.

Time wastes too fast . . . The days and hours of it are flying over our heads like clouds of windy days never to return.

The line from *Tristam Shandy* had never meant much till now. She turned away from the painting, trying to anchor her blurred vision to something else. She would expect not the worst but the best. She refused to let the delay forebode dire things. If Noble Rynallt couldn't turn things in her favor, the Almighty certainly could.

"Lady Elisabeth." The hall seemed to echo. Mistress Tremayne had a way of approaching that was silent as a cat. "Mister Rynallt has asked that you join him in the dining room for supper."

The dining room? At least she was dressed for the occasion. Isabeau had insisted on her wearing her best—her wedding attire—despite all protests. Sadly, the lovely gown was a goad, a reminder of Miles Roth's rejection of her but one of the few garments they'd brought. She tried not to dwell on the melancholy, but after months of fuss over the fittings, she would always associate the dress with her thwarted wedding day.

With a nod, she followed after the housekeeper, trading the portrait hall for the circular staircase, and then Ty Mawr's never-before-seen dining room.

◈

The long mahogany table had been laid, centered with a vase overflowing with peonies and roses from the garden. There were but two places set. Was she to dine with the master of Ty Mawr alone? But of course. Who else could possibly be present? He certainly wouldn't parade her before his fellow Patriots.

Tension ripened in the pit of her stomach. Yet another new hurdle. Never in her life had she partaken of a meal alone with a man, aside from her father.

Candles danced in a wayward draft. Other than a serving girl placing butter pats on a plate with silver tongs, she was alone in the unfamiliar room. French doors were open to the river and portico, making her feel less hemmed in, less awkward.

Crossing to the doors, she looked out on the bricked summer kitchen just beyond the west eave. The windows and door were open wide. Figures in white aprons and mob-caps moved about inside the building. How would it be to stand over a fiery hearth on such a hot day week after week, year after year, preparing food meant for the enjoyment of others?

She'd not seen one slave at Ty Mawr, just indentured servants. No doubt Noble Rynallt was opposed to slavery. Many Patriots were. Yet many Patriots were slave owners too.

How is it that we hear the loudest yelps for liberty among the drivers of Negroes? She'd read the words in the *Virginia Gazette* but couldn't remember who'd written them.

The door behind her opened. Clutched with tongue-tied apprehension, she looked everywhere but at Noble Rynallt. Conspicuous in her bridal attire—and an ill-wanted guest to boot—she wished she could beg for a simple supper tray in the attic.

"I'm sorry I kept you waiting," he said. "I'd thought to meet up with you yesterday."

She smiled. Miles had always kept her waiting. Noble Rynallt was barely tardy. "I'm not mindful of the time, truly."

He came nearer. "You look especially . . ."

She waited, breath held, for his opinion.

"*Eirian.* Lovely."

She softened. Toward the wasted wedding gown. Her host. "Thank you."

He glanced at the clock in a far corner before seating her with an easy grace as if they'd been having supper together for a lifetime. "I wanted to talk with you alone, before I return to Williamsburg tomorrow."

She nodded and placed her serviette in her lap, her plate with the Rynallt crest a safer focus than his earnest face. The rich timbre of his voice, becoming more familiar to her now, was carefully measured.

Did he always take his time speaking? And with such deliberate thoughtfulness? It left her on pins and needles. She was too used to her father's sudden outbursts, his surliness lingering for days.

He shot her a quick glance. "I know hearing about events secondhand must be hard for you. But 'tis only fair you know how things stand."

Her pulse picked up. "You've word of my father, then, and Lord Dunmore?"

"Aye. They're still aboard the *Fowey*, calling it the seat of government and sending communications to the former House of Burgesses from there." His tone told her they were making no headway. "As far as we're concerned, Lord Dunmore has abdicated. A committee of safety has been vested with legislative powers, and we've become the Virginia Assembly."

Eyes down, she asked the obvious. "There's no going back then?"

"To the way things were?"

She nodded, half clinging to the old, half craving change.

"Nay. No going back. Only forward."

She toyed with her serviette in her lap. No going back. Not in Virginia. Not in the other twelve colonies. The Crown wasn't going to let the colonies go without a fight. And her host and his fellow Patriots had helped bring this about. She sensed his resolve and knew she could rely on him to give her an honest answer, even if it wasn't one she wanted.

"Will those aboard the *Fowey* be allowed to leave for England in peace?" she asked.

He reached for his goblet, the glass sweating in the heat. "If they go in peace, aye."

All her breath expelled in a relieved little rush. They grew quiet as supper was served, salat set before them. But as soon as the servants slipped away for the next course, the conversation picked up again. He skewered a piece of lettuce with his fork but made no move to eat.

"'Tis not too late for you to join your father—you and your mother," he said.

Not too late. She felt paralyzed by uncertainty. She who

had hardly been able to make an independent decision in her life now had life by the tail. Questions pummeled her, all without answers.

Where was her mother? Why the delay? She picked up her fork, only to set it down again. "How late is too late?"

He hesitated. "If you don't decide soon you'll have no options. The sea will be unsafe for travel."

His quiet words only underscored the urgency of her leaving for England at once if that was what she wanted. Yet how could she possibly tell him all that pressed upon her heart?

She took a drink. "England might not be the enemy, but 'tis a stranger to me. Virginia is the only home I've ever known."

He looked at her then. The light slanting low across the table caught his hair in its golden fingers, and she saw a glint of silver again. But 'twas his eyes, that rich, burnt umber flecked with yellow light, that pinned her. Rimmed with black lashes, they lent a softness to his hawkish features and turned him so very . . .

She took up her fork again with great effort, only to almost drop it when he said, "'Twould grieve me to see you go."

Truly? Her eyes stung. She kept her attention on her plate, willing herself not to blink lest the tears fall. This sudden crack in his own self-containment was her undoing. Was he moved to see her so . . . lost? *Lost* was the only word that came to mind. But for him she'd be on the street.

Quiet moments passed. Her tears retreated. She forced herself to eat the delicious salat, taken from Ty Mawr's own gardens. Next was salmon, thin slices of Virginia ham, tiny new potatoes, baby beets, and buttered biscuits. The silence, though strangely comfortable, seemed weighted with things still unspoken.

Eyes on her plate, she mustered the courage to ask, "Have

you found out what will happen to my father's townhouse? My maid?"

He cut his meat with a steady hand. "All Tory property is to be confiscated. Auctioned. From the royal governor's country estate of Porto Bello on down."

This was a blow she'd not anticipated. Yet she admired him for his unblinking honesty. The truth must be told.

Her harp sprang to mind. It was no longer hers but would be the highest bidder's. The thought left her slightly sick. Though she tried to school her emotions, she knew they were splayed across her face. "I'm most concerned about my maid."

He looked up from his plate. "I could assume her indenture and spare her—and you—the indignity of the block."

At this came such a rush of relief she wanted to fling her arms around his neck. "You would do that?"

He returned his attention to his meal. "She could go with you wherever you go, or live here if she was willing."

Help Mistress Tremayne? Perhaps even become a lady's maid to the future mistress of Ty Mawr?

Though Isabeau protested being here, Liberty saw through it to the sham it was. Isabeau was as infatuated with Ty Mawr as Cressida was. And the attentive valet didn't hurt. Liberty's thoughts leapt ahead, seeing Isabeau married with children and a home on the grounds.

"Please." Her voice wavered with emotion. "Do that for Isabeau. For me."

He set down his fork. "Consider it done."

A servant came round, pouring coffee, while another served dessert in small silver cups and yet another whisked away empty dishes. She'd hardly looked at Noble during the meal, but she snuck a peek now to see him shunning cream and the fine turbinado sugar so favored in the colonies. So he liked his coffee black. Taking up a spoon, she stirred both cream and sugar into hers, a luxury she would soon do without.

Night was falling fast. A warm wind lifted the edge of the tablecloth and freed a few loose petals from the fragrant bouquet. She couldn't explain the peace she felt here. The almost palpable pleasure. In the last few days even the chair she often sat upon had assumed a sweet familiarity, the view of the James etched indelibly across her mind and heart. Though she would soon leave, it would never leave her.

"I could also," he told her, "try to secure some of your possessions prior to the auction."

Like her harp? She took a sip of coffee, wanting to ask for that and that alone. She wouldn't trouble him beyond this. If she just had her precious harp . . .

"Or you could . . ." He hesitated.

She waited, poised for she knew not what, and found her hand shaking inexplicably as it held her cup. Securing it in its saucer, she waited for the words that never came.

Their eyes locked. Even in the shadows she saw the unclouded invitation in his handsome face as his rocklike reserve shifted and his striking features gentled. He seemed to be waiting for her to help finish the sentence, only she didn't know what she was supposed to say. The silence was riven with tension. It turned her absolutely breathless.

"Libby . . ."

Her eyes went wide. *Libby*. Wherever had he gotten that? Not *Elisabeth*. Not *Lady Elisabeth*. Not even *m'lady*.

"Libby?" she echoed.

"Aye." He leaned back in his chair, his coffee untouched. "Libby."

'Twas said with the utmost ease, a telling simplicity, even an intimacy therein. She felt she would drown in the delight of it. "No one has ever called me that."

"Times are changing." He lifted his shoulders in a slight shrug. "Mayhap it would be best if you go by something else."

She smiled. "Just recently I decided to forsake Elisabeth and go solely by Liberty. Your calling me Libby seems blessed confirmation."

Beyond the perimeter of her sated senses she was dimly aware of the staccato tap of heels in the foyer. Their idyll was broken. Even Mistress Tremayne looked discomfited by the interruption.

"'Tis Mister Henry, sir. He's on the way back from Burwell's Landing and says 'tis urgent."

Liberty fought down her dismay. Noble excused himself, then left the table. She suspected more Patriot business was brewing. What she most remembered of Patrick Henry was her father's rantings.

A Quaker by religion but an absolute devil in politics.

'Twould be a late night for her host. She'd best tell Isabeau the good news. Though what she wanted was to linger at the table till the moon rose and he came back and finished whatever it was he'd been about to tell her.

12

Someone had taken care to light a lamp. Her room, so blue in daylight, held a silvery cast at night. Shutting the door softly, Liberty let her mind roam, surprised that till now she'd not thought much about *his* room. Was it just beneath them on the second floor? Or in another part of the house entirely?

Peeking through the adjoining door to the dressing room where Isabeau slept, Liberty found it empty. She didn't want to be alone with her tumbled thoughts, to try to make sense of what had happened below. Because it simply made no sense.

Libby.

She placed a hand against one cheek and found it fever hot. Her fair skin had ever been an indicator of her emotions. Tonight was no exception. Perhaps Isabeau's absence was a blessing. One long look at her and her maid would know more than dinner had been partaken of below.

Opening a window, she sat on the wide sill and let the night air cool her. 'Twas ten o'clock. The house servants were finishing their duties. She could hear the soft padding of their feet on the floor below. She tried to think of something, anything, to take her mind off the man meeting with Noble in his study. Always her mind returned to the trouble at hand.

Lord, what is in store for me?

The door clicked open behind her and Isabeau appeared. She looked ridiculously contrite. "Mistress, have you been here long?"

"Only a few minutes."

"Who lit the lamp?"

"Mistress Tremayne, likely. Sit down, please. I have good news."

"About your *mere*, your *papa*?"

"About *you*." Liberty gestured to the chair beside her, wondering how to begin. Noble always came to the truth of the matter straightaway. So would she. "You're no longer bound to me, Isabeau. All that has changed. Mister Rynallt has offered to assume your indenture."

"*Aidez moi!*" Her maid's astonishment was so complete Liberty couldn't tell if she was dismayed or pleased. "But I shan't leave you—"

"I'm afraid you have no choice." Liberty trod carefully but candidly. "Our host has just explained it to me. All Tory property is to be auctioned, even the servants. Do you want to go on the block before all Williamsburg?"

At this Isabeau shuddered. She shared Liberty's abhorrence for auctions.

"You'll stay on here at Ty Mawr," Liberty told her. "You'll have a new home, a new life."

"All that is well and good. But what about you?"

The plea in her maid's voice threatened her resolve. "I've been considering what I can do to be independent."

"Independent?" Isabeau's shock underscored the outrageousness of the plan.

"Aye." With a determined wink Liberty rattled her maid further. "Independent. But I shan't tell you my plan till I've told Mister Rynallt."

"Mistress, are you *fou*?"

"Lunatic? Perhaps. Here's another matter. No longer are you to call me Lady Elisabeth but rather Liberty. Now go on to bed. I shall manage." She placed a hand on her bodice, mindful that the gown hooked from the front and not behind, a convenience she'd not planned on. "I have some reading to do . . . a letter to write."

With an aggrieved nod, Isabeau disappeared into the sitting room, and the house seemed to settle with her. Liberty was still upended by all she'd learned at supper, and her thoughts would not let her rest. Not even her favorite passages in her Anglican prayer book sufficed, leaving her wondering what the Presbyterians used, if anything. Her every contemplation returned her to Noble Rynallt.

Toward midnight she heard a violin. Henry had gone then. Though she'd been at Ty Mawr but a short time, she'd learned Noble played only in the dead of night and in very controlled tones. 'Twas him, wasn't it? Who else? He was no novice.

She went to the washstand and poured water into a wide porcelain bowl, scenting it with rose cologne and refreshing her face and shoulders and hands before drying them. The nightly ritual grounded her. Pulling the pins from her hair next, she shook it free of its tight coils. It tumbled over her shoulders to the small of her back as if grateful for release. One hundred strokes and then a loose braid. In the looking glass her reflection was pale. Perplexed.

She held her breath as she went out the bedchamber door, afraid Isabeau would come flying out after her. But it shut with nary a click as she crossed the polished floor to the landing, the music below drawing her as if she was pulled along by an invisible string. Before now she'd been uncertain of just where he was, guessing it was his study, the door now closed.

Sitting down in the attic stairwell, she shut her eyes and listened. Corelli. Haydn. Guarneri. All known, all beloved. In time she matched him note for note as surely as if she accompanied him on her harp. The last piece was somewhat melancholy. "His fiddle weeps," Isabeau had said the first time she'd heard him, complaining that he kept her awake.

He finished the final piece, drawing out the last notes. She pictured his bow sliding free of the strings. Tried to imagine what led to this nightly concert. Perhaps one day he would play for her. And the song he chose would be joyful.

⁊⁊

The next morning found Noble in the stables. His head groom had saddled the Narragansett pacer, which was stomping and tossing his head as if wanting to return to Rhode Island.

"He's a beauty, sir. Tires a bit easy on account o' the heat but can pace a mile in a little more than two minutes," his head groom said with satisfaction. "A fine racer."

Noble swung himself into the saddle, fighting the familiar dread of what lay beyond the safety of the stable doors. It hovered like a dark presence, nearly eclipsing the pleasure he once felt. He'd even considered selling his stock and abandoning riding altogether. But few walked save a vagabond or fool.

No one spoke of Enid's accident here. But they'd not forgotten it. He could see it in their wary expressions when he came round, as if the sight of him resurrected the horrific details of that day. Most of the stable hands had been privy to what happened. And the sight of them set off his own internal alarms.

"You've got company, sir."

His groom gestured to the far stable entrance, looking surprised. Inquiring. Noble felt the same when his eyes fastened on Liberty. *Libby*. Dressed to ride. She could hardly be missed. In scarlet cloth with gilt buttons, the very color of the British army uniforms, she wore a dark little tricorn hat that was twin to Enid's own. Topped with a white feather, it gave her a jaunty air. He was feeling far from jaunty. The resemblance was uncanny. What else did she have in that sole trunk of hers?

He dismounted as quickly as he'd mounted, walking to meet her before she'd ducked into the stable's dusty, manure-laden confines.

"I wanted to ride out with you, if only for a few minutes. I—"

"Nay. No riding." He spoke so emphatically her face fell. "I mean—I—there's no suitable mount. You see . . ."

She looked about in confusion, as if calling him on the blatant falsehood. A half-dozen mares were in stalls on both sides of them. An odd hope skipped through him. Liberty wanted to ride. With him. If not for Enid . . .

As usual, she was graciousness to the bone, sparing him a painful explanation. "Very well. I shan't ride then. I suppose I should have asked about that." She managed an apologetic smile. "There's no need for me to keep to the house any longer. I'm leaving, you see."

Leaving? He reined in his misery. Turning, he instructed a groom to ready the riding chair. It was brought round, and she spoke to the hitched pony in soothing tones as if she'd been raised to the saddle. He helped her up onto the upholstered seat and got in after her as another memory of Enid took hold, darker than before.

Abandoning his plan for a solitary jaunt, they left the stable yard amid the clatter of hooves, much like he and Enid had that last day. But it had been stormy then, and today not a cloud marred the sky. A mile or more they rode in silence, past Ty Mawr's fields and barns and field hands till they reached his property's highest vista.

She looked down at her gloved hands rather than the expansive view. "I want you to know how grateful I am for all you've done. It means all the more when I realize you did it at considerable personal cost."

"Cost? Nay, none worth mentioning." He felt a twist of alarm that she was leading up to something. Perhaps joining her father for good? "Have you come to a decision?"

"You know I cannot stay."

She was looking at him with a strange mix of concern and wistfulness. It tugged at him all the harder.

Of what shallow stuff is the heart made if one can fall in love in a fortnight . . .

He gripped the reins harder, trying to right himself, to return to that passionless place where reason ruled.

"You don't have to make a decision quickly." He swallowed hard, his voice a bit ragged. "Not yet."

"Stay on for a while longer, you mean?"

"Aye, if you would."

Her lips parted, but it was several seconds before she spoke. "Keeping Tory women in third-floor rooms cannot be good for the liberty-loving master of Ty Mawr." Her aim at a little levity fell flat. Neither of them so much as cracked a smile.

He shook his head. "I have another place in mind a short distance from here. Ty Bryn. It means 'hill house' or 'little house' in Welsh. 'Tis well-built. Private. You could live there with your mother."

"Assuming my mother comes." Her look implied doubt. "I want to tell you my plan. It may even make an Independence Man proud."

Would she dismiss his offer so easily? Make her own way? A grudging admiration took hold. "Go on then."

"I am a lacemaker. I learnt when I was five years old after my mother began sponsoring a small group of lacemakers in Williamsburg. Her hope was that these Southern lacemakers would be as enterprising as the ones of the Northeast, like those in Ipswich, Massachusetts."

"Your mother has a head for industry." He remembered Priscilla Lawson was patron of several charities, had even helped establish the poorhouse in Williamsburg. And she was a firm believer that women were more than property and capable of greater endeavors.

"She has a head for a great many things, most of them a bone of contention with my father. She's a little like the late Mistress Franklin and her post office."

"But lacemaking . . . you?" He glanced down at the sleeves of her riding habit, the ends trimmed in the most fetching handwork he'd ever seen. He wasn't given to examining laces but had to admit these were very fine.

"Yes, these lace cuffs are of my making." A smile softened her somber features. She held a sleeve aloft for closer inspection, even admiration.

"You are good at it. But 'tis a trade, aye? Like a common woman would do."

"And I am suddenly a common woman, without a dowry or a means to sustain myself."

He weighed his response. He didn't want to tramp on her hopes. He could only imagine what the haughty former lieutenant governor would say about his tradeswoman daughter. "So you would make lace to barter and sell . . . to maintain yourself."

She nodded, looking up at him so expectantly he didn't have the heart to naysay her. So he stayed quiet. Painfully so.

Her chin lifted. "Friday I shall go to Williamsburg and inquire about work."

Friday. More time with her then. But work? She made it sound blissfully easy. He allowed himself one caution. "You realize what people will say about you. That they might shun you given your family name. Your father."

"I shan't conduct myself as one of the Lawsons. I shall simply be Liberty."

Did she like the unassuming name that much then?

"I shall dress humbly and keep to my rooms—"

"Which would be where?"

"One of the Williamsburg ordinaries, perhaps. I can take in mending and whatnot too."

Her plan was flawed. He wanted to shelter her from what was coming. Warn her. Prevent her. Provide for her.

Marry her.

"Before you set your"—he kicked aside the word *rash*—"plan in place, I'd recommend you see your father aboard the *Fowey*."

"My father? Why?"

For the first time he detected revulsion, even a taint of bitterness, in her tone. He was in no frame of mind to advocate for the earl of Stirling, but he wanted no regrets. "Consider it a means to an end. You meet with him, try to come to some understanding. The encounter will do one of two things. You'll decide 'tis in your best interest to go with him, or you'll resolve to strike out on your own in Williamsburg."

She frowned, obviously as torn hearing it as he was saying

it. A dire proposal indeed. "Very well." She nodded again, the feather atop her hat dancing. "I have no illusions as to how the meeting will go, but I am willing to follow your lead. I shall see him Friday then."

He nodded, considering all the implications. When she left Ty Mawr he might never see her again. Lawson was not above abducting his daughter or making it very difficult for her to leave the ship. Lady Charlotte and her girls were another lure. They might well enjoin her to return to England with them.

"The best outcome would be for Lord Dunmore to return to the Governor's Palace and my father to reunite with my mother and myself at the townhouse. But that is not to be."

Was she a realist as well as an adventurer and dreamer? "Nay. It is not."

Their eyes met briefly. He detected a resigned acceptance there. She hadn't mentioned being reconciled to Miles Roth. And it made her all the dearer to him.

"My coach is yours for travel. Take your lady's maid when you go to meet your father. I can ride along as escort."

"Nay, I'll not have you or Isabeau with me. She's your servant now, not mine. I shall go alone."

Alone. To face her father, the scourge of Virginia Colony. She was made of sterner stuff than he'd thought.

13

There was no disguising the rough edges of York even in the sunlight and bustle of summer. Perhaps it was worsened by the fact that Isabeau was no longer at her side. A lady's maid was security, especially in a seaport such as this, though the grandness of the Rynallt carriage was enough to keep most troublemakers at bay. It rolled through the congested streets with the efficacy of a black cannonball, clearing everyone in its way. Her driver, Dougray, was a man she'd seen at Ty Mawr's stables, a burly coachman who wielded a whip for more than horses, he said. A lone Scot in a sea of Welsh servants. High on his box seat he sat with a decided scowl, leaving her to wonder if it was from the stifling weather or the riffraff in his path.

If she'd not acted quickly, she might have lost the courage to come. Mistress Tremayne had sent word to the stables while Isabeau helped her dress. Not a murmur did Liberty utter about returning. Tonight she didn't know where she'd lay her head, only that it wouldn't be at Ty Mawr. She'd not involve Noble Rynallt further in the fall of the Lawsons.

The coach lurched to a sudden halt. She braced herself for the coming ordeal, nearly wincing as Dougray's Scots dialect grated on her ears. He was arguing with someone, but about what? Gaining proximity to the *Fowey* at the end of the wharf? British soldiers were posted everywhere. She'd likely be searched before the day was done. Might it be she'd come all the way here to be turned away? No sooner had the thought left her mind than the door was yanked open.

Dougray was nearly snarling. "Ye'll no' lay a hand on the lady or I'll have yer lobsterback in a sling."

A red-coated figure peered in, the plume of his helmet colliding with the doorway. A dragoon? "Lady Elisabeth, daughter of Lieutenant Governor Lawson?"

She noticed he didn't say *former*. "Yes, I am she." The familiar refrain, once proudly said, now hung in her throat. She made a move to leave her seat and step out if that was what he wanted, but he slammed the door in her face. The coach jerked forward but at a much slower pace, as if they had a soldier's escort.

"*Och*, we're here, m'lady," Dougray thundered from his perch before jumping down to help her out. "But we dinna have any o' them t' thank."

She thanked him, eyes alighting on the town's Main Street atop a bluff before taking in the glare of sparkling water and an enormous amount of rigging, sail, and wood. Her mind grappled with the enormity of the *Fowey*. Would the king and his ministers of state not send a thousand more warships just like it? Everywhere she looked were redcoats. What chance did Noble Rynallt and the Patriots have in the face of this?

She sent up a silent prayer of thanks the *Fowey* wasn't lying at anchor in the harbor, necessitating a row in a dinghy to reach it. A uniformed officer gave a little bow before her.

Beneath the lace veil of her straw hat, she tried to work up a smile. Chivalry wasn't dead, even in the face of rebellion.

The gangplank was so sun-soaked she could feel its heat through the thin soles of her slippers. It distracted her from the odors—the stench of unwashed men, oil, the sweltering cargo in the hold, whatever it was. She tried to anchor her gaze on the coattails of the officer leading her she knew not where—up, down, and around cramped stairs and passageways like a rodent in a maze.

A cabin door somewhere in the bowels of this great ship was their destination. At last the officer's decisive knock on a far door gained her entry, and she stood looking at her father's bald head. Seated at a desk beneath a porthole, he looked up only when he'd finished with whatever he was writing. 'Twas a full, infuriating minute, a delay she was well accustomed to but that had never set her seething till now.

As expected, his cabin was splendidly appointed. Lacquered white walls were trimmed in gold and decorated with mirrors and copper engravings. A small bust of King George commandeered the ornate desk.

"Daughter." It was said with little surprise or welcome, as if she'd simply come in from the townhouse garden and interrupted him. A deep bewilderment took hold.

Her father was, as always, impeccably dressed. Even without his usual wig, his complexion was powdered, his stock pristine, while her every pore seemed glutted with dust. A trickle of sweat slid from the carefully done coiffure, down her neck to the back of her gown where her stays cinched tight. Having slept little the night prior, she was weary beyond words.

"Would you care for some wine, Elisabeth?"

She shook her head, fighting for composure.

He motioned to a chair. "What brings you?"

She stayed standing. "What brings me?" The words were edged in disbelief. She could scarcely push them past the tightness in her throat. As they faced each other, she could sense his restlessness. His mind was already returning to the letter on his desk, she knew. His entire manner had already dismissed her even if he'd not yet said it. Would he not even inquire about her mother? Or share anything he knew?

"Speak, Daughter, speak."

She fought to keep her voice steady as resentment pooled in her heart. "Why did you flee and leave me that night?"

"Leave you? On the eve of your wedding?" He gave a near roll of his eyes and turned toward a table where he poured himself some Madeira. "I *left* you so that your intended would rise to the occasion and rescue you—"

"Which he did not do."

He swirled the dark liquid around in his glass and took a sip. "Then the fault is not mine, Daughter, but his."

Nay, never yours. Not then, not ever.

Not once had she heard him ask for forgiveness, admit fault. Pride and arrogance had been the pattern of his life and the heart of his every interaction, but it had taken distance and turmoil for her to see it clearly. "Miles Roth may have broken our betrothal, but 'twas you who abandoned both myself and my mother, your wife."

"Your mother was not there that night. Besides, she has long had her own mind in matters." His stare was stony. He brooked no argument. "Would you have me bring her aboard ship once she returns, given her politics?"

"I would have you act honorably."

He drained his glass. "Then you are as lunatic as she is."

"Do you know nothing more about her?" Her voice rose

another notch. "Do you have confirmation she even sailed from England? I—"

He cut her off. "I do not know, nor do I care."

Before his ire she felt small again, the sting of his indifference like the slap of a hand. "No doubt you've had this planned for months now—leaving, being rid of us both. Perhaps Mama isn't coming back. Have you planned that too?"

He fixed her with fiery eyes. "Mayhap you are imagining such things—"

"Mayhap?" She was breathless now. She hated that her voice shook. "I am *not* imagining being left in the middle of the night while drunken men sack my house. Nor am I imagining a betrothal broken or the unknown whereabouts of my mother. Mayhap it is *you* who are lunatic, hiding out aboard a ship guarded by countless soldiers when not one Patriot has taken up arms against you—"

"Enough!" He brought his fist down atop the table with such force the wine bottle overturned. "You impudent girl, you'd do well to remember it was not I who caused this rebellion!"

She recoiled and collided with the shut door before turning and fumbling to open it again. The soldier who had brought her below was waiting outside. Pushing past him, she fled, intent on open sky and sunlight. Once on deck she ignored the stares of a great many men who seemed either amused or sullen at her appearance.

Coming up the gangplank with an armed escort were Lady Charlotte and the girls. At the sight of Liberty, Lady Catherine and Lady Augusta burst into tears.

"Dearest Lizzy, have you come back to us?" They rushed forward, circling her, drawing yet more attention. "Will you sail with us?"

Liberty took them in against the ugly backdrop of York, so far removed from the elegant Governor's Palace they'd called home. Her gaze lingered longest on Lady Charlotte who looked especially wan, even ill, much as she did during early pregnancy. Was she in circumstances again?

Unable to speak, Liberty embraced them, and they huddled together till their wide, beribboned hats were askew and the guard watching was red-faced.

"God bless you all till we meet again," Liberty choked out. Finally pulling free, she took the gangplank at a near run, her blurred eyes on the waiting Rynallt coach down the crowded street.

Dougray was at hand, cheek stuffed with tobacco. "Where to, m'lady?"

"Williamsburg," she said as he opened the coach door.

The hot interior, suffocating all the way here, now seemed a refuge. Without Isabeau near, with the crush of carriage wheels masking any sound, she gave way to all her heartache and exhaustion.

Never had she spoken to her father in such a manner. Since childhood she had accepted his domination as part of the natural order of things, like Newton's laws or the inerrancy of Scripture. Upon her marriage she'd expected to do the same with a husband of his choosing. Though she believed every word she'd spoken aboard ship, it cut her mercilessly to have said them.

The realization that her father viewed her and used her like a pawn in a chess game, only to abandon her when the moves were not to his liking, was beyond understanding. Her respect for him, small as it was, eroded completely in the face of her pain.

He had chosen Miles Roth for her because Miles was a

mirror of his own deficiencies and ambitions. Her whole life might have continued as little more than a game piece if not for the present rebellion. Perhaps instead of railing against the loss of a home and a husband who was grievously wrong for her, she should fall on her knees and thank God for breaking the pattern of destruction in her life.

But at what a cost.

Crying soon gave way to sleeping. They came to the outskirts of Williamsburg at dusk, the exact time the sun would be flooding Ty Mawr's south portico with final light as it swept off the river. Noble was oft here. The thought burrowed beneath her numbness to steady her. Was he staying at the Raleigh? Or at the home of his friend George Wythe along Palace Street? No matter, she was intent on her townhouse.

The footman lowered her trunk, and Dougray shouldered it to a side door, which they found locked. "I canna leave ye here alone, m'lady," he told her. "I dinna see naught but boarded windows and broken shrubs. Master Rynallt wouldna be happy with the arrangement, ye ken."

She said nothing to this, joining him in perusing the lawn of tall grass made ugly by shards of broken glass.

"Besides," he protested, "ye dinna have a way in."

She reached into her indispensable and produced a skeleton key. "Isabeau saved this for just such an occasion."

He rubbed a ruddy brow and looked more befuddled. "*Och*, a smart lass, tae be sure. But what will I be tellin' the master?"

She sighed. "The truth. That I asked you to bring me here after York. Surely there's no crime in that."

He took the key and opened the door, hefting her trunk in after them. The little hall was cool, the shadows deep. She felt a twist of lonesomeness to find it empty when it had never been empty before. The servants liked to gather here at day's end, talking or resting from their labors in the half-dozen chairs scattered about. When she was small she'd sat on soft, aproned laps, partaking of a sweet or some delicacy snuck from the kitchen till her nursemaid called her away.

"Are ye sure, m'lady?"

"Indeed," she said, far from feeling it. "Please tell Isabeau not to worry. And please thank Mister Rynallt for the use of his coach."

He bowed out, the gallant gesture refining his roughness. For a moment she leaned against the door she'd shut after him, ruing her decision, then slowly she made her way to the heart of the house, trying to grow accustomed to the quiet. Had it only been a short time ago she'd awoken to absolute mayhem?

Her heart pulled her to the music room. There in the shadows was her harp. Her broken lute. She stepped carefully over glass and around overturned furniture, took a stool, and positioned her hands to play like countless times before. A Scripture wove through her head like a song.

Therefore my harp is turned to mourning and my flute to the sound of those who weep.

Her hands fell to her sides as if broken. She simply sat, remembering the music of the past, praying she could find a way to keep one instrument at least. 'Twould not be the harp, as large and unwieldy as it was, though it bespoke countless concerts and soirees at the Palace.

Her lute, perhaps. Though damaged, it might be mended by the Williamsburg luthier. She picked it up, gladdened by its familiar weightlessness and elegant lines. Holding it to her chest, she walked about the house, searching for anything of value that was small enough to sell at market. 'Twas clear that she couldn't remain here even for one night. Fearful she was not. But she had no light. Without a fire to kindle or a taper to illuminate her bedchamber, she faltered. But 'twas something else too, something she could not name that bade her leave. There was a profound emptiness here that finally sent her scurrying down the alley behind the house.

Her beautiful, beloved Williamsburg was reassuringly familiar yet achingly strange. The gardens, the rear porches, the stables, and the dependencies along these streets were no different. But she was changed. No longer welcome. No longer a resident. Simply and unalterably an outcast.

Not long ago everyone had vowed allegiance to the Crown. Now the *Gazette*, once notoriously Tory, was printing names of townsfolk found to be sympathetic to England and English goods. But why? She raised a hand and rubbed her pounding temples. She didn't understand independence if one wasn't allowed to have independent thought.

Her footsteps quickened as dusk raced to meet darkness. As she hurried along, her skirt hem trailing in the dust, her hat no longer needed, she was quick to retreat to the shadows if a horseman or carriage thundered by. Few did. Nightlife was centered deeper in town at the Raleigh and the other ordinaries. Passing Palace Green, she was careful not to look down the long drive of catalpa trees to the royal residence. It sat as dark and empty as her thoughts. She tried not to dwell on her lonesomeness as she went, tried not to think of Noble Rynallt, wherever he was.

She felt a bit guilty that she'd left in such a rush, confused about a great many things except that he not be involved with her. Yet even now the exchange between them haunted. He'd asked her to stay on at Ty Mawr. She sensed there was

147

something more behind his offer than simple friendship. Or was she simply craving security? A home?

Even now the ache for something more followed her in the twilight. All the feelings she'd contained so carefully in the fortnight she'd known him were magnified here. She was on the verge of a great many new things, all of them a bit shattering.

A new name. A new home. A new life.

14

Miles Roth was gambling his fortune away. Everyone at the Raleigh knew it. The only question was who would receive the lion's share when all was said and done. The stakes were very high, the men inebriated, Miles most of all. Noble watched from across the smoke-filled taproom, glad his cousin's parents were not here to see their legacy squandered and he had no wife to drag into debtor's prison after him. The rattle of dice boxes seemed to him like dead men's bones. He'd never been a gambler or a drinker, though he had reason aplenty of late. Miles seemed to have received a double portion of the knavishness he lacked. Though he'd intervened in the past—dragging Miles home, paying minor debts, averting quarrels and duels on his behalf—he could do so no longer.

Now, standing in the tavern's foyer with Patrick Henry, waiting for Jefferson and Washington to come down from their rooms, he felt Henry jab him with an elbow. "So ye've cut the leading strings at last?"

Noble eyed the stairwell without comment as more Patriots gathered.

But Henry wasn't letting up. "Ye know, if we were to channel all Roth's wasted energy—and his finances—to our cause, we might well win this Revolution."

"Betimes a man must reach bottom before grabbing hold of what's right."

"Ah, indeed." Taking his eyes off Miles and the mounting tension of the game, Henry cleared his throat. "And how is the lovely Lady Elisabeth?"

"'Tis Lady Liberty now." Noble removed his hat and hung it from a near peg. "Gone."

"Say what?"

Noble turned to him, glad he didn't have a mouthful of ale lest he spew it out in amusement at Henry's comical expression. "Gone. Away from Ty Mawr."

"Blast it, man! I heard you the first time! Where to?"

"To see her father in York."

"Ah, good riddance, I say," Henry replied. "I feared she was about to make you lose all reason. Let us hope all that is in the past. Your involvement with her is so unlike you, so rash. You've always been a man of careful deliberation and sound judgment, the very last to take such a leap."

"I'm in danger of being hung for treason by the Crown. Anything else hardly seems a risk."

Henry chuckled then grew grave. "I need no reminding. As Franklin said, we must all hang together or most assuredly we shall all hang separately." Disgust clouded his face as he studied Roth across the crowded room. "Mayhap her ladyship will even reconcile with the rogue."

"Nay, that is no longer a possibility."

"Well, congratulations on *your* avoiding marital disaster then."

"I have no desire to wed anyone," Noble said with lessening conviction, though one recurring thought continued to nag him. "I'll not leave a widow if there's war."

"Glad to hear it. There might be a great many of those once this is done." Perspiring, Henry gave a tug to his stock. "Well, I must admit at the very least that Lady Elisa—*Liberty*, as you call her—is a fine specimen of womanhood, even dowry-less and a Tory."

"Well said." Noble nodded. "If I was a betting man, I'd wager you'd find her as agreeable as I do."

"I hope not, for the future Mistress Henry's sake," he returned with a wink.

Liberty awoke to stiffness and the scent of hot cross buns carrying half a mile on the Williamsburg wind. What had Mistress Tremayne called them? *Byns y Grog?* Given this, the town's nearest bake shop hardly needed a shingle above its door. Her stomach growled a complaint as she bestirred herself. She should have brought something along from Ty Mawr, a biscuit or apple. She could not spare the few pence in her indispensable for even the humblest bun.

The townhouse's aromatic kitchen stormed her thoughts, all the resurrected spices and sweetmeats. Anything she wanted had been within easy reach. The hollowness inside her deepened. She'd spent the night away from the only home she'd ever known and had finally slept, secreted away in a corner of the Palace gardens known to few but her and Lady Charlotte's daughters, a tiny bower overhung with honeysuckle, as fragrant as it was hidden. Aside from a few insect bites, she hated to leave it to begin her eventful day, but she must.

Half an hour later, having backtracked to the townhouse,

Liberty stood before a full-length mirror in her dressing room, somewhat satisfied. Without Isabeau, managing her underpinnings proved nearly impossible. She'd finally found some front-lacing stays and a gown that didn't need much pinning. 'Twas a simple striped muslin, the plainest she owned. Removing the gauzy sleeves and kerchief, she rendered it plainer still. A simple cambric apron, lined with lace from her own hands, completed her toilette, along with a simple pinner atop her head. With her hair caught back in a tidy bun, not elaborate coils, she looked quite unlike herself. To complete the ruse, she plucked the violets and ribbon off what Isabeau called her milkmaid hat before securing the chin ribbons against the ever-present Williamsburg wind.

'Twas market day and she had little time to waste. Her heart pulsed wild as a hummingbird's wings. Pushing aside all her qualms, she hung a basket from her arm and set off toward the heart of Williamsburg under the guise of an ordinary tradeswoman. Of the many ordinaries in and around town, she'd go begging at all but the Raleigh.

Chowning's was first on her list, far enough down Duke of Gloucester Street from the Raleigh for comfort. She'd enter through the back door to keep her business secret. Yet as she drew nearer, she recalled something her father once said about Chowning's being more alehouse and gambling den. Perhaps she'd best keep going.

Now a part of the milling, hustling market crowd, she glanced about discreetly, praying she'd not see anyone she knew. Likely somewhere in town was Noble Rynallt. The thought warmed her and lined her with lead all at once.

Lord, make me inconspicuous.

Yet she wanted to be seen. To be rescued again. All the implications of her decision to be independent came crashing down, dogging her dusty steps. Though she'd been a part of Williamsburg since birth, she now felt far from the beat of town life. Even with her father away, unaware of what she was doing, she sensed his displeasure should he find out. It shadowed her at every turn. He'd always forbidden her to go out with the rabble, as he called them.

Truly, market days were noisy, boisterous affairs. Along with her identity, the newness of everything tugged at her and bade her tarry. She paused to watch a puppet show, nearly forgetting her mission. The little stage erected in the shade of a giant oak was clever—Punch and Judy painted and provocatively dressed and loudly mocking the king.

Turning away, she was bumped by passersby, her basket nearly upended. Isabeau had oft warned of pickpockets, though any who filched her today would be sorely disappointed.

Making her way up the walk of the King's Arms, a more respectable establishment, she lowered her gaze. Never mind that it was across the street from the Raleigh. A few men lingered outside the entrance, doffing their hats as she went in. A serving girl greeted her and took her to a small office at the back of the ordinary, where Liberty waited, tongue-tied. The pretty speech she'd rehearsed flew right out of her head as other distractions came to roost. A distillation of spirits, stale tobacco, and fried fish snuck into the tiny space and aggravated the queasy flutter in her too empty stomach.

When Jane Vobe, the tavern's owner, finally appeared, Liberty rested her hand on a chair back to steady herself.

"What say ye?" The scowling woman shifted her considerable bulk behind the crowded desk, bidding Liberty to take a chair.

She sat, nearly sighing with relief, basket in her lap. "I've come seeking work."

Sharp green eyes assessed her. "Work? What kind?"

Steeling herself against her rising embarrassment, she mustered as much resolve as she could. "Sewing. Mending."

"For my patrons?"

"Aye. I am a lacemaker too." Liberty opened her basket and withdrew embroidered cuffs and handkerchiefs, even clocked stockings.

Jane rose and looked closely, turning the items over in her plump, chapped hands and making little noises of appreciation. "'Tis a mite fine for my ilk. Ye might have better luck at the Raleigh. Now what did ye say yer name is?"

"Liberty."

"Liberty, aye? More like Lord Stirling's daughter, God's truth." Jane returned to her chair, sitting down so hard her ample body quivered like aspic. "Now why's a lady like you seeking work at an ordinary? Why not be a governess or a lady's companion? Something genteel?"

"Because," she began slowly and with conviction, "I prayed . . . and this was the answer that came to me."

The shrewd eyes softened. "I can't offer ye work, but I can give ye a sound meal. Ye look sore in need of that."

"Nay, please, I'll not trouble you further." Returning her handwork to her basket, Liberty stood—and the whole room spun like a child's top. She made it to the door, only to clutch the handle in a feeble attempt to stay upright.

Jane was close behind, steering her back to the chair she'd just left. "A plateful of eggs and sausages should do, or 'tis off to the apothecary with you."

"But I cannot pay—"

"Nary a ha'pence I'll take."

Resigned, Liberty marveled at the speed with which breakfast could be had. At Jane's bell ringing, a serving girl appeared, then disappeared and returned with a large tray mounded with more than eggs and sausages. A small mountain of biscuits crowded a platter, and a bowl of fried potatoes competed with a dish of grits pooling with butter. Steaming black coffee was set before her with a small jug of cream but no sugar.

Jane heaped a trencher full and handed Liberty a pewter fork. "I don't expect ye to eat like a lady, hungry as ye are, so have at it."

Liberty obeyed, feeling her stays expand with every bite. Jane's eyes remained on her, her hostess appearing sincerely interested in her plight. "Where are ye off to next?"

"Christiana Campbell's."

"Yer too fancy for that establishment. Why not the Raleigh?"

Liberty set her fork down, unable to meet Jane's probing gaze. "'Tis a Patriot stronghold. My presence there would be naught but a joke."

Heaving a sigh, Jane pressed her palms over the wiry red curls beneath her mobcap in a futile attempt to subdue them. "The owner, James Southall, is a Christian gentleman who might well need a seamstress and lacemaker. He sends a great many shirts down the street to the beleaguered tailor and Margaret Hunter, who makes noises about leaving. His clientele is top tier like yerself."

Liberty nearly flinched. "Yet another reason why I cannot go there."

"Pride, is it?"

With a nod, Liberty accepted the candid rebuke. "Perhaps."

"Well, I'd see him right quick before the burgesses—*delegates*—end their session. Word is they'll be tied up till this evening on serious business—something about taking up arms. Sounds positively traitorous to me, but I'm as tired o' the king as the rest o' them."

And Noble Rynallt was smack in the middle of it. After taking a last bite of biscuit, she thanked Jane warmly and exited through a back door, turning left instead of right and wondering if Jane watched her from the window.

On a whim she crossed the street to the milliner's, dodging carts and carriages all the way. She saw a few familiar faces and simply lowered her hat, praying her plain dress disguised her. Fortunately, the mantua maker was in, coming out of the back room at the jingling of the shop door. For a moment Liberty thought her disguise too believable. No sign of recognition lit Margaret's face.

"'Tis me, Margaret. Elisabeth."

"M'lady?" Margaret's prim mouth grew slack. Reaching for her spectacles on a near counter, she peered more closely. "Lady Elisabeth? But I'd heard you were with your father aboard the *Fowey*."

It took a few minutes for Liberty to pour forth the true story. Margaret grew more aghast. "You cannot mean to *labor*? Granted, your handwork is exceptional even by my exacting standards. But a tavern wench—"

"Not *that*. Simply a lacemaker and seamstress. I shan't be in the public rooms but out of sight, doing my stitching, my lacemaking."

Margaret took a stool in back of the counter, resignation in her lined face. "All this rebellion business is simply too much. You might as well know I'm considering closing shop and moving to my father's in Charles Town. Business has dropped off considerably here with the latest trouble." She cast a doleful eye at once stuffed shelves that were now half empty. "Truth be told, your family's generosity has kept me afloat till now. Whatever his politics, your father spared no expense on your and your mother's wardrobes. My going would certainly help in your endeavor to find work."

"But Williamsburg needs a mantua maker. I'm hardly that."

"There's another mantua maker and milliner setting up shop down the street. No one is irreplaceable, it seems."

No one. Not Liberty's father. Not Lord Dunmore. Not even King George. The delegates were meeting now, changing positions and titles. No longer did Virginia have a House of Burgesses but rather Delegates. The terms were strange if memorable. In time they'd be commonplace, she realized, their colonial past like another country's.

"I'd best be going," Liberty told her, taking up her basket again. Though no longer hungry, she felt weighted with trepidation. She wanted nothing more than to turn back time and simply be the highborn girl just arrived for a fitting. She'd even welcome Margaret's scolding about her appetite necessitating her gowns be taken in. Anything but the prospect of near begging before her.

Margaret was looking at her with tears in her eyes. "God be with you, m'lady."

Little else could be said. Afraid she'd break down if she tarried, Liberty let herself out and took the alley to Christiana Campbell's.

The afternoon wore on, one tavern keeper replacing another till they blurred in her mind. Did some suspect she was a Tory—a spy? She read the suspicion in their words and faces, and it cut her. Noble had been right. Yet she had prayed and felt this was her answer. If the Lord nudged her forward, she wouldn't give up till the last ordinary had turned her away.

Who are ye? all asked.

Simply *Liberty.*

15

The Raleigh was her last hope.

Oh, why had she not heeded Jane Vobe's advice and come here first?

As the sun skimmed the rooftops of the Governor's Palace and Bruton Parish Church in its westward slant, Liberty was utterly spent, mouth dry as cotton, bodice stained with sweat from the dwindling summer's day. Though she was Williamsburg born and bred, she'd never walked the length and breadth of it till now, taking in every humble nook and cranny. A new wariness shadowed her every step. Being of the middling sort, if that, was tiresome. She kept her eye on the streets nearest the capitol on her way back to this unwelcome place, knowing the General Assembly might adjourn at any moment.

Entering the ordinary by a side door, she felt a spark of excitement flare. 'Twas the first time she'd been inside. The paneled hall, painted a pleasing melon, was rife with cool shadows. A great many cocked hats and walking sticks hung from a long rack. Supper was well under way. Though she didn't know exactly where the kitchen was, she appreciated its beckoning aromas. Despite having been stuffed by Jane Vobe, her stomach rumbled and she laid a hand there as if to quell it, bumping into a girl rounding a corner.

"Watch where you're goin', miss." Black brows flared over indignant blue eyes. "D'ye have need of direction?"

Pinched with embarrassment, Liberty managed, "I'm here to see the proprietor, Mister Southall."

The girl glanced questioningly at Liberty's basket and motioned her forward. "You'd best be quick about it. 'Tis nearly the supper hour and we're expecting a pack o' Patriots."

Liberty nearly sighed. Her poor timing would earn her no favors. She'd be lucky if the innkeeper agreed to see her. Still, she held on to Jane's words tightly, praying Southall was indeed a Christian gentleman. Meanwhile, the saucy girl—for Liberty could think of no better word to describe her—led her down yet another hall, where she knocked on an imposing door behind a stairwell.

A deep voice bade her enter. With a dismissive glance, the girl disappeared, leaving Liberty to make her own introductions. Pushing open the door, she found no one inside. Puzzled, she took stock of finely crafted bookcases from floor to ceiling, an elaborate desk buried beneath reams of open account books and ledgers, several chairs, and a settee covered in green brocade.

It had the air of a country gentleman's study, refined yet comfortably worn in like an old shoe, the colors reminiscent of Ty Mawr. The comparison bruised her. She needed no reminders.

All fortitude fled. With a swift turn she reached for the door handle to flee and heard a near growl. Mister Southall?

Previously hidden behind a bookcase, a man stepped into view. At the sight of her, he dropped the paper he'd been holding and it fluttered to the floor. Bending low to retrieve it, he promptly lost his wig, which collapsed on the rug in a chestnut heap. Uttering an oath, he snatched the hairpiece up and flung it into the cold hearth before facing her. To his credit, he looked unruffled. His face was cast in craggy lines, his eyes a piercing blue. Slender and bald, he was nevertheless striking, or perhaps it was his air of authority. She remembered hearing he'd served in the French and Indian War under Lord Dunmore himself.

"Lady Elisabeth, I presume."

"Mister Southall," she returned with some surprise. "'Tis simply Liberty now."

"Well, Miss Liberty. Welcome to the Raleigh."

"Thank you." She took a breath. "I'm seeking work." Her voice was tired, her petition flat. Setting the basket on the edge of the desk, she did what she'd done too many times before. But he wasn't perusing her needlework. Just her.

His voice was kind. "Margaret Hunter has explained your situation to me. I've been awaiting you all afternoon."

His melodious Virginia drawl seemed to drag out the last two words interminably. While pride and stubbornness had kept her away, he'd been waiting. *All afternoon.* A bad beginning, this. She bit her tongue to stay her mortification.

"Please have a seat and I'll explain my terms." He waited till she perched on the edge of the settee before he began, arms folded across his chest. "You'll be given room and board in exchange for your services. For every shirt sewn and mended you'll receive your fair share. Embroidery and lacework will garner more. During Publick Times when the courts are in session, you may well do more sewing than sleeping. Other times not so much. What say ye?"

She felt a rush of affection for Margaret Hunter for pleading her case, yet she sensed that, able businessman that he was, Mister Southall was truly in need of her.

"When do I begin?" she asked.

"On the morrow. Nay, 'tis the Sabbath. The day after that. You can lodge here starting tonight if needs be. I'll send supper to your room if you like." He paused and looked almost apologetic. "'Twill be quite a comedown from what you're used to, but I have a dependency—a folly—vacant at present. Maeve can take you out back and show you."

Maeve? The impudent one? She felt an immediate resistance but simply said, "Fine. The folly sounds . . . suitable."

Despite the awkwardness of the moment, he looked like he wanted to say more. She certainly did. But how to school all her angst into a few succinct words? She took a deep breath. "I—if possible, I'd like to keep to myself. Be discreet."

The flash of sympathy in his face told her he'd try to respect her wishes. "I'm sorry for the circumstances that brought you here."

Encouraged, she dropped her gaze to her basket. "And I thank you for dealing fairly with me under the circumstances." Despite his gracious offer, she wasn't yet ready to spend the night at the Raleigh. Not when she might be under Noble Rynallt's very nose. She started for the door, relieved her ordeal was almost over.

Or was it only beginning?

Noble listened to the reading of Virginia's preliminary Declaration of Rights with hands fisted on the table before him. He had reviewed and helped revise the words, and they were knit to his soul in myriad ways. Now, hearing them proclaimed aloud by the Speaker of the House in the echoing chamber of the capitol building previously inhabited by the king's men, he felt hot and cold by turns. Chilled by the beauty and solemnity of the words one minute, he found himself perspiring at their sheer audacity the next.

He was one of the foremost revolutionaries. His signature was slashed across every page. The Crown now had sufficient reason to strip him of his position. Confiscate Ty Mawr. Claim his indentured servants. Ruin his relatives. Hang him.

He shifted in his seat, and the movement caught Patrick Henry's eye. As Noble was normally so still during proceedings, his fellow delegates liked to joke that someone erected a statue in his stead. But the last two hours found him fidgety as a schoolboy. Passing a hand over his face now bristled by a day's growth, he met Henry's gaze and detected a telling amusement there as the Speaker wound down.

Just behind Henry, light spilled from a transom window, but it was fading fast. Two days they'd been in this chamber, and Noble chafed at the time. He'd not spend another night at the Raleigh. He needed to return to Ty Mawr. Leaning back in his chair till it gave a traitorous groan, he folded his arms across his chest and fought another fierce battle with what could only be called desire. It didn't help that every other word served as a reminder of *her*.

Life, *liberty*, and the pursuit of happiness . . . Every man should be the possessor of *liberty* . . . Give me *liberty* or give me death . . .

He nearly smiled at the wry truth of it, then stifled a yawn. Unable to sleep the night before, he'd felt a strange peace about the rash politics before him. While he wished he could be wholly present for the momentous proceedings of the moment, his heart felt cleaved in two.

What had happened with Liberty aboard the *Fowey*? He'd

prayed nearly without ceasing since she'd ridden off in the coach. Now he wished the words back, rethinking the advice he'd given her. Mayhap she was walking into a sort of trap—

"What say ye, Rynallt?" Suddenly Wythe and Henry were at his side, slapping him on the back in celebration and returning him to the matter at hand.

"Lookee there." Wythe jabbed a finger toward a window. "'Tis a mob all right, but an altogether agreeable one."

"Won't ye stay for the firing of the cannon and musketry?" Henry asked with a jab to the ribs. "I'm to parade my regimens of Continentals."

"Nay, I'm needed elsewhere," Noble replied, putting on his hat. The admission ushered in a keen pleasure, warm as Liberty Lawson's presence. He'd often wondered if he'd ever be necessary to someone again. Entwined. At least that was what he'd begun to feel about her.

"Needed? At home, mayhap? Ye have the look of an eager bridegroom," Wythe joked.

"I'm still hearing rumors about a Tory guest," Henry murmured. "Though there are those who may suspect your loyalty to this Revolution, I am not one of them."

"Let this be proof that I am with you," Noble replied, gesturing to the copy of the latest documents in Henry's hand.

He turned away, exited the double doors of the chamber, and rounded the turret to where his horse was tied. There was indeed a crowd, but a very merry, festive one. They waved small Virginia flags and cheered and tossed up their cocked hats when he rode past, causing his pulse to quicken all the more. With a dismissive wave of his hand he turned Seren south and was at a near gallop before he'd cleared Palace Green.

Home to Ty Mawr. Estate business. Personal pleasures. Libby.

Isabeau was beside herself. Not even the competent Dougray knew what to do with a distraught female. The battered hat he twisted in his hands was now misshapen. He eyed Liberty's maid and Noble by anxious turns as he shared the latest news.

Noble cleared his throat, trying to stay atop his dismay. "Her ladyship's gone then. Where?"

"To see her father first, as you well know—which came to no good end." The words were more growl. "I canna tell you what happened as I'm no' privy to that, but from the look o' her, it wasn't profitable. From the *Fowey* we made haste to Williamsburg, to her sacked townhouse. Lady Elisabeth bade me leave and said to thank ye for yer kindness."

"Anything else?"

A shake of Dougray's shaggy head shot down all Noble's hopes. "I rode off and lay in wait to see what she might do next, but there was only the good doctor who stopped me as I left town."

"Hessel?"

"Aye." Dougray looked as disgruntled as Noble felt. "He asked about her. Wanted to know her whereabouts."

Would Hessel come to her rescue? Would she let him? Mayhap no rescuing was needed. Despite Libby's genteel roots, she often seemed as grounded as her British-born mother.

"*Oh là là!*" Isabeau looked stricken. "I knew something was amiss in my very marrow when she went away yesterday without so much as *adieu*. I thought she would return. But no! And she has taken her trunk!"

Noble fixed her with a stony stare that did little to curb the maid's angst. But in the closeted sphere of lady's maids, mayhap a missing trunk was dire indeed.

Isabeau's sobs brought round Mistress Tremayne. "There, there," his housekeeper consoled. "You'll soon see your mistress again, no doubt. For now, let us return to our duties." Slipping an arm around the maid's bent shoulders, the housekeeper led her away, and Noble's study resumed its usual calm.

"I ken something more besides, sir." Dougray's jaw firmed. "The *Minerva* docked and Lady Stirling arrived. There was a ruckus raised and she was whisked away. Where to, I'm no' certain."

"A ruckus?"

"A great many redcoats gathered round when the countess came ashore. With the harbor patrolled so tightly, nary a ship enters or exits without Dunmore's knowledge and approval."

"Did Lady Liberty know her mother was near?"

"Nay. She was still aboard the *Fowey* with her father." Dougray returned his battered hat to his head. "I thought it best to keep her from the fray."

"Wise, that." Noble reached for the round paperweight on his desk, a small, gilded globe. England glared red, the colonies a serene blue, the ocean between.

He felt at sea himself, the glad events of the day crowded out by Liberty's absence and gnawing questions. "You did well to get to York and back without mishap. Keep an eye out for any news of Lady Elisabeth's whereabouts. She is now going by the name of Liberty or Libby. She and I have unfinished business regarding her maid's indenture."

"I'll let you know what I hear, sir." Dougray's words held a promise. He was a canny lad. Scots-shrewd. Between the two of them, Libby would be found.

16

Leaving the townhouse once again with a few belongings in a knapsack, Liberty lifted her face to sullen Sabbath skies, sensing rain. She hardly heard the slight commotion behind her, nor her name.

"Lady Elisabeth, 'tis you?"

She turned to look down at a chimney sweep, his face blackened. Beneath the soot she saw it was Jem. She'd snuck him food a time or two when he'd come to the townhouse begging for bread and work. An orphan like so many. "Jem, are you well?"

"Well enough, miss. I wasn't sure 'twas you goin' about on foot. Yer usually in a fancy carriage or sittin' a horse."

The lack brought another pang. Where *were* the horses? The conveyances? "I'm on foot now."

"Well, I've got news for ye. It mightn't be welcome, but yer mother's ship's come in. The countess fell into a fainting fit at the docks when she was told what's happened here. Doctor Hessel was sent for and is said to be lookin' for ye. I fetched yer mother's maid besides."

She stared at him, letting the words take hold as they

would. She was nearly past hope. Past joy. "Thank you, Jem. Do you know where my mother and Doctor Hessel might be?"

"Aye." He looked down, spiking Liberty's fears. "Publick Hospital, miss." At that, he took off, clutching his blackened broom. His bare, clay-colored feet were all she saw as he raced away from her, as if the bittersweet news, once delivered, was best left alone.

Publick Hospital.

The place of criminals and vagrants and lunatics.

Publick Hospital sat just south of Francis Street. A huge building looking like a brick kiln with a costly weathervane atop it, it seemed large enough to hold all of the deranged in British North America. Hesitating at the front gate in the gathering dusk, Liberty tried to think of it dispassionately. 'Twas the first public institution in the colonies devoted to those "poor, unhappy set of people who are deprived of their senses and wander about the countryside terrifying the rest of their fellow creatures."

That hardly described her dear mother.

Yet her compassionate mother had helped open its doors. Sanctioned in 1773 by a former governor, the dwelling never lacked patients. She could see several wounded souls milling about the grounds now, supervised by staff. *Lost, lost*, their every movement seemed to say.

She rang a bell and gained entry after a few trying minutes. A man—a night watchman?—admitted her. Lights shone from a few windows and left her wondering which room held her mother.

"No visitors after dark," the man told her gruffly, leading her inside nevertheless. "Ye'll have to speak to the matron."

Aggravated, she fell back on her former title. "I am Lady Elisabeth Lawson, and I must speak with my mother as soon as possible."

He grunted an unintelligible answer. Never had she so missed Isabeau. Without her, she felt half dressed. So often she'd let Isabeau take the lead while she remained in the background, allowing her older, enterprising maid to handle things. Isabeau would have put this man in his place by now and bypassed the matron altogether, succumbing to hysterics once inside.

Keys clinking, the man unlocked a heavy door and approached a small room lit by a single taper. A woman sat at a crude desk scratching her quill across paper, pausing to eye Liberty with interest even before she'd been announced.

"Lady Elisabeth, you say? Doctor Hessel is looking for you. I'll take you to the countess straightaway. She's just across the hall."

Liberty thanked her, surprised to find her so young. "Are you the matron?"

"Nay, miss. I'm Septima Ward, the nurse. Mistress Galt, the matron, is occupied."

Taking out a set of keys from her pocket, she dismissed the man who'd led Liberty to her and crossed to an opposite door, then let Liberty in before shutting it soundly and disappearing.

Liberty's heart squeezed tight at the scene before her. Little here but one simple chair, a bed covered with a blue-and-brown coverlet, a writing desk, a pallet in one corner, and a colorless rug. She stared with horror at the iron ring in a wall. For fettered patients? A sole, barred window let in the last of daylight, and a candle sat on the wide sill. Her mother stood looking out, her lovely profile so grave Liberty dared to hope she was calmer than she'd been at the dock.

Seeing her, Mamie got up from a chair with difficulty, reminding Liberty of just how old she was. Yet her worn voice, ever faithful, was full of warmth. "Child, that you?"

Liberty could hardly speak. "'Tis me, Mamie."

She went forward and hugged the round, linen-clad woman tight, all the while assessing the plain lines of the room through wet eyes.

"Doctor Hessel give her a bit o' laudanum earlier today," Mamie whispered as they drew apart. "She ain't been herself since."

"Mama," Liberty called, approaching slowly.

Her mother turned toward her. Her dress, a rich peacock-blue silk, made a mockery of her surroundings. Liberty put weary arms around her, feeling her thinness beneath the elaborate gown. A bandage encased one hand. Had she injured herself when she fainted upon arrival? The sea voyage had gone hard on her. And now this . . .

She clung to her mother longer than she ever remembered doing. Mama felt so fragile, the odor of laudanum strong. How much had Hessel given her? "Mama, I've missed you so." Her voice, sure and smooth for just a moment, began to crack and fade. "You've come home at last."

When she stepped back the candle flickered in a draft, highlighting a single tear trailing down her mother's wrinkled cheek. What little composure Liberty had left crumpled, and she flung her arms around her mother's neck. "Mama, are you sad? Oh please, don't cry." But she was crying so hard herself the words were nearly nonsensical. "'Twill be all right . . . in time."

Mamie came from behind, patting her back, murmuring words of comfort. The barren room seemed to echo the slightest sound. A wild, irrational fear took hold. Would someone come, perhaps at her father's bidding, to lock them in and not let them out?

Mamie took charge, settling her mistress into a chair and bringing Liberty a handkerchief. "Child, you look all done in. If I could fetch you a cup of tea I would, but there ain't no tea to be had here."

Liberty settled on the edge of the bed, the thin mattress giving way to sagging rope beneath. She read a hundred questions in Mamie's old, careworn face, but she couldn't answer a single one. How much should she share? Hold back? She shivered despite the heat, hands in her lap, her mind empty of all but a beloved Scripture.

Whatsoever things are true . . .

With that in mind, she began slowly. "The Lord has been so good to me. He's kept me from harm. People I would not have expected to help have been kind." At this she almost faltered, Noble firmly in mind. "Isabeau is safely settled elsewhere. I've just seen Father . . ."

Silence. And then, "How is he?" Her mother's gray eyes were fixed on Liberty, intelligent and assessing, unclouded by laudanum.

"He is safe, Mama . . . and may need to sail to England soon." Though she could hardly recall their harsh conversation without crying, this much was true at least. She would not share her father's coldness, his complete indifference.

"And the servants? Are they with him?"

"I don't know. I have not seen them."

Her mother's eyes shone and threatened to overflow. Liberty felt an overwhelming anguish. Her mother *knew*. Despite her absence and removal from all the turmoil, somehow she'd sensed everything had changed, that nothing was the same or ever would be.

"I prayed for you, Daughter. Even in Bath I kept you close."

"I felt your prayers, Mama. I believe they kept me safe." Liberty clutched her handkerchief into a hard ball. Even Mamie's chin was trembling, her wise, dark eyes wells of water.

"What of your betrothed? Your wedding?"

At this Liberty said with relief, "I'm not to marry, Mama. My betrothal to Miles Roth is broken."

They fell silent, no more to be said. Mamie began helping ready Mama for bed, and Liberty realized they would have to stay the night in this fearful place. The evening sounds, some reassuring like cricket song and the sigh of the wind, masked those that were strange and frightening.

Shortly after midnight, she awoke to shouting and the rattle of chains. Stiff upon the thin pallet, she was barely aware of the easy rhythm of Mama's breathing next to her or Mamie's soft snoring in the corner. One would need laudanum in such a place—bottles of it. She couldn't stay another moment.

Getting up, she rang a bell as gently as she could for the nurse, who let Liberty out.

❧

Sitting near a broken sundial in the paleness of early morning, Liberty looked upon a patch of untouched ground fringed with daylilies. Beneath the wide brim of her straw hat her eyes burned with dull fire. She'd slept little on this stone bench after leaving Publick Hospital, kept awake more by the plan forming than the town's night noises. And now, as if the fresh air helped clear the cobwebs from her mind, she mulled her scheme in daylight, finding it remarkably sound if scary.

She'd walked the half mile or more from Publick Hospital

171

to the townhouse after midnight, breathing in the solitude of the Sabbath. Once alone in the townhouse garden, out of sight of the street, she sought refuge among a small army of plants once victim to the mob. Now rallying in colorful profusion, no longer keeping to their beds, they spilled over walks and crept round corners with independent abandon.

Therein lies a lesson. Perhaps the Lord was showing her how brokenness could become abundance in the days to come. 'Twas a hope worth holding on to.

Her back pressed against a warm brick wall, she dozed, cast back to Ty Mawr. It seemed a lifetime ago, as if she'd dreamed up her third-floor stay.

"Lady Elisabeth?"

A shadow passed over her. She straightened, overcome with a mad hope. Noble, here? Nay. 'Twas Doctor Hessel's sturdy frame that loomed over her, relief sketched across his face. Disappointment made her chest tight. Try as she might, she couldn't give a greeting.

His eyes were tired, his frock coat rumpled. "I've looked everywhere for you. I'm told you are no longer at Ty Mawr. I've sent word to your father aboard the *Fowey* but have yet to receive a reply."

"I've been there myself to no avail. I've also seen Mama. She seems well enough, but her hand—'tis bandaged—"

"She hurt it when she fainted and fell. I've set it and will oversee its healing."

"Given that, she's hardly in need of Publick Hospital. Or laudanum." Her voice held exasperation. "We must move her somewhere safe. Sane."

He was studying her, his features contrite. "I wanted to bring her to my rooms once I saw her, but it was impossible. No other invitations were forthcoming. I could not secure her at a tavern, given threats have been made against her and your father."

Her spirits sank as she took in the unwelcome words. 'Twas no surprise. She herself had been shunned due to her father's unpopularity. "My only recourse was Publick Hospital. She's resting comfortably there, as you know. Mamie is with her."

She nodded, resignation giving way to grief. She tried to see circumstances in a favorable light. She well remembered the legislation enabling the hospital to be built. Her father had been its fiercest opponent. He had first called Mama lunatic then, as she was its staunchest supporter.

Though Liberty set her jaw till she feared her teeth would crack, her tears ran unhindered. She had not so much as a handkerchief in her basket. In the ensuing silence, Doctor Hessel fumbled in his waistcoat for one. She took it grudgingly. "I saw her briefly last night."

"Then you know I took care to secure a private room for her near the matron." His tone was apologetic. "If nothing else, she's in a safe place. No harm can come to her."

Safe? With so many disordered minds about? She withheld the anguished reply. The suspicion that her father was somehow behind her mother's placement there hovered. It would suit his purposes to declare her incompetent. Was the doctor in league with him? She felt a twinge to assume Hessel guilty of that.

"You know I mean your family no harm. 'Twas a last resort and one that will, I hope, be brief."

Looking away, she focused on the garden and followed the erratic trail of a butterfly in flight. "I appreciate your good intentions." Her next words were so abhorrent she had to utter a hasty, silent prayer before saying them. "I'll go see her again as soon as I can."

He nodded and reached for her hand. The gesture was so unexpected and so uncharacteristic of him she was caught by surprise.

"I'll do all I can to help you, Elisabeth. There's no need to feel alone. I'm confident Providence will aid us." He let go of her at last. "What will you do now? I cannot leave you here sitting on this bench. Where is your maid? Why are you not at Ty Mawr?"

So many questions. She had few answers save one. "I cannot rely on Mister Rynallt's generosity any longer."

"You cannot stay here." She heard the rustle of paper and looked up to see him opening a fresh copy of the *Gazette*. "Notice of the coming auction has just been posted. Trespassers at this address are to be prosecuted."

"I'm no trespasser," she said softly, hurt.

"The authorities may not make that distinction. I'd hate to find you in gaol."

It can't be any worse than Publick Hospital, she nearly said.

Tossing aside the newspaper, he righted an overturned urn and sat beside her. "You were safer outside Williamsburg, and there I'd hoped you'd stay, if not with Rynallt, then the Carters or someone more suitable."

Truly Ty Mawr was unsuitable in the extreme. There she was in dire danger of losing her heart.

"At least till this business with your father is sorted out," he finished.

"I've been to York," she said. "That door is closed to me."

"York? When?"

"A few days ago." The simple question unlocked a storehouse of hurt. "Father has washed his hands of us."

"Please, I know how forbidding he can be. But deep down I know he cares for you—"

"Then why has he made no provision for us? I came here and turned the house upside down, thinking he might have left a few guineas—"

"You have no coin?"

She sighed, taking back some of the blame. "Perhaps he might have given me something had I not left the *Fowey* in such a hurry."

He reached into his waistcoat and withdrew a small pouch. "I have ample—"

"Nay, Bram."

Their eyes locked. He looked taken aback. Never had she called him Bram. Doctor Hessel, yes. Only that. Till now. A ruddy flush stole into his face, making him look more swarthy Scot than fair Dutch. But he recovered well and was soon the good doctor again. Stoic. Professional. Concerned. "When have you last eaten?"

She looked to her lap, her days a scramble. When *had* she partaken of the generous meal at Jane Vobe's? "Eating is the least of my concerns."

"Then we'll breakfast together—now," he told her, returning the pouch to his waistcoat.

The prospect made her queasy. He read her refusal without her saying a word.

She peered up at him again, catching his wounded expression. "'Tis nothing more than this—I don't want to be seen."

"Why? You've done nothing wrong."

"I'm a Tory in a largely Patriot town. I-I want to be invisible, for a while yet."

He nodded, taking off his hat and turning it round in his hands. She noticed it was new beaver felt, not the old cocked hat she was used to. Looking down at her wrinkled dress, dirt sullying the flounced hem, she was reminded she was in

sore need of a bath and change of clothes. Her eyes drifted
to the well house near the stable. Perhaps the copper tub was
still there. She could see the tongue of the coach given her by
Miles Roth lying in the dust before the stable's open doors.

"I don't want you to worry about me." At the risk of
sounding absurd, she added quietly, "Providence has given
me a plan."

He was looking at her with keen concentration—he always
seemed to be looking at her lately—and she nearly squirmed
at his close scrutiny. He took out his money pouch again. "I
insist you take these guineas. Consider it a loan of sorts."
He pressed the coins into her palm and put on his hat. "I
have patients to see for now. Where will you be staying?" One
glance at the boarded-up townhouse dismissed the notion.
"Not here, surely."

"You needn't concern yourself." Truly, she did not want her
whereabouts known, not even by him. Best keep the Raleigh
secret for now.

Before he'd cleared the garden gate she was on her way to
the ordinary. Once her first day's work was done, she would
see Mama again.

17

Y our father and I . . ." Despite the distress in her face, Lady Stirling had recovered her eloquence. "My thought is that your father will sail to the West Indies and the sugar plantation he has there. As for myself, I am done with England and the king's petty policies. I'll seek asylum with the Dickinsons in Philadelphia and stay abreast of the coming conflict."

Wealthy Quakers, the Dickinsons had one of the largest libraries in the colonies, some fifteen hundred volumes. Would Mama make herself known as one of the Daughters of Liberty? The very name that so inflamed her husband?

But Philadelphia? Not once had Liberty imagined this.

"One's true friends are revealed in a calamity such as this." Her mother moved about, gathering her spectacles and a book. "Apparently I have none in Williamsburg. All have closed their doors to me on account of your father's circumstances."

Liberty hesitated. Should she mention Noble Rynallt's generous offer of Ty Bryn, the small house near Ty Mawr?

Had she refused him prematurely? Nay. Those ties were cut. Now she wasn't even his social equal.

"Your father has wasted no time in declaring me lunatic, and Doctor Hessel has inadvertently confirmed it by placing me in Publick Hospital." Handing Mamie a pair of mitts to pack, Mama attempted to tie the chin ribbons of her hat till Mamie stepped in. "You must come with me, of course."

The hospital room door was ajar, their leaving imminent. Had Mama no wish to return to the townhouse? Collect some of her belongings before—

"I shan't return to England Street," her mother continued. "Best leave the past in the past."

Was she aware their former home would be seized and auctioned? Mamie cast her a worried look as if reading her thoughts. Could twenty years or better be dismissed so easily? Did Mamie sense Liberty could not go with them?

"I've set aside some pin money from my publications, enough for a coach to Philadelphia. And I've sent Doctor Hessel a note."

"Mama, I—" She met her mother's silver stare. "I cannot accompany you. Williamsburg is my home, come what may. I've just hired on with Mister Southall."

Mamie's mouth rounded in disbelief, her fingers making a tighter knot of Mama's chin ribbons. "'Tis merciful your father is aboard ship," her mother said. "He'd have an apoplectic fit."

"Which he did over your writings."

"Indeed. Two forward-thinking females in one family are too many." Taking a chair, she studied her daughter. "Let me guess. You are turning to lacemaking and embroidery, am I right? I've long thought your skills exceptional, but I never imagined you would use them in so practical a way."

"I have you to thank, and your cottage industry here, as patron of the Williamsburg Lacemakers and such."

"You could still go north with me and ply your needle in the city of brotherly love." Her mother paused long enough to lift a brow. "Though it shan't be that for long, I fear, peace-loving Quakers or no."

"I've just moved into the folly of the Raleigh Tavern. The proprietor is in need of my services."

"For all those Independence Men, no doubt."

Liberty suppressed a smile. Few could quibble about the Raleigh's clientele.

"Mister Southall is a God-fearing gentleman who runs a respectable establishment," her mother conceded. "I know of the folly. 'Twas his office for a short time years ago. One could do worse living betwixt the bakery and apothecary." Standing, she pinned Liberty with a shrewd stare. "What has become of Isabeau? Run off like the rest of the servants?"

"Thankfully, Noble Rynallt of Ty Mawr has bought her contract." The particulars—the paperwork and payment—had eluded her till now. Would he seek her out to finalize the indenture transfer? And why did she feel a twinge of pleasure even saying his name?

"Very well." Mama raised her splinted hand to brush away a mosquito. "Philadelphia is not far. Should you tire of your work in Williamsburg, you are always welcome to join me." She turned toward the barred window. "The coach has come. Let us say our goodbyes privately."

Because Father abhors public displays.

Even now he seemed to hover, tainting their goodbye. They embraced, not the lingering, heartfelt exchange Liberty longed for but short and sparse with none of the emotion of their prior meeting.

"Please write to me, Mama." Letters had been few betwixt England and Virginia.

"Of course, once I arrive." Her mother's hands clasped Liberty's shoulders with a fierceness that belied her injury. "Promise me this. No matter how much life as you know it changes, I implore you to marry for love, naught else." Woven within the entreating words were years of heated disputes and icy silences, broken dreams and dashed hopes. "Promise."

Marry for love?

Liberty had no wish to marry at all.

18

Noble handed a gold guinea and Seren's reins to Billy. The boy's eyes lit like a match, not from greed but from gratitude. A trifle thin, he seemed in want of the confections wafting enticingly on the sultry air from the bake shop's open windows. As far as Noble knew, Billy was an orphan as well as a lad of all work about the Raleigh. The proprietor, Southall, had an admirable benevolent bent.

Noble took off his hat and slapped it against his thigh to unsettle the dust. "Any news round Williamsburg I might have missed?"

"News, sir?" Billy's freckled face scrunched in thought as he tucked the coin in the bosom of his soiled shirt. "Another litter of pups was just born in the woodshed should ye want one. As for ye Patriots, Mister Jefferson spent the night but was well on his way early this morn to Monticello." Brightening, he gestured toward the back of the ordinary. "There's a new face in the folly."

Noble's gaze shot beyond the fence to Southall's abandoned office. The door to the small outbuilding was thrown open wide, the windows raised. The small Virginia flag that hung to the right of the entrance was now accompanied by a length of lace. It danced in the wind, a frothy, furling, eye-catching white.

Liberty Lawson, lacemaker?

His pulse did a jig. Privately he lauded her for choosing the Raleigh. Though it had been merely a few days since he'd seen her, the longing to do so had not only lingered but intensified.

Billy started toward the back pasture, leading Seren. Throat parched from his ride, Noble nevertheless turned his back on the Raleigh and bypassed both the well and kitchen garden, taking the bricked walk to the folly.

He wasn't above a little sentiment. A burgeoning magnolia bush was to his right. Reaching out, he broke off a showy blossom, drawing the watchful eye of a mulatto woman working among the vegetables. He preferred the meadow wildflowers between Ty Mawr and Williamsburg, but there was something about the magnolia, pure and unsullied, that reminded him of Libby.

He took care to stand on the folly steps and knock on the lintel, averting his eyes from within. In the pause that followed, his anticipation left him a bit breathless. A ray of sunlight cut across the pine floor, and she stepped into it. Libby, at last.

"Mister Rynallt."

"Your first guest, mayhap, this quiet Tuesday morn."

Her cheeks pinked. "Well, sir, you have found me out."

"'Tis not hard in so small a town as Williamsburg. Some two thousand souls at last count." His gaze lifted to the folly's rafters, finding it free of cobwebs at least. "Still, an unlikely place for the daughter of an earl."

"Yet charming, no?" She pushed the door open wider, standing aside to better let him see in. "Perhaps not as grand as Ty Mawr, but . . ."

He smiled, warming to the playful lilt in her voice, glad she had landed on her feet. He handed the magnolia blossom to her.

Her face softened. She breathed in the heady fragrance, her eyes holding his. "Reminds me of when I was a little girl in leading strings. Our gardener had the onerous task of shooing me away from our magnolias. I was besotted by them and bruised the blossoms, he always said."

"Well, I'm no crotchety townhouse gardener, just a man who likes to tie up loose ends." He reached into his waistcoat and extracted the paperwork and money he owed. "For your maid's indenture."

"Isabeau?" Her forehead furrowed. "Perhaps that matter is more for my father."

"She's your maid, aye?"

She pocketed the coin and paperwork, the magnolia still in hand. "How are . . . things?"

Things? He swallowed down a dozen unsavory answers. *Virginia politics are still a-simmer. We'll soon be more in need of soldiers' shirts than lacemaking. Your townhouse goes on the block in July. Isabeau needs a lady to wait on.*

Ty Mawr needs a mistress.

He abbreviated his answer. "Busy." His gaze moved to the overflowing baskets near a small cane-bottomed chair by a window. Her work?

"'Tis my mending. A great many men's shirts from the Raleigh. Any time left over is for lacemaking."

Precious little time left, likely, though her lace pillow was out, resembling a porcupine with its many pins.

"The lighting is perfect, better than the townhouse." She smiled up at him, then her face darkened. "Much has happened since we last met. You should know my mother is on the King's Highway to Philadelphia as we speak. She cannot reconcile with my father."

No surprise there. But Noble wanted to take the hurt from her comely face. "Why Philadelphia?"

"She has friends in the city."

And few here. He silently commended Southall for taking on a Tory. In the span of a few days, Liberty Lawson had waded through the shambles of her cosseted life, shunned Noble's advice, and set forth on a new venture that both baffled and intrigued him.

"Mister Southall has given me leave to travel to Norfolk every fortnight. I'll go to market, see if I can make enough contacts that merchants come to me for orders. I'll need to visit the bookbinder there and beg some parchment for lace patterns."

"The Williamsburg bookbinder might oblige you."

She looked away. "He turned me out. My father owes him, you see."

He sensed her humiliation. So her father had unpaid debts? "You'll be passing by Ty Mawr on your way to and from Norfolk." He hesitated, allowing himself one last chance with her. Would she shoot down his invitation? "Should you need to stop there . . ."

"Thank you. I thought perhaps to stay at Richneck Plantation, but as it stands, those doors might be closed to me."

So she'd come to Ty Mawr as a last resort?

Her smile resurfaced, raising his hopes, then dashing them at her next words. "I might see Isabeau."

"Aye," he said, beginning a slow retreat. He would not ask again. Slowly the door between them began to shut. He canted his thoughts to the upcoming ball at the Raleigh, and the women who would be more obliging than the tarnished Tory before him.

In truth, Liberty Lawson was beyond his reach. Once his social equal, she'd lowered herself to middling tradeswoman, and his political adversary at that. Mayhap he'd best heed Henry's warnings.

"Godspeed." He returned his hat to his head, hating the finality he felt. "I wish you well in all your endeavors."

"*Ffarwel*," she answered in Welsh. *Goodbye.*

He hesitated. Who had taught her that? Her pronunciation was flawless, upending him. Her sunny smile was his complete undoing, somehow tightening the tie that had begun to unravel.

He walked away and didn't look back.

Her days became a blur of work. She measured time by eye strain and back pain. Up before dawn, she labored by candlelight, her foremost priority taking care of the Raleigh clientele. She knew who was at the ordinary by the identifying marks on their garments. Her goal was to finish each forenoon and attend to her lacemaking after, but there were simply not enough hours.

How idle she had once been. How at ease. While those around her had callused their hands and catered to her every whim, she'd given it little thought, simply dropping a polite if rote thank-you like a scattering of crumbs.

As she worked her tiny, mundane stitches—twelve stitches to an inch of cloth—her thoughts ran amok. Had Mama made it to Philadelphia? Was Papa still aboard the *Fowey*? Gossip rumbled like thunder as June melted into July.

The magnolia blossom Noble had given her lay in a windowsill, a dirty, limp brown. For some reason she couldn't bring herself to throw it away. Oddly, the faded blossom seemed a symbol of herself. How many days had passed since he'd pressed it into her hand? She hated that she looked for him, raising her head to peruse the horses in the far field, fixing her gaze on the Raleigh's rear door at busy times to catch his coming or going. But he hadn't come back.

'Twas Saturday. The ordinary bristled with new purpose. If gaiety had a scent, she now smelled it.

Today the rooms' windows glittered from a good washing, and a great many scurrying maids foretold a merry occasion.

"You starin' at that room like you is wantin' to go to the ball."

Startled as much by Thalia's presence as her uncanny ability to read her thoughts, Liberty lost her precious needle. It fell between two floorboards, glinting out of reach. The young mulatto woman promptly dropped to all fours and deftly retrieved it. Liberty met Thalia's eyes and found them warm, the few pockmarks on her tawny face situated like beauty patches. Not even smallpox could dent her comeliness.

"I suppose you deserve a little merriment workin' night and day like you do, just stoppin' long enough to eat or go to the necessary."

"You work as hard or harder," Liberty returned, thinking of Thalia's unceasing care of the Raleigh's kitchen and flower gardens. Nary a weed sprouted before she'd uprooted it. "At least I'm in the shade."

Thalia removed her linen kerchief and caught a trickle of sweat. "We'll likely get no sleep tonight with the dancin' goin' on till dawn. That punch bowl's mighty big besides." The Raleigh's silver-plated bowl and ladle were reputed to be the largest in the colonies.

Setting her sewing aside, Liberty walked to the well, drawing water enough for them both. She'd noticed Thalia limping down rows of leafy lettuce and plumy carrots, rarely pausing for a drink.

Nodding her thanks, Thalia took the wood dipper and drank deeply, offering it to Liberty next. Liberty felt a twist of dismay drinking from a bucket, then took an extra swallow to quell it, dismissing the shiny memory of pewter and silver in the butler's pantry of the townhouse.

"Iffen you like, we can watch the goings-on from over there." Thalia gestured toward a crude wooden bench half hidden by a bed of lofty hollyhocks. "Mister Southall, he give me the night to do as I please on account o' my leg." Lifting a petticoat, she revealed a jagged gash above one garter-tied stocking.

Inwardly Liberty recoiled. How had she come by such a wound? Asking seemed too familiar somehow. Staying stoic, Liberty gestured next door. "The apothecary is at hand. Or I can send for Doctor Hessel."

"Nay, I just needs to rest."

Night was pressing in, the gathering clouds snuffing what little sun was left. The apothecary would soon close.

Without explaining herself, Liberty backtracked to the open apothecary door, nearly colliding with a portly gentleman in black. Like the Raleigh's Apollo Room, she'd never been in Galt's shop before. A servant was always sent for whatever was needed, allowing her a measure of anonymity now.

She breathed in a dozen different potent scents as her gaze settled on Doctor Galt's medical certificates hanging on a far wall. Decorative jars adorned a high shelf, but far simpler containers abounded below it. She recognized a few. Licorice root for sore throats. Tooth powder. Quinine for fever.

"Need something, miss?" No kindling of recognition lit the assistant's eyes. And then . . .

"Lady Elisabeth?"

She turned toward the door, clenching one of Noble's guineas in her fist.

"What are you doing here?"

Doctor Hessel was regarding her as if she was a spectacle. Granted, she'd traded her fancy dress for some of the servants' garments she'd found at the townhouse. But they were clean. Serviceable.

Doctor Galt came out of a back room, hailing Doctor Hessel and regarding her with a mixture of curiosity and confusion.

"I'm in need of a physic," she murmured.

Hessel raked her from head to toe. "Are you unwell?"

"Nay, someone else."

In moments they had exited the shop, and Hessel was examining Thalia's leg in the privacy of the folly. "'Tis deep. A wayward garden implement, you say? A poultice should set it right."

This time it was Thalia who was sent for the remedy, leaving the doctor and Liberty alone. His stoicism flared to exasperation.

"Blast! First your mother leaves and then I can't locate you—"

"But you have." She waved a hand about the folly, making light of his concerns. "As you can see, I'm safely settled and employed."

"I nearly didn't recognize you."

"Glad I am of that." She looked down at her simple attire, appreciating how little fuss it was to dress oneself, though she did miss Isabeau. "I hope in time to be known as the lacemaker and not the earl's daughter."

"You should have gone with your mother to Philadelphia. What is your arrangement with Southall?"

"Sewing and mending mostly."

He reached for her hands. Had he never seen them un-gloved? He studied them as if diagnosing them. His brow creased. "Your lovely hands. They're marred."

"I've been waited on hand and foot since birth." Gently she pulled free. "What are a few pinpricks and calluses now?"

"Please, you needn't demean yourself. This place—" He looked about, appearing disgusted. "You're little more than a scullery maid. A slave. Let me take you away from here. I have new rooms on Francis Street."

Did he? She'd never given it much thought. The invitation seemed unseemly somehow. "Your rooms? Are you asking me to . . ." She hesitated, unsure of him.

Thalia stood on the doorstep, poultice makings in hand.

Hessel took a step back. "I've other patients to see. We can continue our conversation later." With a stiff bow he went out, leaving Thalia shamefaced and untended, as if he'd forgotten her altogether.

"Pardon, Miss Lib."

"No need." Summoning a smile, Liberty felt a sweeping relief. "Let's dress your leg. We hardly need the doctor for that. Now that the day's work is done, you can rest."

From across the garden a fiddle squeaked, evidence of the jollity to come. Listening, Liberty did the best she could with Thalia's wound, binding the leg with a strip of clean linen when done.

Thalia leaned nearer. "You sweet on the good doctor?"

The straightforward question set Liberty oddly at ease. "I feel nothing for him but friendship." There, she had said it. On the heels of this came her mother's voice. *Marry for love, naught else.* "And you?"

A measured nod. "There's a Scotsman, a coachman that serves at Ty Mawr."

"Ty Mawr?" The swell of pleasure Liberty felt overrode the sting of Doctor Hessel's hasty exit. "Would his name happen to be Dougray?"

"Sure enough." Thalia gave a winsome smile. "You met him?"

"In part. Mister Ryn—" Liberty changed course. "I know the housekeeper. Some other servants there."

Liberty looked toward the Raleigh's front entrance. A small dust storm obscured the street as carriages delivered guests. She and Thalia made their way to the garden bench amid the flare of fireflies. A lamplighter passed by, further illuminating the ladies and their escorts stepping through the dusty twilight.

"The Raleigh's nigh to burstin'." Thalia leaned into Liberty, her words a whisper. "You know any o' them fancy folk?"

Liberty kept the wistfulness from her voice. "Most of them." Yet here she sat, hardly believing she'd once been at the apex of the social whirl. "Why do you ask?"

"'Cause you be as fine as them, no matter yo' plain linen and scuffed shoes."

Was it so obvious then? Liberty smoothed a wrinkle from her apron. Would Noble Rynallt attend? More than a few of his fellow Patriots were here. There was no mistaking George Rogers Clark's robust laugh or the scarecrow-like silhouette of Patrick Henry.

A four-wheeled post chaise was slowing, one Liberty quickly recognized. Cressida stepped down from its upholstered interior, the cut of her gown drawing more eyes than Liberty's. Miles Roth drew up behind her . . . in the very coach he had given her, his betrothed. Had he taken it back after all the mayhem? Yet he had discarded her?

For a few excruciating seconds it was too much for her heart and head to hold. She looked toward the Palace, where there had always been a glimmer of light. How long would her father and Lord Dunmore and fellow Loyalists sit aboard ship? Cooped up like the Dominique and Nankin chickens Thalia tended, while the whole of Williamsburg waited and mocked?

Thalia got up from the bench and made her way to the kitchen and the hive of activity there. Liberty watched her slow going, her own stomach cramping in anticipation. She'd been so busy she'd forgotten to eat. The savory aroma of the dishes being carried to and fro was both torment and temptation.

Cressida and Miles disappeared inside the ordinary as other conveyances clogged the street. Biting her lip, Liberty let some of the angst bleed out of her. As raw as Thalia's wound she was. Numb and riled by turns, she had no idea what to do with her fractured feelings. In her mind's eye the decorative jars in the apothecary reappeared, her hands frantically searching. Would that one's unseen hurts be as easily remedied as Thalia's leg.

"Here you be, Miss Lib." Thalia's low voice and open hands reached out to her in the gathering darkness.

How glad she was Thalia's mother was boss of the kitchen house. Thanking her, Liberty took the offering, a small meat pie still warm from the oven, the crust a greasy gold. Gratitude eased her angst. Forgetting her manners, she downed the delicious pie in a few ravenous swallows, brushing the crumbs from her apron and wishing for more.

An opening minuet ended and a jig began. The Raleigh's windows offered an ample view of who danced with whom, the endless imbibing at the punch bowl, the fluttering of fans and side conversations. Miles Roth was not long for the dancing. He soon moved to the taproom and gambling. But Cressida in her celestial-blue silk was the belle of the ball, partnering with every Patriot in sight.

Except Noble Rynallt, who had not come.

19

⁓⁓⁓

T was just past noon when the auction began. Standing in the glare of a cloudless July sun, Noble counted the serious bidders. The crowd was thick, mostly curious onlookers anxious to see the Lawsons' personal lives and possessions paraded before them when they'd been denied the details before. He himself could ill afford to be here. Last year's tobacco crop was less than desired, exports nearly nonexistent now. His purse was stretched at the seams.

John Greenhow stood atop a raised platform in the ransacked garden of the Lawsons' townhouse, sweating and harried. After the usual welcome and recitation of the rules and a reminder that two bids must be made by persons unknown to the other, the Lawsons' belongings went on the block as confiscated Tory property. Furniture. Wine. Art. Saddles and bridles.

"Credit will be allowed until the twentieth of December next for all sums above fifty shillings, the purchasers giving bond, with approved security . . ."

The bidding began. Hands shot up. Beneath a battered

ornamental tree that had somehow survived the ransacking, Miles Roth was adjusting his hat.

Unseen by him in the jostling audience, Noble wondered what it was his cousin wanted here. Simply put, Miles's presence grated. Had he taken Noble's gibe to heart? Was he going to bid on the townhouse?

Item by item, the townhouse's lavish contents were carried out. A beautiful cherry dressing table—was that Libby's own? An embroidered sampler dated 1771—worked by her hand? An enamel patch box. A necklace of ruby glass beads. A complete set of Nanquin tea china . . .

Midafternoon his own wait was rewarded as the remains of the music room appeared. The elaborate harp was the first instrument up for bidding. How had it survived intact?

Noble sent another glance Miles's way, knowing his cousin likely wanted the townhouse, not the contents. When the bidding on the harp began to climb, Noble raised a hand. His number was high enough to deter any but the most covetous.

"Going once . . . twice . . . Sold!"

A burst of elation warmed him. He considered a broken lute and a rare violin with a missing bow. But the harp seemed enough. Dougray waited near at hand to haul it home in a wagon.

Miles was staring at both of them, frowning, as Noble examined his prize before Dougray secured it for the few miles' journey to Ty Mawr. Was Miles expecting him to leave?

The day wore on. The auctioneer grew more hoarse. Carts and wagons toted myriad items away. The sun was slanting beneath Noble's cocked hat now, and he pulled it lower. A drink from his flask revived him, but there was no help for the onslaught of gnats badgering the crowd.

His spirits, high when the harp was his, began to ebb as

the heat climbed and more personal items went on display. Each was part and parcel of Libby Lawson's former life. How would it feel to lose Ty Mawr? To relinquish so many personal possessions? He might well experience it given Virginia's crisis. And not only his estate. His very life.

A quick scan of the crowd assured him Libby was not here. That alone bolstered him. The folly in back of the Raleigh was now her home, for however long it lasted. And God be thanked for that.

The bidding for the townhouse began at last, disrespectfully low. So low Noble nearly flinched. Miles's hand shot up straightaway. So he'd discarded his would-be bride and set his sights on her townhouse instead?

Noble took another swallow from his flask, the tick of his pulse climbing bid by bid. Aye, Miles seemed determined to have it. He'd elbowed his way to the front of the throng, just beyond the reach of the auctioneer's silver-tipped walking stick.

Disgust threatened to unseat Noble's stoicism. God help him, he'd go to the poorhouse before Miles won Libby's former home.

"A thousand pounds more," Noble shouted.

Miles craned his neck and glared, promptly outbidding him. Another gentleman intervened. But not by much. Undeterred, Noble put forth a higher amount, which Miles countered by a measly ten pounds.

Noble was cast back to the wrestling matches they'd had as boys. Miles usually resorted to kicking and biting and looked like he might do so now.

"Going once . . . Going twice . . ."

Noble cast a last bid. The other gentleman topped it. This stranger was from Alexandria. A wealthy lawyer, someone said. Miles was strangely, furiously silent.

Noble held his peace as the townhouse went to the persistent lawyer. Throwing down his snuff box, Miles stalked off into the heated haze of the afternoon.

The folly door was ajar. Would he always find her within? Or would she disappear one day like her father had done? He still wasn't sure of her. Or her loyalties. Her affections.

He paused at the Raleigh's back gate. He had to pass by the garden first, and the woman who tended it was standing guard over a patch of peas. Thalia, Dougray's new sweetheart. He hardly recognized her in her bright kerchief. Sometimes slave auctions were held on the ordinary's front steps, and Thalia had been bought by Southall at one of them months before. Likely Libby had been sheltered from such. If she had witnessed one she might not find the folly so agreeable.

He turned over the serinette he'd bid on and won. French made, it was fashioned of European walnut, capable of playing ethereal tunes. A rarity of a music box. It had gone for only a few guineas while the harp had taken considerably more. He wanted to have something to give Libby. No doubt she knew her former home was on the block. The auction's hubbub could be heard for miles.

Thalia spoke in back of him. "She ain't here, sir. She's gone for pins and thread."

He felt a sudden misgiving. A sewing kit had been auctioned to a woman earlier in the day. Mayhap Libby had more need of that. Both serinette and harp seemed frivolous somehow, an impracticality in her highly practical life. She could fit the serinette in the folly. The harp had already been wrapped in a quilt and was nearly to Ty Mawr.

"I'll leave it here then." He set the gift inside the folly door just as a gentle voice sounded behind him.

"What have you . . . ?"

He turned.

Libby looked past him, eyes widening as she took his gift in. "*Boîte à musique*?" She dropped her basket and reached for it, opening the lid so that a tune floated out. Her delight was worth every guinea. "How did you come by it?"

'Twas the one question he hoped she would not ask. But it deserved an honest answer. "At auction. I did what I could."

"Ah, that. I purposed to shy away from England Street." She shut the serinette. Her eyes shone. "I owe you."

"Nay. There's your harp besides."

"You saved my harp?" For a moment she seemed overcome.

"'Tis on the road to Ty Mawr as we speak, though I cannot testify to its safety in a wagon bed. 'Twill be there for safekeeping till you have need of it again."

Stepping into the folly's shade, she faced him. His broad back blocked the blistering sun, his shirt damp beneath his coat. Sweat trickled down his neck, turning him itchy.

"So the townhouse . . . 'tis gone." Her chin trembled.

"Sold to an Alexandria lawyer, aye." Such pain crossed her face he veered to a safer path. "How was your errand?"

In other words, *How did the shopkeeper treat you? Were you welcomed or shunned?* He picked up her basket and set it inside.

She expelled a breath. "Pins are scarce these days. I'm always in need of them but just learnt that a dozen equal the value of a bedstead."

"Why more pins?"

"The wider silk laces require a great many. I go to Norfolk on the morrow. Perhaps I shall find them there."

He gave a nod. "Stop at Ty Mawr and ask Mistress Tremayne if she has any. Isabeau can even accompany you to Norfolk if you like."

She gave a shake of her head. "No need for a companion. The Quarterpath Road is heavily traveled."

True enough. Still, Noble didn't like the thought of her without an escort. He couldn't rid his mind of pickpockets and rogues, though she had precarious little to steal. Coin, anyway. Her virtue was another matter. "You'll ride?"

"Mister Southall has a gentle mare in need of exercise. But I might lodge at Ty Mawr coming or going."

His hopes revived though her words seemed elusive. "The invitation stands," he reassured her.

Hugging the serinette to her chest, she sat down in the doorway. "What is happening with England?"

The abbreviated answer? "There's still hope of reconciliation. The colonies have extended an olive branch of sorts, asking King George to rein in Parliament and end their unbridled legislation over us."

"And my father? Lord Dunmore?"

"They remain in Yorktown's harbor, or so I last heard." He wouldn't tell her about the death threats. The mounting danger. "Mostly 'tis *clonc*."

"*Clonc?*"

"Gossip."

She smiled, a rainbow in their storm. "A fitting word for tittle-tattle."

Setting the serinette aside, she reached for a dried magnolia in a deep windowsill. The one he'd given her? "How do you say *flower* in Welsh?"

"*Blodyn*." A clumsy name for something so fine, he'd always thought.

The picture of charm, she repeated the word, making it sound almost fetching.

A dozen other words clamored to be said.

Del. Pretty.

Calon. Heart.

Rwy'n dy garu di. I love you.

And his personal favorite—*anwylyd*. Dearest one. Beloved.

He'd removed his tricorn and now slicked the sweat from his brow, ending all romantic musings. Knowing Thalia was near, privy to their meeting, he took a step back. If he wasn't careful he'd be *smonach*. A mess.

"Godspeed, Libby."

His sudden goodbye took some of the light from her face, but he had other, more urgent matters to attend to than delivering serinettes and harps.

"*Ffarwel*," she called after him.

⁂

Weariness followed the next fortnight, draping Liberty like a cloak. Her fingers stiff and sore from so much needlework, she finished the lavender card holding her lace samples. On the back of the card she'd written, *Lace of the kind made in Williamsburg, Virginia, stemming from Buckinghamshire, England*. Thankfully, lace was lightweight and could be rolled into a small bundle and taken to market.

The boycott of British goods was a blessing in disguise, making her own work more sought after, or so she hoped. Women's caps and handkerchiefs were adorned with lace, and colonial women were having their portraits painted while wearing lace shawls, mostly black silk. Her own mother had posed in such only last winter. But even the humblest women often scraped and saved to afford a bit of lace adornment to call their own.

She looked down at the work of her hands, recalling a psalm.

Lord, please bless the work of my hands.

She set what she'd take to Norfolk by the folly door. The only remaining riddle was whether to stop at Ty Mawr. How she'd love to see Isabeau again and have refreshments with Mistress Tremayne.

Opening the serinette, she sat on a stool near the folly's open door to listen and court any breeze. She took a deep breath to settle herself, only she didn't settle. Like a bee in a butter churn she was, ever since the upheaval in June. But 'twas more than this, truly.

Just when she thought she could forget about Noble Rynallt, move past his many kindnesses to her, he'd reappear. Going to Ty Mawr would only fan whatever spark had started. At least on her part.

The serinette's ethereal notes ceased and begged winding. But music was not what was needed. She craved a bath. The copper hip tub from the townhouse. No doubt that had been auctioned off too.

Who was behind confiscating Tory property? Why hadn't they waited to see if England would make amends? Did her father know he'd lost his home?

She reached for the letter newly arrived from Philadelphia.

Dear daughter, I am safely settled in this great city. I wonder that it took me so long . . .

Mama sounded elated. The Dickinsons had opened their home and hearts to her, and she was surrounded by free-thinking Quaker friends far removed from the petty, personal politics of Virginia's capital. If things turned sour, if

Liberty's lacemaking venture failed, she could find refuge in Philadelphia too, Mama restated.

She took up a quill to answer, only to realize she'd run out of ink. And could ill afford more.

Nay, for now, she couldn't leave Williamsburg. Her heart and her hopes were here.

∞

Beneath wide-open skies the precise hue of Cressida's party dress, Liberty's spirits expanded. The folly, so tiny, seemed to clip her wings. Outside its narrow walls she felt she could fly. Norfolk didn't seem so far. Every mile brought a reward. A riot of wildflowers. The capering of lambs. A coastal breeze. The tall, stalwart chimneys of plantations in the distance, ever reassuring.

Her mare was another matter. Little wonder Mister Southall had spared such a creature. Every patch of clover caught her eye, and she was fond of stopping all of a sudden for no apparent reason, nearly unseating Liberty from the worn saddle.

Snapping the ribbons, Liberty coaxed her on again and again. Past the turnoff to Carter's Grove. Past the stately gates of Ty Mawr. Into full view of the James River as it flowed southeast to the Chesapeake Bay.

A great many people traveled this road alongside the river. She breathed their dust, took note of their persons. Noble Rynallt needn't worry about her. She didn't miss Isabeau's company too much. Didn't garner too many inquiring glances.

In her simple linen dress and straw hat she was simply Liberty the lacemaker of Williamsburg.

20

The latest documents from the Second Continental Congress had arrived by express that morning, ink-smeared and smelling of saddle leather. The title gave Noble pause.

The Declaration of the Causes and Taking Up of Arms. Forbidding. Decisive. Final. Everything was inching toward war. He'd be more alarmed if George Washington hadn't been made commander in chief of the newly formed Continental Army. Washington was fearless, a veteran soldier from the French and Indian War. But what was a pittance of colonists against hordes of professional British soldiers?

He looked up as a knock sounded. The door to his study opened.

"You've a visitor, sir." Mistress Tremayne was hard to read, but he detected a glimmer of discontent. "A Miss Shaw has come."

For a few seconds he drew a blank. Miss Shaw . . . Libby's friend? So framed, it made more sense. Out of the social whirl as he'd been, with only an occasional dance at the Raleigh, few women stood out. Had Miss Shaw come carrying news about Libby?

Wary now, he simply said, "I'll meet her in the East Room."

He crossed the threshold to a small parlor seldom opened. At times he felt he needed but three rooms, his bedchamber and his study and the kitchen. At least the whole of Ty Mawr gave him exercise and was large enough for a family, in time.

"Good afternoon, Mister Rynallt."

"Aye, so it is, Miss Shaw."

She stood to his right as was proper, eyes downcast beneath her elaborate hat. This close he was reminded he'd once partnered with her at some function. Where, he couldn't recall. She'd been eager, flirting with him and fluttering her fan. It had made him uncomfortable then. He was doubly uncomfortable now.

He glanced at the parlor's other door, open wide. Mistress Tremayne remained in the foyer, he suspected, for the signal to bring refreshments.

"What a charming chamber." Miss Shaw's gracious words seemed forced, but he cast an appreciative glance at the paneling and carved mantelpiece. She turned in a little circle as if to show herself off to full advantage, taking in the entirety of the room as she did so. The Prussian blue paint was much like the color being considered for the Continental Army uniforms. 'Twas an old room, one of the few Enid hadn't redone.

"'Tis a replica of the family parlor in Wales at our estate there," he said. "My father designed the original." She might not know the local history, as she was a relative newcomer to Williamsburg. Boston bred, if he recalled. Bits and pieces were coming back to him now. Her father was a wealthy merchant. And a fence-sitter regarding politics.

"Lovely indeed." She took something from her purse. A

letter? "I hesitate to be the bearer of bad news, but after much prayer I felt you were the one to consult about the matter."

He felt an immediate check. *Beware the things that come cloaked in prayer.* "And the matter is . . ."

"The letter speaks for itself, though I can vouch for its veracity." She passed it to him. "I've suspected as much."

The letter's seal had been broken. The handwriting was bold. Black. Masculine. In the copperplate style, as opposed to a woman's elegant Italianate hand.

> *Dear Sir,*
>
> *This is to forewarn you of traitors in your midst, namely the daughter of the former lieutenant governor, Lady Elisabeth Lawson. She is guilty of carrying correspondence to her father that will do the American cause harm. Lady Elisabeth has been to Norfolk of late, even Yorktown, under the guise of a lacemaker. Do not be fooled.*

There was no signature. He looked squarely at Cressida Shaw. "The letter loses credibility being unsigned."

Her chin lifted. "These are dangerous times. A signer might implicate himself—"

"Like I did when I signed dozens of documents questioning the king."

She colored at this, her face the hue of her rose dress. "I only want to do my part and warn you."

"After much prayer, as you said." He couldn't keep the mockery from his tone. She had the grace to look down. "Have you spoken with Miss Lawson of late?"

"I have not. Word is she's somewhere in Williamsburg. Just where, I do not know."

Her dismissive tone set him more on edge than the contents of the letter. He glanced at the striking clock. Nearly the hour for tea, a custom he never observed, though many still did. "You'll be wanting to be on your way." He would not thank her. Gut instinct told him there was little truth to the charge, and his heart told him to dismiss it. His head urged a second look.

"I'm in no hurry. Let us speak of more pleasant matters." She was all smiles now. "You were missed in the Apollo Room the other night. With so few Patriots, we ladies sadly lacked partners. Mister Washington, such an able dancer, was not in attendance either."

"General Washington?" He wouldn't say Washington had been in Massachusetts rallying troops, or that he himself had spent the evening revising the final draft of a document first penned by a fellow Patriot but considered too inflammatory. Bold, incendiary language that some members of the committee asked him to revisit. "I've not been in the dancing frame of mind of late."

"Do you ever entertain here at Ty Mawr?"

"On occasion." Was she wrangling an invitation?

She touched his sleeve, removing all doubt. "Should you ever need someone to act as hostess . . ."

He nearly chuckled at her audacity. *Petticoat government.* He had little need of that. She seemed to want to linger, so at odds with Libby's stance. He was in no more mood for her company than he was afternoon tea. The letter sat squarely between them, full of rumor and ill will.

"Good day, Miss Shaw."

When she went out he heard the tap of Mistress Tremayne's heels approaching. "So much for Virginia hospitality, sir." In her arms she bore a silver tray. He smelled strong coffee and bara brith fresh from the bake oven.

He pocketed Miss Shaw's letter and took the tray from his housekeeper. In times past it was his sister he turned to for sensitive matters. Enid was older. Wiser.

Gone.

"Can you spare a few minutes?" he asked. "Partake of some hospitality with a flaming Patriot in need of feminine advice?"

Her answering smile made her seem a decade younger. "Of course, sir. My pleasure."

They went out a door onto the riverfront portico. There he set the tray on a small table and seated her.

"I must confess being surprised at this turn of events," she said. "'Tis not often masters sit down with servants."

"Only in America, mayhap. 'Tis liberty and justice for all, aye?"

She chuckled and reached for the urn of coffee with her usual steadiness. Once she'd filled their cups, he took Miss Shaw's letter from his pocket and passed it to her, knowing she'd never divulge the contents. She read it carefully, thoughtfully, expression unchanging.

"'Tis a heavy charge, that of spy," she finally said, folding it up again. "A little early in the game for such accusations, wouldn't you say?"

"Agreed."

She gave a shrug. "Seems precious little to ferret out and spy about. We colonists are being taxed to death. The despised Dunmore has fled. Virginia simply wants to cobble together a little order in his absence till a new royal governor is appointed and the king makes amends. What's so worthy of spying about that?"

"I'll play devil's advocate." He fixed his gaze on the James River, its calm surface so at odds with his inner turmoil.

"Lady Elisabeth's connections give her instant access to important Tories. She has every reason to be angry with the Patriot cause. Her home has just been confiscated. She's been forced into a trade. Few if any friends are standing by her. And now she's being labeled a spy by a coward with no name."

"You make a formidable case. I forget you were once a barrister before you were a burgess." She looked at him inquiringly, her coffee untouched. "And now you are . . . ?"

"A delegate. Mayhap soon a soldier."

She took a bite of Welsh bread, digesting the news. "War is coming, you mean. There's no avoiding it."

He nodded, tasting his coffee. For once he had no appetite for bara brith. Something Washington had said kept coming to mind, as if made for this very occasion.

True friendship is a plant of slow growth and must undergo and withstand the shocks of adversity before it is entitled to the appellation.

He supposed the same could be said for him and Libby.

Liberty tucked Mama's most recent letter in her commonplace book, which held practical things as well as more winsome ones. A worn sheet of music. Hastily penned poems. Pressed flowers. Prayers. Lace orders and merchants' names. She'd purchased the scrapbook from the Norfolk bookbinder along with more ink from her first weeks' wages.

Mister Southall had kindly given her an old desk, which left her remembering her former Queen Anne tucked beneath her bedchamber window at the townhouse. Though nicked and of inferior wood, the folly's desktop was firm and smooth, and there was a shallow drawer with enough room for her commonplace book. A single candlestick graced a pewter holder, one of the Raleigh's castoffs.

Oddly, she took pleasure in these hard-won things in a way she hadn't the silver candelabra and leather-bound books of her former life. She had little now, but it was enough. Thalia brought her an extra serving of soup or bit of crusty bread from the Raleigh kitchen, and in turn she looked after Thalia's wound.

Tonight a moth hovered near the candle flame as Liberty wrote down her orders in its pale light. Norfolk had been needy while Williamsburg stood aloof. She blew on the ink, for she lacked pounce, and left the book open to dry. Taking out Mama's letter again she reread it slowly, dwelling on one aggravating line.

> *After much discussion with my hosts, we feel you must come immediately to Philadelphia. Virginia is naught but a powder keg.*

Liberty folded up the letter and again hid it in her commonplace book, which she placed in the desk drawer. It was then she heard his voice. How many days since she'd seen him?

Thalia had told her there was to be a meeting of the Independence Men in one of the Raleigh's private rooms. Liberty looked out the folly door with an anticipation that was hard to hide. Noble had finally come. He dismounted from his stallion in the alley, exchanging a few words with Billy before slipping inside the ordinary.

He'd not looked her way once.

Hurt bloomed beneath her tightly laced bodice. Suddenly self-conscious, she pulled off her lace cap, plucked the pins from her hair, and finger-combed the untidy tresses into a top knot at the crown of her head, then pinned her cap back into place. Having settled the matter of Isabeau's indenture, would he now shun her as so many in Williamsburg did?

Pent up, she played the serinette, its airy notes jarring sourly with the lively fiddling in the taproom. Finally slipping out the door, she stepped into the humid twilight and took a turn about the garden, fan aflutter to keep insects away. A few paces took her to the back gate.

Why was she always drawn to Palace Green? Their townhouse had been so close while the Raleigh was a good quarter-hour walk to the Governor's Palace. If she cut across the back onto Nicholson Street her way would be shorter . . .

As always, Williamsburg was bustling even at night. A great many Patriots lived within its boundaries, occupying a cross-section of a few streets. Though empty, the town's crown jewel was still the Governor's Palace and had ever been.

As a child she'd been bewitched by the Palace's bricked gate guarded by a stone lion and unicorn. It hadn't helped that her father said if she was not good she would be the lion's supper. Now she stood outside those gates in the moonlit, mosquito-laden dusk, missing the lanthorn that shone like a star from the balustrade roof high above.

Oh, for another levee! A ball! If only she'd enjoyed her last evening here, not been pent up with worries about tardy fiancés and rebel escorts. If only time wound backward as well as forward . . .

She looked southeast. A full moon was rising, suspended like a gold locket in a darkening sky, casting the empty gardens and outbuildings in ghostly, almost ghastly light.

She wanted to pretend the governor and Lady Charlotte had just gone to Porto Bello, their plantation outside Williamsburg. But even then the Palace had never gone dark. It cut to the deepest part of her. Turning her back on it, she fled down Palace Green to the folly.

&

The next morning found her cradling her teacup outside the Raleigh kitchen, only there was no tea, not even liberty tea, just coffee. Thalia poured the black brew to the brim, a bit spilling into the saucer.

"That's a mighty fancy cup," Thalia whispered, as if Liberty might have snitched it.

"'Twas my mother's," Liberty answered. The puce and cobalt porcelain was Doccia, Mama's favorite, painted with a bucolic scene of a country estate looking disturbingly like Ty Mawr. Blessed she was to have saved even one teacup.

Thalia slipped her not one hot roll but two. The large kitchen had long been astir, half a dozen aproned servants at work well before daylight. Liberty smiled her thanks at Thalia's apron-clad mother at the heart of the kitchen.

"Them Independence Men never went to sleep." Casting a glance at the ordinary, Thalia murmured, "Up all night, the lot o' them, and callin' for plenty o' strong coffee this morn."

Liberty darted a glance at the ordinary. Was Noble still there? She'd lain awake wondering. "I'd best get to work."

Going to the well, she washed her cup and saucer before returning to the folly to set the prized porcelain on the fireplace mantel. Taking her usual position in the doorway, the rising sun her light, she chose her best needle. This morn she was pricking out a pattern, a strip of parchment encircling her lace pillow. If she'd not happened upon a bundle of pins in Norfolk, an answered prayer, she'd have resorted to using fish bones as some did.

She was trying to create a unique design of tiny flowers, leaves, and fans to gather into ruffles for ladies' lace sleeves, as well as adorn a special order for a christening gown. Her linen thread was ready, some new bobbins too. But would she be able to do the work *and* the Raleigh's mending?

Down a pathway came a laundress, a large basket on one hip. She left it just outside the folly doorway, and Liberty saw an abundance of shirts and a petticoat. All freshly laundered but in need of a button at the cuff or a resewn seam.

She set her lace pillow aside and readied a simple sewing needle and thread. The rising sun puddled in the doorway, making the details on the first shirt plain. 'Twas a gentleman's shirt, the twist of fabric very fine, needing only a restitched button at the collar. The discreet monogram at the hem was worked in indigo thread, a pleasing pairing with the snowy linen.

NR.

Noble's own? Her very bones seemed to melt. Lowering her head, she lifted the soft shirt to her face, shutting her eyes and breathing in the welcome scent. It smelled of summer and lye and wind and . . . him.

"Libby."

Her eyes flew open.

Noble's voice rose in question. "Enjoying your work?"

Drenched with embarrassment, she balled up the garment in her hands. Did he know she held his shirt? Surely he did. For all her hasty fumbling his monogram was still visible.

She raised her reluctant gaze to his. His all-night meeting was telling. Shadows lurked, turning his eyes more black than brown but for the strain of red. They warmed with a telltale amusement nevertheless.

"How goes it?" He leaned into the door frame. "Your lace work? The trip to Norfolk?"

Returning his shirt to the basket, she feigned nonchalance. "Well and good. And you? Ty Mawr?"

"The same."

Impatience flared. She wanted to skip past the pleasantries. She craved conversation. Depth. Standing up, she smoothed the wrinkles from her apron. "You've not come for small talk, have you? You're too busy for that."

His curt nod was confirmation. He extracted a letter from inside his coat, and his shifting expression told her it was not glad news. Reluctantly, she took the paper, noting the broken seal. The handwriting was vaguely familiar and tugged on some past part of her. She read it once. Twice. The accusatory tone turned her stomach.

She looked him steadfastly in the eye, but her voice shook. "I am not a spy." Had he shared this letter in his all-night meeting? She cringed at the thought. "Who knows of this?"

"Just you, me, Mistress Tremayne, the coward who penned it, and the letter bearer, Miss Shaw."

Cressida? Her stomach flipped. "She came to you with this? To Ty Mawr?"

"Aye. Yesterday."

Her eyes smarted. Was Cressida not her friend? Granted, she'd not seen any of the Shaws since she'd left the townhouse and had stopped going to church.

Noble was regarding her so intently she felt the need to defend herself. "My recent trip to Norfolk garnered orders for lace and naught else. I saw my father in Yorktown a month ago, and he all but threw me off the *Fowey*." Even now the hurt lingered. Swallowing, she forced mettle into her voice. "I am too busy to act as spy. Besides, I—"

"I didn't say I believed the letter, Libby."

His calm, his calling her Libby, took some of the sting away. "Then why did you bring it to me?"

"To warn you that there are people, supposed friends, who spread untruths about you. If you're thought a spy, bodily harm might come to you. Be on your guard. Go nowhere alone if you can help it."

"But I am alone—" She broke off, the weight of that lonesomeness widening. During her busy days she could bear it. 'Twas the long nights that bestirred her deepest worries.

All around them, the Raleigh was springing to life, people coming and going, the bake shop and apothecary now open. Thalia was at work in the garden, battling squash bugs that bedeviled her prized pumpkins. The laundresses were hanging linens. 'Twas a normal day in Williamsburg, yet Liberty sensed an undercurrent of tension, of something tearing at the very fabric of their ordinary lives. Hers had already been upended. Theirs would be too. She felt it and feared it, but what was she to do?

Her focus narrowed to Noble's sturdy silhouette, the rising sun behind him. She craved his sound-mindedness, his strength. She wanted to thank him for not suspecting the worst of her despite the tainting letter. But the words hung in her throat.

"I want to protect you, but I do not know how." He passed a hand over bloodshot eyes. "I am not your husband nor your suitor, simply a concerned friend."

She sensed all he could not say. She had been warned. Any harm that came to her was beyond his control. To be safe she could join her mother in Philadelphia or—and this next seemed patently unsafe—join her father aboard ship with the possibility of returning to England.

As much to bolster her spirits as to honor him, she said,

"How can I bow to fear when you Patriots risk all you hold dear?"

"I am a man with resources. You are a woman who has lost nearly everything except her ingenuity and pride."

"Pride? Is it wrong to want to make a way for myself? To remain in the place I was born and reared?"

"Nay, but you must not allow those things to override your reason. Your safety. Billy told me you went out in the dark last night down Palace Green."

Billy? "Just who is spying on whom, I wonder?" She flushed. "Betimes these folly walls . . ." She left off. She wouldn't bemoan her lot, or that the folly seemed hopelessly small, all her working hours confined to pins and thread. "The evening was so lovely I wanted to walk about. I needed to see the Palace." Would he understand this? The pull of the past, the yearning to return to a more settled time? She gave the letter back to him. "Have you any guess as to who wrote this about me?"

"Nay. Miss Shaw was not forthcoming. The writing hand is neither Miles Roth nor Doctor Hessel. That's all I know." He returned his hat to his head. "I'm off to Ty Mawr for a meal. And sleep." With a smile he added, "*Ffarwel*."

"*Ffarwel*," she called after him, sorry to see him go. For all she knew he was her one true friend in all of Williamsburg.

21

⁓⁓⁓

The next day fever struck the Raleigh. Thalia and some of the kitchen staff were first to succumb, and Mister Southall begged Liberty's help in the burgeoning garden. Her mending was gladly set aside for the more pressing matter of feeding diners and lodgers. New potatoes needed digging and green beans picked and the like. Salat also needed making, so Liberty filled two baskets with parsley, chervil, lettuce, and scallions.

But for young Billy, she'd have been rather helpless. Checking a grin, he assisted her between leading and fetching mounts for Raleigh patrons.

"Yer not a hand in the kitchen, miss?" he questioned. "Ye've not dug potatoes or picked greens before?"

"I have not," she confessed. "My education has been sorely lacking. But for you, Mister Southall might well turn me out."

He laughed at this, working all the harder alongside her. As they harvested what was needed in the hot sun, another sort of fever burned inside her, the fire kindled by accusation. Her fingers pinched at a stubborn weed, pulling it free of the soil like she wished she could do with the allegation.

Who had written that lie of a letter? Why had Cressida been the one to carry it? What was the reason it ended up with Noble Rynallt?

Spy?

If they were trying to turn Noble against her, they had failed. Or so she hoped. Would he one day believe it to be true? God forbid. For now, she wanted to repay him for his faith in her. Help him and his cause.

The next forenoon she tended Thalia's herb garden, a more pleasant pastime than the kitchen's vegetable garden. Sweet goldenrod stood tall and queen-like, shading sweet fern and spicebush and wild bergamot. Along with the leaves of the common raspberry, these were concocted into a pleasing blend of faux bohea. Her mother had wanted to plant their own liberty garden at the back of the townhouse, but her father forbade it.

How ironic her new name.

She felt anything but at liberty.

⟨⟨⟩⟩

The time was at hand. She chose her attire carefully, unearthing one of her best gowns from former days. Counting a few coins from Isabeau's indenture, she hired a coach and left at first light since the market traffic would soon glut the road. Besides, the daughter of an earl and the former lieutenant governor of Virginia Colony didn't travel on the back of a decrepit Raleigh mare.

Painted sage-green and black, the coach was the best to be had on short notice, the coachman experienced and courteous. The dusty miles flew by, and she was soon smelling the salt air and hearing the cry of gulls.

Beside her on the upholstered seat was a small basket filled to the brim with her father's favorite pastries from the bake shop. She ate one absently, but it was no match for bara brith. Either that or the coming confrontation soured her stomach.

Today the *Fowey* sat at anchor a safe distance from the dock where red-coated soldiers swarmed. It took several minutes, a few coquettish smiles, and the loss of two confections for her to be rowed to its bulk. The dinghy's oarsmen made quick work of the watery distance, and Liberty gave silent thanks for a fair day. The calm water mirrored the clear skies.

"Who goes there?" someone thundered from deck. At her name and request to see her father, she was hoisted up in a bosun chair, clutching her basket in one hand. Glad she was that kid leather covered hands that bore no resemblance to the Lady Elisabeth of before.

Looking back toward the wharf and the waiting carriage brought a cold dousing of dread. She and her father had not parted on the best terms. Would he remember her fury? The words she wished back? At least they gave her good reason to return. Her bun-filled basket would serve as the apology she had no heart to make.

The ship's captain, Montague, eyed her sternly from the bow as her feet touched deck. Smiling at him politely, knowing he could send her packing, she made a wide swath around him and followed a midshipman to her father's quarters below. One knock earned her entry, and she found herself facing the man she'd not seen for more than a month.

"You came alone?" he asked, rising from his desk.

Was he expecting Mama too? "Quite alone, yes." Forcing a smile, she held out the basket to him.

Closing the distance between them, he made a face. "We are in need of meat. Mutton. Pork. And you bring me sweets?"

Her smile slipped.

He set the basket on his desk and leaned against it, crossing his arms. "Why have you come?"

She swallowed down a barbed retort. "I'm sorry, Papa. Please forgive me for being so thoughtless. With Mama in Philadelphia, you are my only family here, are you not?" The sentiment was true, at least on this side of the Atlantic. But it did not dent his stiff demeanor, which made her subterfuge all the easier. "I've come with news . . . from Williamsburg."

At this his gaze sharpened. He gestured to a chair.

She sat, her legs unsteady, the pastry she'd eaten churning. "I thought it only fair to tell you that the rebels are mustering militia, some forty thousand across the colony."

"Go on."

"A plan has been hatched to march to Yorktown and send your fleet up the Chesapeake to prevent you from blocking the supply of rebel munitions from the West Indies."

His expression hardened. She took a breath, sensing his surprise. Her legs nearly cramped from the memory of crouching beneath the taproom's windows as she pulled weeds and tended plants in Thalia's stead, gleaning what she could. Scraps of news. Bits of hearsay she had embellished for this very moment.

"Where did you hear such?"

Her ruse was nearly flawless. "I am in Mister Southall's employ at his ordinary."

"The Raleigh?" His tone was flat. She couldn't tell whether disgust or astonishment was uppermost. "In his employ?"

"I had nowhere else to go."

"So you're in the very nest of the Independence Men, those beardless boys throwing Virginia Colony into woeful confusion."

Beardless boys? Hardly that. She wanted to laugh. "What's more, they have confiscated our home, all our belongings."

"You could have gone north with your mother."

Or to Ty Mawr. That impossibility alone wooed her. But she could hardly tell her father that.

She changed course. "Where are Lady Charlotte and the children?"

"Aboard the *Magdalena* en route to England."

'Twas her turn to be surprised. It meant Dunmore expected the worst. Gone were the carefree hours, the long walks and talks in the garden, the endless parade of new gowns and entertainments, and that full, joyous feeling of belonging, at least when she was with Lady Charlotte and the children.

She looked toward a porthole. "Yet you and Lord Dunmore and fellow Loyalists remain."

"To leave would be to admit defeat." He circled the desk and poured Madeira into a crystal goblet. "We shall soon move the fleet to Norfolk. 'Tis a Tory town full of Scots merchants loyal to the Crown. General Gage, who is headquartered in Boston, is sending reinforcements, but there seems to be a delay. Once they arrive, any colonial rabble bent on an uprising will be quelled." As if realizing he'd said too much, he took a long swallow.

She folded her hands in her lap, committing the details to memory, few though they were. "You spoke of meat. Are you in need of provisions?"

"We need supplies, aye. But we've sent men ashore to gather what we can from various plantations."

At gunpoint, she guessed. Was Ty Mawr a target? "I noticed a great many Negroes aboard ship."

He nodded. "We're offering freedom to any slaves and indentures who join our fleet."

"Then you will strike at Virginia's very heart." The powder keg her mother wrote of had been lit. Virginia's entire economy was driven by slaves and indentures.

"Our strategy is to quell the rebellion at all costs."

The door opened without a knock. Lord Dunmore entered, the smile he had for her reminding her of the one her father hadn't given. She stood. Curtsied. Only at his directive did she sit down again. Courtly protocol still ruled whether she was aboard the *Fowey* or in the Palace.

"A shame you did not sail with Lady Dunmore," he remarked as her father poured him Madeira. "The long journey would have been better for all concerned."

She felt a final qualm. If Noble had gotten her lost letter away from Patrick Henry and returned it in time . . . Nay, there was no room for regret, no turning back the clock.

"My daughter has been telling me news from the capital. The rebels are mustering militia and whatnot. Our townhouse has been confiscated, so I suppose the Palace will be next."

"Porto Bello as well." She suppressed a smile. In truth, she rather enjoyed painting a rosy picture of the Patriots, endowing them with all sorts of furbelows and fancies meant to inspire alarm. But 'twas a sticky web of deceit. She added, "Rumor is the royal residence will serve the new Williamsburg mayor."

Both men studied her. Flummoxed. Transfixed.

She grew bold. "I am confident that will be none other than Patrick Henry."

Dunmore's disgust was unveiled. "Better that than the conniving Washington. Commander in chief of the Continental renegades, or some such nonsense."

Her father's eyes never left her. "What of the Patriots Noble Rynallt and Thomas Jefferson? They continue fomenting sedition with quill and ink, do they not?"

"I am unsure of Jefferson, as I've not seen him around Williamsburg of late. 'Tis no secret he prefers the country—Monticello—to town. As for Rynallt, I know very little." Alarmed now, she felt the need to protect Noble at all costs. "Word is he is keeping company with George Rogers Clark. They are rumored to be going west to enlist natives to help fight the Crown."

This was pure fabrication, but it hit the mark. Her father nearly choked on his drink. She felt vastly pleased. But would they believe it? Dunmore had courted the Indians in the past, was no doubt counting on their help in subduing the Virginians. She'd heard he'd sent emissaries west recently to do that very thing.

"You are certainly a pretty parcel of information." Dunmore set down his empty glass. "Perhaps you should journey to the coast more often. Bring news from the capital. The arrangement might prove beneficial to us both."

"Indeed." Her father reached into his waistcoat and removed a small velvet pouch. "Return in seven days' time, or sooner should the occasion warrant."

Reluctant, she took the money pouch, thereby accepting their terms. Did this make her a spy? Was she now consorting with the enemy? Half sick, she nodded and let herself out, following the waiting midshipman through the bowels of the *Fowey* and beyond.

Across the sun-polished deck she went to the waiting dinghy, all a blur of wind and salty spray and the stare of a great many curious sailors who were witness to her comings and goings.

The waiting coach was suffocating in the July heat. Even with the shades raised she felt she'd been shoved into a bake oven. She needed air. Stillness. As they neared the fork in the road leading to Ty Mawr, her resistance gave way. She could not go another mile. Paying no heed to the surprise of the coachman, she got out and motioned him on before beginning a slow walk along the roadside. Only when he was out of sight did she turn down the gated alley that led to Ty Mawr.

Such beauty here. Such peace. The rustling shade of countless trees was a balm to both body and spirit. She who was accustomed to town life with all its colorful confusion was now starved for quieter places. She walked on slowly, not so much from fatigue as from a heightened awareness. There was so much more to be had on foot than in a conveyance.

Mulberry Island was attached to the mainland by a bridge of land, its command of the James River unsurpassed. Acres of farmland sprawled as far as she could see, some of it tilled and planted, some fallow. Ty Mawr crowned a knoll on the northern end of the island, a quarter mile more at most.

Throat parched, she stumbled over a stone in the roadbed. Once she would have settled for nothing less than a crystal dish of ice cream. A tall glass of lemonade. Now she welcomed well water in a bucket. Never had she felt so unattractive, sweat stains beneath her arms and beading her upper lip, the grit of dust between her teeth. Her gown of silk lustring was lightweight, her skirts rising like a sail in the warm wind, her hem soiled from walking.

The uphill climb to the big house seemed endless. She looked to the ditch, grassy and colored by wildflowers. Exhaustion tore at her. She wanted nothing more than to sit down and go no further.

Lord, help Thou me.

Caught between two worlds she was, belonging nowhere, neither here nor there. Williamsburg was no longer home. Ty Mawr was no more hers than the Williamsburg townhouse.

Yet it rose up in the distance, a sort of refuge, its bricked entrance and porch tower stalwart against the blue horizon. She recalled the crushed-shell path. Circular brick steps. A wide door with a heavy knocker, all very Welsh.

Would the master even be at home?

22

Noble trod a white sand walkway through fragrant flowers he could not name, intent on a brick wall at the southeast end of the garden. Built as a windbreak to protect the planting beds, it now served another purpose, more a redoubt erected for military defense. He stood behind its bulk and raised his spyglass.

The James came into sharp focus, the gold glitter of sunlit water making him squint. Normally the sheer beauty before him would be cause for praise. Now it only reminded him of all that was at stake.

"See anythin' of merit, sir?" A gust of wind snatched Dougray's Scots burr away. "Anythin' at all?"

"A bateaux or two."

"Who'd have thought the high and mighty Dunmore would turn pirate, plunderin' plantations and the like."

"It bespeaks desperation," Noble replied. The white sweep of a gull drew his gaze upward. On such a summer day all talk of Dunmore's pirating seemed laughable as Blackbeard's ghost.

"Nary a redcoat I see by water. But land is altogether

different." Dougray's attention shifted. "Best train your sights on the lane, sir."

Noble turned. The spyglass came down. Across the long sweep of green pasture was a windblown woman, the ribbons on her straw hat a-dance.

Libby?

There was no denying the sudden lift of his pulse. Handing the spyglass to Dougray, he began to walk in her direction. Libby here. Why? And on foot. In a fancy dress to boot.

Gone was the workaday garb. She was Lady Elisabeth again, Williamsburg's bride, her attire from head to toe London made. He knew little about women's fashion, but he knew quality. British goods. The pale yellow of her gown was the ground for embroidered floral sprays, her lace sleeves twin to the lace on her hat, which shadowed her comely features.

He could hardly take his eyes off her to watch his step on the uneven lawn. At last they met beneath an ancient, gnarled chestnut. He said nothing in greeting. His surprise eclipsed words. She knew she was welcome and he wouldn't belabor that.

Unsmiling, she met his eyes. "I've just seen my father." Her voice seemed brittle, empty of emotion. "Dunmore's fleet will soon sail to Norfolk. They're awaiting reinforcements from General Gage and are running low on provisions." She paused, eyes trailing from his face to the small velvet pouch she carried by a silken cord. "They have put out a call for all slaves and indentures to join them in exchange for their freedom."

"So he told you?"

"Indeed. What's more, he asked about you by name."

"Honored," he said wryly.

"I told him you would soon be on the frontier with George

Rogers Clark, enlisting the Indian nations in your cause for liberty."

His half smile gave way to a deep-throated chuckle. "Did you now?"

"'Twas an outright untruth, but I fear you may be in danger with their fleet so near Ty Mawr."

He could believe it. But 'twas the plan to sway slaves and indentures that most nettled him. "Anything else?"

"In seven days' time he expects a report on what is happening in Williamsburg." She dangled the pouch from a lace-mitted hand. "I was given this today."

He took the pouch and opened it, spilling an abundance of gold guineas into his callused palm. "He's rewarded you handsomely."

"I shan't touch it." Revulsion colored her tone. "'Tis meant for the poorhouse my mother founded."

"Why did you see him again?"

"If I'm accused of spying, why not?" She attempted a smile, but it failed to reach her eyes. "Only I'll bring any news to you Patriots. Which means I've chosen sides."

The gravity of what she'd done was not lost on him.

Her expression turned entreating. "Do you believe me?"

The question dug at him. "I'd be a fool not to."

She studied him and softened visibly. "Perhaps at the very heart of this is my desire to repay your earlier kindness to me. 'Tis in my power to help, even in a small way."

"I expect no recompense, Libby." Returning the coin pouch, he came alongside her and took her elbow, steering her toward the house. A backward glance told him she'd not been followed, at least that he could see. "How did you get to Yorktown?"

"I hired a coach but sent it back to Williamsburg. I wasn't

feeling well. Being aboard ship left me so rattled . . ." She left off, clearly shaken.

"You know my door is always open to you." They stepped into the shade of the entrance tower, and then he ushered her into the cool foyer.

Mistress Tremayne soon hurried down the steps, her chatelaine clinking like a chime, her face alight at the sight of their guest. "Lady Liberty? Welcome." She went to a tapestried wall and pulled on a bell cord. "You're just in time for refreshments."

Liberty simply nodded. She'd removed her wide-brimmed hat, revealing a lace pinner beneath. She looked decidedly unwell. Her high flush spoke to the tumultuous events of her morning, her long walk. Or was it something more?

"The Round Room," Noble said, knowing Liberty would like it. Circular and small, the milk-paint walls were the serene green of the millpond in back of Ty Bryn. A calming color, Enid always said.

He moved to open a riverfront door that led to an outer portico. Dougray was still at watch along the wall, spyglass in hand. The irony of the situation was not lost on him. Here sat Liberty in his parlor while her ousted father was raiding plantations along the James, or sending his minions to do the deed for him and Dunmore instead. For all he knew they might all meet at once in his parlor.

Awkwardness threaded the room as he thought their situation through. She had no way back to Williamsburg. He'd need to provide a carriage. Mayhap send Isabeau along, as he didn't want Libby alone. She looked so spent he stayed silent, glad when the promised refreshments were brought. Isabeau came in next, making a lot of noise, and though her former mistress looked happy to see her, Libby stayed subdued.

Isabeau rattled off a string of rapid French, to which Liberty answered so adroitly Noble's curiosity piqued. He understood little of the language and could only guess at the maid's chatter.

"*Vous avez l'air malade.*"

He guessed *malade* was not a compliment. It sounded dire, punctuated with Isabeau's frown. Libby rallied, replying with a musical volley that had no end, making him regret he'd chosen Latin over the Romance languages.

"Pardon." Libby looked his way at last. "Former habits are hard to mend. My mother, being part French, wanted a native maid for me so I could learn French conversation—"

"Which you seem to have perfected," he replied.

A slight smile. "Only to you non-French speakers, perhaps." She finished her lemonade and studied the tray Mistress Tremayne had brought crowded with sweetmeats, then gestured to a small dish decorated with candied violets. "And this is . . . ?"

"Fairy butter, made up of sugar and orange flower water," Mistress Tremayne replied proudly. "It pairs well with the gingerbread."

Though Noble guessed Libby didn't feel like eating, she made over the lovely offering, leaving his housekeeper beaming.

"And these meringues are colored a pale pink with a bit of beet juice," his housekeeper said.

Libby took one, declaring it divine.

"I shall tell the baker, who will be quite pleased." Mistress Tremayne turned to leave the room, a reluctant Isabeau in tow. At the door, she asked, "Will you be lodging here tonight, m'lady?"

A slight pause. Libby looked down at her bodice as if missing her timepiece. Likely auctioned off along with the jewelry case. He rued he'd not bid on more of her belongings.

He spoke in her stead. "In case her ladyship decides to stay, ready the best room on the second floor."

Not the attic. He was expecting no guests, and if there were some, he was done with her hiding. It was now midafternoon. If Libby changed her mind, his stable could supply her with a means to Williamsburg at any hour, but if he read her right she had no wish to go.

"The best second-floor room, sir? That would be the chamber next to dear Enid's then," his housekeeper said. At his nod, both she and Isabeau went out.

Her voice came soft. "You must miss your sister very much."

He wasn't expecting this, though Enid was never far from his thoughts. Somehow Liberty made the mention less sore. "Aye."

"I met her once at a party given by Lady Charlotte. I remember Enid as amiable. Kind." Her gaze lifted to the ceiling's elegant plasterwork with its medallions and flourishes. "She spoke of redecorating Ty Mawr."

"This was her favorite room. She didn't want it altered so left it alone."

"'Tis beautiful, all the greens. Tranquil. Like being in the woods." She sat back, seeming more at ease though her color was still high.

He felt a qualm. Summer fevers were commonplace in the Southern colonies, a few deadly. Hadn't Hessel said she was prone to illness? "Are you feeling unwell, Libby?"

She returned her gaze to him. "Why do you ask?"

"The house is cool. You're flushed. I heard of a fever going round Williamsburg."

"I'm only weary from the day's events." She tried to smile, but it fell far short of the winsome woman he knew. "You needn't worry about me, Mister Rynallt."

Liberty finished a tall glass of lemonade and ate both a meringue and gingerbread spread with fairy butter, unwilling to dint Mistress Tremayne's delight. She sat alone with Noble, too weary to care about any impropriety. Too disturbed by her time aboard the *Fowey* to relinquish the comfort of Ty Mawr. It felt safe to sit here in this lovely old room. It felt familiar and reassuring to be in silk and not the garb of a lacemaker. She was not a tradeswoman. She might never be. 'Twas like trying to fit a round cog in a square hole. Forced. Unnatural. Exhausting.

Lacemaking for pleasure was a far cry from lacemaking for profit.

She pulled off her mitts and looked at her hands. She understood the doctor's dismay now. There was nothing wrong with work-worn hands, but mightn't she use her wits and genteel wiles in a more indispensable way?

"I believe the role of spy may well suit me."

Noble looked hard at her. She read his consternation. To his credit, he stayed silent.

"I take back what I said about giving all those guineas to the poorhouse. They might be of better use in my ruse as a spy for the Patriots."

"You don't know what you're saying."

She lifted her shoulders. "I shall learn as I go."

"And endanger your life in the bargain—"

"While helping many," she said in a rare interruption. "You Patriots must have something afoot, some secret intelligence plan in place."

He regarded her for a long minute, then took a letter from his waistcoat, opened it, and read, "'The necessity

229

of procuring good intelligence is apparent and need not be further urged—all that remains for me to add is that you keep the whole matter as secret as possible. For upon secrecy, success depends.'"

"And the author?"

"General Washington."

"Then why not?"

He returned the letter to his waistcoat. "What are your motives, Libby?"

She felt a little jolt. Did he think her bitter? Rebellious? "You suspect I simply want to strike back at my father." Did he believe her so low? "'Tis unfounded, if so. Granted, I am angry at his actions—"

"Anger is a shaky foundation for espionage."

"You *do* know French," she teased, wanting to lighten the mounting tension between them. "The fact is I've always been at odds with my father. We've been estranged since my birth. I was not the son he wanted. He never forgave my mother, or me, for that. I was seldom allowed an opinion, a voice, till now."

"What makes you more Patriot than Loyalist?"

"My father's rule. 'Tis like the king's and Parliament's. Unreasonable. Tyrannical. Absolute."

Her handsome host still looked doubtful.

She said quietly, "Do you want something nobler?"

"I want you safe. Far from the fray."

"But that I am not, being Lord Stirling's daughter." She toyed with the velvet pouch and finally spoke what was foremost on her heart. "I'm sorry about my father. His character."

"'Tis not your fault, Libby."

"I am still ashamed for him. Of him."

"Let the Lord make a gentleman of him."

She stilled, warmed by the gracious thought. "Can one make a silk purse from a sow's ear?"

"If the Almighty can take an undertrained, undermanned Continental Army and pit them against the world's largest fighting force and win, all else is of little consequence."

"Then I'm inspired to continue my work. 'Tis a perfect ruse, is it not? Discarded daughter turned lacemaker by day. Spy by night." She went a step further. "I wonder what Mister Henry would say?"

The dismay in her host's usually stoic face assured her that Patrick Henry would warm to her plans. He hated her father and Lord Dunmore. What sweeter revenge than to have them brought down with the aid of a daughter?

Noble passed a hand over his jaw. "Look to your conscience, Libby. Aside from the risk, can you live with the consequences? Not only a permanent estrangement from your father but the loss of all you hold dear, an irrevocable cutting of past ties."

"I've been estranged from my father my entire life. And I've just discovered I have few true friends. Besides, *estrangement* seems the word of the day. This is nearly war. Even the most congenial of families are turning against one another. Look at the Randolphs."

"Aye, brother against brother . . ." He left off as if weary of the subject. "Your room is ready for you if you want to go upstairs."

She did not protest. She was the first to break their gaze, let down that their talk was at an end. Only it wasn't truly at an end, not on her part, on account of her new purpose.

'Twas another beginning.

23

"I fear the worst, sir." Mistress Tremayne faced him in the glare of light through the study windows. "Her ladyship has slept through supper and now breakfast, and 'tis nearly noon. Mightn't the doctor be sent for?"

Never had his housekeeper intervened like this. 'Twas a testament to her fondness for Libby. He studied her, weighing his dilemma. Mayhap Mistress Tremayne had a mild touch of Isabeau's hysteria? Had the maid put her up to it? Or was his own calm uncalled for? Granted, his disappointment went deep when Libby had not joined him for supper. She was clearly worn down, the events of the summer catching up with her. And that was the end of it. Or so he'd thought. But women sometimes sensed things men didn't.

Having a recovering Tory beneath his roof was one thing. A dead one, altogether different.

"Have you checked for signs of sickness?" He was out of his depth doctoring. Leave that to Hessel and other physics. "Fever?"

"She seems quite flushed. She's not even awakened to take so much as a sip of water."

He didn't like the sound of that. But call in Hessel? Nay. He mulled his options for a few tense seconds. "Prepare a tray. Broth. Bread. Some of that English tea I suspect you of secreting." She managed a small wince at the mention. "Bring it to me and I'll take it up to her."

"You, sir?"

"Aye. I'll not rest till I see her myself and warrant if Hessel needs sending for."

The tray was promptly brought. Isabeau stood in the foyer, occupied with her usual hand-wringing. When she started up the stairs after him, he balked. "Stay below and help Mistress Tremayne."

"But, sir—" The threat of indecency raised her voice. "*Merci!*"

Leaving her below, he prayed the rest of the way up, pausing to balance the tray in one hand while grasping the doorknob with the other, marveling the servants did it with such grace. Unsure of what he'd find, he swung the door open slowly after a cursory knock, its noisy hinges in need of oiling.

The room smelled stale, the heavy drapes and shutters drawn closed. He set down the tray and opened one window, letting in light and fresh air before turning to the bed with its mosquito netting. Lifting that, he looked down at Libby. Still flushed. Still asleep. Even lovelier than he remembered, if that was possible, her hair loosely braided, the neck of her nightgown encircled with delicate lace trim.

Gingerly, he brought a chair near the edge of the bed. 'Twas scandalous, this. For a moment he had second thoughts. He wasn't sure of her reaction, but his intentions were honorable enough. Sitting there, contemplating an exit, he nearly forgot to breathe. Should he wake her? Surely sleeping round the clock was enough. One needed to eat, do other things . . .

She slept on, allowing him an unhindered look at her. She resembled her mother more than her father, but Lord Stirling was there in the arch of her brow and fair hair. He placed his palm lightly on her forehead, then her soft cheek. Fever, nay. Sheer exhaustion, aye.

He swallowed, wanting to say her name, but it seemed to stick in his throat. Nay, more was needed. He hesitated, on the verge of something momentous, at least to him. Something far sweeter.

"*Anwylyd.*"

He said it once, twice, never having spoken it to another living being. But it came unbidden, rising from his heart to his lips.

She stirred like a cat, eyes shut but stretching her arms over her head as if awakening from the soundest sleep. When she saw him, pleasure trumped surprise, even if his being here was shockingly unconventional. She smiled so broadly the dimple in her cheek all but disappeared. "Are you my guardian angel come to rouse me?"

He chuckled. "Mayhap you've risen from the dead."

A slow awareness came to her then. She half sat up. "What is the hour?"

"Nearly dinner." Two o'clock was Ty Mawr's usual time, at least.

"Then I have not missed it."

Relief turned him lighthearted. "Nay, but the rest of us have been missing you." Reaching out, he plumped another pillow to go behind her.

"I suspect Isabeau has called you to arms." Her face darkened like a storm cloud passing over. "Goaded you into coming up here like this."

"Nay. She is quite put out I'm here. 'Twas Mistress Tremayne's doing."

"Oh. I'm sorry to be so worrisome."

"Never that. I've brought you something from the kitchen."

He rose and served her the broth and tea, now cooled considerably, then took a chair again. "A motion has been made to call the doctor."

"Hessel? Nay, please." She looked grave again, her gaze a troubled blue as it held his. "I am not ill, just . . ."

"Heartsick, mayhap," he said.

A quiver of her chin gave her away, and her eyes filled. Aye, heartsick.

He swallowed, moved by her emotion and the fact that he'd read her so well. "The Welsh have a word for it. *Hiraeth*. 'Tis a longing for home or what once was. A grief for the lost people and places of the past." He went slowly, giving her time to say something if she would. "Just remember, you are homeless but not rootless. A guest, but not unwelcome. If I could fix things for you I would. 'Tis a man's nature to remedy matters. Find solutions. But there is no answer for *hiraeth*, not that I know of."

"This *hiraeth* you speak of, have you ever felt it?"

"Aye. It rises up unbidden at odd times and places." He'd oft felt it over Enid. The loss of his parents. The absence of his brother. Even aboard ship leaving Wales and coming to Virginia long ago. Sometimes it still came over him as he walked about on a lonely stretch of beach or in a field, or felt the sheer expanse of the night. It even came when he let his thoughts drift and foresaw a future alone, without a wife and children.

She leaned back against the bank of pillows. "'Tis as acute as any physical illness." Her sorrow was palpable, and he longed to give her some relief, something to ease the strain and weariness lining her face. "'Tis sad there is no remedy. Not this side of heaven, perhaps."

True enough. But there was a scriptural anecdote at least. *Be thankful in all circumstances.* "To counter it we must make the most of what we have been given."

"Then I must eat. Dress. Thank you for your hospitality."

"No need for the latter."

She attempted a smile. "But I must. You needn't stay. I know you have other things to tend to, Noble."

'Twas the first time she had ever said his name. And it left him flushing like a schoolboy, hardly the seasoned master of Ty Mawr.

Isabeau was rummaging through a wardrobe and finally took out a garment, smiling her pleasure. She had recovered from the shock of Ty Mawr's master in the bedchamber, impropriety aside. "How glad I am we have some female attire here, given your trunk is in Williamsburg." Holding a garment aloft for Liberty to see, she fingered the embroidered sash. "For today you will wear this sultana, *non?*"

"*Non.* Sultanas are for lounging. I must return to Williamsburg. Mister Southall will wonder where I've gone to." No telling what work awaited after a busy weekend at the Raleigh. Her Sabbath rest was over. Reluctant but determined, she pushed back the bedcovers and put bare feet to the floor.

Isabeau frowned. "But, mistress, you are exhausted and must stay on till—"

"I am not the mistress of Ty Mawr, just the lacemaker and seamstress at the Raleigh." Impatience made her sound imperious. "Please go below and ask about a way back to Williamsburg."

Isabeau stood her ground, clutching the sultana to her chest. "First I must help you dress."

"No need. I've learnt to dress myself. Front-lacing stays are a godsend." Liberty softened her tone. "Perhaps Ninian can help with a conveyance. I don't want Mister Rynallt disturbed."

At the mere mention of Ninian, Isabeau brightened and went out, leaving the silky sultana for another day. The bedchamber stilled, and Liberty surveyed it in a way she hadn't upon arrival. In some ways it reminded her of her townhouse bedroom with its bright chintz and cherry furnishings. A sumptuous room, made all the dearer from the memories she and Noble had just made.

Her fingers stilled on the knot she tied in her stays. What had he called her at first? Before she'd opened her eyes? He'd spoken in Welsh, a word she'd never heard. *Anwylyd.* The mystery of it begged unraveling, but the lovely word, the tender way he'd said it, meant she could not ask Mistress Tremayne. For now she would just hold it close. And wonder.

A movement out the window led her to the glass. Noble was down by the river. The spring shad and herring season was over, and the wharf was absent of netting and labor and the reek of fish. He was crouched on shore, boots planted firmly in shell-strewn mud, studying something. Footprints? Trespassers? With the British fleet raiding plantations in the dead of night, no smokehouse or cellar was safe. Her worries about Ty Mawr swelled. She'd not be a burden or distraction for its master any longer.

She dressed, wearing the simple clothes she had on yesterday, a fichu about her shoulders, sturdy shoes on her feet. A look in the glass told her she was nearly ready, but her soul chafed at being on her way again. Now for her hair . . .

Half an hour later she came down the stairs, Ninian awaiting her. Liberty looked out the open front door to the chosen coach, not the one bearing the Rynallt crest but a simpler unmarked one, all black. 'Twas certainly how she felt.

Mistress Tremayne's bustling took away some of the sting of leaving. She appeared with good cheer, carrying a hamper filled to the brim with edibles.

"Might I ask one last thing?" Liberty looked down the long foyer with its many doors, wondering which led to the music room. "I should like to see my harp."

"Of course. 'Tis yours, m'lady." Mistress Tremayne led Liberty to another lovely room, this one holding Enid's spinet. Liberty's harp rested between two tall windows, so placed it seemed the showpiece. "I have a fondness for the harp. And I've long heard you play like an angel. My hope is that one day you'll give us a private concert."

"One day, perhaps." But Liberty had no heart to play. Though she loved her music, it seemed to have little place in her present life.

"Shan't I alert Mister Rynallt, m'lady? Surely he'd want to bid you goodbye."

"Nay, no need to disturb him. I've taken enough of his time."

"Very well then."

Thanking her, Liberty turned to leave Ty Mawr.

'Twould be the last time, surely.

⁂

"Well, I'll be switched." Thalia stood in the folly's open doorway, face shiny from the heat, fully recovered from her fever. "You is back, but there's been a line o' folk to yo' door payin' a Sabbath call."

"Oh?" Liberty poked another pin in the lace pattern she was working.

"The good doctor came first and saw to my fever. And then comes Reverend Bracken. After him was that highfalutin Miss Shaw." Thalia was studying her closely as if gauging her reaction.

Liberty felt revulsion. "Miss Shaw?"

"She likely be back," Thalia replied darkly, returning to her gardening.

And so she was.

The next afternoon Liberty watched Cressida alight from her chaise, a basket in hand. Cressida never rose early, she remembered. She liked to stay up late reading novels when she wasn't out and about, devouring *Tristam Shandy* and *Pamela* like the finest treacle. Watching her approach, Liberty saw her in a harsher light. Cosseted. Fickle. Vain. As she herself once was . . . perhaps was still.

"My dear Lizzy!" Cressida embraced her, the glint of tears in her eyes unsettling.

Who was the finer actress of the two? Liberty squashed a spasm of guilt. Perhaps the both of them belonged on stage.

"My dear friend, how long it has been." Adjusting to her mask, her new identity, Liberty feigned pleasure. "Please, come in, have a seat." She gestured to the only other chair in the folly, a crude, cane-seated one with a short leg. Cressida's dismay was Liberty's delight.

Though she looked askance at it, Cressida finally sat, passing Liberty the basket. "Mama thought you might have need of some sweetmeats."

Liberty settled the offering on her lap, looking to the corner where the empty hamper from Ty Mawr rested. "Please thank her for me." This was heartfelt, at least. Thalia would enjoy them if she couldn't.

"Doctor Hessel told me you were here, and then I met up

with Reverend Bracken." Opening a fan, Cressida waved it at a mosquito, taking the folly in at a glance. "Since you've not been to church I feared you would be fined."

Church. In the tumult of the last month, Liberty had given it little thought except when the bells pealed. And no one had leveled a fine at her either.

"No doubt the reverend came to tell you there's a call for fasting, humiliation, and prayer in response to all the turmoil."

"How fitting." Once glib, Liberty fell into a strained silence. But how could it be otherwise when everything she said might be used against her?

"Tell me, Lizzy. How are you doing all alone here?"

"I'm hardly alone." Liberty worked to keep the chill from her tone. "The Raleigh sets a brisk pace. I have my lacemaking besides."

"But your father is aboard ship, and your dear mother . . ." Cressida reached into her purse and withdrew a pamphlet. "Your family has all the makings of a scandalous novel."

Liberty took the paper, on tenterhooks. A call of men to arms? No—Mama was in print again. And using her pen to pound Parliament and the king. She was even making bold use of her title to boot. *Lady Stirling* was sure to enrage the estranged earl of Stirling.

Liberty read the article hastily, nearly wincing at Mama's heaping scorn on all Loyalists. She lingered on the last melodramatic lines hailing the American Patriots.

> Glory and victory and lasting fame
> Will crown their arms and bless each hero's name.

Liberty handed back the paper. "'Tis old news—she and my father are at odds and have ever been."

"And you, Lizzy? Are you trapped between your Loyalist father and rebel mother?"

Liberty set the basket aside and returned her lace pillow to her lap, adjusting the bobbins. She had little time for idle talk. "I pray for peace." That much was true. "And you? Will you take sides?"

Cressida lifted her chin, her gaze sweeping the folly a final time. "I try not to think about it. My aim is simply to go on with life as we know it. In time I hope to marry and have a family."

"Oh?" Liberty worked her thread unwaveringly. "And your suitor?"

"Don't you recall?" Cressida's fan fluttered more rapidly. "Noble Rynallt of Ty Mawr most intrigues me."

"An Independence Man? Shouldn't you choose a fence-sitter? A Lukewarm like yourself?"

Cressida drew back. "Like your Miles Roth, you mean?"

"Mister Roth is not mine, not any longer. He is yours for the taking."

"Ha!" Cressida made a disagreeable face. "Word is he's in debt to his ears and in danger of losing Roth Hall."

"Then perhaps your family's newfound money can save him."

Snapping her fan shut, Cressida stood, the slur to the Shaws' middling merchant roots finding purchase. "Better *that* than your illustrious family's complete and utter collapse on this side of the Atlantic." She moved toward the door amid a whisper of striped polonaise taffeta and the unmistakable scent of lavender water.

She did not say goodbye. Nor did Liberty.

24

At three o'clock on a Friday afternoon the Raleigh Tavern was mostly empty. A flaxen-haired lad pushed a broom, sweeping up peanut shells and bread crumbs from the midday rush. Noble chose a window side table with a clear view of the folly. The scene was far more picturesque than the ale-saturated taproom.

Beyond the wide windowsill, red poppies and pink hollyhocks softened the fence lines as Thalia picked beans and Liberty sewed beneath the folly's eaves. The clatter from the kitchen house was offset by birdsong and the tantalizing aroma of baking bread.

'Twas hot. The hottest day thus far in a roiling, rebellious summer. James Southall had just run a red Patriot flag up the flagpole, twin to the one flying on the town's liberty pole, sure to inflame any remaining Loyalists in Williamsburg. Patrick Henry was standing beneath it, looking pleased as punch. With an affirming slap on the back, Henry left Southall and half sprinted up the walkway, late for his meeting with Noble.

Henry hung his hat from a wall peg and straddled a chair backward. The barkeep brought him a tankard of ale without his asking.

"So, Rynallt, what say ye?"

"You called this meeting. What say ye?"

Taking a swallow of ale, foam on his upper lip, Henry grunted. "I've a touchy matter to discuss." Letting go of his drink, he looked about and lowered his voice. "What can you tell me about that chit, Lord Stirling's daughter?"

Noble's hackles rose though he stayed stoic. Chit? "Lady Liberty, you mean."

"Liberty, is it? Aye. Who else? I have it on good authority she's spying for her father. Working here and gathering information for the Loyalists while playing Patriot. 'Tis going round in common circles. My maid told me. She's a gabby one, Becky. 'Twill be the talk of Virginia erelong."

Noble sent another look out the window in Libby's direction, glad she wasn't privy to their talk. "I was shown a note about the same from Miss Cressida Shaw. It begs belief. I confronted her ladyship about it. Showed her the accusation. She's not guilty of spying."

"Well, mayhap she can be convinced. We're in dire need of information if we're to outfox Dunmore's fleet and hold Virginia."

"Nay. 'Tis too dangerous."

"'Tis perfect. She's well connected. Comely. Clever. Capable of eviscerating her father's schemes."

"You would do that? Cause lasting enmity between a father and daughter?" Noble stared at him. "Place her in untold danger?"

"I would. These are desperate times. My only question is this—can she be trusted? Are you quite sure she's not working for her father and Dunmore? Spying on their behalf in even the mildest form?"

"Nay." He'd raised the question himself more times than he could count. "I'm a good judge of character. She rings true."

"Only because you're in love with her."

Noble's ale came down with a thud. "You don't know that."

Henry chuckled scornfully. "I'm a good judge of character," he parroted. "But beware. Love scrambles all our brains and casts a rosy glow on even the most undeserving."

"I say leave her alone. Time will tell."

"Time is against us. Meanwhile the British are besieging Boston and plotting more mischief up and down the coast. We need to know Dunmore's plans, whether or not he'll remain in Yorktown or move elsewhere, how supportive of him is General Gage, if there's any truth to the rumor he's about to arm Virginia's slaves and indentures."

"Look elsewhere for your spy then."

"Ha!" Henry drank down his ale and slapped a shilling atop the scarred table. "None have her credentials." Rising, he reached for his hat. "I'll go talk to her."

"Here and now?" Noble stood, his ale unfinished. "In broad daylight? Have a care, man."

"All right then. I'll leave it to you to arrange a meeting."

Noble waited till nightfall, taking Williamsburg's back streets to again join fellow delegates at the Governor's Palace to see what might be made of it. Mayor's residence? Soldiers' barracks? Hospital? Like most everything else, the questions met with no answers, and they soon went their separate ways.

He walked through the abandoned Palace gardens, the

yew hedge scraggly, weeds encroaching on the once pristine walkways. A thick melancholy pervaded the place. Twilight Williamsburg, the stately Palace Green, and all the raucous laughter from the town's many taverns did little to dispel the darkness around him or inside him.

God help him, but he cared enough for Libby that if something happened, if she was harmed or hanged or even spirited away on a ship to England, he'd have no peace the rest of his days. He feared what his fellow Patriots might do. Henry, though brilliant and as fearless a leader as Washington, could be rash, even callous. Libby was dispensable to him, a casualty of war if it came to that. And it would come, aye.

The folly was lit by a single candlestick. Libby could ill afford more light. The soft notes of the serinette threaded through the darkness. Did she miss her harp? Mistress Tremayne had told him she'd asked to see it before she left Ty Mawr.

He tipped his hat to an old acquaintance and pushed the back gate open, his chest tight with anticipation. A full moon shone ten o'clock. She'd likely be abed soon, as the workday started long before first light.

He wished for something to give her, to see a smile warm her face. He had no desire to do what he was about to do. It would only alarm her. Or give her a ruinous connection. Or both.

"Lady Elisabeth." He felt a twinge at the formality. The old address died hard. She'd come to be Libby to him, and he seldom thought of her otherwise.

"Mister Rynallt?"

So she in turn bypassed Noble. "Aye, your humble servant," he said. He looked toward the bustling Raleigh. "Blow the taper out."

A pause, then the requested darkness. "Are you courting scandal, sir?"

"Nay, just honest conversation." He sat down on the door-step, back to her. The scrape of her chair told him she was near. "Beware of Patrick Henry."

"Mister Henry?" Amusement lifted her voice. "Has he gone over to the Loyalists?"

"When Hades freezes over. He means to make a spy of you."

"That won't require much doing. 'Tis already decided."

He felt sick to his boots. "Nay, Libby."

"My father is expecting me, Noble."

"For what purpose?"

"You well know the answer. He's expecting me to play the meek and obliging daughter. Ferreting out information on you Independence Men." Leaning nearer, she pressed something into his hand. "This is an invitation to a ball aboard the *Otter*. My father has left the *Fowey* and is now at anchor in Norfolk."

"A ball?" The words were torn with disbelief. At such a time as this?

"Their fleet has a great many devoted subjects there, more than Yorktown. I received the summons day before yesterday."

He pocketed the note. Yorktown was nearer Ty Mawr than Norfolk. She was moving away from him, well beyond his protective reach. His mind raced with implications. The shortage of women. The debauched Royal Navy. Too many eligible naval officers. A hasty departure to England or the West Indies, never to return.

"I only ask that Isabeau help me dress at Ty Mawr, pro-vided I can find a suitable gown."

He almost swore as Henry's wish came to fulfillment. "Nay."

"I must." Her lovely voice was the firmest he'd ever heard it. She would go, whether he helped her or no.

"If you insist, Isabeau will accompany you. Dougray will drive you there."

"Not in a Rynallt coach," she chided.

He grimaced in the dark. His feelings were overriding his reason. "I'll hire a coach from Yorktown."

"Then I'll ride Southall's mare to Ty Mawr and we'll meet there. At first light."

"Leave a clean trail. Tell no one your plan. Not even Southall. How obliging is he of your coming and going?"

"'Tis the Sabbath, my day of rest. So long as I get my work done by noon Saturday, he is uncaring. It helps that I am a free woman, not an indenture or slave."

"Tomorrow then."

She answered with the sweet notes of her serinette.

❦

Daughter,

Your attendance is required at a ball aboard the Otter. *Eight o'clock, 29 July.*

Norfolk harbor. Bring news.

The note was unsigned but bore Lord Stirling's heavy hand. Holding the paper to a candle flame, Noble watched it blacken and curl to ash.

He had ridden back to Ty Mawr at midnight, leaving Liberty on the doorstep. Once home he couldn't sleep, just lay on his back listening to the whine of insects entangled in the mosquito netting about his bed.

The foyer clock ticked in time to his taut thoughts as he rehearsed their plans for any holes. Patrick Henry would shout with glee at the turn of events. The ball promised a well of information, lips loosened by spirits, a sure way to take the pulse of the British, at least in tumultuous Virginia. But could Libby pull it off?

He'd observed her from afar at social functions as she'd come of age, mistaking her for one of Lady Charlotte's daughters on occasion. Utterly poised, she did her father proud, though it was to her lovely mother's credit she had any social graces. Lord Stirling had the appeal of cold stone.

"Mister Rynallt, her ladyship is here."

His heart jumped at Mistress Tremayne's hasty announcement and exit. He left his study, crossing the foyer to the circular parlor where they'd meet. She adorned it, Libby did. She was the heart of what his home was missing. She had the ability to light up a room.

"Good morning to you, sir."

He shut the door with a rueful grin. "*Sir* makes me feel like your father, Libby. Mayhap use my given name as you recently did, at least in private."

"Noble, then." She smiled up at him in that easy, amiable way he was coming to know. "'Tis a handsome name, however 'tis said."

"A hard one to live up to."

The lament in her gaze was not lost on him. "So is Liberty."

They faced each other, an arm's breadth apart. On precarious ground they were. He trying to be noble and not take her in his arms. Propose marriage. Anything to keep her from going to Norfolk, the Loyalist nest. And she trying to live out her name, free herself from her father's reputation and her family's British roots.

She touched his arm. "I want to tell you something before I go upstairs and ready for the ball."

He waited on tenterhooks, not liking the plan any more than when it was first hatched. "Go ahead."

"I've prayed about my course of action—" She paused, so entreating it seemed she was silently asking for his consent. "I feel 'tis right, this risk. Going to Norfolk again. I've asked the Lord to cover me as only He can. But if something goes awry . . ."

His heart seemed to stop.

"If something should happen—my father is so unpredictable—I don't want you to feel responsible in any way. 'Tis my doing, all of it."

He wanted to lock the door, having thought of all the ways she was hurtling into danger. He spoke with far more calm than he was feeling. "Our aim is to minimize all risks. Dougray will drive you to Norfolk, where Isabeau will lodge at a Patriot-owned inn. You'll alight from the coach a few streets from the harbor. Dougray will stay in sight of the *Otter* and wait for you. I expect the dancing will go on till dawn."

"And I intend to stay till the last reel is stepped."

"Don't be too charming." He tamped down other unspoken concerns. Lord Dunmore himself had a reputation for drunken violence. And Noble wouldn't even start on the Royal Navy.

She touched his coat sleeve again. "My one regret is that you won't be there too."

He softened. Her gaze held his then lowered, denying him the lovely hue of her eyes. He already felt bereft.

She brightened at the last. "Don't look so troubled, Noble. God goes with me. There's no better escort."

※

"Mistress Tremayne said you are to have *carte blanche* with the late mademoiselle's gowns," Isabeau whispered.

"An order was placed for dresses and underpinnings before Miss Enid passed and was delivered after she was laid to rest. These garments have never been worn."

Together Liberty and Isabeau stood before the wardrobe, taking in a rainbow's array of silks and satins and brocades, though the predominant color was blue. "*Magnifique*, no?" Isabeau said.

"Indeed." Enid's taste in fashion had rivaled her taste in furnishings. Liberty fingered a lush sapphire brocade. "I recall Enid being taller than I."

"A little hemming, no?" Isabeau cocked her head. "She was slender as you."

"Most women are till marriage and babies," Liberty mused, admiring a cinnamon silk. "These have the look of a Philadelphia seamstress, not Margaret Hunter. Look at this painted chintz."

"Too dark, no?" Isabeau reached for an ivory gown with a profusion of finely worked lace.

Sighing, Liberty shook her head. "I'll look like a confection from the bake shop."

"Is that not the idea?"

"Perhaps this one." Liberty reached for something behind the bolder dresses. Crafted from silk taffeta the color of sea foam, it reminded her of the wallpaper in Lady Charlotte's boudoir at the Palace.

"Oh, la!" Isabeau clucked her tongue. "Let's try it on and see, mistress. Then we shall start on your hair."

Two hours and a hemming later, the mirror reflected the belle Liberty used to be.

"You are so lovely." Isabeau looked like she might dissolve into tears. "I fear your father will keep you aboard ship."

"Nay, Isabeau. Of what use am I in the harbor? 'Tis Patriot information Papa is after, and that I shall bring him, embellished and misleading. As for tonight, I will mostly dance . . . and listen."

A knock sounded and Mistress Tremayne appeared, jewelry case in hand. "Enid's favorites, m'lady. Mister Rynallt thought you might find something of use."

"How kind," Liberty said as Isabeau took the offering. The door shut softly as the housekeeper went out again, and they examined the burgeoning contents.

Aquamarines. Sapphires and garnets. A circlet of diamonds. Liberty decided on a pearl choker much like her mother once had. For all she knew Father had taken their jewelry when he'd fled. She fingered the pearls once Isabeau clasped them about her neck. They complemented the sea green of the gown and were more elegant than garish, unlike the popular paste gems of the day.

"Your hair lacks powder," Isabeau lamented.

"Never mind. Powder is going out of fashion. Shall we?"

Dougray was waiting beyond the front steps, sitting atop his box, a cap obscuring his Scottish features. With Ninian's assistance, Isabeau got into the coach while Liberty tarried in the foyer near Noble's study door. Why the need to speak to him a final time? Deep down, did she want him to see her dressed in her best as she used to be? If only to make a lasting memory because she feared she wouldn't be back?

Precious seconds ticked by, the London-made clock in the empty foyer marking time. Was he not near? Had he no wish to see her off? Clutching her folded fan, she started for the coach.

"Libby."

She turned. Noble stood behind her, boots muddy. Had he been riding? She found herself wishing he would go with her. Protect her. Cover her.

"Stay, Libby." His words fell flat. He was giving her a last out, eyes dark with intent. "Dougray can return you to Williamsburg instead."

For a moment she wavered. "I . . . just . . . Pray for me."

"Aye, so I have. So I will."

A semblance of peace sifted through her at his calm words. "I don't know when I'll be back."

"I'll be waiting."

This was the incentive she needed, the reward for what she must do. He would be waiting. That alone would get her through.

25

Liberty squinted into the clash of sunlight and gleaming water as dusk drew a curtain about the harbor. If not for Isabeau slipping her a ham-laden biscuit, she'd be ravenous and light-headed. The ham made her thirsty, and the only drink in sight was salt water. Surely there would be punch on deck.

As she was escorted up the gangplank of the *Otter*, she took a last look at the street Dougray had turned the coach down. The inn where Isabeau would be waiting was just beyond.

She was hardly the first guest to arrive. The merchant vessel's expansive deck bore a crush of people, uniformed naval officers and civilians in courtly dress. Overriding everything was the lilt of violins.

Her father's silhouette required no searching. He stood at the *Otter*'s bow, Lord Dunmore near. The sun was just setting off the ship's stern, a fiery palette of crimson and cream.

Red sky at night, sailor's delight.

"Lady Elisabeth."

The ship's captain? She smiled and extended her fan. She felt a wild fluttering in her rib cage. Her ruse had begun.

He gave a little bow. "I heard you might attend."

She avoided his eyes. "If only Lady Charlotte and her daughters were here."

"Agreed. I'm surprised you didn't join them aboard the *Magdalena*. Or perhaps accompany Margaret Gage on the *Charming Nancy*." In his own way, he seemed as probing as her father. "Staying on as you are means courting danger, and in a Patriot stronghold like Williamsburg . . ."

"Oh yes, that. A trifle, truly. The capital seems to have gone to sleep. Much ado about nothing, I think." She smiled and fluttered her fan. "Once the king's reinforcements arrive here in Norfolk, this little uprising shall come to an end."

"Reinforcements?" He shrugged. "They've yet to materialize. No word from Whitehall since May either."

So the king was strangely silent. Or communications had been delayed. Perhaps nobody thought the unrest was of much consequence. Still, the gaiety around her seemed somewhat forced.

"Shall I get you some ratafia?"

She took the captain's offer, gaze sweeping the deck and taking an accounting. She knew few in Norfolk, but there was a heavy Scots presence here, their broad brogues so at odds with the precise, clipped English of the king's men. A small group was moving her way, her father leading.

"Daughter, how good of you to come. Allow me to introduce Lieutenant Ladd, who will be your supper partner, and Miss Phila Siddall, who'll be mine."

Oh? Liberty feigned pleasure as the bosomy woman standing beside her father inclined her feathered, powdered head.

She then turned to meet a tall officer in a blue frock coat and white waistcoat who reached for her hand.

"A pleasure, m'lady," he said while Phila Siddall looked on benignly.

Was this woman her father's rumored paramour? All eyes were on Liberty, perhaps on account of Enid's lovely gown.

"I daresay I've not seen such fine fabric in many a day," Phila said. "With the slowing of imports and such."

"Father spared no expense on my wardrobe," Liberty answered truthfully, knowing he cared little for such matters and wouldn't know the gown was borrowed. "I had not thought to wear this, but the occasion seemed to warrant it. There's little merriment of late elsewhere."

"Then we shall make doubly merry here," Phila said with a sly smile.

Liberty's father was studying her closely, clearly hungry for information. "What news have you from Williamsburg?"

She had a moment to collect her thoughts as the ratafia was handed her. "The burgesses—delegates, now—are mostly away, meeting in Philadelphia."

"The Continental Congress, you mean."

"Yes, these Independence Men change titles like they change clothes," Liberty answered with a roll of her eyes. "Have you ever wondered what George Washington might be called? King George, perhaps?"

This gained a hearty round of dismayed murmurings and an outright gasp.

"Speaking of rebels and upstarts, there seems to have been a bit of division about who should lead the rebellion, but the middling planter George Washington, esquire, won the day," Phila said with a knowledge that surprised Liberty.

Esquire? The slur was not lost on her. The British were

refusing to address Washington as commander in chief, Noble said. And Washington was refusing all correspondence addressed to him as esquire.

"It seems those Patriots are as contentious as they are rebellious," Ladd put in. "What of General Artemas Ward of Massachusetts?"

"Ward?" Her father scoffed. "A military incompetent who is so portly he cannot mount his horse?"

Liberty glanced at Lord Dunmore headed their way. "Ward is now second in command to Washington, or so I've heard."

"What of Henry? Still fomenting all manner of rebellion, no doubt."

"Patrick Henry fancies himself governor of Virginia, if not all the colonies." With another roll of her eyes, she took a sip from her cup. "The man is rabid for war."

"Is he now?" her father said, finishing his drink.

"The very summit of sedition," the lieutenant said.

"Quite," Lord Dunmore replied with thinly veiled disgust. "Another of those beardless liberty boys whose ambitions trump all reason."

The minuet was opening, the crowd parting to make room for the dancers. Sand had been scattered on the deck to avoid mishaps. Already Liberty felt grains in her slippers. Lieutenant Ladd extended his arm, and she took it reluctantly. She preferred the sprightlier reels, but her partner proved a handsome dancer, never faltering. Father had paired her well on that score. A number of other brightly gowned women and their partners joined them.

A few deckhands bore weapons, the ship's cannon trained on the town. Was Dougray watching from the docks as planned? And Isabeau ensconced at the Patriot inn? This brought some comfort.

Despite her wariness, Liberty took a small delight in dancing beneath the stars. The open air was far preferable to a crowded ballroom. Here there was room to breathe. All around them the fleet's sidelights glittered like fallen stars. Singsong cries floated on the salty air as watches were changed and seamen cried the hour.

"There are a great many in Lord Dunmore's fleet," she said during a lull. "How heartening."

"Some two thousand Tories all told, the largest ships being the merchant vessels," Ladd said. "'Tis a bit crowded."

"Why not move south?"

"That's being debated." He spoke without restraint, as she was, after all, Lord Stirling's daughter. "The fleet may well move to the Elizabeth River. Gosport."

She gathered up the little he let fly like bread crumbs, pocketing them for the future. The next few hours became a blur of changing partners and dance steps. She kept asking questions, memorizing names, ranks, associations. But could she remember? Was anything of value?

The midnight supper found her with little appetite. While the majority of guests remained on deck, a few select ladies were escorted below to dine at the captain's table. Seated thus where it was more stilted and formal, Liberty felt shut in, confined, like a bird in a gilded cage.

Phila sat across from her, the only other lady present save the woman reported to be Lord Dunmore's favorite, Kitty Eustace Blair. Liberty felt a bit wide-eyed at the presence of one who had been at the heart of a Williamsburg marital scandal a few years before. Mama had wisely hidden the newspaper accounts of the trial, though the taint remained.

Her mind circled back to Noble, how they'd parted at Ty Mawr. Even now he was waiting for her, perhaps praying for her, while these men were rapidly becoming more sodden and free speaking by the minute. Epithets and innuendo flowed like wine.

"Tell me, m'lady, how are you faring in the rebel town?" Kitty Blair was looking at her, knife and fork aloft over her supper plate. "I gladly extend the invitation to join us and the safety of the fleet."

Lord Stirling frowned. "My daughter can come to us at intervals. For now, she is keeping the pulse of Williamsburg and playing Patriot, is that not right, Elisabeth?"

"Of course, Papa. Being thought an abandoned daughter at odds with her Loyalist father earns me all sorts of attention and information."

"You've a valuable pair of ears and eyes. Would that there were more like you."

"There are still a great many Lukewarms, I'm afraid," Liberty lamented.

A ripple of laughter rounded the table. "Lukewarms, you say?" an officer asked.

"Those loyal to neither side, yes. Those waiting to see how matters turn. I daresay few would step forward as true Patriots if pressed."

"What about the creation of a Continental Navy we've been hearing about? Now that the colonial army is in place?" Dunmore asked. "We've heard rumors of such."

"I know nothing of that, sir. The Continental Army is feeble at best, few in number and fewer in training. As for the navy, where would they get ships and crews?"

"From France and Spain, I fear," her father said. "Though that would take time. If we remain where we are, controlling Chesapeake Bay, we can keep watch and thwart any such activity."

They droned on, talking both hearsay and fact. Liberty wished for ink and paper . . . and better company—Isabeau and Dougray, Noble himself.

"We're most concerned about the leading Patriots. The Virginians." Dunmore set down a goblet as empty as Liberty's was full. "Washington. Jefferson and Henry. Rynallt and Lee."

Noble. Liberty swallowed a bite of mutton with difficulty. "Hades hath produced nothing blacker than the Patriots and their schemes, surely."

Her father stared at her, and she wished the words back. She was sounding like her mother. In fact, had she not read that very sentence in her mother's last broadside? Only it was aimed at Parliament and the king instead?

"'Twould be a fine plan to kidnap those leading the cause and douse the Patriots' fervor, so to speak." This from her father, flushed and full of himself. "A public hanging or two might do the trick."

"A bold plan. I heartily concur," Ladd said.

Her father pinned her with another stony stare. "Bring more news of the main players next time. Their whereabouts."

"I shall do what I can." She raised her shoulders in a disinterested shrug. "Betimes 'tis hard to sort fiction from fact."

"Find out all you can. When we next meet we shall have more." He raised a refilled goblet as if cheering her on. "Are you in need of anything?"

"Nothing I can think of, thank you. I ply my trade by day, tethered to Southall and the Raleigh."

"A clever circumstance, at least for our purposes," Dunmore said.

Phila toyed with her entrée, having eaten as little as Liberty herself. "You should tell her ladyship that the king's standard is about to be raised at Gosport lest she seek us out here and find us gone."

Blessed confirmation then. Southeast of Ty Mawr, Gosport was familiar to her, being the seat of the Sprowles, wealthy Scots merchants and shipbuilders who were old friends of her father. The remove filled her with relief. Yet it likely meant a fleet growing in strength and numbers.

"We must hold Virginia at all costs," an officer said.

"If we could only silence the press," another replied, flushed with anger. "Shut down the *Virginia Gazette* and that endless drivel coming out of Norfolk."

"That matters little once our eminent guest arrives," Dunmore said. "Hopefully in time for the coming fete in Gosport."

"Ah, the Sprowles' ball, aye. Mark the date, Daughter. Your presence is duly expected."

"Guest, indeed," the captain said, raising his goblet. "A toast to an imminent change of fortune!"

The conversation grew heated and less tense by turns, but no more was said of the expected guest. Liberty forced herself to eat, wondering where they'd gotten such fine meat, being short of provisions. The meal lasted two hours, and then the dancing resumed. When she rose from the table she was more stuffed with news than supper, both unpalatable.

At five o'clock in the morning when the stars were fading, Liberty left ship, another coin purse in hand. She walked down the gangplank, transfixed as night gave way to a bloodred sunrise, the very color of his majesty's red-coated men.

Red sky at morning, sailors take warning.

26

Never had she been so glad to see Isabeau. Or climb into an overheated coach. Yet cocooned so she felt slightly sick, head pounding, glad her maid dozed all the way to Ty Mawr. Dougray managed admirably despite his sleepless night watch on the pier, and soon they crossed over onto Mulberry Island.

'Twas the Sabbath. The very day General Washington called for fasting and prayer. She missed Bruton Parish Church, the scent of old wood and candlewax. Would she never again sit in their box pew alongside rosette windows beneath that soaring ceiling? Somehow the Sabbath hardly seemed the Sabbath without church.

At the long shaded avenue leading to Ty Mawr, the coach took an abrupt left, round a bend and up an incline rife with honeysuckle vine. They had bypassed the big house. But why?

She stared out the coach window. How fragrant this path would be in season when the honeysuckle bloomed. The trees were thinning, the morning air humid and noisy with birdsong. The changing country was like a gift as they passed beyond a low stone fence.

Through a narrow break in the trees a stone cottage opened up on the hill before her. Two-storied and surrounded by a flower garden and orchard, it unfolded like a storybook setting, perhaps a Welsh fairy tale.

Dougray jumped down from the box and opened the door. "Welcome to Ty Bryn, m'lady."

Liberty expected to find it overgrown, as Noble had told her it sat empty. But this . . . this was as well kept as Ty Mawr. And far more charming with its Welsh slate roof and small entry door. And lo and behold, a regal gray cat swished its tail on the front stoop.

"The cat . . . is it a resident?"

"Madoc?" Dougray grinned. "He acts like he's king o' the manor, but he mostly prowls the stables. The master doesna ken how he came to be here. He just showed himself one day and has been lurkin' ever since."

"I've always wanted a cat." Her father had denied her the pleasure, finding cat hair disagreeable and disdaining felines underfoot.

Dougray smiled and glanced back in the direction they had come. "I'm certain no one followed."

She took a last look down the drive, but all she saw was the raised dust from their coach wheels. Remembering Isabeau, she nearly had to shake her maid awake. Sleepy and silent, Isabeau climbed out of the conveyance, as unsurprised to see Ty Bryn as Liberty was surprised.

Dougray slapped his hat against his thigh to dispel the dust. "The master hopes all is to yer satisfaction."

Pondering this, Liberty led the way. The cottage door was reached by a flagstone walk rimmed with elfin, low-growing herbs. Beneath her heels came the pleasing scent of crushed thyme and mint. At the door stone she bent, intending to run a hand down Madoc's velvety back, but the big tom eluded her. Skittish of strangers then.

As her shoe cleared the last step the door swung open to reveal a ginger-haired maid, one she recognized from Ty Mawr. The white-capped girl gave a quick curtsy, then welcomed them into a small white foyer swept clean of all adornment save a Queen Anne table and a bench opposite. Up the west wall climbed a staircase to rooms unknown.

Liberty felt she'd stepped into a dollhouse, a very elaborate one. "How charming this is."

The maid smiled her pleasure. "Aye, 'tis that, m'lady. Let me show you to your rooms."

Up they went, Isabeau following. The hall was narrow but not confining, the carpet soft beneath her feet. The maid opened a door at the top of the stair, allowing Liberty to enter first. All the windows were open, giving the room an expansive feel. From where she stood, Liberty saw the reassuring tip of Ty Mawr's tower rising above the trees. Beyond this spread the James in all its blueness, backed by a patchwork quilt of green pasture and hills. Ty Bryn seemed to be on top of the world. *Hill house* indeed.

"My name's Nell, m'lady. Short for Penelope." She softened her next words with a bit of a smile. "Mister Rynallt has gone to town. There's been some trouble in Williamsburg."

"Trouble, you say?"

"Aye, I'm afraid I know very little." At this, she went out, leaving Isabeau to take charge.

"Did you know of this move to Ty Bryn?" Liberty asked as her maid plucked the pins from her hair.

"Only that Monsieur Rynallt feels it is safer for you here," she said tersely, leaving Liberty with the impression that her maid was missing Ninian and Ty Mawr.

In a quarter of an hour the undressing was finally done. "To bed with you, mistress." Isabeau took on the tone of Mistress Tremayne. "When you awake we shall have a proper Welsh tea."

Too weary to argue, Liberty climbed the bed steps of the room's centerpiece, a chintz-hung bedstead. The bold floral design was of costly Indian cotton, not the English imitation. Of varying hues of blue and green, it matched the striped papered walls. Some of the furniture looked new, and flowers graced a side table as if picked just for her. Noble had spared no expense on this place or her coming here.

Isabeau adjusted the mosquito netting, then went out on quiet feet. Though the room was warm, Liberty felt chilled, drawing the linen sheets up under her chin.

Sweet dreams she did not have.

∞

Noble smelled smoke long before he saw the ruins. A crowd gathered in back of the Raleigh, the heat of the flames scorching and wilting the surrounding flower and vegetable gardens. His gaze swung to the Raleigh's mansard roof and those of the outbuildings. Tinder-dry as the weather was, it seemed a miracle the fire had not spread. On a windy summer's day, aye, but 'twas still as the grave.

He kept to the Raleigh eave, watching and waiting. The folly, once so charming and picturesque, was now a blackened, smoky crater, the only evidence something stalwart had once stood.

James Southall surveyed the damage, hat in hand, expression vexed. The gardener, Thalia, was shaking her head.

"You do not know the lacemaker's whereabouts?" Southall asked.

"No, sir. Who can say?" She dabbed her eyes with the hem of her apron, a small pile of what looked to be Libby's few belongings at her bare feet. The serinette and lacemaking kit. A commonplace book.

Noble felt a surge of gladness nearly as great as his relief that Libby wasn't present.

"So long as she's not inside." Southall kicked at a charred beam. "You saw nothing, you say? No one suspicious about?" At the shake of Thalia's head, he muttered, "'Twas no accident. That much is plain."

Noble passed into the ordinary, mindful of the Sabbath. The bells of Bruton Parish Church were pealing as if announcing the calamity, not simply the end of divine service.

He'd wanted to be the one to meet Libby at Ty Mawr once she returned from Norfolk. Now the stench of sour ashes storming his senses gave rise to the deeper worry that someone meant her harm.

Before he'd cleared the hall and stepped into the taproom, Southall's riled voice reached out to him like a tug on his collar as he followed Noble. "Blast! You can bet I've been torched by a Tory. It has less to do with Miss Lawson than myself, owner of an inn infested with rebel rats, as Dunmore calls them."

Or a Patriot thinking Libby was a spy. Noble said nothing. To reply would only fuel Southall's ire. All he wanted to do was quench his thirst, learn all he could about the fire, and return to Ty Mawr. The few shillings he'd paid Billy to bring him any news had been well worth the cost.

"So what brings you to Williamsburg on the Sabbath if not to attend church?" Southall asked him. "There's been a curious lull among you Independence Men lately."

"Most are in Philadelphia."

Southall poured them both ale and slid Noble's to him across the scarred counter. "The Continental Congress, aye? I've yet to understand why some of you venture to Philadelphia and some of you stay."

"'Tis simple enough. Some are elected delegates whose presence is required. I chose to remain."

"You wouldn't know the whereabouts of Miss Lawson, I suppose. I'm not unaware of hearsay that she might be in league with her ousted father."

"Don't believe it."

"Many do."

"Buck the norm," Noble told him.

Their eyes locked. Southall was the first to look away. "She was a fine hand with a needle."

"Why are you talking about her in past tense?"

"I can no longer keep her in my hire." Southall took a long drink. "The fire seems a warning. Wouldn't be surprised if she doesn't turn up."

Aye, that was Noble's greatest fear. Leaving his ale unfinished, he parted with some coin. "Send word if you learn the culprit behind the burning, or anything else related to her ladyship."

Southall grunted his assent and Noble went out. Thalia was gathering up Liberty's belongings. He wanted to take them with him to Ty Bryn, but to do so would raise suspicions. For now, best keep their association quiet.

With a last look at the smoking folly's remains, he went to the green in search of his horse.

☙

"He's come, your ladyship." The maid, Nell, was at the bedchamber door as Liberty had requested, though it wasn't necessary. She'd heard a horse and rider on the drive, her spirits soaring along with it.

Despite being up all night aboard ship, Liberty had dozed lightly since, sensitive to any sound beyond her open bedchamber windows. Thanking Nell, she took a last look at herself in the mirror. Clad in a sultana, the lovely embroidered sash in place, she was ready to receive visitors, even the master of Ty Mawr. But where?

"There's a service stair there," Nell told her, pointing to a bookcase to the left of the bedchamber's mantel. "It leads to the parlor."

Liberty approached as Nell pressed a small lever beneath a shelf, which cracked open to the passage behind and a narrow stairwell. Liberty descended alone, gripping the unpainted handrail, drawn by the light illuminating the bottom steps.

She entered the unfamiliar room through a small door, again by the hearth. Noble stood by the largest window with his back to her, spyglass trained on the James. The surprising presence of Madoc relieved a bit of her angst. On sight of her, the cat approached with a swish of his tail, rubbing against her skirts. Noble stayed intent on the river as if he hadn't heard her enter.

She said softly, "You might well see the fleet move south. To Gosport."

He turned toward her, erasing every doubt she'd ever had that she was a nuisance, an inconvenience, a traitor. There was something alive in his face—a depth of feeling, even a profound relief. Or was it only because she had news he and the Independence Men needed?

Nell entered then, carrying a tray, reminding Liberty she'd missed breakfast. A small Welsh repast was the offering, even the delectable bara brith. And a pot of independence tea, from the scent of the steam, reminding her of Thalia's garden and Williamsburg.

"Welcome home, Libby," Noble said. "Or at the very least, welcome back."

Home, indeed. She looked to the enticing tray, awash with a hunger and all sorts of sweet feelings that had nothing to do with her empty stomach. Did he sense how glad she was to be here? Immersed in a refuge like Ty Bryn? Hidden away on Mulberry Island? At the Raleigh she felt a bit exposed. A target. Never quite comfortable or at ease.

She expelled a breath she hadn't realized she'd been holding. "I should tell you everything I know straightaway lest I forget."

"Aye, but have a seat first."

She sat, fingering the sash of the sultana absently. 'Twas a relief to share what she'd observed and heard, names and faces and myriad impressions. She felt lighter at the telling, spurred on by his interest. Impressed by his well-placed questions.

"There's one last thing that troubles me. My father and Lord Dunmore spoke of the imminent arrival of a mysterious guest. I sensed they believed it would alter everything for them. They even raised a toast."

"But no name? No more details?"

"Nothing," she lamented. "And because of it, I feel the need to go to Gosport. To take part in the fete they spoke of. My father said he duly expects me." She withdrew the velvet pouch from the folds of her sultana. "From my father. The fleet seems to be low on provisions but swimming in currency. Once I return to Williamsburg I'll see that it goes to the poorhouse."

"You won't be returning to Williamsburg."

She let go of the pouch in surprise, the coins jingling. "What do you mean?"

"Last night someone set fire to the folly. Southall doesn't know who yet, but he has no more need of your services."

Though it was gently said, she still felt stung. Fire? Her winsome folly? Had she been . . . dismissed? "Was I of no use to him then?"

"On the contrary. He said you're a fine hand with a needle."

"But . . ."

"Someone means you harm or means to send a message. Williamsburg is no longer the place for you."

She poured tea with hands surprisingly steady. The amber liquid sloshed into the porcelain cups so like her mother's fine china. Her thoughts whirled. Once again she was without a home, seeking a place to call her own.

Where shall I go? The unspoken question hovered between them.

"Do you like Ty Bryn, Libby?"

The simple question seemed almost ludicrous. She looked about the lovely room. She'd not seen all of Ty Bryn yet, but how could she not like it? "Very much."

"And the Welsh fare?" There was subtle teasing in his tone as she served them both bara brith.

"'Tis pleasantly un-English," she replied.

"What about Ty Mawr's master?" His gaze canted toward the window, but his question went straight to her heart. "Might you grow used to an Independence Man with noble intentions?"

His design came clear. She took a sip of tea, unable to answer. The silence lengthened, so expectant it rent her heart.

"In other words, I'm asking for your hand. For you to marry me. To make Ty Mawr your home in time. To come under my protection."

She listened, disbelieving. "Noble, indeed."

He swung his gaze her way. The smile she was coming to know, the one that touched her in ways she could not fathom, warmed his bewhiskered face. Had he forgotten to shave in the tumult of events? She rather liked him swarthy. He had the look of a smuggler. A pirate.

She bit her lip, still at a loss for words. He'd just proposed marriage, and here she sat thinking of his whiskers.

"What say you?" he said, somewhat tenderly.

She felt little more than a puddle of delight. "I suppose this proves you do not think me a Tory spy." How she had fretted about that. And how easily she now tucked that worry away. "You believe I am Patriot to the bone."

"Aye. And as such, you would be imminently safer taking the name of Rynallt and bidding goodbye to Lawson."

"So this is a marriage in name only?"

He hesitated. "'Twould be a marriage of whatever you want it to be."

The enormity of that engulfed her. "But what of my spying?"

"I'm against it. The danger remains."

"Should we keep our marriage a secret? Till the time is right to make it known?"

"Probably wise, aye."

"And the servants? Suppose someone talks?"

"They're a tight-mouthed group of Welsh, mostly. The few Tories I've employed have been dismissed or disappeared. Keeping you at Ty Bryn means you're mostly out of sight and mind."

"But the banns must be read—"

"Not any longer. Colonial customs are dying. All that is needed are witnesses and a preacher."

"Not from Bruton Parish?"

"Nay, a Presbyterian preacher who is a tenant of mine. He occupies the farm next to Ty Bryn and pastors a small church."

"No banns . . . a Presbyterian rite." Her perplexity nearly seemed a refusal, or so his guarded expression seemed to say. "Would it be legal?"

"Aye, a hundred times aye." He gave her a wry smile. "You can pass, Libby, say nay."

Nay? There was not a *nay* bone in her body. Her very soul was shouting *aye*. Could he not sense it? Tea forgotten, she looked about the winsome parlor, trying to make peace with her swirling emotions and strange surroundings. Why was she pinched with surprise, less from his asking than her own heart's cry? Was she being rash, wanting to wed him? Was it not a mad leap when she was unsure of his feelings for her?

She met his eyes. "There's something else that needs knowing. A Welsh word."

He waited, perfectly still, his eyes holding hers.

"Anwylyd," she said softly, finding it poetic.

"Anwylyd," he repeated, voice lowering melodically. "It means . . . 'beloved.'"

Her heart turned over. This was her answer then. "Shall you call me that?"

"If you want me to."

"Say it again . . . slowly," she said.

"An . . . wylyd."

The tender word cast her back to something Mama had said at the last.

I implore you to marry for love, naught else . . . Promise.

She set her empty cup down. "Seven days hence. On my birthday."

'Twas his turn to be surprised. "Your birthday?"

"Soon, yes, lest you change your mind." *Or I do.*

"If you're sure."

"More sure than not."

"'Twould work well, as I need to travel to Richmond on business between now and then. You can stay here and . . . prepare."

She scoured his handsome profile, searching for some sentiment. Tenderness. She found resolve. An honest, straightforward proposal seasoned with *anwylyd*.

"Send for your pastor-tenant then," she said, a bit shy at the turn of events. Her sultana would hardly do. "I shall see about a proper wedding gown."

27

*Q*uelle?" Isabeau gaped. "*Madame* Rynallt?"

"If all goes as planned." Liberty's outward calm belied her careening insides. "On my birthday."

Isabeau's shock gave way to practicality. "We must have a proper gown, no? One sent up from Ty Mawr?"

'Twould be another of Enid's, out of necessity. Yet a gown seemed frivolous in light of their circumstances. A marriage on the fly. Her future changed in the beat of a heart, a breath. *Both* their futures.

Liberty said nothing, hands folded in her lap.

Isabeau continued to regard her with wonder. "What news from your father you must have brought Monsieur Rynallt to come to this!"

Liberty smiled, suffused with a joy she'd not felt in months. She pushed all thoughts of her estranged family aside, refusing to allow even the slightest shadow on her present happiness.

"What of your hair?" Isabeau asked.

"Something simple, perhaps just ribbons. Best send word to Mistress Tremayne about a gown."

Isabeau brought out straight pins for the gown's hem. "Where are you to wed? The downstairs parlor?"

"In the garden, I hope," Liberty replied. "At sunset. If the weather is clear."

She would not allow herself to think beyond the ceremony, yet her thoughts ran ahead to the hour the servants retired and the bride and groom were left alone to begin their honeymoon.

Noble's gracious words now haunted.

'Twould be a marriage of whatever you want it to be.

What *did* she want? Moreover, what did he?

※

"You have need of what, sir?" Noble's pastor-tenant was regarding him with amazed amusement even as he reached for his Bible.

"I need you to officiate at a wedding, if you will." Noble stood, hat in hand, feeling far more awkward groom than master of Ty Mawr. "Mine."

"And who is the blessed bride, sir?"

"Lady Elisabeth Lawson. Or simply Liberty."

"*Gwych!*" came the enthusiastic reply. "A most worthy choice. Congratulations to you and your lady."

"Thank you. Plan on seven days hence. I'm still unsure of the time. I'll be away on business till then."

Standing in the small parlor behind them, Gabriel Tannant's wife was aglow, their brood of children, mostly girls, giggling.

"You are welcome to come to the reception after, impromptu as it is," Noble told them, glad Mistress Tremayne was amiable on short notice. Even now she was in the kitchen while most of the staff was away on the Sabbath. "See you soon."

Smiling, Noble went out. Theirs had been a lightning courtship, so they would marry in the same vein, with few trimmings.

He rode back to Ty Mawr at a steady clip, galloping the few miles beneath cloudy, breathlessly hot skies. Thunderheads rode the eastern horizon, turning the normally blue James a shining pewter.

Would Libby be ready in so short a time? She wanted to wed in the garden, Isabeau had told Ninian. A fitting spot. But would she change her mind between now and then?

And what sort of marriage would they have once they said "I do"? He craved a union in all the fullness the Almighty intended. Heart, body, soul. Had he given her too much leeway in deciding the terms of their relationship? How patient could he be if she decided their coming together would be in name only?

Despite all his wondering, the elation he'd felt at her response stayed with him. He'd expected outright refusal, even a wait-and-see. Somehow the timing seemed right. If the folly's burning had done anything to turn things in his favor, he was glad, despite Southall's losses.

Soon there'd be a mistress of Ty Mawr, or rather Ty Bryn for now. Glad he was he'd given Ty Bryn a thorough grooming of late. He'd had it in mind for Libby all along, even if she hadn't agreed to marry him. Few came here. Fewer knew it existed. To reach it one had to pass by Ty Mawr.

The next days were a blur of heat, dust, and expectations. At last Noble returned home from Richmond. He stabled his horse before going in Ty Mawr's side entrance, then taking the stair from his study to his bedchamber.

Ninian greeted him with a word that all was well. "Your bride is making ready at Ty Bryn, sir."

At the washstand, Noble rinsed the dust from his face and decided to bathe. A day's growth of beard needed banishing, and he owed his bride his best suit of clothes, at least. Remembering a detail, he opened the lone drawer of his shaving stand. His mother's ring was cocooned in a scrap of velvet.

Don't let them bury me with it. Keep it for your bride-to-be.

She'd prayed to that end, she'd told him. Was Libby an answer to his mother's prayers? And Libby's own mother—what would her reaction be?

The afternoon waned and he rode to Ty Bryn, stabling his horse with Dougray. As twilight descended he found himself in the miniature garden, walled like Ty Mawr and arguably the most fragrant, as if all that hot brick hedged in the intoxicating scent of blooms and herbs.

Soon Gabriel Tannant joined him at the wall, looking outward on the James, the river mostly empty save a familiar batteau and skiff. Its calm surface was a striking counterpoint to Noble's unrest. Not because of Libby but because of her father, Dunmore, and the simmering colonies.

"No river pirates on the Sabbath, I hope," Tannant said.

"Nay, thankfully. Not on my wedding eve." Noble gave him a searching look. "Everything in order for the hasty ceremony?"

"Indeed." Tannant smiled, thumbing through the open Bible in his hand. "Why wait, truly. You either know you want to wed or you don't. Times are changing. I just heard word the rector of Bruton Parish has struck the king's name from the church Bible."

"He's a Patriot then."

"Aye, little time left to take sides."

The clouds shifted, revealing a rising moon, just light enough to see the silhouettes of Mistress Tremayne and Isabeau following in Libby's wake. His eyes were for his bride, the lacy lines of her veil flowing about her and turning her almost ethereal.

His birthday bride.

Though she was a small slip of a woman, she had a gracious carriage. And even the gathering darkness couldn't hide that she was looking at him. Her hands were empty—ludicrous amid so much color. He began picking flowers, robbing the recently weeded beds. Lilies and roses and hollyhocks. By the time she reached him he had a generous, unkempt bouquet. Clearly delighted, she took the blooms, cradling them in her arms.

He made introductions. For all his earthiness as a farmer, Tannant was a fine preacher, his poet-pastor roots coming to bear. The opening words rolled off his tongue like a prayer. Noble stood stone still and took in Libby's bent head, the fall of her veil. If she wore one of Enid's dresses, he didn't remember it. The thought tightened his throat. His sister should be here. Libby's mother should be here. In a perfect world, all their parents would be. This felt right, but it wasn't easy. This act required courage. Hope. Faith.

Love.

Liberty was aware of a great many things. How calm Noble seemed. Tennant's Welsh and English vows. The fly bedeviling Isabeau, who was trying not to bat at it but stay still. The look of satisfaction on Mistress Tremayne's face. Liberty lowered her gaze to the blooms Noble had gathered for her. She could not meet his eyes. Doing so seemed an intimacy not yet warranted, yet his gift of flowers was a gallant gesture that made her insides dance.

The pull to look at her groom, weigh his reactions, gauge his thoughts, was nearly irresistible. She knew him well enough to rule out any impulse or rashness. Noble Rynallt of Ty Mawr was of sound mind taking a Tory bride. He'd thought it through like the barrister and former burgess he was in ways she hadn't. The ring he slipped on her hand was proof. It left her wishing for more light to better admire it.

Following the pastor's lead, Noble spoke the words Liberty had never thought to hear. "With this ring I thee wed, with my body I thee worship, and with all my worldly goods I thee endow."

She was penniless. Dowryless. No matter.

"I, Noble, take thee, Liberty, to be my wife . . ."

Together they knelt on a small, brocaded bench someone had brought from the parlor as the final prayer was said.

Finally, her gaze found her groom's, her shadowy veil between them. There was no call for any bride kissing. A question rose in her eyes. Her heart. He started to raise her veil then stopped, as if paralyzed with uncertainty as to what she really wanted from him.

"Noble and Liberty Rynallt of Ty Mawr," Tannant proclaimed as they rose from the bench.

"God be praised," Mistress Tremayne exclaimed. "Now if the bride and groom will lead the way to the parlor, we shall celebrate."

∅

She had shed her Tory name. No longer was she Lady Elisabeth Lawson but Liberty Rynallt. Mistress of Ty Mawr and Ty Bryn. Everyone's continuous smiles were a reminder of the sudden, surprising change. Isabeau's was especially broad, as it signaled her return to lady's maid.

A wedding cake was served, its icing soft in the heat. The delightful confection was small but beautifully done, adorned with candied flowers and orange and lemon peel. A marvel. The Williamsburg confectionery could have supplied no better.

As she sipped her punch, standing to the right of her groom, she took note of guests. The pastor's wife and children were sprinkled about the parlor, the youngest girls enamored by some glass figurines on a small table. There was Ninian shadowing Isabeau and Mistress Tremayne speaking with Nell and Dougray. Glad she was it was the Sabbath and so quiet, the ceremony hushed.

Still, she wondered. What if the news of their marriage seeped to her father? It took but one loose-lipped servant . . .

Lord, protect us, please.

"A toast to Ty Mawr's master and new mistress." This from Ninian, wearing merino broadcloth.

All raised their glasses. The toast was made in Welsh, the valet's eyes shining his pleasure. He looked jubilant, though their marriage meant a change to his routine, surely. Liberty took his measure. Old enough to be Noble's father. Immaculate in dress. Neither portly nor thin. And by all appearances as besotted by Isabeau as she was him.

As she pondered it, a new qualm beset her. What of their wedding night? Would they dismiss the servants? Be alone? If only Mama was near enough to ask about what came next. She could well imagine Cressida's reaction, having set her sights on the handsome Welshman now married.

"Your ring—how lovely!" This from the pastor's wife looking at her hand.

In the rush, Liberty had forgotten it. She slipped the ring free of her finger, admiring the trellis pattern of gold and silver, squinting at the tiny engraving within. But alas, 'twas in Welsh.

Noble intervened, not looking at the ring but at Liberty. "'No heart more true than mine to you.'"

Returning the ring to her finger, she smiled up at him, a bit bashfully, aware of a great many eyes on them.

"'Twas my mother's ring given by my father on their wedding day," Noble remarked when Mistress Tannant had moved away to chasten one of her children.

"And a happy marriage it was, forty-eight years long," Mistress Tremayne said. "I was privileged to witness it myself."

"I wish I'd known them," Liberty said.

The housekeeper gave a smile of expectation. "You'll see them in the faces of your children, surely."

"A lovely thought."

Beside her, Noble was noticeably silent.

The cake was cut and served on fine china bearing the Rynallt monogram. She appreciated it like the stranger she was, at sea with all the little details new to her. Someone had placed the flowers Noble had picked for her bouquet in a silver pitcher beside the china. Coffee was served, and also something finer and far more fragrant and forbidding than liberty tea, as if it had been secreted for a special occasion.

He took a bite of cake, murmuring something about preferring the savory to the sweet. Another small revelation. Everything he did surprised her—because she knew him so little.

Oh, what had she done, marrying a stranger?

Was he thinking the same about her?

Conversation swirled then stalled. Ten o'clock sounded from the lofty case clock in the foyer, and Mistress Tremayne and Nell began tidying up. The guests gave the happy couple their last best wishes, and soon the newlyweds were left facing each other. The lovely room seemed to shrink. Or was it only because they were standing so close to each other?

"A guinea for your thoughts," he said.

She set down her empty cup. "I'm finding it hard to believe I left my father's ship only a few days ago an unmarried woman, and now I'm standing here and 'tis a very different story."

"One that has a far happier ending, aye?" For a moment he looked stunned about what they'd just done. "We'll take it as it comes. One circumstance at a time."

She liked that he said *we*. It sounded solid. Enduring. Far safer than going to and from Norfolk with the circumstances' changing tides.

"I'd still like you to allow me one important consideration," she ventured. "I do want to go to Gosport." His troubled expression nearly stole her courage. "'Tis critical, I feel."

"One last spying mission, so to speak."

"Yes, the very last. Think on it, please." Leaving his side, she crossed the room to stand at the window looking out on the James. Daylight had eroded completely, and the rumble of thunder sounded far off through the darkness. Summer thunderstorms were a favorite of hers. She used to watch them from the oriole window of the Williamsburg townhouse.

"If I could, I'd take you to honeymoon in Wales."

"How I'd love to see your native land." A sudden whim turned her impish. Or perhaps it was the ratafia seldom drunk. "Why don't we turn the tables on my father and steal away in one of Dunmore's ships and sail there?"

He chuckled. "Don't tempt me."

Together they took in the night as the storm sent a jagged slash of lightning over the garden, illuminating the flower beds and fountain with eerie light. But she was far more conscious of his nearness than the storm outside. This moment, this new, wondrous oneness, would never come again.

"You must be tired."

She smiled up at him. "Mostly I am happy."

His answering smile reassured her that he was too. "Happy birthday, Libby. I've been pondering what to give you."

"Your lovely wedding ring will do."

His hand caught hers, her fingers enfolded in his warm grasp. "I'll see you upstairs."

Her heart skipped. Would he take the lead? Take her in his arms and forever silence her doubts about his devotion? Slowly they climbed the steps, and she heard Isabeau humming. So he'd not dismissed the servants. She'd hoped 'twould be just the two of them. But he bid her good night at her half-open door before continuing down the hall to his own room, bypassing the connecting sitting room. Perhaps 'twas best. Exhaustion pummeled her in little waves, making her crave the comforts of her new bedchamber.

"Ready to retire, sir?" came Ninian's muffled words two rooms away. The respectful question rose above Isabeau's humming in the dressing room.

Curiously let down, Liberty faced her maid.

"*Oh là là!*" Isabeau came forward to unpin her veil. "You are now mistress of Ty Bryn *and* Ty Mawr. I can hardly take it in!"

Through the connecting door, Liberty saw Noble shed his fine coat. He turned around right then, his eyes meeting hers from a distance. Her heart skipped again. And then Isabeau and the valet unwittingly moved to shut the door between them.

Hoofbeats? At this hour?

Noble yanked at his stock as Ninian went to investigate. He returned and said, "Mister Henry to see you, sir."

His resistance roared. On his wedding night? Only Henry wasn't privy to that intimate detail.

Though Noble said nothing in response, Ninian read his displeasure. "He's insisting on a meeting, I'm afraid, having been to Ty Mawr first."

Reluctant, Noble retied his stock. Tight as a noose it felt. Noble dismissed Ninian and took the stairs to the study, bypassing Libby's closed door, only to slow and take a step back. The feminine, floral fragrance of her seemed to linger, wafting beneath the door. Or was it merely the essence of his own mounting yearning?

He reached the landing. Henry had better be prepared for a hasty meeting. And have a sound explanation for his midnight intrusion.

"Rynallt. Finally." Henry fanned his cocked hat about his flushed, damp face. "I nearly had to threaten your housekeeper with gaol to learn your whereabouts. You're hiding out here in this cottage, no doubt, because you're first on the Tories' latest blacklist to be hung." He sighed in the face of Noble's continued silence. "You look . . . frustrated."

Frustrated? And why might that be? Because his bride waited upstairs and he wanted no interruptions should she decide to share their wedding eve alone with him? What would she think if he spent the night with Henry instead?

"What brings you out in the dead of night?"

"Intelligence that the British are planning a major rendezvous at Gosport. When I heard the news I thought immediately of Lord Stirling's daughter, that she might be of use to us. Trouble is, no one seems to know what's become of her after the folly fire."

28

The remainder of Noble's wedding night—that brief hour between Henry's leaving and daybreak—consisted of lying on his back in a strange bed, the mosquito netting billowing from the damp wind charging through an open west window, his own thoughts just as chaotic as the storm outside. The strength of it bespoke the coming hurricane season and all that needed to be done to batten down both Ty Mawr and Ty Bryn.

But his foremost concern was his bride's safety. She now wore his ring, bore his name, was his responsibility. He was dead set against her going to Gosport despite all of Henry's arguments to the contrary. There was only so much he could control once she was there. He had no power once she entered Tory strongholds. No sway with her father or Dunmore or Patriot-hating Tories.

What would Lord Stirling do if he learned about her marriage? Send her to England, most likely. And Noble would probably only hear of it secondhand once she didn't return to Ty Bryn.

Dawn rode the horizon, a crimson scar to the east. He

got up and donned breeches, leaving his nightshirt hanging and his feet bare. He pushed open the sitting room door and then the door to her bedchamber, where he stood transfixed on the threshold, his heart beating breathlessly fast.

Libby stared back at him from the middle of her bed, sitting half upright, a bank of pillows behind her. The bed seemed too big and she too small, her pale braid falling over one shoulder like hemp rope, the bound end buried in the linen sheet. Unlike their first bedside meeting, she was fully awake this morning—and married. The storm had cooled the air and turned it more humid. He ran a hand through his own hair, the dampness making it unkempt and curled.

He had never been much ill at ease in her presence, and he wasn't now. But did she somehow sense he'd slept little, weighing their future?

"The storm kept you up?" she asked, as if he charged in at dawn every morning.

"Nay. You did, Libby."

At this she smiled, and he nearly flushed from the irony of it. Kept up all night for all the wrong reasons. Grabbing hold of a chair, he sat down by her bedside.

"I slept little," she said, eyes on her ring finger. "And prayed much."

A stitch of guilt nicked him. She had him there. He had stewed much and prayed little.

She looked up at him. "'Tis almost time to go to Gosport and see my father again—"

"Nay, Libby. I've thought it through. As your husband—"

"Just once more." She raised her gaze to his, something so entreating in her face he melted like candle wax. "Once more is all I ask."

"Once more will lead to yet another meeting, other dangers."

"I must find out all I can while I can. Something huge is in the offing that will decide all our fates. Perhaps I can be of help in even a small way to you. Your cause." Her gaze held his. "*Our* cause."

His opposition, whittled down by her entreating and Henry's sound arguments, began to shift. He'd sworn Henry to secrecy about their marriage and restated his opposition to having Libby act as spy. "If do you go you'll simply be Lady Elisabeth, unwed, with no ties to Ty Mawr. If your father has any inkling of what we've done . . ." He left the thought unfinished. It sounded underhanded somehow when all he wanted was to protect her. "I feel concerned enough about Gosport that I'm going with you, but I'll travel ahead at a distance and on horseback."

Alarm filled her face. "But—"

"I'll keep occupied visiting the warehouses along the waterfront that once stored Ty Mawr's tobacco and indigo. My presence there isn't unusual, though I've not been since last shipping season."

"'Tis too risky." Distress turned her paler. Hardly the bride on her wedding-after morn. "Someone might do you harm."

"Better me than you."

She began fidgeting with her long braid, breaking the composure he found so remarkable. "Now I know how you must feel when I go."

He took her hands, entwining their fingers. He had never touched her save escorting her to the Palace ball and then yesterday when they'd married and he'd taken her up to her room. "Anwylyd . . ."

Her eyes softened. She liked that he called her that. He

could tell. His own soul felt softer saying it. The endearment held an intimacy that tightened their tie and had even turned his unexpected marriage proposal in his favor. Beloved she was.

A slight commotion and then Isabeau stormed through the door, a pair of lace mitts in hand. "Mistress—" Seeing them together, she blushed a bright poppy red. Slowly she began backing up. "Pardon!"

With a slight smile, Noble stood and gave Liberty a last, lingering look. "Till supper, aye?"

"And how is the groom this evening?" his valet asked for the first time that day.

"Still stunned," Noble replied truthfully. "At least matrimonially."

Ninian chuckled. Only a few servants had come up the hill to Ty Bryn from Ty Mawr. He wanted to send them all back again. But he and Libby—his anwylyd—must eat. Dress. Try for a return to normalcy, whatever that was.

"I've brought the papers from your study and the latest post, sir."

"Leave them on the table there, and then you're at your leisure."

Ninian looked startled. "On a Monday, sir?"

"My honeymoon Monday, aye."

Noble turned toward the window to see Libby waiting for him in the rear garden, a wicker hamper on the stone bench beside her. At her request, Cook had packed a picnic supper. He couldn't have ordered a better evening. The wind had died down, and the recent rain cooled the heat of August considerably.

"Should I come up the hill tomorrow, sir?"

"Only should the need arise." Noble gave his valet a grin. "I'd like to shut the world out a little longer."

"Of course, sir. One more concern. Mistress Tremayne said a courier came. Some matter about the militia. Good day."

Ninian disappeared. The militia matter remained. But at the moment all Noble could think of was the countdown to Gosport.

He leaned out the window, unable to take his eyes off Libby. She was looking up at him, clad in a gauzy summer dress, a wide, beribboned hat hiding her comely features.

"Are you not hungry?" she called.

"What have you in your basket?"

She smiled and lifted the lid. "Fried chicken and smoked ham. Scotch eggs. Cheese and pickles. Butter wrapped in lettuce leaves and warm bread. A feast!"

A door slammed below. Isabeau appeared with a quilt. In the stable courtyard, Dougray waited with a pony cart. It had been Noble and Enid's in childhood, its battered box painted a fresh green and bringing an avalanche of memories, most of them pleasant.

Noble went downstairs with his riding whip, ready to return the remaining servants to Ty Mawr. In so small a house they seemed forever underfoot. Or mayhap it was only his need for privacy that made him wish for time alone with Libby.

"Just the two of us?" she asked with what seemed no small satisfaction.

"Not entirely." He nearly smiled as Madoc wended his way around his boots.

"He's quite a handsome cat."

"Aye, he's a tom with an independent streak." He helped her into the cart before securing the picnic basket and taking a seat beside her. Madoc jumped in at the last, and they laughed as he sniffed the contents. "Out with you."

Noble returned him to the ground and they set off, taking the path nearest the James, the most secluded part of the island. Tobacco and cornfields spread to one side, the water on the other. The day's work was done, and few hands could be seen save an overseer repairing a fence at a distance.

"One could almost believe there was no discord anywhere," Libby said, her eyes on the river as if expecting to find a fleet of warships there.

"None on our island," he replied with a new contentment. The waiting post flashed to mind, but he blocked it. "A more serene eve I've never seen."

"How much land is yours?"

"Ours, you mean?" At her look of surprise he said, "All of Mulberry Island and two thousand acres on the mainland."

"You hardly have need of my lost dowry then."

"You need no dowry, anwylyd." The words came easy despite his lack of practice saying such. "You are enough."

"I hope you can say that in another ten years, or twenty." She untied the chin ribbons of her hat and put it in her lap. "How long must I stay out of sight at Ty Bryn?"

"I can't answer that yet."

"Well, it shan't be a hardship to be Ty Bryn's mistress, though I do wonder what I'll do with all these hours."

"What did you do in Williamsburg at the townhouse?"

"Shamelessly little. I'm amazed at how much time I devoted to taking tea and playing the harp."

"You'll miss your lacemaking then."

"I do love my laces, not for profit but for pleasure. I suppose all of that burned in the folly fire."

Thalia flashed to mind, and his retrieval of Libby's belongings a few days later. Only he'd forgotten to give them to her. "Start a little enterprise sewing shirts for the militia and knitting stockings. Just leave off the lace."

She brightened. "Like something my mother would do, one of her charitable endeavors."

"Libby . . . about Gosport." He swallowed, eyes on the lush lines of the sunset. "I'm more concerned about it than you think."

"Have you any news from there?"

"Only that Dunmore has commandeered Andrew Sprowle's fine residence and is quartering soldiers in Sprowle's warehouses along the waterfront."

"Who tells you these things?"

"Patriot spies."

"My father is right there in the thick of it, no doubt, raiding the wine cellar and carrying on with his mis—" She stopped, a decided edge to her voice. The taint in her tone was so unlike her, Noble was more surprised by that than her father's peccadilloes.

"Your father has a mistress?"

"I'm sorry I spoke of it." She looked contrite. "I cannot cast stones. 'Tis bad enough my father is being played the fool with my going aboard his ship, pretending to be who I am not."

"Another reason to abandon Gosport."

She sighed and he frowned. Their conversation had taken a negative turn. Before he changed course, she pointed to a blue heron. "'Tis good to be away from town. There are no herons in Williamsburg proper."

"The country agrees with you."

"'Tis peaceful. Beautiful. I welcome the quiet."

"You don't miss Williamsburg or the folly then."

She smiled. "Not when I have Ty Bryn—and its master."

They crossed a shallow creek, the cart's wheels skittering over stones. Ahead was a small glen, the place he had in mind. The picnic was Libby's suggestion, something Enid had often wanted but he'd no time for. Now his priorities had shifted. His and Libby's time was so limited. He wanted everything to be perfect. Memorable. No regrets.

He applied the hand brake as she took up the quilt and basket. Helping her down from the cart, he surveyed their surroundings. The peace of the scene was jarringly at odds with their circumstances. He was now wed. To Lord Stirling's daughter. The colonies were in rebellion against the king. War was imminent. His new wife was acting as spy. He himself was a wanted man.

"What a lovely spot." Liberty yanked him back to the immaculate present. "I can't remember when I last had a picnic."

Fireflies began winking in the twilight. He was glad for the gloom. The privacy. Though he felt safer behind walls, he'd enjoy this one outing, given it was their honeymoon.

"You look much too serious for a new groom," she whispered.

"It happened so fast I half forget I am one. But I regret none of it," he added, in case she wondered if he did. "I've wanted to marry, share my life with someone, for longer than I can recall. Yet I never met anyone who seemed to fit what I'd envisioned here at Ty Mawr and Ty Bryn. Till you."

"Glad I am of that. Being Libby Rynallt is far more agreeable than plain old Lady Elisabeth Lawson." She spoke with lowered lashes and a teasing lilt. "Your words could well be my own. For as long as I remember I've dreamed of this day. A husband. A happy home." She reached for his hand a bit tentatively, and he gave it without hesitation. Her gentle touch was the most pleasant thing he knew.

They said grace and she began unpacking their picnic, tempting him as much with her gracious, feminine movements as the fare. "Tell me how you acquired Ty Mawr."

"My grandfather acquired it through royal patent. But the land was originally tilled by John Rolfe."

"Rolfe? He wed Pocahontas."

"Aye. They were among the first settlers here, planting the sweet tobacco that made them prosperous. Mulberry Island has a rich history."

Her brow creased. "I hope 'tis yours—ours—for years to come."

She was thinking of the confiscated townhouse, no doubt. "Lord willing, it will be ours for generations." He had no fear of losing the land, more his life. His wife. But that was in the Lord's hands as well.

He dared a somewhat safer subject between swallows of meat and bread. "I think all this picnicking is good for me. You're good for me. I suppose we're having a sort of backward affair of the heart."

She smiled—and sighed. "Somehow we did manage to marry without a proper courtship."

So she minded? She was looking at him so bewitchingly, he certainly did. "We could remedy that."

She gestured to the hamper. "This twilight meal for two is a fine start."

"Your idea. Just who is courting whom, I wonder?"

At his teasing she returned to her supper, still smiling.

It was the kind of flirtatious banter found in ballrooms, a remnant of the not-so-distant past.

He turned his attention to the river. The rising moon was full, the gathering dusk idyllic for poets and dreamers. His own musings were decidedly unpoetic. Patrick Henry seemed to shadow him. Once they'd returned to Ty Mawr, he'd look at his correspondence and his papers in the small study below their bedchambers.

But all he wanted was his wife. Children. A fuller life.

29

Was there ever a lovelier garden? Once Liberty thought the Governor's Palace gardens sublime, a work of art, but now Williamsburg's best seemed stilted and formal, even Ty Mawr's too grand. Ty Bryn's was near perfect, even with a few weeds showing, and definitely whimsical with a child-sized stone dragon at the gate. *Draco*, Noble called it. This morning, the day after their picnic, she sat on a teal garden chair with a leaf design, feeling like the queen of her own little kingdom, caught up in her own fairy tale.

White sand walkways divided nine planting beds, hemming in a glory of larkspur and columbine, hollyhocks and snapdragons. A tiny, tinkling fountain was at the garden's heart, a cherub at one side. The garden's wall provided a windbreak as well as privacy, hiding her from the drive. Whimsical indeed.

She felt protected. Blessed. The wedding band glinting on her hand was a constant reminder. But with two nights in separate rooms it seemed she was only half his. She'd thought—hoped—Noble would indicate his desire to make her wholly his wife. Or was he indeed leaving it to her? If so, how would she approach him? On tiptoe at bedtime, breath held? Or did he prefer a more direct overture?

Noble, can I be near you tonight?

She flushed even thinking it. What if he was content with their marriage being in name only? His absence a second night seemed to say so. And she was bound for Gosport on the third . . .

Her gaze trailed to the kitchen house, a miniature of Ty Mawr's. The rattle of crockery foretold dinner was in the making as much as did the chimney belching smoke. She spied Dougray leading out the quarter horse Noble had given her, a beautiful red sorrel mare. The horse whinnied as he walked her, for she'd been newly shod. Isabeau was hanging the wash while Nell beat rugs at the parlor door.

And Noble?

He had gone down the hill to Ty Mawr long before she'd awakened. Years of habit and early rising had made him quiet as he left the house without so much as a footfall. But his absence was keenly felt.

She'd risen at half past seven, stealing to his room as he'd done hers yesterday, hoping to find him sleeping and surprise him. But he was gone. She'd then hurried downstairs, thinking to overtake him at breakfast, only to find Nell dusting the parlor, her broad face lighting with pleasure at Liberty's greeting.

"Good morning, m'lady." Nell ushered her into the study. "The master had me bring some things up from the big house for you."

For a moment Liberty just stared. Her harp? And her serinette. Beside these were her sewing basket and lace kit. All that remained of her former silken, cosseted life. Her lace pillow protruded, the bobbins still in place from that last complicated piece she'd been working. Someone had saved it from the fire. Thalia? A rush of gratitude wet her eyes.

Picking up the basket, she smelled the smoky contents.

The purple lace cards were a tad brown at the edges, but the laces were unscathed.

"A buttermilk wash and all should be well," Nell said. "Shall I?"

"Please. But I'll see to the lace pillow and finish what I started."

Last was her commonplace book. What kind of business-woman was she? Within its pages were lace orders aplenty and she'd all but forgotten them.

The clock chimed, reminding her time was against her. She didn't want to spend her honeymoon filling lace orders, if one could call this chapter of her life a honeymoon. She sat down at her harp, tuning it to an open C chord. The strings seemed good as new. Should she ask Noble to bring up his violin from Ty Mawr? Together they would fill Ty Bryn with music. Life. Memories.

A half hour passed and she grew restless. Her gaze strayed to the empty drive and tower of Ty Mawr through the lush trees before taking in all aspects of the small, unfamiliar parlor.

Ty Bryn was still a bit of a mystery. Nell had told her of an attic. She decided to explore, but halfway up the winding stair she nearly changed her mind. The heat pressed down like a steamy blanket, the scent of dust overwhelming when she opened the attic door.

A spiderweb caught in her hair and she brushed it away, next dodging a pesky fly. The attic itself was dark, its contents made visible by two windows at each end. Her gaze landed on an old trunk. A chair with three legs. A battered armoire.

A cradle.

Kneeling beside it, she examined the spindled wood. It was finely crafted if whitened with dust, hooded end engraved with a fleur-de-lis. It looked lonesome, somewhat forlorn.

Nay, no longer.

Dare she bring it downstairs? Would Noble even notice? Ty Bryn had a room across from their bedchambers. Newly cleaned and smelling of milk paint, it sat empty. Waiting to renew its purpose.

Half bent, she walked beneath the heated eaves, debating. Here was another trunk bearing a brass nameplate. A Windsor chair. A figurine or two. A forgotten painting. With a little loving care she would have her nursery.

Next she inspected a rolled-up carpet. Aubusson, the colors still bright. Mama had a penchant for such rugs.

She imagined her mother's delight at a grandchild. Her dismay if there was none. The weight of Liberty's responsibility shadowed her. Now she understood her father's disappointment with a girl. His legacy, their family name, had come to an end. She wanted to ensure the Rynallt name lived on. Noble needed an heir.

But her own longing went far deeper. Since she was in leading strings she'd loved her dolls and wished for a brother or sister. Denied that, she found great delight in Lady Charlotte's brood. A loving mother, Lady Charlotte had taught her much, involved as she was in her children's lives despite their many servants. Despite an oft absent husband.

Ty Bryn needed a family. A son or daughter, whatever the Lord deemed fit. But at such a time as this? With effort, she shuttered all worrisome thoughts of war away, knowing such was sin. She'd trust in God's perfect timing. Had He not shown Himself faithful? Even amid the tumult? *Especially* amid the tumult?

Looking back, she could see how even divinely timed politics had prevented her from a disastrous marriage to Miles Roth. Living in the folly, seeing him about town if only from a distance, had shown her this. Though she didn't judge him, she had no wish to be his wife.

She took a handkerchief from her pocket and dabbed at her damp hairline and upper lip, then called for Nell. Joy bubbled inside her and banished any fear of the future. A new chapter of life had opened, every blank page full of possibilities.

Including a nursery for Ty Bryn.

⬤

Noble glanced at the clock on his study mantel. The midday meal was almost upon them. He could ride up the hill to Ty Bryn in ten short minutes on this, the third day of their honeymoon, and spend time with Libby. Or he could finish the paperwork before him. Away since dawn, he had a curious itch to return to her.

As he shrugged on his coat and tucked the courier's latest post in his breast pocket, Mistress Tremayne appeared at the door, abject apology on her face.

"Mister Roth to see you, sir."

Miles? He felt a sinking to his boots. He'd not seen Miles since—

"Morning, Cousin." Miles swaggered in, bearing a lopsided, sheepish grin. Unshaven, his stock soiled, he looked like a caricature lampooned in the *Virginia Gazette*, the reek of spirits in his wake. "I've come to beg a loan—see that new quarter horse everyone's abuzz about in Williamsburg."

"I've no loan to give you," Noble said. "But I'll show you the stables on my way out."

Without asking, Miles poured himself a brandy. Noble made a mental note to do away with the decanter or hide it till Henry or Clark came by.

Downing the drink in two swallows, Miles set the glass down so hard the table rattled. "I've been sent by a select group of gentlemen to ask about reinstituting the races. Another subscription plate, if you will."

Revive the most popular race in Williamsburg? "Gambling, you mean."

"Come now, Cousin. Even you wagered once upon a time."

Noble remained silent.

"How much can you contribute to the purse? We're hoping one hundred pounds for the winner, a handsome saddle or bridle for second place, and a whip for third."

"Not to mention substantial side betting, aye?" Noble started for the door. "And glutting the local courts with cases of unpaid debts?"

Miles frowned and followed him out. "You're no doubt thinking of my being held in gaol on account of all that."

"I was, aye."

"You can't deny you've enjoyed a bit of betting—"

"I was never hauled to gaol. Or court."

"Well, nay, but you *have* lost several pounds playing the ponies."

They entered the stables, the sudden shade and scent of leather and horseflesh welcome.

Miles kicked at a tuft of hay. "What say you, Cousin?"

"I'm sorry to dent your enthusiasm," Noble told him, "but Article 8 of the Continental Association seeks to 'discourage every species of extravagance and dissipation, especially all horse-racing, and all kinds of gaming, cock-fighting, and other expensive diversions and entertainments.'"

"Bah!" Miles spat as they reached the stall of the quarter horse in question. "Burgesses and barristers have no sense of sport."

"Delegates now," Noble said, extending a hand. "And here stands the pride of Ty Mawr. Romulus is said to be the finest bloodstock in all Virginia, if not the entire thirteen colonies."

Miles gaped. The stallion stamped. Two grooms slowed to admire the horse.

"How's his temper?" Miles asked.

"Like yours. Fractious. Unpredictable."

"Thank you," Miles returned drily. "Sounds as if you still haven't forgiven me for breaking my betrothal to Lord Stirling's daughter."

"Forgiven you?" Noble checked a smile. "'Tis the wisest thing you've ever done."

"Well, fancy that." Surprise washed Miles's face. "A compliment from you at long last." He ran a hand down the horse's sleek side. "There's been no sign of her since the folly burned down in Williamsburg. I'd heard she was living there, working as a lacemaker. Quite a comedown for the daughter of Lord Stirling. Perhaps she's rejoined her father."

Noble turned toward the other end of the stable, where a groom waited with Miles's own mount. "Give my regards to your cronies in town." It was tantamount to a dismissal, but he wanted to be with Libby. "Now, if you'll excuse me, I've other business."

He tarried long enough to watch Miles ride off before turning up the hill toward Ty Bryn. He was late for dinner, but his bride, bless her, was not one to mind.

He envisioned Libby waiting at the door when he dismounted, holding out a hand to him, eyes shining. He prayed she'd be as favorably disposed to the news he had to tell her. But he'd wait till they'd eaten before he shared Washington's summons.

30

The storm of hooves on the drive told Liberty her new husband was well aware he was late. Feeling she'd swallowed a swarm of butterflies, she rushed to her bedchamber window to make sure it was him before taking a last look in the mirror.

Pale. Blue-veined. Slim as a riding whip. The lace ribbon woven in her upswept hair and her filmy fichu did little to soften her sharp edges. Gaunt she was. What man would find her appealing? Is that why Noble kept her at arm's length?

She took the stairs two at a time. Nell was in the kitchen and the other servants were occupied, so she met her new groom at the door, her warm welcome lost in his.

He tossed his hat onto the foyer chair. "I've not kept you waiting, I hope."

He looked so contrite, her heart squeezed. "The master of the house need not apologize, surely."

"Only to the mistress, mayhap," he said with a wink.

They went into the dining room where he seated her at a table, and they made small talk as Nell swept in and out, replenishing glasses and removing empty plates.

Liberty ate two of everything, raising Noble's curiosity.

There was teasing in his tone and query. "The country life agrees with you."

"Well, I . . ." Feeling gluttonous, she looked down at her empty plate. "I've decided I'm too . . ."

The sudden silence turned awkward.

"Too what, Libby?"

"Boyish."

She raised her gaze to see humor cross his face. "You, boyish?" He shook his head and forked a last bite of fish. "Mayhap Doctor Hessel should be sent for."

"Doctor Hessel? Why?"

"You're obviously in need of spectacles."

"My eyesight is in question, you mean."

"Aye. *Boyish* is not how I would define you."

"Oh?" The playful cadence to her voice was an open door inviting him in. "How would you define me?"

"Delicate. Feminine." He took a drink of ratafia. "Lovely. Alluring."

"Perhaps *you* are the one in need of spectacles."

"Nay." He frowned. "The attention you're sure to garner in Gosport is a worry to me."

Gosport again. She nearly sighed. But he was not finished.

"The British Navy is a debauched lot for the most part, and Andrew Sprowle's wine cellar is deep and wide. Add a highborn *geneth*, a lass like yourself . . ."

She picked up her dessert spoon as her former anxiety took hold. Was she walking into a trap? Should she abandon her plan?

She forged ahead. "No man would dare behave unseemly with my father present." Taking a bite of dessert, she fixed her attention on the fluted glass. "I shall leave at the first sign of trouble. Promise."

"One more meeting," he said quietly, his eyes unyielding. "And then you're done."

"Well and good. I'm ready to move on. Settle into married life." Should she tell him about the nursery? She'd sworn Nell and Isabeau to secrecy. Till the time was right she'd keep the door closed and decorate and rearrange to her heart's content.

He leaned back in his chair. "I've news to share that may be as hard for you as Gosport is for me."

She looked up as Nell brought coffee. Their dessert dishes were whisked away, steaming cups in their wake.

As the door closed, Noble took a post from his pocket. "I've been commissioned as major of the 2nd Virginia Regiment."

Her first swallow of coffee went awry. Sputtering, she said, "*Major* Rynallt?"

"Aye, at General Washington's request. Originally I'd been considered captain of his Life Guard, but . . ."

"One of Washington's personal bodyguards?" She'd heard talk of such things while at the folly but never dreamed he'd be among the chosen few.

"Washington is recruiting men for their sobriety, honesty, and good behavior. Men of some property. None but native-born Americans." He gave her a wry, regretful smile. "I am not native born. And there is one other difficulty. I am too tall."

"What?"

"Candidates are to be between five feet eight and five feet ten inches, 'handsomely and well made.'"

"Well, you satisfy on that score, though I'm guessing you're a tad over six feet."

"Aye, so I'm a mere major. The Committee of Safety is raising an army in Virginia's defense. Come September, recruits from every county will encamp behind the college of William and Mary, and there we'll drill."

She set her cup down, trying to come to terms with all the implications. An absent husband. Perhaps an absent father, if she conceived. Was this why there'd be no honeymoon? Would it not be best to remain childless during war?

"I'm not surprised at your commission. You're well respected and esteemed. I'm proud of you. Honored for you." She meant every word. "Men like you are needed, never more than now. I'd best start sewing soldiers' shirts. Knitting stockings like you said."

"Aye. For now I need a good rifle, tomahawk, bayonet, cartouche box, and three charges of powder."

The harsh-sounding words seemed out of place in their small yet elegant dining room. She thought of all the weapons in the foyer of the Governor's Palace in Williamsburg. Were they still there? September was not far. Soon he'd be gone. First to muster in Williamsburg, then on to face the British if the worst was realized. All the more reason to go to Gosport and learn what she could of Dunmore's plans.

He set the post on the table, his coffee untouched. The day was too warm for coffee, but she craved another bracing cup. She sought to fill the silence.

"Perhaps one day when all is said and done there'll be a Noblesburg or Noblesborough." Her attempt at levity fell flat. She knew he didn't care about such things, nor did she.

"All I want is to return to Ty Mawr and Ty Bryn." He looked more earnest than she'd ever seen him. "And you."

Their eyes met again. She was in need of her fan, warm more from his words than the coffee and summer's heat. "I'll be waiting."

He looked away, toward the windows and the James. "Pray for me. I have much to learn. I know books and law. I'm not a military man."

Did he doubt his call then? "You have all the makings of a fine soldier. In fact, long ago when I first saw you . . ." The girlish remembrance sharpened. "I thought you were an officer, you stood so straight and true."

He smiled. "And you, anwylyd, are a charmer through and through."

"'Tis the truth." She laced her hands together in her lap. "I've always thought uniformed men dashing. What will yours be like?"

"Rebel blue." There was truth in his teasing tone. "General Washington has recently appointed a clothier general."

"I can tailor it if you like."

"You'll put Prosser and Nicholson out of business."

"I'm no table monkey," she returned, remembering the lowest rung of the tailoring trade. "More a cutter and finisher. We'll need to purchase cloth."

"Henry sent a bolt." He rolled his eyes skyward. "The man is already at war."

"I'll need to learn the cut of your uniform. How about sherryvallies?" she mused, thinking of overbreeches. "I'll take your measurements now, if you like."

They went into the parlor, and she took her measuring tape from her sewing basket, then stood to one side while he shrugged off his frock coat.

"All this makes me think of poor George Bosomworth, who barely eked out a living tailoring in town. He died with a sad estate of twelve pounds not long ago." She stretched the tape across his shoulders, noting the width with satisfaction. "You saved me from all that, you know."

"What?"

"Poverty. Want."

"Would you make me some knight in shining armor, Libby?"

"More a noble soldier," she returned. He held still while she ran the tape from shoulder to wrist. "I suppose I should call you 'Major Rynallt' in company."

"Since you rarely call me by my given name, I wouldn't worry with 'Major.'"

She noted the subtle sorrow in his words, then shook off her pleasure for practicality. Circling his middle with the tape, she pinched it off between his weskit and trousers. His measurements were easily remembered—nay, treasured—now that time was short. She would write them in her commonplace book. 'Twould be simple enough to cut a pattern from an old coat. "You said Mister Henry sent cloth."

"Colonel Henry now."

She expelled a breath. "The whole world's turned upside down when misters become majors and firebrands become colonels."

His chuckle cut into the tenseness. "My commanding officer is Colonel William Woodford from Caroline County."

"I've not heard of him till now."

"You will henceforth."

She finished her taping, a bit lost in the pleasure of it.

He was looking down at her, thoughtful. "So you think you're boyish . . ." He took the tape from her hands and circled her middle. "Just how small is your waist?"

All his detailed measurements flew out of her head. He stood so near, nearer than he'd ever been, even the mornings he'd sat by her bedside. Even closer than when they'd wed. So near now that he was perfectly positioned to . . . kiss her. She'd never been kissed. But she'd oft wondered what it might be like. All she wanted was for him to put down the tape and take her in his arms and end all speculation.

"Eighteen inches." Hanging the tape about his neck like

a true tailor, he placed his hands about her waist, nearly encircling it. "Easily spanned by my hands."

She sighed. "And that, sir, is the trouble."

"Trouble? Nay," he said with a wink as his hands fell away. "A bit more bara brith should do the trick."

She focused on a buttonhole of his shirt, thoughts full of far more than gussets and seams. "I'll get to work right away. Do be so kind as to send the cloth up when you return down the hill. And your violin."

His face lit with interest. "Are you in the mood for music, Libby?"

"Have you never heard the harp paired with the violin? 'Tis sublime." She stepped back, watching him put on his frock coat again. Their eyes met, held. It seemed he touched her in glances, sending a little shiver through her each time.

"Give word to Ninian should you need me. I'll be in my study at Ty Mawr till supper."

"That seems rather . . . far." The words were out before she'd given them thought.

He studied her, looking surprised. "Would you rather I be here? Occupy a study no bigger than the necessary out back?"

"Aye, aye, Major." She entwined her hands, feeling coy. "Necessary or no, you are necessary to me."

All afternoon she measured and cut and pinned, pausing long enough to read the post Noble had left on the dinner table. Congress had originally adopted brown as the official color for uniforms, but there was a scarcity of brown cloth and thus the chosen color was blue. What Henry had sent was a hardy wool of good quality, gotten from some unknown merchant. She would make Noble a blue coat with blue facing laced with white around the buttonholes till she knew more.

Uniforms would instill pride in the company or regiment, Washington wrote, even if only officers wore them. 'Twas certainly her desire that Major Rynallt of the 2nd Virginia Regiment have one.

A little before teatime, she climbed the stairs to the nursery. Now completely furnished from the attic, it was charming, even cozy with its corner fireplace. 'Twas hard to imagine the heat of a fire in the dog days of summer, but winter was coming. The fireplace insert was of iron, embossed with angels that only small children could see at eye level, adding a touch of whimsy.

She went about the room, feeling a tad silly as she rearranged a pillow here and straightened a picture there. There was no baby coming. No call for a nursery. But her mother's heart wouldn't stop beating.

She moved toward the door and turned to take a last, contemplative look.

"Mistress!" Isabeau exclaimed as she entered the nursery. "Is there something you are not telling me?"

Liberty started, her pride and pleasure in the room hard to hide. "No secrets, nay. I simply want to make ready for when the time comes."

"A charming cradle, no?" Isabeau ran a hand over the polished mahogany edge, setting it to rocking slightly, and then her face clouded. "While you are busy sewing Major Rynallt's new uniform, I am nearly finished hemming your dress for the ball. You must try it on."

Liberty's happiness dimmed as they crossed the hall into the dressing room. The gown of silver tissue was draped across a chair, a feast of silk woven with silver gilt threads. Though sumptuous, the alterations near perfect, it left Liberty cold.

Isabeau was fawning over Enid's jewelry. "These sapphires set in silver are a perfect pairing, are they not?" She lifted the glittering necklace from the velvet case, noting the looped ends for the silk ribbon to tie around one's throat.

Liberty said nothing, trying to remember the details. Noble would ride ahead of them to Gosport. Dougray was to drive the coach. They would meet at a certain spot if there was trouble . . .

Once in the gown, Liberty turned in a slow circle as Isabeau's practiced eye examined the dress for loose threads or any flaw.

"*Enchante!*" Her expression shifted from approval to near panic. "You resemble cake in so fine a gown . . . and all those hungry soldiers!"

"*Mais no!*" In a tone that would stand her in good stead as a mother, Liberty said, "Speaking of cake, is it not time for some bara brith?"

"Mistress! How can you eat at such a time?" Isabeau was tottering toward hysteria the longer they dwelt on Gosport, her voice slightly shrill. "All I can think of is your papa. Now that he has gone away, I can tell you how he frightened me with his black moods. Like a funnel cloud he was! What if he should keep you aboard ship? Force you to wed a sailor?"

"I am already married, remember." Checking the tiny watch pinned to her bodice, Liberty brought her maid's moodiness to an end. "I'll ring for Nell. Please have a seat and we'll refresh ourselves."

"Refreshments—and then?" Isabeau sat with a disgruntled sigh, looking as if she was facing the guillotine, as Liberty gave a gentle tug on the bellpull.

Soon Nell bustled in with Ty Mawr's tea set, and Libby

presided in silver tissue. The bara brith was delightful, the china exquisite, a gentle reminder of more serene times.

Below, the foyer clock chimed, ticking unceasingly toward Gosport.

The appointed time was at hand. They stood in Ty Bryn's small study adjoining the first-floor parlor. The octagonal walls were lined with bookshelves, Noble's desk in the room's center. From where Liberty stood she could make out a few unsettling titles atop her husband's desk.

A Treatise of Military Discipline. An Essay on the Art of War. The Military Guide for Young Officers.

His half-finished uniform coat lay across her sewing basket. She longed to complete it. Longed to shed this elaborate gown and simply savor his presence now that he'd moved his study to Ty Bryn, small as it was. Even his violin brought up from Ty Mawr begged playing. But for now, more pressing matters stole their time and attention.

"I prayed for cooler weather," Noble said as calmly as if he was discussing a legal document.

"Cooler weather we have," Liberty replied. She glanced at Ty Bryn's open front door. The clatter of the black coach on the drive was impossible to ignore, looking much like the hearse she'd so often seen about Williamsburg, the somber warners handing out death cakes in passing.

Could he sense her ripening dread? Her desire to flee out the back door to the shade and comfort of the portico? Despite his prayers and the slight ease in temperature, the ride would still be sweltering from Ty Bryn to Gosport.

He took one of her gloved hands. She'd rather he take her in his arms and quell her churning stomach instead. The scent of rosewater, a generous dousing by Isabeau, wafted between them.

"I've prayed for safe travel," he said. "That the gathering be civil. Orderly."

She knew what he was thinking. No excess of spirits. No moral lapses. That officers and officials be gentlemen.

"Your prayers have no end," she breathed as his fingers tightened around her own. "They're so needed. And appreciated."

He looked down at her, a telltale wariness behind his stoicism. "Two doors down from Sprowle's mansion is a warehouse bearing a blue sign labeled 'Merrick's.' Remember, if the night turns troublesome and you need to go there, the door will be unlocked. I'll not be far, nor will Dougray."

"A blue sign," she echoed. "Merrick's."

"For now, you need praying for, anwylyd."

At her nod he rested his hands on top of her head, lightly enough not to disturb Isabeau's artful coiffure but almost symbolic as if covering her. Eyes closed, he spoke in Welsh. Quiet words full of power and poignancy. The meaning was lost to her, but the emotion of the moment was not. 'Twas a husband's prayer for his wife. For protection and blessing, surely. A holy moment.

"Amen," he said, finally taking her in his arms.

She laid her head upon his shoulder, hearing the rustle of leaves outside the open windows as summer hinted of autumn. Since childhood, she'd always imagined the wind sounding like the rush of angels' wing. Once again the nursery came to mind, and the charming angels on the fireplace insert. What if the room remained empty? Nay, that she could not bear. Best empty her mind of the worry and savor Noble's nearness. For long moments he held her as if he wanted to mark the memory. Leave nothing undone. For now she felt safe, at home in the haven of his hard arms.

His breath was warm against her ear. "I'll ride ahead of you some distance. Once in Gosport I'll go about my business till you're done at Sprowle's."

It came to her again that her husband, traveling to a Tory stronghold, was in more danger than she.

31

In Gosport the odor of brine and pitch was stronger, the sea wind hotter. His majesty's sloops glutted the water, but there were no British warships. Not yet. Once they came the spirit of sedition and rebellion would be crushed. A lone sloop was patrolling the bay, its white wake like fluted lace on the calm Elizabeth River.

Sprowle's mansion faced the water, its neighbors naught but stone warehouses some five stories high. It bespoke industry and Scots fortitude. Liberty spied Merrick's and anchored it to memory. Dunmore's troops were quartered at a near shipyard warehouse. Their presence and their bright uniforms were plain enough.

Liberty alighted from the coach a block or more away, stripped of all ties to Ty Mawr. The door to the Sprowle mansion was open wide, a butler at the entrance. He announced her arrival over the din of a hundred or more cultured voices, her father's foremost. Lord Stirling stood with his host, Andrew Sprowle, at one end of the ballroom while she was met by Sprowle's wife, whose smile of greeting did not reach her eyes.

"Ah, Lord Stirling's lovely daughter," she murmured, drawing Liberty into an alcove brimming with ferns. "I believe we've met before, at a garden party given by Lady Dunmore."

"I remember, fondly." But the mention was melancholy, at least for Liberty. She faced her hostess warily. Kate Sprowle had a feisty reputation, her high color in keeping with what Liberty recollected. Yet there was an edge to her tonight that had been missing in the Palace gardens. "Are you . . . all right, Mistress Sprowle? Is the current company too much?"

"Indeed, m'lady." Kate looked hard at her as if deciding whether to vent her angst. "The current company is indeed too much. Lord Dunmore and his retinue have descended on my house and my provisions and are rioting in them."

Liberty had only to look at the throng in the ballroom to imagine what went on behind the scenes. Was her father a chief troublemaker?

Kate continued with an agitated flutter of her fan. "His lordship refers to my husband as Gosport's new lieutenant governor, which only incenses Lord Stirling."

This Liberty could well imagine. Her father's pride had always been in play. "So his lordship feels Gosport is now the new capital, not Williamsburg."

"Precisely," Kate replied. "And here his entire entourage behaves like the worst of heathens, treating my household effects and my servants in the most uncivilized ways."

"Surely that will end soon with the arrival of British warships."

"God send them then," she murmured, turning toward an alcove window. "His lordship and your father watch daily for their coming."

Liberty scanned the horizon, fixing on the outer harbor and mouth of the river. "Tonight may well be the night."

And if they came? What did that spell for the likes of Washington and Henry? Noble and other Independence Men? She knew the outcome of treason. Death. This crisis had taken a personal turn. Once these politics had been little more than newsprint. Gossip. Hearsay. But now?

"And what of your eminent guest my father and Lord Dunmore spoke of entertaining here?" Liberty pressed in genuine interest.

Kate shrugged silk-clad shoulders. "I've seen nothing on that score."

"Daughter?" Her father stood behind them.

She and Kate turned away from the window. "Greetings, Father." Liberty's smile was false. Had she ever been glad to see him? It was as Isabeau said. Like a funnel cloud he was, full of bluster and fury. Even now she sensed his irritation with her, his impatience for whatever news she had brought.

"Let us dispense with formalities and adjourn to the study." He took Liberty by the sleeve, his firm hand more pinch. "Excuse us, Mistress Sprowle."

'Twas nothing short of a curt dismissal. Liberty felt a qualm for Kate, who bristled visibly. Taking a last look about the crowded ballroom brought no ease. Lord Dunmore was at the far end with his paramour, Kitty. Thank heaven Lady Charlotte had sailed. Liberty had yet to see her father's favorite, the ginger-haired Phila.

She followed him to a private room made stale by spirits and smoke, its paneled walls ponderously heavy with books. Though the study was as dark as it was strange, she was glad to be away from the crush of Tories. A shuttered window gave little light, just enough to showcase a dark silhouette.

Doctor Hessel?

He turned. "Lady Elisabeth." Dressed in his impeccable best, he came forward and kissed her hand.

A dozen questions begged answers. Had Hessel chosen sides? Aligned himself with her father? Tonight he was formality itself, as starched as the Raleigh wash, hardly the easy, affable physic. For her father's sake, likely.

The door closed. "Tell me what you know," her father said.

And so she did, mixing in as much truth as untruth lest she be called a liar. They listened intently, betimes questioning her about the newly formed Virginia Regiment, slaves fleeing and crippling plantations, the *Virginia Gazette*'s continued printing of inflammatory articles.

When she finished, her father said nothing for a long, tense minute as if digesting all she had told him. And then, "The time has come, Daughter, when you are of more use to me here than there."

"Here, as in Gosport?" She reached for the back of the chair she stood beside, its ornate rococo back hard beneath her gloved hand. "You mean I'm to stay on?"

"Indeed. You'll occupy a second-floor bedchamber in this very house and be present at all social functions."

"But I—I have business. Lace orders to honor—"

"That ruse is done." His voice held the finality of a locked door. "Doctor Hessel tells me the place you were living has been burned to the ground. You'll not hear any more Patriot secrets at the Raleigh." He paused a moment and looked directly at her. "You've been found out."

They were both looking at her, expecting her to elaborate. Ice lined her spine. Did they suspect she was with Noble? Living at Ty Bryn? She scrambled for an answer. "But this house—'tis teeming with people—"

"Your tenure here will likely be brief. Once the warships arrive we'll move further up the Chesapeake and raise a defense there."

She took a step back, toward the closed door, but Hessel circled behind her.

"If you refuse to comply with my plan, the doctor will administer a calming drug. I shall tell everyone you launched into hysteria and had to be confined to your chamber. Given your mother was recently admitted to Publick Hospital, no one will doubt it."

She whirled to face Hessel and saw a glimmer of compassion on his face, but then it vanished quick as it had come.

Her father moved to the door. "Once you compose yourself you may rejoin the dancing. Later you'll retire upstairs."

He went out, shutting the door firmly behind him. Her thoughts veered to the footmen at the front entrance, no doubt armed and aware she was not to leave Sprowle's teeming mansion. Every exit would be watched. She was trapped, plain and simple, as bound as if her hands were tied.

Nothing had prepared her for the irreversibility of this moment. She looked on, stricken, as Hessel rummaged in his pocket and produced a vial. For once she felt as hysterical as Isabeau.

"There is no need, Bram." Her voice was dulcet, so at odds with her brimming panic, returning them to the familiar address of old. "If you are my trusted friend, a fellow believer, you will not obey the whim of my father, who is neither."

"Elisabeth . . ." He looked down at her. "Joining us here is far preferable to lacemaking, surely. Plying a trade is so far beneath you."

"Nay. 'Twas of my choosing and is honorable. This"—she waved a hand about the room—"is not."

"It is what it is. Your father and Lord Dunmore have elevated me to personal physician, and I shall do everything in my power to retain that position."

Since when did he care for such? She stared at him, weary of rank and social position and pecking order, all decidedly more British than American. She could offer no sincere congratulations so said with finality, "Do as you wish but leave me out of it. I must go." Turning, she tried the doorknob. Locked.

"Go where?"

"Back to the ball." Her hand stayed on the knob. She'd put on a brave face and return to dancing, if only briefly and to fool them, then make her escape.

"Not until you're calmer. I've opium here laced with brandy."

She spoke over her shoulder. "Then I shall be too drowsy to mind my steps."

"So be it. I cannot stand those navy men fawning over you. Yet I sense your father's ambitions to parade you about in hopes of an advantageous match."

"Those ambitions are ill placed." She faced him, fear giving way to fury. Should she say what was uppermost in her mind? Her heart? She could scarce believe it herself. "I am already wed."

His gaze sharpened. "Married?"

"To one of the Independence Men."

"You—*what*?" Disgust rivaled his surprise. "Surely you jest."

"I do not." She held tight to the details, wanting to protect Noble at all costs yet wanting to distance herself from the doctor and any romantic notions he had for her. If he knew his hopes were for naught, might he let her go? "We wed a few days ago, and quite happily at that."

He regarded her in stunned silence, then looked to the vial he held. "Do you know what your father will do once he learns this?"

"I do. And if you betray me by telling him, you shall live with the consequences."

"Betray you? Have you not betrayed us?" His fair features grew ruddy. "Whom exactly have you wed? Not that traitor Rynallt, surely."

"One who has always had my well-being, my best interests, at heart." Saying it, she nearly choked with emotion as Noble's many kindnesses and sacrifices stood tall in her memory. Even now, at great personal risk, he was near at hand. "My husband is above locking me in and threatening me with laudanum."

Hessel grabbed her wrist, dropping the vial in his haste. It hit the plank floor with a clatter but did not break. "Elisabeth, *who*?" His grip sent a spasm of pain up her bare arm. "Tell me and perhaps some deal can be struck."

"Deal?" She shook him off. "How like my father you sound. Not everything has a price. Not even Lord Dunmore can untie a marital knot."

He bent to retrieve the vial, his jaw a hard line. He was no longer the doctor she knew. Each of them had crossed a line fraught with complications and irreversibilities.

"You are a good man. A fine physic." She softened yet stood her ground. "Do not make an enemy of my husband or this cause. Despite the odds, these Patriots will be victorious in the end." She did not have the gift of second sight, of predicting the future, just a sudden, unswerving confidence that the colonies would prevail because men like Noble were freedom's foundation.

Hessel looked shaken. Sick. He returned the vial to his weskit and took out a key. "A scattering of turncoats will not prevail against the mightiest fighting force known to man.

319

Nor can I commit treason against the king." He unlocked the door. "I leave you to your delusions."

He went out, and she heard the scrape of the key against the lock. Penned in again, she flew to the window, a closed rectangle that overlooked the river and Sprowle's vast shipping enterprise. Painted shut it was, the glass dirty. Half a dozen red-coated soldiers talked and smoked in the near dark along the waterfront below.

God in heaven, help me.

Was Hessel now telling her father everything? Would Papa come in like a whirlwind and abuse her? The music in the ballroom swelled as a minuet gave way to a country dance.

Her heart seemed to beat out of her chest. She struggled to breathe. She should have heeded Noble. Should have shunned Gosport. Oh, to be back at Ty Bryn. Her haven. This dark study was a prison, unlit and oppressive and shabby from use.

She sat down hard on a settee, trying to replace panic with prayer and reason. Noble was not far, nor were Dougray and Isabeau. The mantel clock struck nine. Supper would likely be served at ten, followed by dancing till dawn.

Would they leave her here all night? She got up and went to the ornate hearth, running her hands over the woodwork in search of a lever or secret spring. But this was not Ty Bryn with its secret stair or service door.

A quarter of an hour dragged by. She paced. Prayed. Tried the door again. Only the Lord could extricate her from Gosport.

Atop a table was a heavy vase capable of breaking glass—and attracting the attention of one too many redcoats. One seemed intent on the window. Or was she simply overwrought and imagining it?

Her bodice grew damp, the heat of a stifling August night pressing in. The music ceased. Lightheaded, she sat down again. A sound at the door set her on her feet. Her father? Hessel? At last the door opened, and a housemaid brought in a tray of supper items being served in Sprowle's dining room, none of them appealing.

In back of the maid was Kate, looking no less agitated than she had at first. "Why have you been locked in my husband's study?"

Was Kate her ally or her enemy? "I'm held here against my will. My father insists that I stay on." Skirting the supper tray, Liberty inched her way toward the door. "Had I known his intent, I would not have come."

Kate ordered the maid out and turned to Liberty. "One more person in the mayhem of this house is one too many."

Could it truly be this simple? Would irascible, overburdened Kate retaliate for Dunmore's commandeering of her house with this slight to Lord Stirling's pride and plans?

Kate waved a hand. "Leave now—quickly—and I'll say nothing to your father."

Liberty moved past her hostess, thanks on her lips, and sought the foyer and the mansion's front door. At Kate's insistence the guard let her pass. Liberty descended the front steps at a near run and ran smack into Noble at the first lamppost. Joy sang through her, so at odds with their predicament.

"Keep moving," Noble told her as the redcoats along the waterfront turned and watched them hasten past. "I sensed you were in danger so I kept close to the mansion."

The darkness was a blessed disguise. She could see the outline of a coach ahead. Dougray? Isabeau would be within, the safety of home in reach. She wanted to weep with relief.

"There was some trouble." Her voice was wavering, as

were her legs, a latent response to the turmoil of the past hours. "My father wanted to keep me at Sprowle's."

Noble put an arm around her shoulders, imparting the strength she so needed. Leaning into him, she stepped around a shattered gin bottle on the cobblestones. The way was poorly lit, the street strewn with garbage.

Almost there. Isabeau got out of the coach and held open the door, waiting for them. Perched on his box, Dougray looked like he was ready to fly.

"Rynallt, is that you?" a voice rang out, chilling in tone. It bore as much of a challenge as did the figure springing from an alley and knocking Noble off his feet. A scuffle ensued, both men rolling in the muck atop cobblestones, startling both wharf rats and gulls.

Stunned, Liberty backed up as the fracas intensified. She was aware of Dougray jumping down from his box and starting toward them just as a second man emerged from the shadows, blocking him.

With effort, Noble got to his feet, as did his attacker, who lunged for him again. Liberty stepped nearer, torn between fleeing and helping if she could. They'd not harm a woman, surely. But a woman could do harm. Yet she had no weapon.

Hands unsteady, she bent and pulled free a hat pin in her garter. She'd thought to bring it at the last, its needle-like point now of far better use securing a husband than a hat. She leaned in as Noble pinned his opponent, but in a heartbeat the thickset man thrust him aside, thwarting her aim. Finally, frantically, she drove the hatpin home, rewarded with a howl of pain.

Dougray rushed forward, having bested the second man who'd joined the fight. Together, he and Noble drove the first assailant backward with a punch and a shove. Off the dock he went into the dark water with a satisfying splash.

Trembling, breathless, Liberty kept to the light beneath a street lamp. And then the fierce tug of her husband's hand was enough to send her running, done with Gosport for good.

32

"Let me tend you," Liberty said. 'Twas a woman's task, a wife's. Not a valet's.

Noble's jaw bore a mean gash from his waterfront scuffle, a purplish bruise marring his right eye. Still, he winked and looked askance at her as she approached him in the privacy of their second-floor sitting room. "Just what was it you were wielding there at the last?"

She gave a satisfied smile. "A ferocious ivory hat pin of cut steel. Nearly as formidable as your sword or bayonet."

"Beware hat pin–wielding women then." He sat down in a chair with a little groan that did not escape her notice. "I didn't think you had it in you."

"I'm not all ribbons and roses."

"Nay, you are not. The poor man will never be the same."

"Poor man, indeed. Who do you think he was?"

His slight shrug was more wince. "One of any number of Tories."

She sniffed at the ointment Mistress Tremayne had given her, breathing in comfrey and rosemary from Ty Mawr's herb garden. Gently she applied it with a clean cloth.

Patient beneath her gentle hands, he mused, "Who needs Doctor Hessel when Nurse Rynallt will do?"

"I don't know that I will ever see the doctor or my father again."

"Does that make you melancholy, Libby?"

She shifted, her gown of silver tissue rustling. "It makes me fear for my father eternally. He knows no saving grace, no Savior. On the other hand, all this simply makes my loyalties clearer. My true ties dearer."

"What about that guest Dunmore and your father were expecting? Did he or she ever arrive?"

"'Twas naught but a ploy to bolster Tory spirits and raise flagging expectations, I suspect."

The evening played out in her mind like a sordid stage production. She was exhausted now at nearly two o'clock in the morning, but she continued to apply the salve, Noble's comfort foremost.

"I've posted a guard in case someone followed."

Alarmed, she stilled her hands.

"A precaution, 'tis all. You were wise not to tell them you're my bride. As it is, you've stirred their interest and eluded them, with a little help from irate Kate."

Truly, if not for the exasperated Mistress Sprowle, she'd likely still be in the locked study. She gave him a sheepish smile. After tonight, she felt rash. Foolish. Embarrassed. "I pray, if worse comes to worst, we'll billet no redcoats here."

He stood. "I'll send Isabeau in."

She set the ointment aside, wishing for a little coffee or tea despite the heat. But they needed to be abed. "You're not going to rest?"

"Not yet. I've unread correspondence to see about."

She'd oft seen the stack of posts from Philadelphia, even

Boston and New York, some delivered by secret courier. Likely more had arrived today. She got to her feet, hoping her disappointment didn't show. She wanted nothing more than his help with her dress and underpinnings. While romance wasn't on her mind, comfort was. He was her refuge in all the ways that mattered.

"I'll be below if you need me," he told her.

She nodded and began removing the sapphires from her neck and ears, listening for Isabeau's soft tread on the stairs. When she finally came, bearing a tea tray with the lovely Ty Bryn china, Liberty looked at her in astonishment.

With a shrug, her maid said, "Tea on a hot summer night is *fou*, but if the master says so, it is so, no?"

Liberty clasped her hands together in delight, more from Noble's thoughtfulness than the favored brew. Tea or no tea, sleep would be long in coming, if at all. Perhaps she would wait up for him. Finish sewing his uniform.

Relieved, she shed the heavy dress and its heavier memories. "Take it," she told Isabeau, who favored the ornate French style above any other. "'Twould make a fine wedding gown."

Isabeau's blush was telling, her thanks profuse. She went out, arms full of silver tissue, leaving Liberty in her sultana with her tea.

Adversity is a school in which few men wish to be educated.

Noble awoke as the cock crowed, the words of a letter he'd been reading at the last still circling in his sleep-numbed brain. His first thought was of Libby. *Anwylyd.*

Ty Bryn was quiet, no servants about like at Ty Mawr.

The candelabra on his desk was gutted, the spent wax a hardened puddle atop his desk. A small drift of ashes in the fireplace bespoke burned correspondence. The stakes were climbing higher. He'd been delivered a map taken from the British, identifying Ty Mawr as the estate belonging to "the patriot Rynallt." Another confiscated letter from British officials spoke of "sending Rynallt and Henry to Boston in irons." There General Gage held sway as the commander of British forces in America. No longer was there any question Noble was a marked man, yet all that filled his thoughts was the woman upstairs who made all these politics dry as dust.

He took the stairs two at a time, eyes adjusting to the hall's dimness. Most of the second-floor doors were kept closed, as were his and Libby's. One door at the hall's end was cracked open, a beam of sunlight cutting across pine planks.

Curious, he trod down the narrow passage, avoiding the one board in the floor that creaked loud as a horn. Had the maids been cleaning and forgotten to close it? Madoc stepped out, swishing his tail and purring contentedly.

To his recollection this particular room had always sat empty. He pushed the door open wider to sunlight and the scent of lavender. Small bunches of it lay about to sweeten what was now, without any doubt, a nursery.

Half a dozen warring emotions slid through him. Was this Libby's doing? He'd neglected his bride of days, thinking she needed more time to adjust to marriage. Believing she wasn't ready for the intimate side of two becoming one. Wanting some encouraging sign from her.

Man, are ye daft?

So she wanted children. Was a family not his dream too? Aye, in safer, more settled times. His worst nightmare was not war nor capture nor death but leaving a widow and baby behind.

He stood stone still, letting his emotions settle, aiming for an objective view. Libby had spoken of her admiration and affection for Lady Charlotte and her large brood. For an only child with an estranged father and absent mother, the prospect of a happy family would be more than appealing. For a kin-starved young woman, it would seem like heaven on earth.

This nursery, though privately arranged, seemed an open invitation. And here he stood, so unaware of his new wife and her hopes that an odd sadness took hold.

Stepping around Madoc, he entered the room, trying to imagine what his firstborn and an entire family might be like. The cradle looked small if sturdy. Everything in this readied space bespoke loving care. Madoc's presence even seemed approving.

"So . . . what do you think?"

The soft voice was as alluring as ever. He turned around to find Libby in her sultana, feet bare and hair plaited. He forgot all about the intimate business at hand.

She looked contrite. "I hope you don't mind that I robbed the attic."

He winked. "'Tis yours to rob, Mistress Rynallt."

"Then I shan't feel guilty I didn't ask first."

"Nay." His focus returned to the room. "An unexpected surprise but not an unwelcome one."

Her face flushed the pink of her sultana, and he knew he'd given the right reply. "Here we are," she said quietly, "and we've hardly discussed children."

"They usually arrive without much discourse," he murmured.

She laughed, and it was his collar that heated. "True enough."

"You've obviously put thought behind this room." His fingers curled over the back of a rocking chair. "No doubt you've considered a name or two."

She was beside him now, Madoc in her arms. Shoulder to shoulder they surveyed the workings of her head and heart. "A Welsh name should do."

"Spoken like an obliging wife."

"Yet you're pleased," she said, smiling up at him. "I can see that you are."

"What you see is a man in need of breakfast." He ran a hand through unkempt hair. "Coffee, at least."

"Did you spend the night in your study?"

"Foolishly so."

"I—I waited up for you . . ."

Had she? She looked from him to the cradle. What he'd give to read her thoughts. A wealth of emotion lay behind her blue gaze.

She set Madoc down. Neither of them made any move to take his offer of breakfast. Slowly he turned toward her. Ever since their wedding day he'd regretted he'd not kissed her. He'd merely lifted her veil before letting it fall back around her shoulders in lacy folds. There was no veil between them now. No gardenful of guests. No cake to eat or toast to be drunk. No awkwardness. If love was palpable it was here, in this quiet room that held so many hopes—his and hers. *Theirs.*

Encircling her waist with his hands, he felt the warmth and fullness of her. Without her usual stays and underpinnings, the sultana she wore seemed an invitation. Tilting his head, he brushed his lips against the pale slope of her neck before moving to her ear, where a pale tendril had slipped free of her braid. If spring had a scent, it was her. This close, she seemed the piece that had been missing from Ty Bryn, created to fit against him and fill every empty place.

Her hands stole about his shoulders, fingers lacing together where his stock buckle sat at the back of his neck. He was having trouble catching his breath, the race of his pulse at full gallop. He bent his head and kissed her parted lips, once, twice, her response as ardent as his own. Time . . . the room . . . spun away.

And then Libby let go of him, hands sliding down the length of his weskit. She half turned toward the nursery door at the sound of a footfall in the hall. The clink of Mistress Tremayne's chatelaine was unmistakable. Arms full of linens, the housekeeper passed the nursery's open door on her way to the linen closet at the end of the hall.

"Will you join me?" He offered Libby his arm in what he hoped was a gallant gesture.

Flushed, eyes alight, she simply slipped her hand in his, returning his thoughts to the empty nursery and what it would take to fill it.

"Some independence tea and bara brith, perhaps?" She recovered her composure and shut the nursery door behind them. "Though a strong cup of coffee with cream and sugar will do. After that, I'll return to my handwork."

"Your last lace orders?"

She nodded. "Though my time is better spent imitating those Daughters of Liberty my mother wrote me about. She's busy supervising mass spinning bees and boycotting tea. She says the colonies must become a coffee-drinking nation."

"You'll write her that we've wed?"

"Now that Gosport is behind us, I shall. She'll no doubt crow the news from Philadelphia's rooftops."

"She's welcome here."

"Should I return to Ty Mawr as its true mistress first?"

"Nay." He said it so forcefully her eyes widened. "Ty Mawr has been targeted by the British. I don't know what will come of it, but for now you're safer out of sight at Ty Bryn, especially when I'll be away—"

"Away?"

"Tomorrow we muster in Williamsburg." Even as he said it he was planning another occurrence of what had just passed between them. "And Patrick Henry has called for a meeting at the Raleigh this afternoon."

She looked as crestfallen as he felt. "'Tis our goodbye breakfast then."

"Of sorts." It had the feel of the Last Supper. Grim. Final.

"I've nearly finished your uniform."

Good news, that, yet why did he feel weighted with rocks?

They went into the breakfast room, bypassing Nell, who hastened to the kitchen. A silver pitcher of flowers graced the table, their perfume reminding him the gardener and overseer needed meeting with before he left. Libby leaned in and breathed the flowers' heady fragrance, eyes closed, and he thanked God for his efficient staff. His wife would not want in his absence.

"Coffee, please," she said with a smile when Nell served them.

He took his black and watched as she added sugar and cream. Their plates overflowed with sunny eggs, fat sausages, and thick slices of toasted bread slathered with butter and honey from Ty Mawr's creamery and hives. To his surprise, Libby said little while Madoc watched them from the doorway.

She finished every bite. "How long will you be away?"

"A fortnight, likely. We'll encamp behind the college, Henry's orders." William and Mary's buildings made a fine base. But Williamsburg wasn't home. And it was too many miles from Libby. "All this makes me wish I had a townhouse there—and you in it."

"A good soldier shouldn't be distracted by a needy wife."

"True enough, though I'd hardly call you needy. Not after the hat pin incident." He forked a last bite as she refilled his coffee. "Send word to me at any time should the need arise. I'll have my head buried in military books when I'm not drilling." He leaned back in his chair. "I don't want to tie you to the house, but I must, at least for now. Have your last lace orders delivered by the servants, aye?"

"Of course." She set down her cup. "Ty Bryn will miss you. I'll miss you."

Their eyes locked. He had half a mind to dismiss all orders and stay home, Patrick Henry be hanged. "Hopefully the separation will be short and all will come to naught."

But he didn't believe it, and the look in her lovely eyes confirmed she didn't either.

33

Dear Mama,

By now you must be wondering about my lack of letters. Since I last wrote, the folly in which I lived and made lace burned to the ground, and I have been in contact with Father, who is entrenched with Lord Dunmore in Gosport. Unbeknownst to many, I have wed Noble Rynallt and hereby declare my allegiance to our cause. What will come of all this talk of liberty and rebellion I do not know. So many lives and fortunes are in jeopardy.

I am safely settled on the James River at my new husband's estate. We covet your company when time and circumstances permit. My prayer is that you are well and Philadelphia is as much to your liking as my new home is to me.

Your affectionate daughter

The ink glistened as Liberty sprinkled it with pounce before folding and sealing the letter, still feeling the pleasure her new name wrought. Her mother would be relieved and pleased. Her father, once he found out, would be neither. And he would find out. Virginia was not vast and spies were everywhere. Daily she prayed he'd sail away for good.

Noble had been gone a week in Williamsburg. Finished with her lace orders and his uniform, she began to knit stockings for the militia, spurred on by reports that ninety-two members of the Daughters of Liberty in Massachusetts had brought their spinning wheels to meeting and together spun 170 skeins of yarn. She would do her small part.

Madoc stayed close, playing with stray yarn and jumping into her lap when her needles stilled. "You are good company," she told him, stroking his silvery ears. "'Tis a shame I can't set you to knitting. Together we might make happy a great many more soldiers."

Always she wondered how Noble fared. When the sun was blistering and no wind ruffled the James, she fretted inland Williamsburg would be hot as a bake oven. When word of another summer fever reached her, she worried that he might have succumbed yet not sent word to her.

At last a post came.

Dearest Anwylyd,

I found your note in my uniform pocket, and that is where I left it so that I shan't have to part with it. It does me good to hear that my image is imprinted on your heart. I hope your concern that your letters might miscarry and fall into the wrong hands does not deter you from writing, especially if we are to endure longer separations. Forgive me if these scribblings are illegible and all too brief. They are contrary to my all-consuming thoughts of you.

For now, I enjoy good health. God be praised our

company is hardy despite the heat. The military manuals I have read are standing me in good stead.

I subscribe myself your
loving husband

'Twas her first letter from him, and though necessarily brief, she found it to be like the sweetest dessert. Besotted, she went to bed, tucking it beneath her pillow. She would write to him upon awakening, savoring the anticipation of that too. But every expectation seemed fraught with uncertainty.

Sometime in the night Isabeau woke her from a sound sleep. "Mistress, come away! Quickly! Something is burning. There is talk that the British fleet is setting fire to rebel plantations."

Sleep fell away. Liberty reached for her sultana before rushing to the window where Isabeau stood pointing. On the horizon was a fiery smudge of orange and crimson that seemed to expand before their eyes.

"I fear 'tis Carter's Grove," Liberty said. The great house was of brick like Ty Mawr and Ty Bryn, its interior boasting some of the finest woodwork in the colonies. By the time help came, would more proud plantations be rubble? All of Virginia's forces were marshaled in Williamsburg.

Liberty turned away from the window. "Perhaps 'tis only a barn or outbuilding."

"*Oui*, perhaps. With the weather so dry . . ." Isabeau touched her forehead as if she felt faint. "But what if they come here? What if they set fire to this very house—"

"Nay, surely not." But she was not sure, her voice fading at Isabeau's next exclamation.

"*L'aide de Dieu!*"

Beneath the light of torches were a dozen or more silhouettes on the grounds below. A cold finger trailed down Liberty's spine when Nell came in and said, "Dougray has roused all the tenants and the overseers."

Armed with hoes and axes and muskets, Ty Mawr's ragtag army was headed to its gates. "Ninian and several tenants are armed and surround Ty Bryn," Nell added. "The master gave orders before he left."

So Noble had thought of everything. Liberty wasn't surprised. Though he'd said but a few terse words about potential trouble, she knew there was a great deal he'd left unspoken. For the first time she was glad the nursery was empty.

The three of them left the bedchamber and moved to the landing. Ninian was below, a holster pistol in one hand, its steel barrel a-shine in the candlelight. As Isabeau and Nell joined him, Liberty bent her head. What could she, a sole woman, do at such a time? Prayer seemed the greatest need they had.

◈

Liberty never left his head, quite a feat when the unfamiliar names of his men and countless military maneuvers filled his days and wartime correspondence his nights. Noble had just lain down on his cot beneath the canvassed arch of his military tent when the unwelcome news came.

Fire on the James.

Fire in August was an onerous thing, no matter how it started. Never had he stood on his feet so fast, his premonition that Dunmore would strike like a rattler when the militia was inland coming to bear. He heard a commotion as his adjunct readied his horse outside. He wasn't the only officer given leave to return home. Colonel Woodford was sensible and shrewd, well aware the British fleet had taken control of Chesapeake Bay and had a malicious eye on Patriot plantations.

Noble emerged from his tent to a moonless night.

"Major Rynallt, betimes the road is safer for two than one, especially in the dark," his adjunct said.

"Aye, but I know the way even at night and you do not," he replied as he swung himself in the saddle. "A false alarm, mayhap."

But he scarcely believed it. He rode hard the few miles home, his horse soon flecked with foam. Providence guided him as the night was so black. He kept off the main road, taking fences across fields and bending low in the saddle amid copses of trees. His riding whip was scarcely needed save for the mastiff at the mill right before the road gave way to Ty Mawr. The barking dog rushed at him, but he kept on, going at a precarious gallop till he neared home. A gathering of his tenants met him at the gate. No one seemed to know yet where the fire was or how it had started, though his overseer had gone out to find answers.

"No harm's come to either house, sir," Dougray said, his face shining beneath a torch's light. "Nor any of your dependencies or horses."

Relief coursed over him like rain. He turned up the treed lane to Ty Bryn, drawn by the sole light shining like a star in a second-floor window—Libby's own.

"Major Rynallt, sir." One of his ablest field hands cast a bulky shadow near the stables. "All's quiet here."

"Good. We'll soon learn what's afoot. Till then keep watch and you'll be rewarded."

"I'll see to your mount, sir."

Noble dismounted and led Seren by the bridle to the man's outstretched hand. Once on the steps of Ty Bryn, he exchanged a few words with Ninian before Nell met him at the door, eyes wide. "God be praised, sir! I never expected to see you on such a night as this. Lord Dunmore's river pirates, mayhap, but you, nay."

"How is Mistress Rynallt?"

"Calm as a summer's morn." Nell cast a glance upstairs and rolled her eyes. "But her maid, nay."

He envisioned Isabeau's hand-wringing, which Libby never seemed to mind. Mayhap Ninian would be a calming influence during his absence.

"Be you hungry, sir?"

"Just thirsty."

"I'll fetch something then."

Before he'd set foot on the stairs, a slight noise in the hall caused him to look up. Isabeau? Nay. A smiling Libby, looking sleep-disheveled and delighted in the candlelight. And as glad to see him as he was her.

∂◯

She rushed down the spiraled staircase to meet him, feeling oddly like a heroine in a novel. Trouble lurked but here was her hero, pewter buttons glinting, the deep blue of his uniform reassuring. He smelled of horses and sweat and leather, but she cared little. She all but threw herself in his arms, finding him as steady and unmoving as one of the columns on the riverfront portico.

Above, Isabeau hovered at the balustrade and Madoc yowled before Nell scooped him up and disappeared, allowing them some hard-won privacy.

"You've come all this way." Admiration laced her tone. "In the dark."

"'Tis not far." Turning round, he kicked the door closed. "And to be completely honest, I can think of little but Liberty."

She took hold of the lapels of his uniform coat. "Your cause."

"Nay." His smile was warm, even a bit sheepish. "My wife."

"You flatter me when a mysterious fire is burning but a few miles away."

"Colonel Woodford has sent patrols to investigate. We'll soon have our answer and mount a defense if we need to."

She worked free the top button of his uniform coat. "You need a change of clothes. Something to drink."

He shrugged off the heavy coat, the linen shirt and weskit damp beneath. Nell came with a candelabra and they retreated to his study, where he set the light on his desk. Taking a chair, he stared down at his dusty boots as if wanting to tug them off. The perry cider Liberty poured him was gone in a few swallows. Did it steady him somehow? He seemed about to tell her something important. She took a seat on the footstool beside him.

Reaching out, he clasped her hands in his. "You need to know there's a royal bounty on my head. I received confirmation of it in Williamsburg. Miles Roth is said to be one of those who mean to waylay me and claim it."

"Miles?" She drew back, stunned. "Your own kin?"

"He's deeply in debt and in need of ready cash. Some suspect he's a British spy. There's another to be wary of as well. Cressida Shaw."

Liberty stayed silent. Cressida had ceased to be her friend when she tried to brand her a Tory spy, but somehow Miles's perfidy seemed worse. Miles was family, a longstanding neighbor. Perhaps he and Cressida were acting together.

"Dunmore has a ring on the mainland looking for Patriots. They mean to make an example of us once we're caught." He hesitated, and she sensed he held a great deal back. "I'm telling you this because everything I have will be yours should the worst happen. My attorney in Williamsburg drew up papers to that effect. It gives me peace of mind that you're provided for." He attempted another weary smile. "You'll be as wealthy a widow as Martha Custis Washington once was if it comes to that."

"I'd rather be poor as a pauper and have you instead."

"Glad I am of that. For the time being, those of us who've been targeted have been offered a measure of safety. Washington has assigned us a few of his Life Guard until the worst of the danger passes."

She looked toward the dark foyer. "And yours is . . . ?"

"On the way." He got to his feet and she followed, stung with regret as he put on his handsome blue coat again. "I'll be back as soon as I can. I'm awaiting orders from Colonel Woodford. Don't leave the house unless it's burning down."

"I shan't tell Isabeau that."

He checked a laugh. "Nay, downplay the danger."

"Aye, aye, Major." She forced lightheartedness, not wanting him to leave on a sour note.

When he went out she thought of all he hadn't said. He'd seemed on the verge of something at the last. Something tender, perhaps. Something memorable if he didn't return. He'd not yet said "I love you." Yet he called her *anwylyd* . . .

She stood on the stoop as he mounted Seren. So straight in the saddle he sat. So controlled. 'Twas easy to envision him at the head of an entire army. Crossing her arms, she swallowed past what felt like a live coal burning her throat and fought the impulse to run to him and unravel completely. But she must stay strong. Must be a credit to a man who was willing to risk so much and provide for her so well.

Lord, if anyone should be hunted down like a criminal for treason, let it be me.

34

She waited up, strangely exhilarated by the combination of coffee and circumstances, her knitting needles flying. Every so often Isabeau would come in, but she seemed more settled as Ninian had come up from Ty Mawr with more weapons nearly as formidable as the master's own. They conspired below, leaving Liberty alone with Madoc in the upstairs sitting room. She could hear them moving about downstairs, occasionally communicating with someone outside.

Dawn painted the James with wan light before she heard the beat of hooves. At the door again, she was as overjoyed to see Noble as she had been before. Only now, hours later, he looked more haggard—eyes bloodshot and jaw bewhiskered—but still straight and soldierly.

She met him on the bricked front steps, the taint of smoke on the sultry air. The coastal wind stiffened and threatened to remove his hat. She put a hand to her skirts lest they set sail as well.

"Anwylyd," he said simply, and took her hand.

The endearment and his touch sent her stomach somersaulting all over again. Ever since their nursery tryst, she'd relived both a thousand times in her memory. But like the sudden intrusion of Mistress Tremayne, the news he brought was unwelcome indeed.

"A British frigate landed soldiers at Hartwell and demanded a large supply of provisions. The factor refused, so they laid the plantation in ruins."

"Was anyone hurt?"

"Thankfully the family was away in Richmond, but a great many slaves turned Tory and joined the British fleet." He ran a hand through his hair. "Captain Graves of the *Savage* is headed our way."

Graves? She remembered him from Gosport. "Best teach me to shoot then."

"Shoot? I've a mind to dispatch you to your mother in Philadelphia, but I doubt you'd be much safer there."

Would he send her packing? Everything in her balked. "I'll not leave you. Or my home here." 'Twas easily said but less understood. Why did Ty Bryn seem more her home now than the Williamsburg townhouse of twenty years?

A sudden gust shook the eaves and sent Noble's gaze past her to the back door with its sidelight and view of the James. "You said you've been praying about all this. You've not asked the Almighty to send some sort of independence hurricane, have you?"

She smiled as the wind struck another lick. "I've been praying the Lord would curb whatever mischief my father and the British fleet mean to make. If that includes a storm, so be it. But I do apologize for any damage incurred."

"Seems like we're still recovering from the damage dealt us in '69."

She shuddered at the memory. "I well recall it." There was no way to prepare for such weather, but might it keep them safe from enemy hands?

"No matter." He tugged at his stock. "We know who controls the weather and we're home together. Let's make the most of it, aye?"

While a northeaster rattled windowpanes and moaned about Ty Bryn's corners, Noble slept after two days on his feet. But only briefly and only after battening down the estate as best he could against the weather. All the livestock was sheltered, every wheeled conveyance under cover, the barns and outbuildings barred shut. His crops and gardens he could do little about. His dependencies—summer kitchens, smokehouses, icehouses, dovecote, necessaries—were all as sturdy as brick could be.

The ancient, towering oaks and chestnuts took the brunt of the storm, weakened by rain-soaked roots and buffeting winds. None were near enough Ty Bryn or Ty Mawr to damage either, but the tree-lined drive and lane might be littered with limbs and leaves by morning. Noble felt a sense of loss already. He loved these old, stately trees, planted by John Rolfe and kinsmen, a part of his own legacy. And now Noble's children's legacy, Lord willing.

On a whim he confined all the servants at Ty Mawr, even Isabeau, who looked a bit put out to be separated from her mistress. With a last goodbye, he left the big house and began the walk uphill to Ty Bryn, which was hidden from sight by so much green, the place stripped bare and exposed only in winter. Rain slashed sideways, the ground a sponge beneath his boots.

His empty belly grumbled like low thunder, and he fixed his eye on the frantic weather vane atop the garden's wrought-iron gate. It spun like a child's top, the copper bird Libby found charming threatening to take wing.

Beyond, the usually picturesque James was surly and dark. The river had been named after a British king, and Noble wondered if that would change if independence was gained. For the moment the water seemed a reflection of the shifting times, as angry and white-capped as he'd ever seen it.

God preserve us.

Though his hat dripped water and the wind shoved him sideways, he felt a bone-deep contentment, almost chuckling at the telling crack in the front door just ahead. But it was only the wind. For once, Libby did not look out at him. He'd not seen her since his nap, as he'd spent the bulk of the day riding about the estate, making sure his tenants were safe before the worst of the storm hit.

He let himself in, the wind masking his movements and the shutting of the door. He locked it, the ring of skeleton keys jingling.

Was she even here? Beyond the foyer's far back door and sidelight the garden was taking a beating, rose petals scattering, the once proud hollyhocks twisted and toppled. Even an iron trellis was askew.

"Anwylyd?"

Another gust shook the eaves, and then he heard, "In here, Husband."

His study?

He found her seated atop a buffalo-skin rug before an empty hearth, where a fire waited kindling in a colder season. Lush and thick, the buffalo hide was soft as Madoc's fur. He'd not expected to find Libby there, fingers flying, a basket of stockings near at hand. She usually sat in the small wingback chair by the window.

She smiled up at him, never missing a stitch. "Sitting down low to the ground seems safer somehow. I fear getting blown out of my seat."

"There's always the root cellar."

"Oh my . . . I hope it shan't come to that." The candle on the footstool beside her danced in a vigorous draft. To her right was a hamper reminding him of their honeymoon picnic, if they'd even had a honeymoon. Did a kiss count?

He was a patient man. Or a fool.

Libby patted the basket. "Don't laugh, but Mistress Tremayne sent up a basket from Ty Mawr so we wouldn't suffer for supper."

"And the offering is?"

"Fried chicken and biscuits. Cucumbers and radishes. Even your favorite peach tart."

She looked surprised when he sat down beside her. "You must be hungry," he said.

She set her knitting aside. "Yes. We shall have another lovely picnic despite the weather."

As the roof's shingles took a pounding, she sounded positively gleeful. He nearly chuckled at her delight. Betimes she showed the pleasure of a child at the simplest things.

"Shall we say grace?" She extended her hands to him expectantly.

They bowed their heads, and he cobbled together a boyhood prayer. "Give us grateful hearts, our Father, for all Thy mercies, and make us mindful of the needs of others, through Jesus Christ our Lord. And we ask for special protection from the storm. Amen."

She passed him his supper on a linen napkin. He eyed the

tart and wished for coffee to wash it down. But two pewter cups with cider sufficed, a good beginning.

"Thanks be to Mistress Tremayne," he said.

"Indeed. She spoils us. I'm not used to such. When I was growing up, Mama was always too busy reading and writing to make much sport, and Papa was mostly absent. Whatever frivolity I had was at the Palace with Lady Charlotte and the children. Many a picnic we did have in the Palace gardens."

"My boyhood was spent traipsing after estate factors and overseers when I wasn't in the schoolroom. They were too busy balancing ledgers and tallying accounts for much merriment."

She picked at her chicken daintily and finished off a biscuit. In the brief time she'd been his, beneath his roof, she'd bloomed. His anwylyd was pale and rail thin no longer. He recalled the feel of her in his arms that day in the nursery. If Mistress Tremayne hadn't interrupted them, no doubt he wouldn't be sitting here now, interested in more than supper. He was done with interruptions.

"Speaking of overseers and factors, where are Isabeau and Nell and your manservant?" she asked, as if reading his thoughts.

"Banished to the big house."

Her brows peaked. "Are we all alone then?"

He cast a glance about for Madoc. "Save one feline, aye."

"Madoc doesn't like storms, it seems, and has been in hiding all day."

"All the better. I have you to myself." He raised his cup, and she followed his lead, clinking rims. Her eyes sparkled and the candle sputtered. Soon they'd be in the dark.

He all but forgot the howling wind. The magnolia torn to shreds beyond the nearest window. The candle that needed replacing. A drowsy goodness filled him along with the supper. He was locked in with the woman he loved. What more could he ask for than that? This moment was all they had.

Finished eating, Liberty sank her fingers into the lush buffalo fur. "I've never before seen such a rug, save the skins the Indian delegations brought to Williamsburg to treat with the government."

"This is from the Kentucke territory, a gift from George Rogers Clark. Enid thought it uncivilized, so I moved it here from Ty Mawr."

"Well, I like it. No fashionable turkey carpet can compare." She stroked the fur like it was Madoc instead. "I might just stay the night in your study."

"Then I'll do the same."

She reached for his spyglass and turned it on the James. The storm was building, the wind keening with a rare intensity. Was the *Savage* making its way upriver? No British vessels marred the water. In this weather, everything was against even the ablest sailor. The enemy might come by land. If so, Noble's sword and pistols were near at hand but tucked out of sight for her sake.

"Are you afraid, Libby?"

The spyglass came down. "Afraid? With an officer of the Continental Army guarding me? I've never been less afraid in my life."

"Well said."

"I do mean that. I plan to curl up on this wild-skin rug and sleep the night away."

"That sounds a bit . . . dull."

"Dull indeed." She tilted her head. Held his gaze. Her earnestness worked more powerfully than being coy ever could. If she'd swished a fan and lowered her lashes he couldn't have been more undone. Her voice came soft. "What do you have in mind then? A game of chess? Cards? Hunting for Madoc?"

"Nothing that requires light," he said wryly.

At this, the candle went out. Shadows draped the room as summer's dusk crept in.

Her voice, when it finally came, was a mere whisper, but he heard it over the force of the wind. "Count me in then."

He stilled. There was no longer any doubt as to her intent or his. A faint outline of light graced the study's windows but was fast fading, the storm's gray foremost. Despite the buffeting wind, the silence between them was breathless.

She sat facing him, her silken skirts a blue valley between them. His heart seemed to beat out of his chest. Need made him bold. He leaned nearer for a kiss. Her lips met his, her arms encircling his neck. They drew apart, and he realized how damp he was from his long ride. Her nimble fingers began untying his stock.

He longed to take the pins from her hair. He'd never seen it unbound, only plaited. Pearl tipped, the hairpins were easily found. Down her hair tumbled about her shoulders in gentle waves, shocking his senses.

A woman's hair was her glory, Scripture said. Truer words were never spoken. His Libby looked . . . radiant. This was his bride. The woman God had created for him since time began. The mother of his children, whenever they came.

She was his, come the storm. Come the war. Come what may.

Anwylyd.

35

Liberty slept curled on the lush rug, Noble's body warming her. Occasionally, a loud bump or crash beyond Ty Bryn's bricked walls would shake her awake. But she knew no fear. She knew only her husband. His scent. His touch. His feelings for her. In the span of a single night he had satisfied her every longing and spoken the words she so wanted to hear.

I love you, Libby.

She'd spoken them back to him in both English and Welsh.

Rwy'n dy garu di.

Never would she forget them or this night. If the war took him away, the words would remain, a gift to warm her on the longest days and coldest nights.

Wonder kept her awake more than the wind. She turned gently so as not to awaken him and lay on her back, looking up at the frescoed ceiling and envisioning the nursery above it. Inexplicably, she knew her prayers had been answered. For a husband. A home. A family. Deep within, where soul and spirit lived, she sensed a quickening. A child. Though she knew little about such things as babies and begetting, something wondrous had just happened. She was changed, a wife in the truest sense, and soon, she sensed, to be a mother.

As dawn came, the storm seemed to wear itself out. Birdsong lit the garden, fragile at first as if fearful the storm would reawaken, and then strengthening into what amounted to a tittering symphony.

Beside her, Noble stirred, coming slowly awake. This close, she could make out the fine lines in his tanned features like tiny cracks in an earthenware jug.

She gave a sleepy smile. "I now seem to know nearly everything about you but your age."

"Old enough at thirty." He kissed her soundly, then focused on a leaf-spattered window. "I had meant to stay up with the storm, but . . ." Concern washed his features as something outside gave a resounding thud. Their idyll was over.

"I pray nothing is beyond repair."

"'Twill be a long day riding about the estate, taking toll of any damage. I'll send the maids up to be with you once I reach Ty Mawr."

"Is it safe to venture outside? There were a great many noises in the night."

"I'll take a look around first." His lazy smile told her he was in no hurry. "You make it amazingly difficult for a man to resume his duties."

He dressed and went outside. Soon the maids came cautiously up the hill, Ninian leading. Liberty dressed and ate, but nothing seemed the same, neither outwardly nor inwardly. Could she be wrong about this night? A child? She went about the house in a bit of a heavenly daze.

As the morning stretched to noon, Liberty stood in Ty Bryn's garden with Nell and Isabeau. If ever there was cause for hand-wringing, 'twas the storm's aftermath.

"Will you look at that . . ." Awe laced Nell's tone. All eyes followed her pointed finger to the riverfront.

Beyond the trammeled garden, half of Ty Mawr's wharf had been torn away on the frothy James. A capsized schooner was washed ashore, no sign of life aboard.

Both land and water were ravaged, the shock of it nearly unseating the beloved memories she and Noble had just made. Liberty held on to their fragile beginnings, the bliss of their honeymoon night, though needs cried out everywhere she turned.

She went about the battered garden, righting this or that, Isabeau scolding and trying to shoo her inside. Their lovely world was badly shaken, but both houses and the dependencies had stayed strong.

She wished for a little sunshine. A hint of blue sky. But the heavens stayed a sullen gray.

For once politics faded into the background as the *Virgina Gazette* and *Norfolk Intelligencer* nearly ran short of ink reporting storm damage.

The James River postboy had been washed off his horse into a swamp. At the last he grabbed hold of a tree, saved by a passerby who had a rope. Trees were torn up by the roots and littered roads. The damage to port towns such as Norfolk was inexpressible. Nearly forty ships were lost or damaged. During the storm, Lord Dunmore's sloop tender that had been used to patrol the bay was grounded near Hampton and immediately burned by the citizenry.

Was her father safe? How had they fared in the hurricane?

More tragic reports reached them. Hundreds of sailors drowned. Livestock lost and fields flooded. No one asked who or what was Patriot or Tory. Suddenly such divisions ceased to matter.

She watched for Noble from Ty Bryn's wide windows as Nell cleaned the glass and Isabeau fretted about Ninian, who had gone out with Dougray in search of a few stray horses. When the sun poked a few pointed rays beyond the clouds, they all felt like cheering.

"God be praised!" Nell said, finishing her window washing.

Smoke soon puffed from the summer kitchen, and Liberty watched it spiral toward hard-won blue sky. Would Noble be home for supper? With the servants about, they'd not spend another night on the buffalo rug in his study. Unless he banished them to Ty Mawr again.

Cook butchered a chicken, that much Liberty knew. A savory mingling of broth and thyme and rosemary spilled out of her brick domain, along with the aroma of baking bread. Nothing, however, would ever be as satisfying as their stormy picnic.

"What shall you wear this evening, mistress?" Isabeau began rummaging through her wardrobe. All of Enid's new gowns had been brought up from Ty Mawr. Somehow in wearing them Liberty felt closer to Noble's sister.

"The blue chintz." Blue was his favorite color. 'Twas her eyes that first drew his notice, he'd told her in the night. She'd been strolling down Palace Green with Lady Charlotte and her girls years ago when he'd come out of a legislative session and they'd nearly collided. She had no memory of it, but he'd not forgotten.

Aye, 'twas your eyes. Blue as Llyn Llydaw, a lake in Snowdonia.

"And how do you want your hair?" Isabeau was saying. "Curled with the tongs and pinned up, no?"

"Leave it undressed, simply tied back with silk ribbon."

"Is that not risqué?" Isabeau's face scrunched in dismay. "Might you just as well appear in your underpinnings?"

"Ty Bryn is informal. For now let there be little fuss."

Isabeau began brushing Liberty's hair with vigor as if making up for lost time. "I have heard beauty spots and patch boxes are going out of fashion. Imagine! Next men will no longer wear wigs. Ladies will abandon their stays—"

"Nonsense," Liberty chided gently. "I prefer my stays. But I do abhor wigs. Noble doesn't own one."

"Then he is indeed a rebel."

They laughed. A generous splash of rosewater followed, and then her simple toilette was complete. The lines of her gown settled into place as Liberty stood, extending both elbows while Isabeau pinned on lace sleeves and adjusted a frill here, a furbelow there.

"You seem . . . different, mistress."

"Different?"

Isabeau clasped a pearl choker about her neck. "Dreamy. Something has changed for you. I can sense it. No longer are you in your father's shadow, no longer are you missing your mother. You are content being the mistress of Ty Bryn."

Liberty laced her fingers at her middle and tried not to smile. "You know me well."

"Do I? I think you have secrets you are not telling."

Liberty laughed. "Just who is being dreamy?"

Leaning forward, Isabeau whispered, "My desire is to see the nursery overflowing. I think we shall be banished again tonight." Her complaint was tempered by wistfulness. "Sent again to the big house so the master of Ty Mawr can have you to himself."

"Ah, so that is it." Liberty moved toward the door, certain she heard a horse. "So long as you go with Ninian, does it matter?"

Isabeau gave her own secretive smile, remaining behind as Liberty went below, joy singing through her.

She opened the front door ahead of Nell, almost expecting a face full of wind but finding it dead calm. It was not Noble, nay. A smiling, uniformed stranger instead. His bodyguard, on loan from General Washington? Liberty took Captain Hodge in at a glance.

Blue coat with white facings. White waistcoat and breeches. Black stock and black half gaiters. Round hat with a blue and white feather. Except the white parts of him were now a dingy, storm-speckled brown.

"Please, come in," Liberty told him, feeling her world shifting again. "My husband should return any moment."

He entered the foyer as Nell came down the stairs, toting a pistol. Liberty sent her a glance to put the weapon away, but she only had eyes for the young officer.

"Please, Nell. Our guest is wearing a blue coat, not a red one."

Captain Hodge chuckled and swept off his cocked hat, bowing to them both. "At your service, ladies."

The still-staring Nell curtsied back.

"'Tis a miracle you came through the hurricane unscathed," Liberty remarked. To Nell she said, "Some refreshments for our guest shall do nicely."

"Ah yes, the storm." His expression foretold a mishap or two. "Most roads are blocked by debris, but I came on. 'Tis of small consequence compared to the storm that is coming."

"I'm sure you bring news from headquarters."

"News aplenty, though I'll try to reserve most of it for Major Rynallt and spare your sensibilities."

By the time they reached the parlor, Noble had returned. Liberty had a private moment with him in the foyer. "Your Life Guard has arrived, and Nell is setting an extra place for supper. I assume he'll be sleeping outside your door."

"*Our* door. Nay." He winked. "Ty Mawr has guest rooms to spare. Life Guards aren't needed on honeymoons."

"No doubt 'twill be a late night nonetheless."

"Aye." He bent and kissed her cheek. "But not on account of Captain Hodge."

She flushed like a schoolgirl. Elated, she went into the dining room where Nell was now arranging a vase of the few remaining flowers that had survived the storm. Her ginger hair had been tucked anew beneath her cap, her apron changed.

"I've served the refreshments, m'lady."

"Thank you. I feared you'd shoot our guest first."

The amused words turned Nell ripe as a raspberry. "These men in uniform . . . one never knows what to expect." She cast a glance toward the study. "I wonder how long Captain Hodge is to stay on."

"Perhaps you should ask him. Offer to clean the soiled whites of his uniform. Or knit him some stockings."

"Mercy, m'lady!"

Cook had prepared a fine supper. Roast chicken. Gravy. Potatoes and peas. Wheaten bread. Even a berry trifle. The storm had not dented her enthusiasm or her skills.

Captain Hodge's appreciation knew no bounds. "A vast improvement over salt beef and hardtack." He took second helpings with relish, his manner polite and obliging. Liberty caught sight of the white of Nell's cap as she hovered behind the service door.

"Do you have a family, Captain Hodge?" Liberty asked over dessert. "A wife and children, perhaps?"

"Nay, but if I should find a liberty lass, who knows?"

Talk soon moved to more somber matters. Should she excuse herself or stay on? At the pressure of Noble's hand beneath the table, she stayed.

"In Boston, Admiral Graves has ordered the captain of the *Asia* to seize and keep in safe custody any delegates to the Continental Congress and any rebel general officers or the chief radical leaders," Hodge told them.

"So I heard," Noble replied, leaning back in his chair. "There aren't enough Life Guards to prevent that."

"Washington feels a special concern for officers like yourself who serve without pay and are considered a prime target."

"Is there any truth to reports that Lord North and the British Cabinet plan to employ an army of eighteen thousand in New England and another twelve thousand to act in Virginia and the middle provinces?"

"True, aye." Hodge took a drink, his cheer slipping. "Meanwhile, General Washington struggles to recruit our own ranks, partly on account of the British hatching a plan to send smallpox victims to Patriot lines."

Their talk ended and they passed into the parlor. Wanting to give the Life Guard some entertainment for all his trouble reaching them, she sat down at her harp while Noble tuned his violin. Till now they'd only played together briefly. She looked at her new husband expectantly, the allure of music taking hold. Could they manage an unrehearsed duet?

"I trust my wife will cover my lack of finesse," Noble murmured with an apologetic smile as he slid his bow across the strings.

"My harp is hardly needed," she chided. "You manage as well as Mister Jefferson, 'tis been said."

They began a sonata, playing with such *joie de vivre* it left Hodge smiling. Another delightful hour passed. Drowsy, stifling a yawn, Liberty excused herself, seeking the stairs and her own bedchamber. Pausing at the oriole window on the landing, she took in the James, still muddy if calm. A full moon rose in skies that had been a serene robin's-egg blue.

Isabeau had laid out a nightgown but was absent. Helping Nell, likely, and discussing Captain Hodge. Or having a few moments alone with Ninian. Undressing was simple enough with front-lacing stays and a simple muslin gown. Liberty climbed the bedsteps, parted the mosquito netting, and fancied she smelled pipe smoke. The men were no doubt having a last peach brandy.

She settled beneath the linen sheet as the clock in the foyer chimed nine. A slight commotion in the foyer was punctuated by Isabeau's airy laugh. Throwing off the bedcovers, Liberty made for a window, delighted to find Captain Hodge and Ninian squiring both Nell and Isabeau down the hill. Dougray was no doubt still in the stables caring for Hodge's horse.

The house settled into an unfamilar quiet, and then Noble's tread on the stairs sent her spinning. How tired he must be, having been out riding all day. She'd not blame him if he fell sound asleep. And yet the wonder of the night before couldn't be denied. She craved his closeness. His strength. The sheer newness of him.

A splash of water told her he was at the washstand. And then the door to the hall opened and he trod away, down the steps, out the riverfront door, and onto the dusk-shadowed lawn. He bypassed the garden, a towel trailing behind him. Befuddled, she looked on, and then his intent came clear. A bath?

What was good for the gander was good for the goose, her mother used to say.

She took the stairs by twos. How scandalized Isabeau and the servants would be, her husband nearly naked save his breeches, she in hot pursuit. Years from now, would she and

Noble look back and laugh? Or would she alone hold the memory close?

She tried to step carefully, tried to sneak up on him. The ravaged wharf had created a cove of sorts, shoving back sand as its huge timbers fell into the water at odd angles. These she stayed clear of lest they shift.

His back to her, Noble was submerged to the waist. His pistol rested on his towel atop the sand. If she was a redcoat . . . The flicker of fear was snuffed as he swung around, his muscular frame flexing defensively.

When he saw her, the wary lines of his face gave way to pleasure. Surprise. He opened his arms wide and she rushed toward him, the chill of the water making her gasp. Legs tangling in the damp hem of her nightgown, she tripped and fell headlong into the river. At his hearty laugh she came up sputtering, an unladylike mess, and his sturdy arms wrapped round her.

"The James is just settling. Beware angry frogs and box turtles and mud daubers."

She swiped the water from her eyes. All she saw were a few fireflies. "I have no fear of the river. Not with you here."

"So our adventure continues." He looked up at the sky, the moon overhead, a few stars blinking. "Most couples marry and honeymoon quietly, but here we are braving both a hurricane and a war."

"But the hurricane is over and the war has not begun."

Their eyes met. "True enough." Reaching out, he smoothed back her wet hair, then looked beyond her to the house and landscape. He seemed extraordinarily wary. What else had Captain Hodge told him? "Can you swim, anwylyd?"

She sighed. "I'm no mermaid."

"Mayhap a Welsh water fairy then. One of the *Gwragedd*

Annwn." Spanning her waist with his hands, he pulled her toward deeper waters, the sand disappearing beneath her feet. "They haunt lakes and rivers and live in castles that sometimes show their battlements and towers above the waters." His lips brushed her damp temple. "One lake maiden is said to be a wondrous beauty with hair long and yellow, who rows up and down gently in a golden boat with a golden oar."

She hung on his winsome words, a bit lost in the tale. "You make me wish I was in Wales."

"Someday, Lord willing, we will go."

"I should like to meet your brother, heir to the true Ty Mawr."

"The true Ty Mawr, aye?" Both teasing and indignation rode his handsome features. "Am I an imposter then, a counterfeit Contintental, like the false paper money being forged by the British?"

Her high spirits dimmed. "So every artifice is used to injure us."

"Aye, Libby. Our cause is akin to David and Goliath." He started swimming out beyond the broken wharf, still embracing her. "As for my brother, I've yet to send word we've wed, given the post is oft compromised. Since Elon has yet to marry, I have the prize."

Elon Rynallt? And she thought the name Noble poetic. As for being his prize . . . no longer did she feel like the penniless daughter of the enemy. More Welsh princess.

Together they bathed in the cool water, the sticky heat stripped away. Daylight had eroded completely before they returned to the house. Nell had left a light burning in the oriole window, a golden starbust in the blackness. Hand in hand, they trudged up the sloping hill toward that light, Liberty's head and heart a-dance at another night alone with him.

This was what it must be like to be without servants. Able to do as one pleased without shadows. Able to run down hills and splash and laugh like children with no one watching. Able to kiss in the foyer with abandon, and then all the way up the stairs till you were breathless and no longer remembered your clothes were dripping wet and leaving little puddles atop the plank floor, conscious only of each other, not even the cat.

This was bliss.

36

And then, just like that, he was gone. No tearful parting. No protracted goodbyes. Captain Hodge was looking on, after all. They were only going to drill in Williamsburg with Colonel Woodford. Why did it feel as far as the Orient instead?

Liberty missed him more intensely now because her room was no longer just hers, nor her bed, nor her body, nor anything else. Truly, two had become one. She felt a bit lost. Upended. Perhaps the first day apart was the hardest. His very scent seemed to linger. She wrapped herself in his banyan to try to stay close to him.

He'd left a letter for her atop her dressing table, secured with an indigo blue seal. She broke it open hungrily, craving something of him, even his elegant, bold hand.

Dearest Anwylyd,

You've given me a rare gift upon leaving. I no longer go alone but take the memory of you with me. It is the deepest pleasure to think of you waiting for me, peering out Ty Bryn's cracked door, or waiting on the stoop and looking down the lane in expectation. I retain a deep

*affection for you, which neither time nor distance can
alter, nor words do justice.*

*I know not the time of my return. We will soon move
from Williamsburg to confront the opposition in another place. Till I come home, keep yourself safe. Take
extra care, knowing my prayers have hemmed you in.*

*Continue to fill our home with your unearthly music.
Let the hospitality of the house with respect to the poor
be kept up. Let no one go hungry away.*

Your entire,
NR

A teardrop spattered his initials. She wiped it away, staring out the window at the James, now a tranquil blue. Workmen were repairing the wharf, their hammering an exclamation point to her angst.

She sensed what he did not say. Virginia's newly formed Continental Army would soon move against her father and the British fleet. She pictured her husband beneath the blistering Indian summer sun as companies enlisted, stores were gathered, and preparations were made for the coming conflict.

Lord, he is but a barrister. Once a burgess. Now he is a soldier leading other men, some to their deaths.

What had he said to her at the last? Before Captain Hodge came round?

"The dangers we are to encounter I know not, but it shall never be said to my children that their father is a coward."

She pressed hands to her cinched middle, feeling the familiar restriction of stays. He spoke of children like he knew her secret, yet she had breathed nary a word. Was this mysterious sixth sense part of the bond between husband and wife?

She took solace in the nursery. The little christening gown she'd just begun lay on the wide windowsill, the lace she'd made to trim it alongside. The chamber was filled with light. It pushed back the darkness of the unknown, blanketing her with peace whenever she stepped into its warmth. As if the presence of the Lord was here, in this very place, the embodiment of her hopes and dreams.

Sitting in the rocking chair, she had a view of the summer kitchen. A man was below, clothing ragged and bare of foot. She'd given Nell several pairs of stockings to hand out to needy souls along with Cook's provisions of meat and bread and whatever the kitchen offered. Since the storm there'd been more arrivals at Ty Mawr's back door. All the staff was aware of the hospitality of the house in regard to the poor.

She sewed the afternoon away, pausing only to read a post from her mother, who gushed about her marriage. A wedding gift was forthcoming, if one could be found in trade-deprived Philadelphia. While she reread it she took a turn in the walled garden, savoring her mother's delight. The flowers were righting themselves, most of the damage cleared away. How was it for Noble in such weather? Did the officers wear full uniform on the hottest days?

Pocketing the post, she swung her gaze wide, taking in the river beneath her bergère hat. What memories they'd made! In her mind's eye she could see them swimming or boating with their children in the years to come, a whole, happy family, enjoying the very best of Ty Mawr's bounty.

"M'lady, d'ye want to dine in the master's study again tonight?" Nell was at her elbow, squinting in the sunlight.

"That shall do nicely, thank you." No doubt the staff found it strange to shun the dining room, but it held a lonesome echo, even for Ty Bryn. She felt closer to Noble in his study.

Besides, there she had his broad-nibbed pens and ink pot near at hand. Each night after supper she penned him a letter, giving an account of her days down to the humblest details.

He'd surely want to know about the recovering winter wheat. And that his prized oxen, the Ruby Reds, had finally been found after they'd bolted in the storm. Or that a valued mare had foaled and was being celebrated by Dougray and everyone in the stables. And then, just today, they'd inspected the orchard trees that had survived the hurricane, a few remaning peaches and cider apples left hanging. She mustn't forget to mention that she'd heard from her mother, who extended felicitious greetings on their marriage.

She wouldn't write that the house yawned empty, the bed seemed too big, and she even missed his slight snoring. Nor could she say she'd begun to feel a little topsy-turvy, her nose and stomach turned by the coffee Nell brought round in the morning. And that when she got to her feet all of a sudden, Ty Bryn seemed to spin round. Or that she was overjoyed by these discomforts because she hoped they meant the nursery would soon resound with a baby's cries.

Nay, she would save these things for him in person, once she was in his arms again.

⌀

Noble had never seen such a company of riflemen. He himself had always been considered a fine shot, but these frontiersmen took powder and bullet lead to a new level. That some were cronies of his old friend George Rogers Clark didn't surprise him. General Daniel Morgan's sharpshooters were equipped with the finest Pennsylvania rifles instead of muskets, improving accuracy at up to ten times the distance. This corps of sixty-nine men was on a special detail to join the northern army.

In linen hunting frocks they made quite a show, bringing down impossible targets at a hundred yards or more amid the cheers and huzzahs of the men. According to intelligence and the *Virginia Gazette*, the British fleet was threatening to bombard the coastal towns if frontier riflemen entered the fight. Lord Dunmore had even convinced his troops they would be scalped if they fell into the hands of these frontiersmen, the most warlike people in America second to the Indians, 'twas said.

"This may well be the edge we need to end the conflict." The usually stoic Colonel Woodford stood beside Noble, his appreciation plain. "I'd rather they stay with the southern army, being Virginians. But orders are orders."

"I suspect they're welcome anywhere," Noble said, turning toward a courier who handed him a post.

Woodford and Hodge looked on, Woodford nonchalantly, Hodge almost enviously. Noble quietly slipped Libby's latest letter inside a pocket as the rifles reverberated around them, the humid air writhing with white smoke.

"I do believe the army should make exceptions for honeymooning officers," Woodford said.

Noble gave a slight smile. "Or allow the ladies to visit their husbands in camp, at least."

"I suspect that is exactly General Washington's intent for officers' wives should they wish it, even his own."

"But far from the danger." Noble couldn't imagine Libby in such conditions, even in Williamsburg. Several hundred men encamped here, as well as a few female camp followers, including Thalia, fresh from the Raleigh Tavern. Dougray was ready to enlist. Many a servant entered the Continental Army to substitute for an unwilling master.

In the fortnight he'd been in Williamsburg, the short distance to Ty Mawr seemed both an eternity and a torment. All sorts of hearsay reached them, a persistent rumor being the British fleet's plan to not just pirate provisions but commandeer coastal plantations in the future till they'd regained control of Virginia.

He'd feel better if she was here in town, but Libby would not be moved. The servants were on high alert, and there was an escape plan in place. Still, his prayers seemed to be unceasing for her safety.

With a quick word to his superior, he left the sprawling encampment behind the college and took a back street to the armory. James Anderson's smithy was rarely idle, the coal fires and bellows from its seven forges burning far into the night. Journeymen and apprentices scurried like ants amid all the clanging, clad in leather aprons and besmirched with charcoal. They'd all but forsaken the simple tools and accoutrements of colonial days. Any passerby would note the difference. These men were preparing for war.

Pausing under a shady eve, Noble withdrew Libby's letter. Devoured it. Held it to his nose when no one was watching. How could paper be so fragrant? As if she'd captured the very essence of Ty Mawr's garden and tucked it within.

"Good afternoon, sir."

He turned, the voice vaguely familiar. Cressida Shaw stood behind him, her wide hat shading her unsmiling features. "A quiet moment, Major Rynallt?"

The pleasure of the letter soured. "Not any longer."

His curt words failed to turn her away, though she did stiffen visibly. "I simply wanted to congratulate you on your nuptials."

Unease clutched him. "Thank you," he said flatly.

"You're welcome." She smiled, but it failed to reach her eyes. "You'll soon be the talk of Virginia, marrying a Tory.

Though I don't know where you're keeping her. Rumor is that she's not at Ty Mawr."

"And how did you come by your knowledge?"

"I have confidants in strategic places, mind you. Too many to count. I simply wanted to call on your new wife, offer my felicitations."

"No need since, as you've said, the lady of the house is not at home." Cressida's accusations of Libby spying leapt to mind, along with the accompanying dislike he always felt in her presence.

"How unfortunate." She looked away from him at the noisy clatter of a carriage. "Of course, everyone knows why you wed her. Either that or she'd be as destitute as the poor that I hear flock to your door."

He folded the letter and returned it to his breast pocket. "Miss Shaw, for a woman of small standing you have an acid tongue. I've beheld more gracious beggers."

He entered the smithy, bending his thoughts to the task at hand—an order of muskets for his regiment. But the bitter taint of his exchange with Libby's onetime friend remained.

⁂

The fortnight ebbed and Noble did not come home. His letters, nearly as frequent as hers, hinted at a movement of troops. She prayed they would not join Washington in the northeast. Surely Virginia needed them right here. Since the hurricane, news of Lord Dunmore and her father had dwindled to a few reports of damage to the British fleet. 'Twas rumored her father had come ashore at Westover farther down the James, paying a visit to Mary Byrd, the Loyalist-leaning wife of debt-ridden William Byrd. But rumors were as thick as dandelions dotting Ty Mawr's fallow fields.

Noble's latest letter came cleverly concealed in a bobbin made of artfully engraved walnut. Somehow he'd gotten hold of imported pins and thread. Smuggled goods? She turned the extravagance over in her hands, marveling.

In her idle hours, she returned to lacemaking. The christening gown only needed trimming. By the wide nursery window she worked, her hands moving rapidly, even rhythmically, the wooden bobbins creating a chime-like sound. Every so often she would rest her eyes and take in the cradle. Being in this room, believing she was already a mother, made her heart overflow.

Here she sat when the brass knocker sounded on the front door below. Had she misheard? 'Twas rare anyone got past Ty Mawr. She'd begun to think of the big house as her guardian, the first line of defense for Ty Bryn. 'Twas Mistress Tremayne's voice she heard mingled with Nell's quiet tones, and then a masculine voice filled the whole foyer.

Leaving the nursery, she trod down the hall and looked over the banister. Gladness was swept away by suspicion and surprise.

Doctor Hessel?

Gosport and all its what-ifs still shadowed her. If the doctor and her father had had their way, she'd still be with the fleet, perhaps foisted upon some officer or even en route to England.

He looked up, hat in hand. "Lady Elisabeth."

The old address fell flat. Mistress Tremayne and Nell exchanged glances, clearly ill at ease with his coming.

"Good day, Doctor." Cool as a frosty morn she was. Once he had been her friend, her physician. Now he was neither. Grief cut her that it had come to this.

He made a move toward the first step. "'Tis imperative that I speak to you—alone."

She made no move to leave the landing. "Why alone?"

"I bring word from your father." His tone was earnest enough, but he seemed irritated by the two women on either side of him. "A private matter."

The silence grew more prickly as they awaited her response. Liberty was torn between refusing him and making him state his case here in the foyer before them all.

"Please . . . we haven't much time," he said.

She could imagine Noble's reaction. She'd always felt he had no great liking for Hessel. She asked the question he surely would have. "How did you find me?"

His fingers clutched his hat. "You said you'd wed when we last met. I recently spoke with Miss Shaw."

Her alarm spiked. How did Cressida know? She started down the stairs. "I'll see you in the parlor. Mistress Tremayne, if you wouldn't mind waiting in the foyer."

Nell slipped down the hall, resuming her tasks.

Liberty led the way and left the parlor door open, the doctor following. "Elisabeth, please. We parted on poor terms. I know what you must think of me. Let us be done with all that. I come today on behalf of your father, who is quite ill."

She faced him, saying nothing, weighing everything he told her as suspect.

"He's asked that you come immediately." Doctor Hessel's blue eyes seemed to drill into her. "He desires to see you one last time."

"And his malady?"

"A throat catarrh. Likely fatal. Your mother is with him now."

"My mother?" This struck her harder than if he'd announced her father's demise.

"She's just arrived from Philadelphia. Her chief desire—

and his—is for the three of you to be reunited, perhaps for a final time. Let bygones be bygones."

Her parents were now of like mind? Disbelief tugged at her. "Where are they?"

"Aboard the *William* in the Elizabeth River."

"Why did my mother not come here first?"

"Urgency required she sail. Traveling overland is too risky."

He had an answer for everything. She looked down at the patterned rug without seeing its bold design, her thoughts aswirl. The nausea that had begun to bubble up had recently intensified, sometimes so unexpectedly she was embarrassed. She'd have to carry a bowl in the carriage . . .

He took a step nearer. "They've asked that you come with me as your escort—"

"Have you any proof? Perhaps some note in my mother's hand, begging me come?"

"Only my word." He flushed, whether from the blatant distrust in her question or his lacking proof, she didn't know. "For God's sake, Elisabeth. I am your lifelong friend, politics aside. Will you not go with me?"

"Only if my husband allows it."

"He won't. There's no time—"

"If you are my father's attending physician and he is as ill as you say, why are you here and not by his bedside?"

"Because he thought a courier—a stranger—too threatening, that someone known to you should deliver the news and then accompany you safely. Given his precarious health, it was uncommonly kind of him."

Kind? Such a courtesy was unheard of. But dying men did unusual things. Might her father finally be receptive to the Savior and His message of forgiveness and grace? What kind of daughter would she be to ignore such a plea? Still, she felt a restraining hand, a check not to heed him.

Doctor Hessel stepped back. "Come away with me. Now. There's precious little time left."

Mistress Tremayne stood in the doorway, looking as conflicted as Liberty felt. "Perhaps if Isabeau accompanies you and Dougray is your driver. I can go along also if you like."

"Nay." Doctor Hessel swung toward her. "'Tis a private family matter—"

"I cannot come," Liberty interrupted, finding some solace in simply saying no.

He looked disbelieving. "You refuse me then? And your father's dying wish?" Anger spiked the heated words, but she held firm.

"My place is here." *With my husband.* Though Noble wasn't present she knew he would be against her going. Just like with Gosport, the risk was too great.

A Scripture sprang to mind, confirming her decision.

Therefore shall a man leave his father and his mother, and shall cleave unto his wife: and they shall be one flesh.

She looked toward Mistress Tremayne, who appeared relieved at her firm stance. Without so much as an adieu, Hessel went out, pushing past Ninian and Nell in the foyer to make a hasty exit, leaving a great deal of ill feeling after him.

✍

She spent much time in Ty Bryn's garden the next few days. Doing so helped keep her mind off her father's health and Hessel's disturbing visit. Gathering an armful of daisies, the flower that had rallied the best after the hurricane, she sought out a vase in the pantry attached to the summer kitchen. Given it was the Sabbath and the servants were not close at hand—save Ninian and Isabeau in the house—she was left to her own devices.

Pushing open the keeping room door, she spied a shelf of glassware and a simple piece of crockery that would suffice. But first water. The well was behind the summer kitchen, and she carried both crock and flowers there, glad for a simple task. Always thoughts of Noble were foremost.

What was he doing on so cloudy and close a day?

Lord, please hedge him in behind and before, and place Your hand of blessing on his head.

"Pardon me, miss."

The unfamiliar voice made her turn. A man in ragged homespun stood in back of her, near the closed kitchen door. Her heart squeezed. Was he hungry? Wanting to be fed, as did so many displaced by the storm and the conflict?

"Are you in need?" she asked, but it seemed a silly question. At his nod, she started for the kitchen. "I'm sure Cook has some bread and meat on hand." Turning her back to him, she gave a twist to the doorknob.

What had Noble insisted upon?

Let the hospitality of the house with respect to the poor be kept up. Let no one go hungry away.

The man came closer. She could feel him shadowing her, a bit too closely mayhap, and her nose wanted to curl at the smell of his unwashed clothes. Shamed by her reaction, she put one foot over the kitchen's threshold—and was overcome with a great smothering blackness.

37

If he had been at home that fateful day, none of this would be happening. The recurrent thought was like a sharpened sword through his soul. Would he go to his grave laden with regret? Why had he not left his Life Guard at Libby's side? Now, three months later, her disappearance—and his ongoing fury with Hessel and her father—had become as much a stronghold as the earthworks thrown up by his men. Rage crowded out reason and whittled down his faith.

God had let this happen. While he'd acted honorably in defense of his wife and his country, a Tory spy posing as a beggar had separated them, mayhap for good.

A cold, late November wind rattled the paper he held, the ink smudged from repeated reading and the emotion of those first moments. Ninian had delivered the news to him immediately after Libby's disappearance, and then came confirmation of what had happened.

Major Rynallt,
  Intelligence suggests your wife has been captured by Tories associated with Dunmore. She has been taken aboard an unknown vessel in Gosport. Word has also

come that Lord Stirling is alive and well. No other de-
tails are forthcoming. Will advise if otherwise.

The note was unsigned but had come from reliable sources, through that spiderweb of intelligence the Patriot cause had constructed.

He'd just been about to go home, ready to tell Libby in person that their troops would move to Hampton to counter an anticipated naval attack by the British. By the time he reached Gosport the ship on which her father was aboard had vanished. No one would tell him where he, or Libby, had gone.

He returned to a solemn household staff, Libby's maid more hysterical than he had ever seen her.

And then, adding insult to injury, Patrick Henry appeared, his blistering tongue intact. In the canvas closet of his army tent, Henry had the audacity to take him to task. "I warned you, did I not? I knew wedding her would cost you dearly. And what is this talk of her being captured? Methinks she is Loyalist to the bone and has played you false—"

"Nay, not that." Noble's pain was so great the words were hoarse. He'd not believe she'd turned on him. Not his Libby. She loved him as he loved her. Politics played no part in matters of the heart.

Henry took a piece of paper from his pocket. "I've done what I could and confirmed what you already know. Lady Elisa—your *wife*—is supposedly being held aboard an unnamed schooner somewhere in the Chesapeake. There are recent reports she'll be transferred to a frigate bound for England or taken to New York to one of the prison ships moored near Long Island."

Noble nearly swore. The last was new. Horrific. "I've spoken with Elias Boudinot about a prisoner exchange."

"Washington's commander general of prisoners?"

Noble gave a nod. "I proposed to exchange myself for her release—"

"Are you daft?" Henry stared at him, beads of sweat pearling on his brow. "You are considered one of the most active and virulent of British enemies. You'll be hanged without delay. Or worse, the British authorities will try to sway you to join them in fighting against us Patriots."

"And what if it was your wife? Would you not do the same?"

Silence. Henry took out a handkerchief and wiped the sheen of sweat away. "General Washington will have none of it. He will not even allow British soldiers to be traded for American citizens, as this only legitimizes the British capturing more citizens."

"I am an American officer, not a civilian."

"Aye, aye. And you are indeed bereft of all reason if you disobey orders—"

"No order has yet been given." To his credit, Washington was gravely concerned about Libby, but his hands were tied. "My circumstance is beyond military law."

"You will set the precedent then. And win Washington's fury and disfavor."

"So be it."

Henry balled up the paper in one fist. "I understand your dilemma, but I'll take no part in your plan."

Beyond the tent's sweltering confines came the all-too-familiar rat-a-tat of a drum.

"Next is Great Bridge," Noble said, though Henry well knew that too. They were now at Norfolk, twenty miles distant from Fort Murray, where Dunmore held sway with a small army and confiscated military stores from ongoing coastal raids.

Noble's mind was made up. If he could at last communicate

with the British authorities in the Chesapeake where the coming conflict was to be, he might determine just where Libby was.

And he would, Lord willing, set her free.

Liberty's space aboard the HMS *Sapphire* was more closet, but Providence had spared her from being crammed in the hold with a great many men. The rebel rabble, as the ship's crew called them, were mostly Continental militia with a few civilians thrown in. She was the prize aboard this floating hulk of a prison ship, the sole female, oft invited to the captain's table. When she declined, a moldy biscuit, a half pint of peas, and a half gill of rice was given her. Water was brought in a chamber pot.

Each morning she awoke to the hoarse cry, "Rebel, turn out your dead." As the autumn weather turned sweltering and disease raced like rats among the prisoners, more fell. Desperate, still nauseous, she fixed on the meagerest blessing. She had a bull's-eye window. A moldy mattress. Privacy. Most miraculous of all, she had been snuck a lace kit from the plundering of a near plantation. Though she'd wondered why it fell into her hands, she now saw it as God's provision.

What else was she to do, cooped up all day? Not only did the routine ground her and fill her hours, she bartered and sold bits of lace to the crew, who were greedy for gain. They, in turn, brought a piece of cheese or unmoldy bread or extra ration. She must keep her baby well. Already she was showing, her soiled gown hiding nothing. Pared down again she was except for her middle, the memory of the delectable bara brith excruciating. A hasty look in a cracked mirror bespoke a scarecrow in blue silk. If she lived to get off this ship . . .

Noble's last letter, delivered to Ty Mawr in September, was tucked beneath her stays, the lettering a ghostly gray from repeated perusing. Was she still his anwylyd? Did he pine for her by day and dream of her by night? She did him.

Her one regret was that she had not told him her secret. He was to be a father in late spring, by her reckoning. But perhaps Providence had kept her from telling. Mightn't her absence be all the more troublesome if he knew that not only was her life at risk but their unborn child's too?

What a conundrum she was in. He had no idea just where she was, nor did she. When she'd been taken captive that day at Ty Bryn, she'd been whisked to a ship at anchor in the Chesapeake in sight of Virginia's shore, an insignificant schooner amid the mighty British fleet. Not a word was said about Lord Stirling, nor did she see Hessel, though she believed they were behind her abduction. Her father was not ailing or dead, she soon discovered. 'Twas a lie told to get her here. The ship's captain confided that, unable to capture Noble, they'd dealt a blow to him by capturing her instead.

The light from her window was fading. She had no candles and would soon see utter darkness but for the tiny pinpricks of gold aboard other surrounding ships.

A tap and a muffled voice came at the door. "Yer supper, m'lady."

A key grated in the lock as her one shipboard friend delivered her scant supper, a greenish biscuit and a square of pork pooling with grease. She looked past him to the empty companionway. His opening the door seemed to have uncorked the vilest of the ship's smells. Bilge. Dampness. The reek of unwashed bodies.

Ignoring them, she smiled. "Thank you, Nathaniel." He was but a boy, stolen from his family and pressed into service.

His own misery and the abuse he suffered from the crew made her more mindful of her own. Betimes hers seemed small in comparison.

"I remember when you first came aboard, and rumor was you were a high-minded lady married to a Patriot. At every meeting I expected you to hurl insults my way, but 'twas only a kind word."

A rat scurried past. She pressed the soles of her worn slippers to the plank floor, resisting an unladylike shriek. By now rats were commonplace. Sometimes she felt the brush of them in her bed.

Lightheaded, she sat down on an upturned barrel. "You are a fellow captive, not my enemy."

He nodded, staring at the tray as if sorry he had brought her such swill. "Yer prayers seem to be helpin', m'lady. The crew's not beat me of late. And only two rebel dead this morn."

Only two. God rest their souls. "I've not thanked you properly for all your help to me." She took a roll of lace from her pocket and handed it to him.

His eyes shone with rare glee. "'Twill fetch a fine price in Norfolk."

So they were closest to the Tory town? They moved about quite a bit as if to confuse or elude. At the slightest heave of the ship she feared they'd set sail for England. "Any news?"

He leaned into the doorway, a grubby finger caressing the pale lace. "Dunmore's preparing for battle. There's talk ye might be switched to one of the sugarhouses along the waterfront soon."

Surely the joy she felt must have shown on her face. To be on land again! There she might have a chance of escape. Here, afloat, there was little hope.

378

"Might you smuggle out a letter for me?" Only recently had he snuck her writing tools, at great personal risk.

"Aye, m'lady."

"If you think 'tis too much a danger for you—"

"For you, aye. Nobody else." The conflict in his mind was evident on his pockmarked face. "Yer held here, against yer will, with yer babe. 'Tis not me I fear for but yerself."

"Very well then. I'll have a letter for you tomorrow, meant for someone on shore sympathetic to the American cause. If it lands in the right hands they'll see it safely delivered."

But the wrong hands? She wouldn't think of that. She would pray for safe passage. That somehow the letter would reach Noble. Time was running out. Soon, she sensed, an irrevocable shift in their plight was coming—and not for the better.

Breaking through their low talk was a rising storm of voices toward the front of the ship. Nathaniel's face fell. "Best hie to the forecastle and help feed the miserable crew."

At the edge of the field where Noble's regiment was drilling stood his adjutant, looking impatient, something in hand. Without a break in his commands, Noble finished the manual exercise, his voice loud and distinct.

"Poise firelock . . . Cock firelock . . . Take aim . . . Fire!" Then, amid the acrid swirl of black powder, "Rest."

He left the field abruptly, the sun in his eyes, aware of his men's scrutiny as if they too detected something afoot.

Alarm lined his adjutant's face. "This just came, sir. Delivered by a washerwoman out of Norfolk."

Noble's fingers nearly shook as he took in the scrap of unsealed paper. On the outside was his name, penned in—could it be?—Libby's elegant hand. But without the costly, fragrant foolscap from Ty Mawr, she'd crowded a brief message on the back of a wrinkled receipt for molasses.

His eyes stung. Disbelieving, he moved into the shade of a hickory, his shoulder cutting into the ragged bark. All the sounds and smells of the busy encampment faded away.

Dearest husband,
   I am not far. Your child and I—

He stopped cold. Reread that telling line. Child? Their unborn child. *Lord, nay.* He stared at the leaf-strewn ground, a fiery carpet of color. This was the first indication he'd had of her whereabouts. He devoured the rest of her words as if he'd been denied a meal for months.

   Your child and I have come to no harm aboard the Sapphire.
   Captain Graves is in command. I may be moved to the sugarhouses in Norfolk soon. Till now I've had no ink and paper.
   I love you with all my heart and pray my way into your arms again.

Anwylyd

Three months it had been since she'd left Ty Mawr. He knew the day, the very hour. His ache for her never lessened. All his searching with the men he'd hired to find her had come to naught. He'd been left with prayer and prayer alone. And now with a few tersely penned words, his flagging hopes revived.

Not only was she near, she was carrying his child. The son or daughter of his heart. The heir to Ty Mawr.

Father in heaven, help us.

Just like that, the daily nausea ebbed and Liberty felt that flutter deep inside her, a soul-stirring motion that brought to mind the sunny, white-walled nursery with its walnut cradle and the angels on the fire screen.

Nathaniel had carried away her letter the week before. 'Twas now the last of November. A dismal, damp cold had descended and a frigid wind blew through the ship's timbers, causing her to wrap herself in the moth-eaten blanket given her.

When Nathaniel next came below, his cheeks were fiery with cold. "Some soup, m'lady. Though I don't know what's in it."

He entered and set the bowl on her bunk. No steam rose. The soup was nearly as cold as they were. She thanked him, wishing for more lace to give him. Of late her fingers had been too stiff to do much work.

He looked to the companionway, lowering his voice. "Dunmore and the British in Virginia are gathering at Great Bridge."

She stared at him, the flutter inside her bolder. "Will there be a battle, do you think?"

"Aye, the rebels are setting up defenses there, a great many breastworks and such—"

His eyes flew upward at a sudden commotion above. Without warning, the schooner heaved leeward, along with her stomach. They were on the move.

But to where?

38

Dawn. December 9. Noble's breath plumed like white feathers as he observed his forward sentries creep toward the hastily erected British stockade dubbed Fort Murray. *Hog Pen*, the Continentals were calling it. The 2nd Virginia Regiment was encamped near the local church, the Patriot Main Guard positioned behind a seven-foot-high palisade wall. A bridge spanning the Great Dismal Swamp separated redcoats and bluecoats.

Weary of Dunmore's coastal raids of military stores, Colonel Woodford's forces had arrived the end of November, exchanging musket and cannon fire ever since. They were running low on munitions. Perilously low.

God, hasten the artillery train. It became his constant prayer.

Once they had the needed cannon, Hog Pen would fall to splinters and the Patriots would drive Dunmore and the British out of Virginia for good. Or so they hoped.

Shadows moved in and out of the icy mist, obscuring the bridge.

"They're putting down the planks on the bridge floor they tore up in the night," a lieutenant said, his spyglass sweeping from left to right.

"Then they mean to advance," Noble replied with a backward glance at his men.

Above the ping of buckshot came the Patriot command, "Hold your fire!"

Within seconds, Noble saw British captain Fordyce press forward with the shout, "The day is ours!"

An alarming swarm of redcoats ran up the narrow causeway toward them, only to be met with a sudden roar of Patriot fire. Noble steadied his hands and sighted, dropping the British officer leading the charge. Someone's son. Mayhap brother. Husband. Father.

God forgive him, but if this was war he wanted no part in it. Losing Libby had worn him down like a wasting disease. He had nearly lost the will to fight. Yet he reloaded. Misfired. Fired again in haste, nearly choking on the dense smoke.

Within minutes, Colonel Woodford had brought up the main Patriot force, and the battle began in earnest.

But Noble's own personal conflict was yet to be won.

'Twas nearly Christmas. The snow foretold it as much as Nathaniel's timekeeping. Liberty stood by the bull's-eye window, hearing the crisp aristocratic tones of gentlemen, so different than the rough rasp of seamen. Lord Dunmore? She'd not seen his lordship since the ball in Gosport months ago. Nathaniel said he had gone on to Great Bridge to fight.

A knock at the cabin door followed by the scrape of the key made her turn. At Nathaniel's stunned expression all her weariness fell away.

"Lord Dunmore's leaving Virginia, m'lady. But first he's come aboard to make a prisoner exchange. 'Tis you he's asking for."

Before he'd finished speaking, she was in the companionway. How long it had been since she'd left her cramped quarters. She'd first come aboard ship in September, and now 'twas December. Nathaniel followed, hard-pressed to keep up with her even though her legs were so unsteady from lack of use they quivered like twigs.

Up the ladder she went and into the spitting snow of early winter. The broad deck was slick, and Nathaniel put out a hand to steady her. She blinked at the fierce glare of daylight. Through narrowed eyes she saw a great many seamen and British soldiers, a great blur of redcoats . . .

And one blue.

Her heart—*oh, her heart*—seemed to stop. Not twenty feet away stood Noble. Just as handsome as she remembered. Just as stalwart. His expression was stoic and tender by turns. His arms open.

She started for him, still trembly-legged, joy pushing her forward. She had eyes for no one else, not the stone-faced lord who had called her on deck, nor the surrounding swarm of gawking men.

Locked in Noble's arms, her cheek pressed to his cold, damp uniform coat, she was suddenly aware of how bedraggled she was. Tidy, yes. But bereft of a bath for long weeks and in the same soiled blue dress. And very pregnant to boot.

"You're all right, anwylyd?" His head was bent, his mouth near her ear. "No harm has come to you? Or our child?"

"None," she replied through tears, trying to keep herself in check. "But 'tis good to be on deck. To breathe fresh air." Her voice broke. "To see you."

He nodded, stroking her filthy hair once so fresh and finely dressed by Isabeau. "Your maid is waiting in the coach with a basket of provisions. Dougray will return you to Ty Bryn."

Dazed, she stood a bit straighter, so glad to be going she would not even fetch her few belongings. Why did he tarry? She clutched his sleeve, starting to shake from the cold.

He unfastened the clasp of his wool cloak and draped it around her. So large it was it dragged the deck, but 'twas warm. So warm, recalling Ty Bryn's hearth fires. Murmuring thanks, she locked eyes with him. "Let us be away then."

"Nay." He swallowed, eyes damp but jaw resolute.

"Nay? But Great Bridge . . ." She looked hard at him. "You Virginians won the battle."

"Aye, but not the war." A gust of wind nearly unseated his hat, and he clamped the tricorn down. "I am to stay. You are to go."

Stay . . . go. The biting wind flung his words away, her whole world along with them.

Go? Alone? She met his eyes briefly but he looked away, as if he could not bear another separation. A sick sinking feeling clawed at her as all the implications came crashing down. Overcome, she threw her arms around him. "Nay!"

As her clutch on him tightened, men sprang into action, shackling him in irons. She whirled to face Lord Dunmore—to beg for mercy—but he had disappeared. Nathaniel and Captain Graves himself came forward to escort her off the ship she now had no wish to leave.

"Nay!" she shouted again, her ladylike reserve shattering. Twisting her head, she tried to gain a last look at her husband.

But he was being led away below deck, the rebel blue of his uniform obscured by fast-falling snow.

❧

"Did Major Rynallt not tell you his grandmother was a twin?" Mistress Tremayne asked.

Liberty shook her head, no less awed than at first. In the crook of each arm was an infant, one in a lace cap with blue ribbon, the other in pink. Both babies, though small and a month early by her reckoning, were sound, their matching features belying their diverse temperaments.

Three days old they were, the pride of Ty Bryn and Ty Mawr—and of their grandmother newly arrived from Philadelphia.

"We shall send for a second cradle," her mother said. "Though for now this one will do."

Isabeau hovered, taking her turn with the bellowing boy. "*Oui*, he is a noisy fellow! His poor sister will get little sleep and less milk."

Truly, they had to coax the littlest Rynallt to wake and eat. She seemed content to doze while her brother claimed the lion's share of nursing and cuddling.

"What shall you name them?" her mother asked gently.

"I shan't," Liberty replied. "Not till their father returns home."

The older women exchanged glances. Four months it had been since Liberty stood on the *Sapphire*'s deck as part of the prisoner exchange. Not one word of Noble's whereabouts had leaked since then, though all feared he'd been transferred to the ghastly hulk *Jersey* in New York's harbor.

"'Tis not odd to delay naming them," Mistress Tremayne said, settling a supper tray on a side table. She kindly refrained from saying why. Many infants died before their first birthday.

Liberty surveyed the familiar Welsh fare, and dismay cut in. What did Noble eat? 'Twas a recurring question. She herself had only just begun to recover from her lean months aboard ship. 'Twas an outright miracle she'd produced two healthy babies, the midwife said.

Her life, so barren and lonesome over the stark, snowy winter, was now full and lush as spring, the births ushering in a new bittersweet season.

Once again Liberty latched on to her blessings. *Count it all joy.* Her babies were here. The nursery was full. The Lord had given them a double portion far beyond her wildest hopes. Mama had come. They were all safely at home with plenty to eat, a lovely stretch of summer before them. All because of Noble.

Her days overflowed with little room to ponder. 'Twas her nights that the magnitude of what he'd done overwhelmed her. He'd traded his life for hers. For his children. For his country.

In the meantime Norfolk had burned. The British had withdrawn from Boston. All the united colonies were poised to strike or defend their ground. Ty Bryn seemed an island to itself.

A silver rattle arrived by April's end from Lady Washington at Mount Vernon. Her gracious letter put an end to all Liberty's wondering about Noble's commission and his standing in the army. Martha had written, "Greater love hath no man than this, that he lay down his life for his friends, or in this case, his wife and children."

After that, Liberty found her feet. "I cannot lie abed any longer." Not with two babies to care for, a blooming garden to walk through, and shirts to sew for the needy army.

"Mistress, you are too busy," Isabeau fussed.

"Betimes busyness is a blessing," Liberty returned, walking the floor with her son.

Sometimes weariness overtook her, and she could do little but partake of a cup of coffee and listen to Madoc purr as she watched her unnamed babies sleep or wave fat fists and make endearing newborn noises.

"I hate to leave you," her mother said at the end of a fortnight. "When you are stronger and the twins are fit to travel, you must come to Philadelphia. I've let a house there, large enough for us all. In the meantime, do consider a wet nurse."

Liberty said little to this. Neither prospect held any appeal. What a gift it was to provide her babies with nature's own nourishment. Was this not a part of mothering? Besides, Ty Bryn had her heart and at Ty Bryn she would stay. And wait. And pray with every breath she took that Noble would come home.

The hardest part was not the scant food nor the close quarters nor the sickness but that Libby, his anwylyd, seemed distant as a dream. Aye, *that* was the hardest part. The not knowing. Their shipboard reunion and prisoner exchange last winter had been numbingly brief. With the shifting of the seasons came new questions.

Had she delivered their child? Was she well? Were Ty Mawr and Ty Bryn standing strong? What of his tenants and servants? His tobacco and cash crops?

His world had shrunk to shades of gray. He knew so little, only that he and forty-some other Patriots were imprisoned on the *Packhorse*, a schooner afloat in Charles Town's harbor. Daily the ship's captain offered him his freedom if he would renounce his cause and sign an oath of allegiance to the king, thus enlisting in the British army. Daily he refused. Twice he had received a caning and a fierce blow to the head on his way back to the hold. They'd not hang him if they had the chance to shame the Patriots by making him a turncoat.

Soon the fine uniform Libby had made him hung like a discarded rebel flag on his lean form. Ravaged by cholera, he survived while many didn't. The sandy shore of Charles Town's bay was littered with graves.

Were Libby's prayers keeping him alive?

As spring turned to summer, the heat intensified but the portholes were fastened shut, the iron bars glinting beneath a merciless sun. Beside him now stood Charles Pinckney, equal in rank and recovering from smallpox, his sunken face a mass of open sores.

"There's talk of torching the ship." Pinckney's voice was low, weak. "Better a quick death than this."

Noble studied him, his one true ally. A man of prestige and means in South Carolina, Pinckney seemed about to give up.

"I heard those of us who refuse to enlist are to be taken to the West Indies, where we'll be put on ships of war."

"I say we overpower them first." Noble rubbed his jaw, his full beard itchy and vermin ridden. "Before they take us south."

Pinckney blinked bloodshot eyes. "Are you mad? What chance have we of that? They need no provocation to kill us—"

"There are sixteen of them left after the smallpox. Most are unwell, including the captain. There are thirty-three of us." He spoke like an officer, their predicament demanding bolder action. "Numbers alone give us an edge."

"How do you propose we do the impossible?"

Noble pushed past Pinckney's skepticism. "I've been praying about it. You know our captors hate any sign of patriotism."

"Aye, I watched Laurens get thrown from the gunwale for humming 'Yankee Doodle.'"

"Exactly. We'll set up a roar and sing patriotic songs in the middle of the night, which will cause them to open the hatch—"

"And cut us to ribbons with their knives and cutlasses."

"I'll lead," Noble continued calmly. "The rest of you will stand close behind. Once the hatch opens we'll storm it."

Pinckney frowned. "We've not tried such before. We always act like the officers and gentlemen we are."

"That's partly the trouble." Noble sometimes rued there were no rogues or cutthroats among them, mostly just the cream of South Carolina turning to Patriot corpses, a lone Virginian like himself among them. "We need to act in a most ungentlemanly manner. The crew won't expect it, and therein lies our advantage."

Pinckney passed a hand over his own unshaven features. "And if we fail?"

"Leave no room for failure. The alternative is death. We'll not survive the coming summer in this hulk. Prepare yourself and the men. And pray."

39

For days now Liberty had felt an odd dread. The unwelcome feeling had come on the heels of the babies' christening, a mostly joyful occasion. Both wee ones had been quiet, their blue eyes open and watchful during the short ceremony as they adjusted to many an admiring glance and unfamiliar arm. The sun had shone. Cook prepared a feast afterward, and though Noble's place sat empty, the thread of joy was undeniable.

"Perfect cherubs they were," Mistress Tremayne said. "How pleased and proud their papa would be."

The advent of June was as full of thunderstorms as the christening had been clear. Mistress Tremayne came up from Ty Mawr more and more, on account of the twins, she said. Or was there another reason?

"You've not been yourself of late," she confessed, lingering in the doorway of the nursery.

Liberty stood by the cradle, her hand gently rocking. "Oh?"

"You're quieter, lost in thought." Concern was sketched across the housekeeper's lined features. "No doubt on account of Major Rynallt."

"My husband never leaves my thoughts," Liberty said. "I don't know where he is. How he is. 'Tis as if he's vanished from the face of the earth. Lately all I feel is a terrible foreboding."

"You've not felt such before?"

"Feelings come and go, but this . . . 'tis like being caught in a bad dream, as if something momentous and terrible is about to happen, only I don't know what it is."

"Then we must pray like never before." Mistress Tremayne bowed her head in the doorway. "Gracious heavenly Father, our sight is so limited and our hearts are so full. We take comfort knowing You are with the major wherever he is. We continue to ask for a hedge of protection about him, that no weapon formed against him shall prosper. We boldly ask that You bring him home. These babies need a father. The mistress needs a husband. Comfort her heart and quiet her thoughts. In Your gracious name, amen."

"Amen," Liberty echoed. Her daughter startled and began to cry. Scooping her up, she felt her milk let down, so she settled into the rocking chair to nurse, pondering Mistress Tremayne's unexpected prayer.

Would Noble come by land or by sea? The particulars mattered little. Dare she hope again?

Lord, please let it be.

The last of spring's daylight slanted across Liberty's lap, creating a halo about the babe's head. While her brother slept, the tiny girl regarded her mother with wide-eyed wonder.

Noble's dark hair wreathed her pale face in wisps, but she had Libby's coloring and dimple. More than a month old and in need of a name, she was near perfect. Liberty stroked her flawless cheek, trying to recall the Welsh lullaby Nell had taught her and Mistress Tremayne's recitation of Welsh names.

"I shall call you Rhian Hope Rynallt." She kissed the baby's smooth brow. "Because Rhian means 'maiden,' and Hope because I have hope your father will return to us. When he comes home, he shall name your brother."

The din they were raising was deafening. It hurt Noble's own ears. Their combined voices, weary and disease wracked, gained in strength as the words to the song reached a crescendo.

> Torn from a world of tyrants beneath this western sky,
> We form a new dominion, a land of liberty.
> The world shall own we're masters here, then hasten
> on the day.
> Huzzah, huzzah, huzzah, huzzah for free America!

His own heart seemed to beat out of his chest, his pride in his new nation was so great. These ragged, irrepressible men surrounding him spurred him on, as did his love for his wife and home. Virginia. Their larger cause.

He braced himself for the opening of the hatch, the crack of light on deck penetrating the darkness of the hold. When it came, what would follow? Expectation oozed all around him as his fellow Patriots pressed near, ready to spring up the ladder toward fresh air. Freedom.

They sang another chorus, louder and warmer and more proud. The battered ship shook with a sudden storm of motion on deck.

At last the hatch cracked open.

Noble led the charge with a resounding shout. "Liberty or death!"

If she had dreamed it, she could not have made it more memorable. There she was, looking out at the James just feet from where she and Noble had gone swimming after the storm all those months ago. Unlike that day, this twilight eve was pure gold, not too hot, with a wind rising off the water that ruffled both the chin ribbons of her hat and her dress hem. Her thoughts were full of him. And she kept pondering Psalm 139, that bulwark of Scripture that spoke loudest to her these lonesome days. She took to heart one verse especially.

If I take the wings of the morning, and dwell in the uttermost parts of the sea; even there shall Thy hand lead me, and Thy right hand shall hold me.

The twins were asleep in the nursery. She knew Dougray was not far. Since her abduction, he and Ninian seemed to shadow her, though they tried their best to keep a respectful distance. She herself had turned more watchful, more wary. Because of it she saw the dark speck on the horizon coming over a gentle hill at the back of Ty Bryn when she might not have noticed it before. A stranger. On horseback.

As she studied him he dismounted, leading his horse on foot. With a slight catch in his step.

Squinting, she tried to make out more details. Ninian had come out from the garden wall. He began walking toward the stranger. And then, in a rapid about-face, he swung round to look at her before vanishing completely.

What?

She began to walk toward the approaching figure, her heart picking up in rhythm. She felt oddly breathless, nearly tripping over a stone in a tuft of grass, her attention was so fixed on him. And he . . . he'd let go of the reins of his horse and was coming toward her as fast as his limp would let him. Over the greening grasses and then the tiny stream that meandered between rustling oaks.

Her heart—her whole heart—turned over in such a poignant rush that all the strength seemed to leave her. 'Twas like being aboard the *Sapphire* when Noble had come to free her. His life for hers. Only now there were no soldiers. No slippery, wintry deck. No taint of salt water or treason. Just the two of them in the open meadow with the warm wind and fading sunset. She was running toward him full tilt, her hat dislodged and dangling down her back, her chin ribbons barely holding it.

"Anwylyd," he called. His voice held laughter and joy and a disbelief every bit as strong as hers.

"Noble." She kept saying it as if he would somehow vanish if she stopped, as if this was all a dream like the many she'd had of this day, this reunion.

But the feel of his hard arms around her was real—and the distinct manly scent that was his alone and that she'd not forgotten but had craved day in and out during his absence.

She was crying and laughing and talking in short bursts while he continued to hold her, appearing too moved to do anything much at all. And then . . .

"I've come home. For good."

Their eyes met through a blur of emotion. *Home.* The finality of his words seemed a promise. *For good.* No more absences? No more separations?

Cupping her chin in his roughened hands, he kissed her. Not the tentative kiss of their backward courtship but a wild, firm declaration of a new tie borne of love and loss and hard-won devotion.

She could hardly take it in. "You're free? How—when—"

"Three days ago we stormed the hatch of the ship. 'Twas either that or face the fate of being moved to another prison ship or taken to parts unknown. There were more of us than the crew. I thank God the rash plan worked."

She touched his thigh. "But you're hurt—"

"I'll mend. Not all were so fortunate."

She lay her head on his chest, taking in the rough homespun shirt he wore. "You might have been killed. I can't believe you're here, an answer to countless prayers."

"'Twas prayer alone that saw us through. We locked the crew in the hold and ran the *Packhorse* aground on an isolated beach in North Carolina. It took awhile for us to reach any sympathetic to our cause, but those of us who came away with only minor wounds were given food and clothes. I even managed to bathe and shave and borrow a horse."

"Very thankful for that. Does your commanding officer know? Any of your fellow Patriots?"

"Not yet. I wanted to reach you first. Ascertain you were safe. See our firstborn."

"They're asleep in the nursery with Isabeau and Mistress Tremayne near at hand—"

"*They?*" His utter astonishment made her laugh.

"Indeed. A perfect pairing. We shall wake them up. They need to meet their father." A dozen more things clamored to be said, but she held her tongue, not wanting to overwhelm him with too much at once.

They fell into step together, hand in hand, the faithful horse following. Toward Ty Bryn and Ty Mawr.

Home. At long last.

EPILOGUE

Twas the bitter that made the sweet all the sweeter.
Now six months old, the twins were chewing on
their fat fists as they sat in countless laps, their antics
a source of endless delight. Rhian was even-tempered and
oft smiling, her sole dimple on display, charming all of Ty
Mawr down to the humblest stable lad. Ewen, Welsh for *warrior*, was indeed that. Tyrant of the nursery he was, Mistress
Tremayne boasted, with a bit of fiery red in his dark hair.
Ewen was his father's pride as much as Rhian was his joy.

"'Tis the workings of Providence that keeps me home with
you at such a time as this," Noble remarked as they walked
through a scattering of autumn leaves down Ty Mawr's lane.
"I'll not bemoan my injury, painful though it is."

"Providence—and our prayers—spared your life." Still a
bit disbelieving, she looked at their son in his father's arms
as she carried their daughter. "You can do just as much for

397

liberty and the cause off the field as on it, now that you've been called to help draft the Articles of Confederation."

Patrick Henry and other Independence Men oft came by, and Liberty sometimes visited Williamsburg with Noble for meetings at the Raleigh. The folly had not been rebuilt, and she was glad to let it go, along with all its tarnished memories.

"We'll travel as a family to the next Continental Congress and stay with your mother in Philadelphia," he told her, shifting Ewen in his arms.

"Let's not think yet of that. 'Tis so far in the future. Let's savor the present, the coming holidays." 'Twould be their first Christmas together at Ty Bryn. "Hard to believe just this time last autumn I was held aboard ship and you were on the field. What a difference a year makes."

"And next year? What shall it bring, do you think?"

She squeezed his hand, content to dwell in the moment. "So long as we're together, we four, it matters little."

"Well said, Libby." He smiled, kissing the back of her hand. "*Cael rhad Duw, cael y cyfan.*"

"Amen," she said with deep contentment, taking his Welsh to heart. "To have God's blessing is to have everything, indeed."

Fairy Butter

Receipts (recipes) for fairy butter are found in cookbooks beginning in the mid-eighteenth century. In *The Art of Cookery Made Plain and Easy* (1747), Hannah Glasse says it is "a pretty Thing to set of a Table at Supper":

Take the yolks of two hard eggs in a mortar with a large spoonful of orange flower water, and two tea spoonfuls of fine sugar beat to a powder; beat all together till it is a fine paste then mix it up with about as much fresh butter out of the churn and force it through a fine strainer full of little holes onto a plate.

Bara Brith (Speckled Bread)

Many recipes exist for this traditional Welsh bread. My favorite is the one I've adapted below. Some versions even call for tea as an ingredient! But I prefer tea with the speckled bread once it's baked. The bread is simply wonderful sliced, toasted, and buttered.

1 cup milk
¼ cup brown sugar, divided
4 teaspoons yeast

1 pound flour
1 teaspoon salt
3 ounces unsalted butter
1 teaspoon allspice
1 egg, beaten
12 ounces mixed dried fruit

In a saucepan, scald the milk and pour it in a bowl. Whisk in 1 teaspoon of the brown sugar and the yeast, then leave the bowl in a warm place for about 20 minutes. Sift the flour and salt into a separate large mixing bowl, then stir in the remaining sugar. Cut the butter into the dry ingredients until the mixture looks like fine bread crumbs. Stir in the allspice, add the beaten egg and scalded milk, and mix into a dough. Turn the dough onto a floured surface and knead for about 10 minutes. Return the dough to the bowl and cover. Leave in a warm place until it has risen and doubled in size, about an hour.

Punch the dough down, then knead in the fruit. Grease a loaf pan with butter. Pat the dough into a rectangle shape, then roll it up from the short side and place it seam-side down in the loaf pan. Let it rise again for about 45 minutes.

Preheat oven to 375°. Bake on the lowest rack for 30 minutes. Cool the loaf on a wire rack. Slice thinly.

ACKNOWLEDGMENTS

While writing *The Lacemaker*, I came across something Pastor Chuck Swindoll said that has stayed with me: "Being totally committed to Christ's increase . . . means letting our lives act as a frame that shows up the masterpiece—Jesus Christ. And a worthy frame isn't tarnished or dull, plain or cheap; yet neither is it so elaborate that it overpowers its picture. Instead, with subtle loveliness, it draws the observer's eye to the beautiful work of art it displays."[1] It is my ultimate hope that anything I write reflects the beauty of Christ, not my limited abilities as a storyteller. And I hope you as a reader sense the sweetness and nobleness I found in these pages and these characters while writing this particular novel.

So many hands go into making a book. Heartfelt thanks to all—from my agent, Janet Grant, to my publishing house, Revell, to myriad booksellers. No contribution is small or

---

1. Chuck Swindoll, quoted in Melinda Schmidt, Anita Lustrea, and Lori Neff, eds., *Daily Seeds from Women Who Walk in Faith* (Chicago: Moody, 2008), 30.

wasted. I'm always in awe of the publishing process and still pinch myself after nine books!

I invite you to enjoy another lacemaker's story in *A Refuge Assured* by Jocelyn Green. Jocelyn and I had fun creating a tie between Vivienne and Liberty and their French ancestry in our newest novels, after discovering our heroines share a lovely and highly prized eighteenth-century skill!

During the writing of every book, certain people come alongside to make the journey sweeter and the story stronger. Susan Marlene Kinney is one of those remarkable friends. She shares my love of the eighteenth century, colonial Williamsburg, fiction, and the Lord. I'm forever grateful for her sunny spirit, ongoing generosity, and timely encouragement. I see Christ when I look at her. She is a beautiful framework of our Savior.

This book wouldn't be possible without the existence of colonial Williamsburg, the College of William and Mary, Welsh-English helps, and many primary and secondary sources—too many to mention here. The more I study colonial life, the more I agree with Ronald W. Michener, an associate economics professor at the University of Virginia, who said, "Viewed from the twenty-first century, life in colonial America was like living on a different planet." Yet for me as an author, this is exactly what makes this fascinating time period so rich and worthy of remembering, even in fiction.

Lastly, heartfelt thanks to beloved readers who have embraced my books. As Philippians 1:3 says, I do thank my God upon every remembrance of you.

Love *The Lacemaker*?
Read on for an Excerpt of Another
Revolutionary War Story
from Laura Frantz

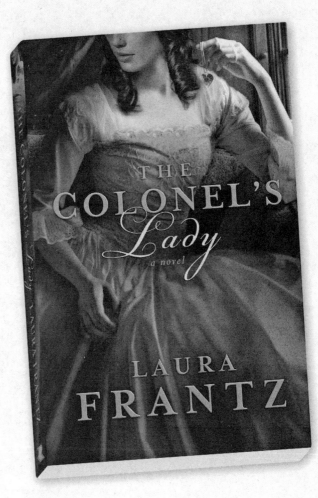

1

This is madness.

Roxanna Rowan leaned against the slick cave entrance and felt an icy trickle drop down the back of her neck as she bent her head. Her right hand, shaky as an aspen leaf, caressed the cold steel of the pistol in her pocket. Being a soldier's daughter, she knew how to use it. Trouble was she didn't want to. The only thing she'd ever killed was a copperhead in her flower garden back in Virginia, twined traitorously among scarlet poppies and deep blue phlox.

An Indian was an altogether different matter.

The cave ceiling continued to weep, echoing damply and endlessly and accenting her predicament. Her eyes raked the rosy icicles hanging from the sides and ceiling of the cavern. Stalactites. Formed by the drip of calcareous water, or so Papa had told her in a letter. She'd never thought to see such wonders, but here she was, on the run from redskins *and* Redcoats in the howling wilderness. And in her keep were four fallen women and a mute child.

They were huddled together farther down the cavern tunnel, the women's hardened faces stiff with rouge and fright. Nancy. Olympia. Dovie. Mariah. And little Abby. All five were looking at her like they wanted her to do something dangerous. Extending one booted foot, she nudged the keelboat captain. In the twilight she saw that the arrow protruding from his back was fletched with turkey feathers. He'd lived long enough to lead them to the mouth of the cave—a very gracious gesture—before dropping dead. *Thank You, Lord, for that. But what on earth would You have me do now?* A stray tear leaked from the corner of her left eye as she pondered their predicament.

The Indians had come out of nowhere that afternoon—in lightning-quick canoes—and the women had been forced to abandon the flatboat and flee in a pirogue to the safer southern shore, all within a few miles of their long-awaited destination. Fort Endeavor was just downriver, and if they eluded the Indians, they might reach it on foot come morning. Surely a Shawnee war party would rather be raiding a vessel loaded with rum and gunpowder than chasing after five worthless women and a speechless child.

"Miz Roxanna!" The voice cast a dangerous echo.

Roxanna turned, hesitant to take her eyes off the entrance lest the enemy suddenly appear. Her companions had crept farther down the tunnel, huddled in a shivering knot. And then Olympia shook her fist, her whisper more a shout.

"I'd rather be took by Indians than spend the night in this blasted place!"

There was a murmur of assent like the hiss of a snake, and Roxanna plucked her pistol from her pocket. "Ladies," she said, stung by the irony of the address. "I'd much rather freeze in this cave than roast on some Indian spit. Now, are you with me or against me?"

The only answer was the incessant *plink, plink, plink* of water. Turning her back to them, she fixed her eye on the ferns just beyond the cave entrance, studying the fading scarlet and cinnamon and saffron woods. With the wind whipping and rearranging the leaves, perhaps their trail would be covered if the Indians decided to pursue them. They'd also walked in a creek to hide their passing. But would it work? Roxanna heaved a shaky sigh.

I'm glad Mama's in the grave and Papa doesn't know a whit about my present predicament.

At daylight the women emerged like anxious animals from the cave, damp and dirty and wild-eyed with apprehension. One small pistol was no match for an Indian arrow. But Roxanna clutched it anyway, leading the little group through the wet woods at dawn, in the direction of the fort they'd been trying to reach for nigh on a month. By noon the women in her wake were whining like a rusty wagon wheel, but she didn't blame them a bit. They had lost all their possessions, every shilling, and hadn't seen so much as a puff of smoke from a nearby cabin at which they could beg some bread.

Were they even going the right direction?

The dense woods seemed to shutter the sun so that it was hard to determine which way was which. When the fort finally came into view, it didn't match the picture Roxanna had concocted in her mind as she'd come down the watery Ohio River road. The place was dreary. Lethal looking. Stalwart oak pickets impaled the sky, and the front gates of the great garrison were shut. Drawing her cape around her, she stifled a sigh. It needed fruit trees all around . . . and a hint of flowers . . . and children and dogs running about, even in the chill of winter.

But not one birdcall relieved the gloom.

As they came closer, she could see the Virginia colors flying on the tall staff just beyond high, inhospitable walls. And then something else came into view—something that matched her memories of home and made a smile warm her tense face. A stone house. She blinked, expecting the lovely sight to vanish. But it only became clearer and more beguiling, and she drank in every delightful detail.

Solid stone the color of cream. Winsome green shutters with real glass windows hiding behind. Twin chimneys at each end. And a handsome front door that looked like it might be open in welcome come warmer weather. Situated on a slight rise in back of the fort, the house was near enough to the postern gate to flee to in times of trouble, though she doubted even the king's men could penetrate such stone. Who had built such a place in the midst of such stark wilderness?

Papa never mentioned a stone house.

Roxanna was suddenly conscious of the company she kept—or rather was leading. It wasn't that she was afraid to be seen with these women in their too-tight gowns and made-up faces, or that she felt above them in some way. Glancing at them over her shoulder, she pulled her cloak tighter as the whistling wind of late November blew so bitterly it seemed to slice through her very soul.

Her skittishness was simply this—she feared the reaction of her father. Stalwart soldier that he was, what would he think to see her arrive in such flamboyant company? He hadn't an inkling she was coming in the first place. But to see her roll in unexpectedly with doxies such as these, and a pitiful child to boot . . .

"Is that Fort Endeavor, Miz Roxanna?" The weary voice was almost childlike in expectancy. Dovie, only fifteen, had attached herself to Roxanna with the persistence of a horsefly in midsummer's heat from the moment they'd met on the boat.

"Yes, that's the fort, or should be," she replied as the girl clutched her arm a bit fearfully. "Best keep moving lest the Indians follow." Roxanna looked to her other side and grabbed hold of Abby's hand. The child glanced up, ginger curls framing a pale face buttonholed by bluish-gray eyes, her dimpled cheeks visible even without a smile. "We'll soon be warm and dry again—promise."

At the rear, Olympia laughed, and the sound tinkled like a tarnished chime in the frozen air. "I aim to be more than that, truly. Or I reckon I'll turn right around and find me another fort full of soldierin' men—or an Indian chief."

Ignoring the babble of feminine voices, Roxanna looked over her shoulder warily as they emerged from the woods. How in heaven's name had it come to this? She realized she was running from discomfort to danger. Virginia no longer felt like home, and she was desperate to leave its hurtful memories behind. But *this* was far more than she'd bargained for.

Oh, Lord, was it Your will for me to leave Virginia . . . or my own?

Every passenger on the flatboat they'd just forsaken seemed to be running from something. Even Olympia had confessed she'd left her life at the public house because she was tired of the lice and the stench of the river and the men who man-handled her. Her sister who had worked alongside her had died, leaving a child behind. To her credit, Olympia wanted a better life for little Abby. The girl hadn't spoken a word since her mother's death a few months before, and Roxanna wondered if she ever would.

"I've heard that in Kentucke, women are so scarce even a

fallen one like myself can take my pick of any man I please,"
Olympia had announced aboard the vessel one evening. "And
he'll treat me decent too." She smiled with such satisfaction
that Roxanna almost envied her.

"I just want me a little cabin with some chickens and a plot
of corn. Seems like that ain't askin' much," Mariah added.

Beside her, Nancy arranged her tattered skirts and purred
like a cat with a pot of cream, "I'm partial to a soldierin'
man myself."

Dovie's faded blue eyes lingered on each woman, her round
face full of expectancy. "Why, Miz Roxanna, you ain't said a
word about why you're travelin' to the wilderness."

A hush fell over the group as they huddled about the shanty
stove. Roxanna expelled a little breath. "Well . . . my father's
at Fort Endeavor serving as scrivener. He's always writing
letters telling me how beautiful Kentucke is, how you can
see for miles since the air is so clear, that even the grass is a
peculiar shade of blue-green, and the forests are huge and
still. Not leaping with Indians like some folks say."

"Sure enough?" Mariah murmured as the other women
huddled nearer.

"My coming to Kentucke is a surprise. Papa's enlistment
is near an end, and we'll be going somewhere to settle, just
the two of us."

"Don't you want to find a man—get married?" Mariah
asked.

The innocent question stung her. Roxanna lifted her shoulders in a show of indifference. "I'm not so young anymore—
spinster age, some say."

The women exchanged knowing glances and began to titter.

"Seems to me you're comin' to the right territory then. A
frontiersman ain't gonna let a gal who's a little long in the

tooth stop a weddin', " Olympia said, her smile smug. She reached into the bosom of her dress, withdrew a Continental dollar, and waved it about. "I bet Miz Roxanna with her fine white skin and all that midnight hair won't last five minutes once she sets foot in that fort."

There were approving murmurs all around. Roxanna smiled ruefully as Nancy reached over and snatched the bill out of Olympia's hand, tossing it into the stove. "That dollar's worthless and you know it. Show me somethin' sound."

Still chuckling, Olympia lifted her soiled calico skirt and took a pound note from her scarlet garter. "Now, who's to wed after Miz Roxanna?"

"I say Nancy 'cause she's so sweet." Mariah sneered, rolling her eyes.

This brought about such feminine howls a riverman stuck his head in the shanty doorway.

"I ain't sweet but I'm smart," Nancy said, tucking a strand of flaxen hair behind her ear. "I'll take the first man who asks me, so long as he ain't wedded to the jug and don't beat me."

Mariah rubbed work-hardened hands together, the backs flecked with liver spots. "I've got a hankerin' for a cabin in the shade of a mountain with a spring that never dries up, not even in summer. If a man won't take me, I'll make do myself, just like I've been doin' since I was nine years old."

Roxanna felt a stirring of pity for every scarred soul around the hissing stove. "Why don't we pray for husbands—for all of you?" she said on a whim, watching their faces.

Olympia smirked and shook her head. "With all due respect, Miz Roxanna, the only experience I've had with prayin' women is the ones who've prayed me and my ilk out of one river town after another."

"I ain't never prayed before," Mariah confessed.

"I like the idea. It ain't gonna hurt none," Dovie said quietly. "Maybe it'll help."

Reaching out, Roxanna squeezed her hand. Despite their worldly ways, these women could be surprisingly childlike, and they responded to any compliment or scrap of kindness like a half-starved cat.

"Praying isn't hard," she told them. "Sometimes when I can't think of what to say, I just remember the words I learned as a little girl." Opening the door of the stove, she added some dry willow chunks. "It goes like this. 'Now I lay me down to sleep, I pray the Lord my soul to keep. If I should die before I wake, I pray the Lord my soul to take.'"

Nancy nodded. "I learned that a long time ago in settlement school back in Pennsylvania."

"Well," Mariah urged, "keep on a-goin'. Might as well add that we're all needin' husbands."

"Maybe we should hold hands," Dovie suggested, reaching for Nancy's. "Once I peeked in at a prayer meetin' and it seemed that was what they did."

Self-consciously they bowed their heads. Roxanna stayed silent as they made their petitions before adding her own at the very end. "Father, You know what we have need of before we even ask. But we ask anyway, knowing You are patient and kind and the giver of all gifts. I ask that You send each of these women a husband—but only men who are honest and kind and good. Help them to be the women You made them to be. Help them to know You." She looked up, eyes searching the shadows. Curled up on a cot against a far wall, Abby was fast asleep. "And please bring Abby's voice back—let her speak again. Amen."

Dovie didn't let go of her hand. "Why, Miz Roxanna, you left yourself out."

Swallowing down a sigh, Roxanna dredged up a smile.

Truly, some things are past praying for.

"I ain't goin' to bed till you're prayed up," Olympia said, crossing her arms.

They joined hands again, the only sound the stove's popping and water sluicing under the hull beneath their feet. One by one they all prayed again, this time for Roxanna, and it seemed she'd never heard such sincere whispered words. But it was Dovie's petition that lingered the longest.

"Help my friend Roxanna, Mister Eternal. Prepare her a man she can't take her eyes off of and who can't take his eyes off her. And let it be right quick, if it pleases Ye."

Laura Frantz is the ECPA bestselling author of *A Moonbow Night*, *The Frontiersman's Daughter*, *Courting Morrow Little*, *The Colonel's Lady*, *The Mistress of Tall Acre*, and the Ballantyne Legacy series. She lives and writes in a log cabin in the heart of Kentucky. When she's not writing novels, she enjoys cooking, letter writing, traveling to Scotland, hiking, handwork, Bible studies, and flying to the West Coast to visit her firefighter son. Learn more at www.laurafrantz.net.

Glimpse into History

WITH NOVELS FROM LAURA FRANTZ

══ MEET ══

LAURA FRANTZ

Visit LauraFrantz.net to read
Laura's blog and learn about her books!

 see what inspired the characters and stories

 enter to win contests and learn about what
Laura is working on now

tweet with Laura